D1696265

Roll the Bones

edited by Ignatius Ümlaut and Del Beaudry

illustrated by Mark Allen

ISBN 978-0-9833119-2-8

Co-published by Golden Dawn Studios: 20 East 15th St. Covington, KY 41011. Email us@goldendawn@insightbb.com.

The cover and all interior illustrations are from the talented hand of Mark Allen. You can check out his website at marjasall.com.

The illuminated initials are by Hans Holbein, from his Dance of Death Alphabet, and are in the public domain.

The editors would like to offer their special gratitude to Gabor Lux and the staff of *Fight On!* magazine for invaluable critical and editorial assistance.

Similarities between the characters and situations depicted herein and real persons living or dead or actual historical events are in fact completely unavoidable, in all works of fiction in any medium. However, these are tales of fantasy, and the names and situations that occur within them 'refer' to imaginary beings. They are not direct or coded references to real world persons or situations and as a consequence cannot be libelous.

www.fightonmagazine.com

stores.lulu.com/fighton

Table of Contents

Index of Illustrations

Foreword

Roll the Bones grew out of a contest sponsored by *Fight On!* magazine. Our aim was to assemble an anthology of the kind of fiction we most enjoy: stories of swords, sorcery and weird adventure that veer on occasion into the darker precincts of human imagination. We sought bloody tales of witchcraft and treachery and plunder, where life is cheap and fortune or death turn on a roll of the bones. In short, the kind of stories which these days have become so devilishly scarce in the popular marketplace.

We have succeeded at this and more.

To our amazement and delight we received hundreds of entries. Here, amidst a tableau of weird enclaves and black pits, you will meet dreadful foes and deranged minds; desperate gambits and narrow escapes; dungeons, dragons and golden hordes; and the certainty of fate's inexorable judgment. Twined throughout are the fragile dreams of would-be heroes, often frustrated but also sometimes fulfilled.

But a true banquet needs more than just red meat. Its menu should reflect a certain piquancy of the imagination. To that end we have chosen several stories which range well into fantasy's contested borderlands. We believe the collection is richer for charting the byways of heroic fantasy alongside its hard core.

As to the larger value of this enterprise, our hopes are modest. Good fiction has been ascribed an array of noble ends, but foremost it is an entertainment and a luxury. The latter is especially true these days. To read for pleasure first requires time, a resource that grows increasingly scarce. We very much hope the tales within will provide good fun in your idle hours.

More than this would be fortunate indeed. Yet perhaps, on fleeting occasions, you will catch a sense of something more: something that moves you to introspection – or even wonder.

- the Editors

Weregild

Kristen Lee Knapp

he dropped pine needles into her small fire. The flames crackled and sweet smoke sizzled and drifted away. Tall twisty pines loomed above, blocking all but faint patches of starlight. Icy winds rustled their needles and cut through her furs.

Shadows shifted at the edge of the firelight. Feral eyes shone in the dark. Black shapes loped closer, pink tongues lolling from jaws bristling with yellow fangs.

Igral stood and drew her sword. Firelight gleamed down the sharp steel blade and the frayed length of her blond hair.

A huge wolf padded forward, sword clenched in its jaws. Its fur vanished and its paws became hands and feet. A naked man rose from the ground, a muscular, grinning savage with pale skin and a murderous gaze. "Little girl," he said, "I am Vargwr. This is my forest."

He grabbed his crotch and pointed at her with his sword. "You will bear me many children."

Igral ripped open her jerkin, bared her breasts, and slapped them with the flat of her blade. The wolves howled with laughter.

1

Vargwr spread his arms. "Come. I will not hurt you. Let us be friends."

She charged. Steel met steel. Sparks flashed, then fizzled on the frozen earth. She slashed but missed. He grabbed and locked her wrist, twisting the sword from her hands. His amber eyes glowed and he growled out a laugh.

She smashed his nose in with her forehead and he stumbled back screaming. She dropped, grabbed the sword, hacked – an arm spiraled loose, spurting red.

Vargwr's body folded inward. He was a wolf once more. Big yellow eyes stared up at her, pleading. A dog's whine escaped his jaws.

Down came her sword and clove head from shoulders. She knelt, seized the head, and hurled it at the other wolves. She slapped her breasts again with her bloody sword.

The wolves melted away into the darkness. Long after the flames died, Igral lay awake, clutching her bloodstained blade.

The sun breached the horizon and spilled its light down through the thick canopy. Snow drifted through the forest, dusting trees, wandering on the wind. Igral rose and buckled on her sword.

A few logs yet smoldered in her fire. She stamped the embers out, shouldered her goods, and set out. She ate as she walked, chewing strips of jerky and spitting gristle.

She came to a narrow river. Ice crusted both banks; dark water flowed between. She filled her waterskins and walked upriver, boots crunching on packed snow.

She spotted the craggy grey mountain through the mist. Snow buried its sheer cliffs and sharp boulders. A halo of dark clouds circled the frosty peak. The grim cadence of her blood- and melt-soaked boots quickened.

The maw of a huge cave gaped at its base. Spars of stone and mineral hung from the ceiling like mammoth tusks; snowmelt drizzled down them in bright rivulets. Light glowed in the depths of the cavern. She drew her sword and clambered down.

Blue flames erupted all around her. An old man with a white mossy beard and dark eyes stood before her, frowning.

"Who are you?" he said, then sniffed. "You stink like a werewolf. But you're human. Hmm. Well, come this way. What do you want?" He hobbled to the wall and pulled open a small wooden door. Igral followed him in.

Workbenches and tables were scattered through the chamber, every surface strewn with arcane paraphernalia: bundles of roots and herbs; potions in cork-bunged vials; crystals, both rough and cut; skulls of many kinds. Books and scrolls were stacked to the ceiling. Igral gaped.

"Speak up," said the old man. "I am occupied."

"Are you the Wizard Under the Mountain?"

He nodded, sat, and began crushing something with a mortar and pestle. "I am. I have dwelt here forever. Kings have come seeking my wisdom. What do you want?"

"If you lie, I will kill you."

He smiled and raised his caterpillar eyebrows. "You are welcome to leave."

She frowned. "No." She showed him her sword. "This is Akjik. It was my father's sword. It has slain a hundred men."

The wizard looked at it and flicked the blade. "A sharp piece of metal," he said. "No more deserving a name than your boots or a piss pot." He handed it back. "Now state your business. My time is precious."

"I must kill the man that killed my father".

The wizard rolled his eyes. "Not interested."

3

"I have fought with this man already," she said. "But I was…beaten. His sword was bright like the sun and blinded me."

"He spared you, did he?"

Igral gnashed her teeth.

"Some manner of light incantation. An old spell." The wizard thrummed his fingers along his beard. "A very old spell. Interesting."

"Will you help me?" she said.

He wove his fingers, spotted and wrinkled with age, together. "I may. But you must bring me this light sword after you kill him. Agreed?"

"Yes," said Igral, holding Akjik's hilt out to him. "Work quickly."

He looked at it and chortled. "No. No. This will take years, child."

"Years?"

"Years. What did you expect? For me to mutter some words and speed you on your way?" He tsked and shook his head. "Foolish girl. No. Learn some patience or abandon your vengeance. But do not waste any more of my time."

"I cannot wait years."

The wizard frowned and scratched his jaw. "Oh, enough, enough. Here." He walked over to a shelf and plucked a tiny leaf from a potted plant. "Eat this. You will sleep the years away and never age. I will wake you when your sword is ready. And then you will bring me this magic sword of light."

"Why do you want it?" she said.

The wizard made an easy gesture. "A professional interest. No more."

"I will chase you to hell if you try to cheat me, wizard." She sniffed the leaf, bit. The taste was bitter. At once her head felt heavy.

"Yes. Fear not," said the wizard. He helped her over to a bed of straw. "I will try and remember to wake you."

The dim lights went black and she saw no more.

Igral opened her eyes and immediately hauled herself upright.

"Well. You're awake now," said the wizard. He walked over and handed her a gourd. Igral drank. Spiced wine burned her throat; heat rushed into her limbs.

"I was successful," he said. "Though it took longer than I expected."

"How long?" she said.

"How long have you been asleep, you mean. Thirty years. You will no doubt appreciate the extra care I took preparing your sword. It is most formidable now."

She grabbed his throat. "Thirty years!"

He smiled and nodded. "Thirty. I offer no apology. And you have profited from our bargain – as you will see." He handed her a sheathed blade.

"It looks no different." Igral let go of the wizard and made to draw it.

"No!" His eyes crackled with blue fire. "You must never draw this sword unless you mean to kill. It must take a life before returning to its sheath – or it will take yours."

"What manner of sorcery is that?"

"I have nurtured a demon to live in your sword, woven its binding with many spells. The steel is very strong and will never dull. But the demon hungers for flesh and thirsts for blood. No foe is beyond its power. Seek your enemy's flesh." He paused. "Remember your end of the bargain."

"I do not even know if my father's killer still lives. Suppose he is dead – what good is the sword then?"

The wizard shrugged. "Kill his children. It's no matter to me." He glanced back towards a bubbling cauldron of blue-green liquid. "Your young blood was very useful these past few decades. Very seldom do I encounter such a vigorous specimen. No wonder heroes' blood is in short supply."

Igral examined her forearms, crisscrossed with a latticework of unfamiliar scars.

"But a deal was made. I expect you to uphold it, or I will not be so kind," said the wizard.

She drew the sword. Red light throbbed down its length of polished steel. She thrust it into the wizard's chest and twisted. His eyes went wide and he screamed, grabbing at her shoulders feebly. Black blood gushed from the wound. When she withdrew the sword only smoking bone remained of the Wizard Under the Mountain.

Outside were blue sky and bright sun. Green grass poked out from beneath a blanket of thawing snow. Warm winds blew up from the valley; birds sang and skirted through budding trees.

Igral hiked down into the forest and made camp. She kindled a fire against the coming night and sat in front of it, rubbing her callused hands against her cold, pale flesh. Sleep came quickly.

She woke before dawn, covered her fire, and set off into the forest. Her stomach snarled for a bloody haunch of meat and her throat screamed for a flagon of wine. She was beginning to feel every year of their long absence.

Tracks were scattered across the forest floor. Igral knelt, dusting the snow until she uncovered a trail. She followed it, mind flooded with memories of hunting with her father. It had been simpler with bows.

A young doe sipped water from a creek. Igral plucked a stone and carefully climbed a nearby tree, finding secure perch on a stout lower branch overhanging the gamepath. Stretching herself out quietly along the bark, she drew her long knife. Then she cast the rock onto the streambank behind it. The yearling bolted straight for her and she dropped, slitting its throat smoothly as her bulk crushed it beneath her. She held it fast while it bled out.

Horses trampled through the woods. Two men emerged from the trees. Each wore a metal helmet and carried shield, axe, and lance.

"Who are you?" one of them said.

Igral rose from the forest floor. "Who are you?"

"Mordren, and this is Borzum. We are Lord Auric's housecarls. Who are you?" he repeated. "By what right do you hunt in this forest?"

"This land belongs to me."

They laughed. "Queen of the Forest, are you?" said the other.

"I am Igral. Hastald was my father, whom Auric slew by treachery. I am your Lord, and soon I will drink Auric's blood from silver goblets."

The two men looked at one another. "Hastald and his ilk have been dead thirty years," said Mordren. "Do you think this is a game, whore?"

She drew her sword. Red light played down the blade; a hard smile bloomed across her lips. "Come and play, eunuch."

Mordren cursed and raised his spear.

"Leave her!" said Borzum.

Mordren spurred his horse and charged.

Igral rolled under the spear thrust and hacked the horse's legs, sending it screaming to the ground. Mordren crawled from the saddle and drew his axe from his belt.

"That horse was worth more than your life," he growled, leaping to the attack.

Igral danced backwards, parrying his strokes. The sword felt strange in her hands, moving against her instincts, pulling her to the attack.

Akjik struck, a backhand cut that yanked her along by the tendons. It hewed the axe-head clear from its haft. A blink. The sword pierced Mordren's bowels, the thrust too quick for her eye to follow. Blood gushed from the wound. The sword pulsed red, swallowing it. Howling, Mordren shriveled. Flesh sloughed away like candle wax, leaving a scarecrow: clothes draped over naked bone. The skeleton clattered to the ground.

"Sorcery!" Borzum shouted, fighting with the reins. His horse shrieked, reared, and spilled him from the saddle.

Igral strode over, raising her sword.

He pulled off his helmet. Borzum was an old man, his beard the color of iron. His face was grey with shame. "Please," he begged. "Spare me! I served your father."

"Traitor."

"No!" He rolled over onto his knees and bowed his head. "I fought for you and your father thirty years ago. I did not recognize – could not believe –"

"You serve Auric now?"

Borzum pressed his face to the ground. "After the war he…he offered me mercy. I took it. I wanted to live!"

"You should have fallen on your sword," she said.

"Your father was dead and you had vanished." He looked up and there were tears in his eyes. "I have a family. Hungry mouths care nothing for honor. Take me in your service, I beg of you."

"What would I do with an old man?" she said.

8

"You may take my horse and weapons. I have food and –"

"Wine?"

He nodded. "A skin of Gossian red."

They built a fire, gutted and skinned the doe, and cut spits from hornwood branches. Soon Borzum had it roasting over crackling flames. Igral sucked at the wineskin and bit steaming venison off the bone in fat hunks. Blood sluiced down her chin. She washed down the meat with more wine.

Borzum spoke cautiously. "Mordren was one of Faylek's greatest warriors."

"Mordren," she said. She poured some wine on the ground.

Borzum frowned. "What did you do to him?"

She touched the hilt of her sword. "It is a demon blade. The Wizard Under the Mountain forged it."

"I did not know he truly existed."

"He doesn't, not any more. I slew him."

"Why?"

"He tricked me. Gave me a drug, then left me to sleep for thirty years."

Borzum's green eyes were wide with wonder. "So that is the secret of your youth."

Igral grunted indifferently, spat gristle into the fire.

"And now you will slay Auric? You won't need a demon sword for that. A pillow is enough. He's old, on his deathbed some say. His sons rule."

"Then I will kill his sons," she said, wiping her mouth with the back of her hand. "Which one is nearest?"

"I was sworn to Faylek's service. He rules from a castle a few leagues east. War is brewing with his brothers."

Drunk already, Igral drank more and more, heedless of intemperance.

"I heard tales of the battle at Muradk," said Borzum, staring at her. "They say you were a demon that day, that you killed fifty men at least. But then you disappeared. What happened?"

"Auric defeated me," she said, standing. "Take me to this castle."

Borzum shook his head. "That would be suicide. Faylek will kill you on sight."

"Do not defy your lord and master," she said. "Take me there."

Faylek's castle proved to be a timber fort set atop a mud-slopped hill. Men teemed around the stockade like ants, digging ditches and sharpening stakes, gawking as Borzum and Igral rode past. Their horse picked a slow path around bubbling brown pits and puddles.

A spearman stopped them at the outer gate. "Alone?" he said to Borzum. "Where's Mordren?"

"I slew him," said Igral as she dismounted.

He smiled. "Oh. No small feat. What's your name, lassie?"

"Igral. Daughter of Hastald. I have come to kill your master."

A pause. The spearman laughed and winched open the gate. "Go on through," he said.

Borzum stabled the horse and they walked up to the fort proper. Four men in steel coats and crested helms barred their way.

One spoke. "No weapons in the hall."

Igral nodded. The custom had been the same in her father's house. The guards took their weapons. Igral's hands tingled as she gave Akjik away.

They walked into the dim smoky hall. Multicolored banners hung from tall wooden beams. Burning torches cast dim light on log walls. Guards armed with hooked halberds stood at attention.

Faylek sat on a tall oaken throne, a fat man, well past youth. His dark hair and beard rusted white over his flabby jaw. A slim woman in a grey gown stood beside him. Her long russet hair was tied back in a simple braid, and her blue eyes scrutinized Igral as she approached.

"What do you want, Borzum?" Faylek snapped. "And why did you bring that slut? We teeter on the brink of war!"

Borzum grabbed her arm. "This is suicide!" he whispered.

"Borzum – where is Mordren?" Faylek's eyes narrowed.

"I slew him," Igral said. "I am Igral, and I've come to destroy your family."

A chasm of silence opened wide in the hall.

"Impossible," said Faylek. "She would be sixty at least, were she still alive."

"She tells the truth, my lord," said Borzum.

The fat man laughed. "A joke."

"No," said the woman at his side. "Look at her, look at her eyes. She is not joking."

"Fight me, if you are no coward," said Igral.

Faylek chuckled. "Gout stole the strength from my sword-arm long ago," he said. "But even were I hale, I still would not fight you. Whoever you are. I have no courageous bone in my body." He lifted a finger. "Take her."

11

The guards raised their halberds and converged. Borzum stepped forward to bar their path. Steel blades rained down, hacking him apart.

The guards closed in on her. A halberd whistled down. Igral ducked the cut, seized the shaft, and twisted it loose. She drove the butt into the guard's solar plexus, knocking him flat. Another stepped in to fill the line. She windmilled the pole and brought the axe face down on his helmeted pate. Blood squirted from his head like juice from a crushed fruit.

Something swept her legs from under her and she hit the ground. Men piled on, pinning her by sheer weight. The halberd was pried from her hands.

"Such a fierce creature," someone said.

Igral growled like caged lion. "Cowards!" she screamed. "Fools! Who would serve a man afraid to fight a woman?"

Faylek laughed, slapping the bulge of his gut. "Throw her in the dungeon."

The jailer's dull bovine eyes watched her through the iron bars. Igral regarded him stoically. She had never seen a man so huge. His arms were like tree limbs, his legs fleshy pylons. Belly fat hung to his knees in concentric folds.

He shambled forward, unbarred the gate. "Going to scream?" he asked. His tone was both good-natured and indifferent. He might have been talking to livestock.

Igral didn't bother answering. Once more she yanked at the chains, hoping to pull them loose from their moorings in the ceiling. They held firm.

He shrugged, unbuckled his britches and came at her.

She lifted herself by her chains and clamped her legs about his neck, driving her knees into his throat. He choked, grasping pitifully at her thighs as his face turned pink.

A chain snapped. Igral lost her hold and went sprawling to the ground. The jailer staggered back and leaned against the bars, huffing to catch his breath. He wiped his face, spat and came again.

Igral whipped him with the loose chain, gouging his blubbery haunch with rusted iron, but the jailer barely seemed to notice. He lumbered inside Igral's guard and bore her down.

Her face was trapped in a slick buttery burrow. She couldn't see, could hardly breathe. The jailer's hot breath roiled across her neck. She felt him tear away her shift, probe her thighs, stiff, unyielding. Vomit trickled from her lips.

A door opened, closed. The jailer looked up and cursed. Igral drove her fist into his temple and heard a satisfying crack. He crawled away, moaning.

Two figures descended into the dungeon. "Leave us," said a woman's voice. The jailer stumbled to his feet, clutching his head, and staggered out.

"Are you injured?" Another voice, a man's.

Igral inspected the newcomers. Faylek's red-haired woman stood before her with a stranger at her side. He was a tall, lean man with dark unkempt hair and green eyes. He wore a shirt of iron scales and a sword at his hip.

"Who are you?"

"Cerwyn," she said. "Faylek's wife."

"Royac," the man said with a half-bow. "Auric is my father. I hear you mean to kill him. Me, too," He smiled. "Your methods are somewhat unorthodox. Did you really expect to succeed like that, disarmed and surrounded?"

"I have waited too many years for revenge. I will not wait a moment longer."

Royac grinned. "A little more subtlety might improve your chances. Unless you want to end up like your friend Borzum."

"Better to die than live like a leech." Igral bared her teeth at him.

13

Cerwyn spoke. "I've come to make you an offer."

Igral tested the chain around her left wrist. The iron bolts still held. "Speak," she said.

"We free you from this cell. Then we deliver you my husband, to do with as you please."

"In exchange?"

"Marry me," said Royac.

Igral smirked.

"None of Auric's children have clear title to these lands," said Cerwyn. "The people do not support them. If you wed Royac, his claim gains legitimacy. Your father is fondly remembered. Folk will remember you as well. They will follow you. That will tip the balance in the coming war. "

"Not such a bad deal," said Royac. He scratched his jaw. "It's your only real chance, you know."

"I will not bargain away my honor," said Igral. "My answer is no. I will kill Auric and all his children."

"Listen to reason," hissed Cerwyn. "You have no money, no support, no friends. You are condemned to death in the arena. Your corpse will go to feed the dogs. Take my word. Royac is the youngest of his brothers and the best of them. Faylek is cruel; Altor is grasping and useless."

"We are done," said Igral.

Cerwyn stalked back up the stairs, but Royac lingered. He slipped a leather skin from his shoulder and tossed it to her.

"Wine," he said, winking as she caught it.

She pulled the cork, sniffed, and drank deep.

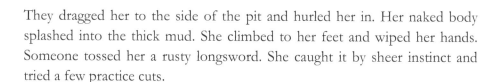

They dragged her to the side of the pit and hurled her in. Her naked body splashed into the thick mud. She climbed to her feet and wiped her hands. Someone tossed her a rusty longsword. She caught it by sheer instinct and tried a few practice cuts.

A crowd of men shouted at her from above. She scanned their faces and found Faylek in the masses. Cerwyn sat at his side, face drawn tight.

A horn sounded; a gate opened. Three slavering hounds rushed in, dragging their leashes behind.

One leapt straight for her throat and she impaled it, quickly tossing its bleeding, yelping mass aside. The other two circled her, wary. She pivoted, mirroring their movements to protect her flank.

They struck from either side. The dog to her left clamped its teeth to her forearm and shook it viciously. The other pounced at her legs. She skipped backwards, swinging her sword wildly. She caught its foreleg with a lucky cut. It howled, foundered in the mud. Igral clove its head in two.

The first hound still had its grip. She hammered the sword's pommel down below its neck, snapping the dog's spine. It yowled and fell, broken. The crowd cheered, hooting and shouting her on.

Again the horn blew. The gate opened again. In tramped a massive bear, snout wrinkled in annoyance. Pink scars laced its heavy brown fur. For a moment it was placid. Then it scented Igral and with a snarl charged straight for her.

She danced away, sweeping her blade back and forth as she went. Its tip nicked the bear's snout, drawing a sliver of red. It pulled away as if stung. She kept her distance. Blood leaked from her left arm with every step.

Her foot slipped in a puddle of mud. The bear lunged. Igral rolled away, spinning and sliding in the thick mud. The sword slipped from her hand.

15

Now the bear occupied the center of the ring while she was she was close by the wall. She leapt for a handhold halfway up the wall and tried to lever herself higher. The audience booed and gasped; guards rushed over and jabbed at her with pikes. She seized one just below the spearhead and ripped it away, falling back into the pit.

Her new weapon was well suited to her foe: now she had the advantage of reach. Igral circled her quarry, poking, prodding, taunting. At length the bear grew frustrated and hurled its great mass forward. The point caught its throat, tearing tissue. It staggered back.

She stabbed, stabbed, stabbed. The bear groaned and slumped onto its side. She kept stabbing until it stopped breathing.

The crowd thundered its approval.

Faylek stood and raised his arms. "Send it in!" he shouted. The crowd went wild. Several horns sounded in unison, and the gate opened a third time.

A grey-skinned ogre lumbered into the arena. It was at least eight feet tall and muscled like an ox, with skin like an Oliphant's hide. Tusks jutted from its lower jaw and it carried a massive axe and a shield the size of a door.

Igral howled and charged, leveling her pike at the ogre's face. Perplexed, it raised its shield. Quick as a snake, she swiveled the spearhead, driving it into the ogre's ankle. Green blood bubbled free.

The ogre slammed its shield down, snapping the pike in two. It snarled and hewed at her with its axe. Igral slid under the arcing blade and shimmied right, claiming her bloody sword from the mud. As the ogre lumbered around for another swing she slashed its hamstring

The monster moaned and fell backwards. Igral clambered onto its chest and thrust the sword into its eye. The ogre twitched, then lay still.

"Seize her!" shouted Faylek.

Guards rushed in by the dozen from the tunnel to beat her down with hardwood cudgels. Igral lay stunned. They pried the sword from her hand.

When she came to her senses Faylek stood in the ring, Cerwyn at his right hand. Akjik hung from his side. Igral's eyes fixed on it.

"An impressive display," he said. He rested a hand on the hilt of her father's sword. "Perhaps you truly are Igral, returned after all these years. If so your reputation is deserved." Faylek smiled cruelly. "Yet for all your skill, it is I who am greater." He drew the sword and took a fanciful cut, then held the tip to her throat.

"If I wished, I could spill your blood all over this arena. But to kill you is beneath me. You are my slave now. It will please me to see you raped a hundred times a day for the rest of your unnatural life." He smiled and sheathed the sword, turning –

Stopped. The veins in his face and neck bulged. Blood spilled from his eyes, nose, ears, mouth. His skin sloughed off his flesh and piled at his feet. His body crumpled like wax over a flame.

Someone screamed. Everyone stared.

"Release me," said Igral. The guards let her go. She stood, walked over to the corpse, and claimed Akjik from the smoking puddle. She looked at Cerwyn, standing ashen-faced and aghast.

"I accept your offer," Igral said.

Wine poured from the cup, spilling across her lips and chin. Igral grunted and wiped her mouth with the back of her hand. Blood from the wound in her arm seeped into the leather lining of her new ringmail shirt. Her father's demon-haunted sword sat across her lap, throbbing in time with her heart.

"Perhaps those wounds…" began Royac.

She thrust her cup at him. "More wine."

"As you please," he said amiably, and filled her goblet. Their eyes met. She drank.

Igral said to Cerwyn: "Shouldn't you be wearing black and weeping?"

Cerwyn looked, startled. "Oh. No. Faylek kept me as his slave. Auric seized my family's lands when I was only a girl. I was a gift to his son."

Igral nodded. She looked at Royac. "How many men are here in this castle?"

"One hundred and thirty fighting men. A few dozen laborers, also."

Again she nodded. "And weapons? Armor?"

Royac sighed. "You're getting ahead of yourself. How precisely do we proceed? Faylek's men will not follow me. And I doubt they will follow you."

"We pay them."

"Not all are mercenaries," said Royac, rubbing his jaw. "Though many will be swayed. But who will pay them?"

"You," she said. "Consider it my bride price."

Royac grinned. "I have certain chests of coin set aside."

"What of your own men? How many can you rally?"

"Twenty-five housecarls. Plus fifty conscripts, given a few days' notice." He paused. "What are you planning? We cannot possibly attack."

"No," said Cerwyn. "That would be suicide. Altor can summon a thousand men to fight for him – Auric twice that."

Igral was not deterred. "The people must learn of my return. Then our numbers will grow."

Cerwyn shook her head. "But what hope is there if we —"

"I have won your husband's lands and your soldiers' loyalty in a day. Now I will win this war."

Two guards dragged in a prodigiously fat bald man. "Here's the one you wanted," said one.

The jailer looked up at her and screamed.

Igral drew her father's sword.

The green-robed cleric spoke, voice sere. "You are now husband and wife. What is here joined together, let no beast, man, or god tear apart." Down came his hammer and crushed the lamb's skull. It slumped to the ground.

Igral and Royac raised their joined hands. The gathered mass roared, soldiers and commonfolk alike. Colorful banners waved as flower petals filled the air and pipes blew long trills.

Igral and Royac turned and ascended the path toward the house on the hill. Fiddlers skipped ahead of them in whirling celebratory song.

"A day ago you were a prisoner," said Royac, loudly in her ear. "Now you are the master. I should worry."

She caught his gaze. "But you don't."

"I am incapable."

Guards cast wide the longhouse doors. In they went, and on to the bedchamber, shutting the door behind them.

Igral let loose her yellow hair and pulled off her white gown. Royac stayed her hands. "We met once before," he said. "Do you remember?"

Her eyes narrowed. "No."

"It was long ago. I was a boy then." He smiled. "You were exactly as you are now. I remember you hunched in a corner, nursing a wine cask. You glowered at me." He squeezed her hand. "I did not fight against you. What my father did to you, and your father, was wrong. I have never been your enemy." He looked at her longingly. "You don't believe me. I have no reason to lie to you."

"Like father, like son," she said.

His smile changed, grew grim. "I do not care if you think me a liar. I have loved you since I was a boy. Your face has stayed with me for thirty years, haunting every woman I take to bed."

"You have my pity." She turned away.

He grabbed her wrist. "I know what you have suffered. I know what my father did at Muradk."

"It was war," she said, tearing her hand away. "That is the way of it."

His smile fell. "Still you do not comprehend. My bloodline means nothing to me. Take your revenge. Kill until you are satisfied. I will love you all the more." His tone was frigid.

She cleared her throat. "Will you consummate our vows?"

"When neither honor nor vows demand it."

Igral slipped the gown back over her head, took up Akjik, and left the chamber.

Mist clouded the vale. Igral rode a chestnut mare, Royac and Cerwyn at her side. Behind marched a haphazard army clad in iron, leather, and skins. They beat brave drums and waved bold banners. They numbered barely a hundred.

Igral glanced at her husband. He was staring ahead, grinding his teeth.

"Where are we going?" said Cerwyn. She looked uncomfortable on horseback.

Igral sucked wine from her skin. "There are villages nearby."

Cerwyn nodded slightly. "Yes. Minor estates."

Igral watched her. "Tell me how revenge feels."

Cerwyn pulled her cloak tight about her. "I spent so long hating him. I grew that inside of me. Like some kind of...egg. I wish I could have slept those years away like you." She smiled wanly.

"Will you go home?"

Cerwyn shook her head. "Who waits for me there? My family is dead." She looked away.

"Tell me about your father's sword, Royac. That blade of light."

"A family heirloom," he said. "Forged five hundred years ago by dwarves, from the strongest iron, dragon's gold, and sunlight. But they tricked my ancestors and sealed their creation in stone, never to be removed."

She drank. "Yet it was. How?"

Royac shrugged. "My father pulled it from the rock. He will say no more. My brother carries it now."

"Tell me about him."

"I have not seen Altor in years. He is my father's favorite. He..." Royac trailed off.

Hovels appeared ahead, emerging from the fog. Igral spurred the mare ahead and looked around. The homes looked deserted, with shuttered windows and barred doors.

Cerwyn and Royac rode up beside her. "They flee the coming war," said Cerwyn.

A door opened. A boy emerged carrying a piglet in his arms. He saw them, shouted, and ran away down the street. Igral followed him, cantering through the fog.

She came to a meadow. A hundred people crowded beneath the drooping arms of a titanic willow. They stared at her in confusion and fear. A big-gutted man with a bushy beard pushed to the front. "Who are you?"

"Igral. Hastald's daughter," she said.

The man was silent a moment before he spoke. "Clear off. We want no part of your madness." The crowd murmured its agreement.

"Who are you?" Igral asked.

"Storn Barrelmaker." He folded his arms over his chest. "Chief of these villages when the housecarls are called to war."

"That time is now. I require your men and women of fighting age."

Some in the crowd shouted in outrage; others whimpered or jeered.

"Why?" roared the barrel-maker. "What will you promise us? Gold? Land? Glory?" He pointed at the ground. "We want only peace."

Royac rode up beside her. "You will not move them," he whispered. "Leave off. Take their food for the army and leave them to their fate."

Igral shook her head. "Your village is a reed in a storm," she said. "Sooner or later you will be overwhelmed. Better you fight for me than someone worse."

"You are as bad as the rest!" A shout from the crowd.

"No," she said firmly. "I seek revenge for my father and death to his usurpers."

Storn spoke. "I did not know your father. When I was born his body was already cold in the grave."

Igral raised her voice, speaking to the whole crowd. "Your fathers fought with mine for what is right. Your coward's peace dishonors them. I ask only that you honor your forebears by fighting with me now."

A long pause. A few stepped forward; then a few more. Storn wavered, scratching his beard.

Igral pointed at him. "You are a barrel-maker?"

"I am."

"Instead be a man."

Storn sucked in a breath and stepped forward.

Igral stared out over the ragtag mass of villagers and soldiers. Rusty billhooks and pitchforks bristled like a porcupine's quills.

"A logistical nightmare," groused Royac. "We have almost no food left. We've eaten this town to the ground and more volunteers arrive every hour. We need to march or we'll starve."

He glanced at Igral sidewise. "You look like you're about to smile."

She didn't answer. Instead, she unslung the battlehorn and blew a long note. "FORM!" she roared.

Their forces gathered in ragged clusters of several dozen men each.

Royac was not impressed. "Those levies of yours aren't worth much. Give us another hundred fighting men and forty more housecarls and someone might mistake us for an army. From a distance, I mean."

Igral blew her horn again. "FORWARD!"

Knots of men advanced, shouting and screeching at the top of their lungs. Royac cocked a brow. "That's the most bloodthirsty pack of cobblers, gardeners and gong farmers I've ever clapped eyes on."

She snorted.

He grinned at her crookedly. "So you *can* laugh."

"Will your brother march out to meet us?"

"You are openly challenging his rule. Suborning his subjects. He must fight or the housecarls will desert him."

Igral nodded. "What of the rumors?"

"Which ones? That my father is dead? That his housecarls rise up in revolt? Unlikely. Wars starve the commons, but they breed rumors as dung breeds flies."

"Your father. When my father died at Muradk I could think only of revenge. I took Akjik from his hip, rode into the press. We fought. I lost.

"Auric raped me right there on the battlefield, and again at the camp. His housecarls watched. Then I had to pledge my allegiance or he would keep Akjik for a war prize. So I swore him fealty.

"He demanded other things, too. Title to my lands. To know where my father had buried his hoard. I gave whatever he asked. Then, when I had Akjik once more, I fled."

Royac looked at the ground. "Do you miss Hastald?"

"Not now, so close to vengeance. When I was alone in the wilderness I did. Every minute; every smile."

A horse and rider galloped towards them and skidded to a halt in a flurry of dust. "They're on the march!" he yelled. "Altor comes!"

"How many men?" Royac asked.

"At least a thousand," gasped the rider.

"Time to go," said Igral.

Last night's rain had drenched the green hills where they had bivouacked. Fog coiled about the highlands, a bed of bloated white serpents. A chorus of frogs and insects chirred their primal song from the flooded vale below.

The army slogged through a drowned meadow and up onto the ridgeline. Igral raised a hand. The army halted. She unslung her horn and blew a long wailing blast. They fell into formation: cavalry on the flanks, footmen in the center. Three adjacent wedges like the prongs of a fork.

She glanced over her shoulder and took stock of her followers one last time. Storn Barrelmaker, pensive-seeming, wooden mallet in one hand and rusty knife in the other. Dar Quickshot, a tall, thin man busily stringing his bow. Gared Blockman, armed only with threshing-hooks and chisels. Hundreds of others, strangers mostly, that she had somehow coerced into service.

Spears sprouted from the hill to the east. Armed men poured over it, flanked by housecarls on horseback.

Royac pointed out the various factions. "The ones in the feathered caps – Ossland archers. And there – Langovarts – see the long beards and axes?"

Igral nodded. "And on the right?"

"The little ones are Gisqwiks. Javelin-throwers and slingers. The ones in chainmail are Bosfin swordsmen."

Cerwyn rode up to join them. She was soaked. They all were. "Gods," she muttered, "so many." Then: "Look."

Three horsemen had split off the main army and rode toward the sunken vale between them. One carried a white flag.

"A parley," said Cerwyn.

Igral clicked her tongue and her horse trotted down the slope. Cerwyn and Royac followed close behind. The parties met on a narrow spit of ground still above water.

She knew Altor at once. He had his father's eyes, blue as robin's eggs. A wedge of white beard hung below his jaw. His face was narrow, cheeks gaunt, eyes weary. A gold-hilted sword hung from his saddlehorn.

And there was something else, something that rippled the air around him: a transparent aura, like heat from a bonfire. He looked at her – not angry nor afraid. Curious? Something in his gaze unsettled her. She looked away.

It was to Royac that he first spoke. "Is it true that Faylek is slain?" he asked, a gauntleted hand on the hilt of his sword.

Royac nodded. "Burned to death from inside when he set hand on her blade. Few deserved it more."

Altor looked to her. "My father is dead. He succumbed to illness several days hence."

For a moment Igral's heart ceased to beat.

"We hear rumors of revolt," said Royac. "Any truth to them?"

"Riots more like. Minor insurrections. All put down." Altor spoke again to Igral. "You are Hastald's daughter?"

She nodded.

"I knew your father. Did you know that? It is true. I spent a summer at his hall when I was a lad. Before you were born. A good man. Wise, fair."

"Murdered. By your father."

He made a noncommittal gesture. "So they say. But I was not at Muradk. So how should I judge my father's deeds?" He sighed, a sound of sheer fatigue. "But I understand your need for vengeance. Blood for blood."

Igral said nothing.

Altor spoke. "Am I what you expected? An old man, bent by taxes, famines, disputes and rebellions?"

"No," she said.

He smiled sourly. "It makes no difference now. Battle is unavoidable."

"There is a way," said Igral. "Single combat. I will fight any champion you name."

"No," said Altor. "Every day my housecarls grow more defiant. Some want to destroy you. Others – more, probably – yearn to join you, to carve out new estates for themselves from the wreckage of my kingdom." He rubbed his forehead. "I am tired. I do not sit a saddle half as well as I once did."

"Will you accept a truce?" said Igral. Both Royac and Cerwyn looked at her in astonishment.

Altor smiled mirthlessly. "Are you frightened? Or has revenge lost its savor?" He shook his head. "No. My situation is precarious. More men desert each day. You must be crushed, and quickly, or I will have no more army."

"Yield," said Royac. "You will be spared."

"Do I have my brother's word?" Altor ran two fingers through his white beard. "Do you know what father told me on his deathbed? He said that when this sword was created, it was prophesied that he who freed it from the stone would be the one to ruin his family."

Royac rolled his eyes. "Nonsense."

"I agree," he said, smiling. He looked at Cerwyn. "My lady. I offer you a proposal. You would not know it, but you have kin who live not far from

28

here. Two of your younger sisters and your uncle, Fralyn. They hold a small estate two days' ride northeast. Let me provide you an escort there."

Cerwyn's face blanched. She raised her hand to her throat. "I…"

"No trick, my lady. This field is no place for such as you." He gestured invitingly. "I am happy to see you freed. My brother was a beast."

Cerwyn looked at Igral, blue eyes wet with tears. "Thank you," she said, and rode off.

"I will look for you on the field," said Altor to Igral. He turned his horse and trotted back to his army. His spearmen followed.

Igral and Royac rode back through darkening floodwaters.

By the time they returned to camp black clouds hid the morning sun and the storm was almost upon them. Thunder rumbled across the hillsides. Spears of lightning forked between the thunderheads. By its flash, they watched Altor's army lurch forward, a rising iron tide.

Igral's cheek twitched.

Royac put a hand on her shoulder. "Come on. Time to go."

She looked into his eyes, nodded. Then she drew her sword and raised it. Akjik throbbed sensuously. Warmth surged into her hand and up her arm. She brought her horn to her lips and blew long and shrill. Roars rose from her army. She led them forward.

Arrows rained over their advance. Men fell, pinned to the mud by goose-feathered shafts. They shouted and wailed and died. The advance stalled.

Royac pulled up alongside her. "Lead them," he shouted. "You are their captain. Lead them or we will all die."

She searched for her ancient molten rage and discovered it missing. But she did not want to die. So she put the horn to her lips and blew another note. Men shouted battle cries and surged forward.

Altor's men had entered the bog, foundering through knee-deep muck. "Archers!" someone shouted. Arrows sprang from her line this time. Men toppled, another obstacle for Altor's force to overcome.

Howls of bloodlust rose up at her rear. A dozen men charged. Then fifty. Then the ranks gave way in a mad stampede. Igral's army fell on Altor's like wild dogs.

Igral watched, reins tight in her fist as bodies piled in the marsh. Akjik pulsed in her hand, throbbing, coaxing her towards the fray.

From across the vale a trumpet blared. Altor and his housecarls barged forward, riding into the press. Igral spurred her horse towards them. Royac and his horsemen charged close behind.

Through the steel bramble of swords and helmets and spearheads she saw a beacon of light. Altor rode through the very heart of the battle, sword flashing its balefire, carving down her soldiers like grain at harvest.

Akjik thrummed. Altor looked up and saw her and their eyes locked.

Altor raised his sword. White light poured from within, bright as the sun, and she went blind.

She felt her horse surge forward. It whickered in panic. By instinct Igral raised her own blade.

Steel met steel. Her whole body trembled from the force of their clash. Akjik fought on its own now, using her strength, pivoting in her grip, pulling her arm this way and that. She felt Altor near, smelled his stink. Their blades clashed again, razor edges grinding together, screeching. Akjik pulled her closer. Igral screamed and hewed with all her strength.

A crack like shattering glass. The world fluttered from shadow to color.

Altor still sat his horse. Shards of steel bristled from his throat. Blood flowed down his lacerated chest and drained into the bog. In his hand was a broken sword.

Igral looked down at her father's blade. Akjik was a splintered ruin. All the fire inside was gone.

Altor slumped from the saddle, fell. His horse reared, then trotted away, dragging the body by a stirrup until it came loose and sank into the bog.

Igral gnawed at a chicken leg and stared into the fire. She spat gristle onto the coals. It sizzled and popped.

All around were sounds of celebration. Pipers piped; drunken voices sang; men and women grunted towards satisfaction. Igral looked up. The stars watched. She tore the last shred of meat free with her teeth and swallowed.

Gar Quickshot sat nearby, waxing his bowstring. A mangy black and brown dog lolled against his thigh. She tossed the bone to him, then stood and walked off. She came to a large tent. Two guards stepped aside and she passed through.

Royac lay on a blanket. Physicians hovered over him, inspecting his wounds. They saw her and bowed. Royac looked up at her. Dried blood stained his face. He smiled weakly.

"Leave us," she said.

The physicians went away. Igral drew the broken sword from her belt. Candlelight flickered on its jagged edge.

Royac coughed. Blood dribbled from the corner of his mouth. "Do you remember…what I said at our nuptials?"

She leaned down over him and held the sword to his throat.

He winced. His dressings were soaked red. Yellow pus oozed out here and there from under the gauze. "If you're going to kill me, might I suggest a more pleasant method?"

She paused.

"If we were to couple," he said. "I'm quite certain my dressings would tear loose, and I would bleed to death."

Her lips twitched into a hard smile.

How Pell Left

A. H. Jennings

ik paused at the lip of the stone pathway and scanned the dense forest that clothed the mountain's lower reaches. Away to the west, a white swathe of beach reclined beside a vast expanse of purple ocean. Several specks bobbed on the water – boats and rafts on which boys sat or lay fishing for food or pleasure.

Several yards on, the path drew in against the mountainside and narrowed into a dangerous ledge. Nik hugged the wall and sidled carefully on – not for fear of the drop, but because he was tired, and would rather not spend however long making his way up again.

At the end of the ledge, Nik jumped the five-foot gap to a sort of natural stone porch that jutted from the mouth of his cave. He stood quietly for a moment and bathed in the perfumed sunlight, listening to the birdcalls of new boys gathered around the Naming Spring.

Nik turned to duck inside and stopped short as the feathers on his war bonnet rustled against the sun curtain. He slid the bonnet from his head and carried it into the cave.

Nik had lived here for as long as he could remember. The marionettes, the dusty spinning tops, and the dried mantarangs, he had stolen fair and square – but the stone nesting dolls, the miniature skeletons, and the earthenware pottery all seemed to have belonged to someone else who had lived here before his time.

Crawling on three limbs, Nik made his way across the sleeping cushions to a shelf set with model soldiers and the bust of a dour-faced sea bishop. Nik set his war bonnet on the merman's head and nodded gravely to him. Satisfied, Nik flopped onto his back and laced his fingers behind his head as he stared up at the cave's domed ceiling. Now he thought if it, it might be nice to build a ladder and paint a mural up there.

Before long, sleep swept in and carried Nik away to float on the surface of a dark pool. The water was warm and secret, and above it stretched an irregular stone ceiling limned with constellations of iridescent lichen.

A school bus: the green vinyl seats, the scrolling suburban scenery, a fat boy stuffed into the seat beside him. Everything breaking. Silence. The smells of blood, wet hair, and too much rain.

Nik gasped awake to the rattling of his speaking cup. Night filled the chamber with a liquid darkness. Nik took a breath and moved to grab the receiver. "Hello?" he said.

"Nik?" It was Goz. "Are you back?"

Nik rolled his eyes. "No, Goz," he said. "I'm still gone."

"Well, Pell wants to see you when you get back."

Black howlers cried out in the forest canopy, but none of them seemed interested in throwing anything tonight. Nik could have walked this trail even without his brine lantern. He knew without thinking that if he struck out to his left and walked seventy paces, he would find the cache of buried pebbles which, held under the tongue, would allow him to breathe underwater. After ninety paces, the path bisected a grassy clearing that gave way to the clean white beach and the wine-dark ocean.

Most of the time, Pell lived in a grass hut situated some thirty yards shy of the tide line. Tonight, a hundred or so half-wild boys had built a bonfire nearby and most of them sat around it sucking the yolk from beer eggs. The wind changed direction, and the smell of roasting meat told Nik that some boys must have killed a boar or two to eat along with the fish.

Pell stood near the water, listening to a captured night clam as it sang for its life. The clam's song was sweet enough, but it sounded tinny and far-off, as if it issued from the bottom of a tiger pit.

"What do you think?" Pell said as Nik approached.

Nik shrugged. "Roast it. I've heard better."

Pell's bronze skin looked even darker tonight, contrasted against the white linen wrap his mermaid friend Mura had given him when they parted.

"How are the Koahoma?" Pell said quietly.

"We were winning when I left."

"Did you win anything while you were gone?"

Nik grinned hard enough to show the gap left by his missing right incisor. "A war bonnet," he bragged. "It has eight eagle feathers."

Pell didn't seem to hear the answer. "How old are you, Nik?" He said.

"Eleven."

"Are you sure?"

Nik smiled. "Sure I'm sure," he said with a shrug, then dropped into a cat stance. "Wrestle me."

Pell ignored the challenge. "Haven't you been here longer than you were in the Other Place?"

Nik's smile faded. "I dunno. I guess so."

35

Pell bit his lower lip. "I think I was nine when I came here, but I've been here a long time."

Ugh. No fun to be had with Pell tonight. Nik looked across the beach, where groups of boys wrestled or tossed mantarangs back and forth.

"I don't know how long. Nobody knows."

"Yeah, that's... Yeah."

Pell shut his clam with a snap and sat Indian-style in the sand beside its sandy hole. "Nik. Pay attention. Sit with me, please."

Nik wavered for a moment, then sat.

Nik stared at the moon over Pell's shoulder. It hung fat and yellow, magnified to an impossible scale by the moisture in the air. As Nik watched, its pocked surface reminded him of a skull face – no! A boy's face, painted like a doll. Like – !

"There's talk that you keep time," Pell said.

Nik frowned. "That who does? Me?"

"Yes," Pell said.

Nik made a rude noise. "Talk is talk," he said.

"Then it's not true?" Pell said. "You don't know how long I've been here either?"

Nik would have laughed if not for the strain in his friend's voice. "How would I know a thing like that?"

Pell nodded solemnly. "Of course. It was silly of me, to..." He grinned like a hound, showing his teeth, then kicked to his feet to take a cat stance of his own. "Come at me."

In the morning, Nik rolled out of bed and grabbed the speaking cup.

"Goz!" he said. "Goz! Hey!"

Nik waited a beat, then grabbed an ordinary beach pebble from the shelf. He dropped it into the cup and shook it experimentally. No answer.

As Nik took a seat on the sleeping cushions, the sour smell of his own sweat clogged his nostrils and made him squint. He was due for a swim. He shook the cup again, harder this time, the pebble rattling dry against the smooth stone.

Finally, "Hello?"

"Goz?"

"No!"

"Who, then?"

"This is Pekk! Goz left!"

"Where did he go?"

"Yah! Broken City!"

The Broken City was three days away on foot. Nik could have climbed to the highest cliff and caught a kite there, but Goz was terrified of kites, and Nik hoped to catch up to him on the way.

As he walked, a voice Nik hated spoke from the back of his mind: Why is it so important that you speak with Goz?

Shut up, Nik thought.

What would Goz know that you don't?

Someone had told Pell stupid lies about him, and Goz very well might know who.

Before the day was out, the forest path became a crumbling stone road. Nik knew that the road forked several miles on and that if he took the left branch, he would soon reach the Clothes Farm. If you are eleven, said the Voice, how have you had time to learn the things you know?

On his second day walking, Nik left the road to push through high grass toward the sound of running water. Before he could locate the stream, the grass gave way, and Nik found himself standing in a clearing.

Here, the vegetation had been beaten down into a reedy carpet, at the center of which stood what looked like a sand castle half melted by the tide.

The lobster hive was mostly dark, but that was no surprise — brine honey glowed only at night. Still, as Nik approached the hive, he heard the hum and snap of lobsters about their lobster business.

Nik knew that if he stood here long enough a lobster would emerge from the hive and, seeing him, cry out in surprise. He even knew which one it would be — a zebra-striped bug with spotted rainbow wings and sapphire blue eyes. He and the arthropod would regard one another intently for a time, and then the lobster, its name an incomprehensible mess of clicks and whistles, would retreat inside to warn his brothers that a thief had come to steal their honey.

But stealing honeycomb was a two-boy operation, and Nik had left Pell far behind. He stood very still and felt the world trembling around him. One wrong move and everything would shake apart.

Nik reached the city wall by sunset on the third day. Built from enormous red blocks, it rose so high that if Nik stood close enough to touch it, he could not see the top.

Without having to consider his course, he headed west toward the only entrance, a giant jagged hole. Fallen masonry blocked the city gates, and even if it hadn't, the hydraulics that powered them in ancient times had long since gone dry.

Carefully, Nik made his way through the breach into a residential district. Nik hated the look of these houses, of the red stone from which they were made. Their windows, eroded by time, gaped like silent mouths.

Where would Goz be? Nik realized now that he knew nothing of Goz's interests or passions. Goz didn't fish, he didn't hunt, he didn't ride the kites, and he never accompanied the Nokhami on raids. Like the rest of the boys, he disappeared from time to time, probably to come here.

Night brought a mad wind wailing across the plain. Nik could hear it even from within the city. Who had built all this? Surely not boys. The dead gardens, the houses, the staircases joining each level of the vast metropolis, seemed built to too large a scale. It was not impossible for Nik to make his way, but it was just difficult enough to unsettle him.

And did shades of the Broken City's long-gone inhabitants still haunt its shops, its homes, its markets and thoroughfares? Nik had seen ghosts before – when he followed Pell and Mura aboard a sunken galleon outside a Sea Ape village. Ghosts of boys, human ghosts, would not have frightened him, but the things hiding in the rotten ship were black, diaphanous like sheetfish, and their touch was brutal cold.

Just before sunrise, Nik found Goz sitting on the rim of a dry fountain at the center of a piazza surrounded by stern buildings with oversized monumental stairs. He slumped like an abandoned doll.

Goz had worn a patch over his right eye for as long as Nik could remember, but would never explain it when asked or even acknowledge it in conversation. For all Nik knew, the boy had another working eye under there.

He was slight, blond, maybe eight years old. His thick hair grew down to his shoulders and his broad tanned face was dusted with freckles now nearly invisible in the dim of the predawn. He wore only a pair of tattered buckskin pants.

Nik kept to the shadows and watched Goz without approaching. He could have sworn he'd come through here not even an hour ago, and he couldn't escape the sense that he'd only found Goz now because the smaller boy had allowed it.

Goz came to life as Nik stepped out of the shadows. "Nik! Hi!"

"Hi, Goz."

"Is there anyone else?" He made a face, shook his head as if to answer his own question. "How long have you been here?"

"Well, I just…not long."

"Would you like to see my Place, Nik?" Goz said. "It's wonderful. It's so wonderful that – it's so wonderful that I hate it sometimes, I think. Did you say you would come with me?"

"Where?"

"To my Place. I'll show you." Goz rose from his seat and turned to bound up the front steps of an enormous columned building.

Nik knew that he could no more follow Goz than he could swim to the moon. A cold terror had stolen over him, and he felt as if he stood in the path of a falling tree. He ran after Goz not because he wanted to but to escape his own fear.

Inside, a blue stone walkway wound through a vast overgrown garden where plants huddled around the bases of enormous trees and fought each other for a pale and sourceless light. Goz waited by a plant whose royal purple leaves were as big as the oars of a canoe. "The garden is bigger inside than out," he said. "I used to wonder how all the plants could have survived so long on their own, but I think it's the books."

"The books?"

Goz glanced at Nik over his shoulder, then nodded, looking away again. "Every page is an hour, I think, and there must be a thousand million pages."

Nik opened his mouth and shut it with a snap. He realized with a sort of sinking sensation in his belly that he was more scared now than he had been outside.

Together, the boys passed through the garden and stopped before a fresco that showed a swarm of human figures climbing up an enormous vine. Not all of them were boys – with a shock, Nik recognized men, women, even girls.

"I don't know where they went," Goz said. "The books don't say."

"The books," Nik said without realizing he had spoken.

"Down the hall and through the big doors," Goz said. "I taught myself to read them."

"How long have you been coming here?"

"Down the hall and through the doors."

Lanterns hung from an invisible ceiling, glowing lambent in the dim. Some shelves stood full of volumes, their spines crowding one another up and down as far as Nik could see, but others were partially vacant, and the books on them leaned, supporting one another like weary boys after a hunt.

As he wandered through the aisles, Nik began to realize that he no longer cared about Pell's question. He didn't care what Goz knew that he didn't, and he didn't care who had told Pell stupid lies. But it was too late for all that, wasn't it? Here he was. It would be sheer cowardice to turn back now.

I hate this place, Nik thought savagely. It's old and it's boring and no one should ever come here!

The need to sleep took Nik by surprise. He swayed on his feet, so tired that he was almost sick, then climbed onto a long, low table in the stacks. He was uncomfortable with nothing to cradle his head, but sleep sent him dizzening down.

Tall figures stood to either side of the table and stared down at Nik's sleeping body. He clawed against the blackness of his dream, but try as he might, he could not wake up. Beach. Forest. Desert. Farmland. The shift and creak of hollow bones. The snap and ripple of paper skin. Nik found himself sitting astride a kite as it rode the strong winds just beneath the clouds.

The kite folded its wings and dropped into a dive. Nik howled, weightless and overjoyed, but his sleeping body dragged him back into himself. He groaned, aware once more of the table beneath him and the library all around. He smelled lilies and perfume.

Nik opened his eyes to find Goz standing beside the table.

Someone had washed Goz's face and painted it a waxy pink. Red spots of color stood out on his cheeks, and his hair, shorter than before, lay plastered against his skull. Both of his eyes were whole and uncovered, but they looked glazed and sightless.

Nik was too surprised to feel afraid. "Why are you painted like a doll?" he croaked. His mouth tasted bad, and his tongue was still swollen with sleep.

Goz grinned like a hound.

"Goz?" Nik said.

Goz wore a black suit two or three sizes too big, lustrous brown shoes, a dress shirt. An impeccably knotted blue and yellow striped tie hung nearly to his waist, and a red carnation stood brilliant on his right lapel.

Those are my clothes, Nik thought.

"Hey," Nik said, and sat up.

Before Nik realized what was happening, Goz grabbed Nik's hair at the back of his head and yanked him from the table with surprising force.

Nik struggled as Goz pulled him into a tight embrace. Lillies. Perfume. Incense. The sound of weeping. The sound of metal in distress.

Nik found his breath, but the hold Goz had on him kept Nik's arms pinned to his sides. Goz brought his forehead down on the bridge of Nik's nose. Numbness spread across Nik's face, and in his panic, he wriggled like a landed fish.

The boys fell together, and Nik landed hard on his back. The breath rushed from his lungs, and he made a breathless keening sound. Goz pursed his lips and inhaled loudly.

Light exploded across Nik's eyes as Goz bashed his forehead into Nik's face again. He didn't notice when Goz climbed off him – one moment, they were still struggling, and the next, Goz had him by the hair again and was pulling him down a long, dark corridor.

Tears poured down Nik's face, mingling with the blood from his nose. He tried to say, "I don't care anymore," but the words came out mangled, and not even he could understand them.

Sorry, Nik, Goz said without speaking. *Now all your questions will be answered, and when they are, your world will end.*

Nik shut his eyes and found himself standing on the Great Plain Road. Goz knelt next to him, huffing his displeasure as he extracted a stone from his right moccasin.

"And why don't we eat kites?" Goz said.

"They're made of paper," Nik said without thinking. "Besides, they're too smart. They have feelings."

"Boars have feelings."

"Boars are stupid, so their feelings don't matter."

Nik tensed. His hands moved on their own, fitting a stone into his sling. He turned his upper half, let the stone fly, and a choked cry rose up from the tall grass to his right.

"Let's go," Nik said.

Goz, on his feet now, made a face. "I want to check the body."

"There will be more. Let's go."

"I've never seen one up close."

Nik shook his head. "Nazis are no good."

"Please, Nik. Please. I'm newer than you."

Nik's expression darkened.

"I'm sorry."

Nik considered, fingering his stump. "The hunting's no good here," he said. "I want to show you something in the City before we head back."

"What about the Nazi?"

"We'll check the body together, then head straight to the City."

"Yes!" Goz bounded from the road.

Nik followed as a nauseous anticipation soured his belly. He moved around Goz to lean over the body, staring at its ruined face.

The Bush Nazi was bald, and his body was painted black with soot. A red ochre swastika stood out across his chest, and he wore only a faded pair of blue jeans stolen from the Clothes Farm. His big feet were bare, with thick, yellow toenails.

Nik's stone had spoiled the Nazi's once-sharp features, but Nik could still barely make out a Roman nose. Like his own, the Nazi's eyes were a stark, uncluttered blue.

"He's bigger than we are," Goz said softly.

"All Nazis are," Nik said without looking up.

"Because they're not boys."

"In the Other Place, boys grow. They become youths, then men."

The Nazi sat up. He and Nik stared calmly at one another.

"Nik," said the Nazi.

With a quick dip of hand to waist, Goz produced a stone dagger. Without a word, he slashed the Nazi's throat. He tried to dodge the spray of blood, but his right arm came away wet.

The Bush Nazi fell back, twitching, as Goz stepped away from him, an absent look of disgust on his face.

"Yah, Bush Nazi," he said. "I am Goz, and Goz always wins."

Nik opened his eyes and lay still for a time, considering. Was that sky above him, or a high and intricately decorated ceiling? Beyond the lanterns hanging above the table were stars arranged in unfamiliar constellations.

Nik sat up and kicked to his feet when he saw Pell standing by the table. Nik made a face to hide his embarrassment and sat on the table's edge, letting his feet swing slightly as Pell stood watching.

"You're not eleven."

"No," Nik said.

Pell smiled and took a breath. He held it in his mouth and let it pooch out his cheeks. He exhaled slowly, still watching Nik as if waiting for a response.

"I didn't lie," Nik said. "I forgot."

"There were girls once," Pell said. "What happened to them?"

"They left because they didn't like how we played."

"Where are they now?"

"Not even I know that."

Pell turned and pulled himself up to sit beside the bigger boy. For a long time, they were quiet, but Nik could feel Pell readying himself to speak.

"I loved Mura because she reminded me of my sister."

"That's not so foolish," Nik said. "I once suspected that our girls fled into the sea and became mermaids there."

Pell paused to examine a fresh scrape on his left knee. "My sister's name is Maggie," he said. "I must have been from one end of our world to the other. It's big – is it ever – but it's too small because Maggie isn't here."

"Maybe she was never here. Maybe she's still in the Other Place."

"Then I'll go back."

"No one has ever gone back," Nik said. "The boys who go too far and lose that something we have that keeps us young and lets us forget…they're crazy like hurt animals."

"How many Nazis do you think there are?"

"Two hundred and fifteen," Nik said without thinking.

"That's not many." Pell said. "So, if boys go, most of them stay gone."

"You've made up your mind," Nik said.

"Yes," Pell said. "But I'll sleep before I go. Goz says that if I sleep here the books will tell me something."

Nik was silent for a long time, gathering his thoughts. Finally, he said, "Growing up is learning things you don't want to know. If you leave here, you'll grow up."

Pell shrugged, then leaned forward and let his mouth hang open. Seeing him that way, Nik wanted to hit him, or at least shake him very hard.

Instead, Nik closed his eyes and sat back, concentrating on the feel of his palms against the warm wood of the table.

Eyes still shut, Nik said, "In the Other Place I am dead, but here I am Nik, and I am not afraid of anything."

"Is that why you stopped keeping the time?" Pell said, and the sound of his voice filled Nik with shame.

Finally, Nik opened his eyes. Pell had taken no notice of his rage, and for that, he was grateful. "Yes."

"Then forget again," Pell said. "You have everything you need."

"Pell."

"Don't cry," Pell said and touched Nik's cheek.

Nik shook his head, but he couldn't feel his face. "I'm crying?"

He swung his legs up onto the table and scooted over to let Pell lie beside him. Together they stared up at the constellations spread across the library sky. Nik saw a serpent menacing a man.

"You don't have to stay," Pell said.

"I know."

When next Pell spoke, his voice was slow with sleep. "You'll be better off without me."

Nik didn't answer.

Pell's breathing grew slow and even.

Nik gazed at a constellation of a girl holding a slingshot. His eyes burned, but he did not close them. Before he fell asleep he wondered idly whether he should return Goz's eye.

When he awakened, Pell was gone.

A Secret of the Trade

Lance Hawvermale

ariya blundered through the bustling market, trying to stay on her feet. *Foolish lass*, said Nifkin's voice in her head. *When will you ever learn?*

"Never," Mariya whispered, then stopped to fight down another wave of sickness.

This one doubled her over. Braced against a nearby stall, she bent at the waist and opened her mouth, expecting the worst. But all that came up was a sour trickle of bile. Damn the jeweler for coating his lockbox in tomb-oil, and damn her for not noticing! What a fool she was – and now she had earned a fool's death.

"Hands off, riffraff!" growled a voice from within the stall. She looked up. A big bald man in a bloody apron leaned across the counter, cleaver in hand "Last thing I need is street scum like you trying to filch mutton!" He shook the cleaver meaningfully. "Now get back before I call the foggers." He meant the Fog Watch, the town guard, so named for their gray uniforms. Foggers were famously brutal; Mariya wanted no part of their attentions.

"Excuse me," she mumbled, doing her best to sound polite. The poison had inflamed her tonsils and left her short of breath. "I'll just be on my way."

She lurched back into the press, blinking back sudden stinging tears. Panic rose in her: wild, ungovernable. She pitied herself; she did not want to die.

51

Then do something about it! Nifkin spat, exasperated as usual. Death hadn't cooled his temper: two months gone into the Bonegarden and he was still irascible as ever. *Think, lass. Think.*

"I'm trying."

And so she was. But after only three days in Swordsport, she did not know where to go for help. She was on her own now. Her family dead of plague; Nifkin dead too, likely slain by assassins.

And now Mariya would join them all in the Bonegarden.

Unless…

Something red caught her eye: a headscarf of fine scarlet silk that shimmered in the sunlight. Its wearer, a curiously attired dwarf, bustled past. A leather lanyard hung across his darkly furred chest, from which depended an assortment of small glass bottles: tangerine, turquoise, lambent blue. Vials and canteens hung willy-nilly from his jerkin. Pouches ringed his waist.

Perhaps he was an alchemist, or a healer…

Mariya pushed through the crowd after him. He jangled like a windchime as he walked, but made good speed. Mariya had to jog to keep up. He paused at a trader's stall to examine an earthenware pitcher, hefting it experimentally.

Mariya put a hand on his shoulder. "Excuse me, sir."

The dwarf gave a cry of alarm and jumped aside, nearly dropping the jug. "Pelora's heart! What is the meaning of this?" He handed the pitcher back to the merchant, keeping his eyes on Mariya. "If you're a beggar, you'd best move on. The only largesse I've got for you is a dusting of powdered basilisk bone in the face. Turn your eyelashes straight to stone, it will!" He shook a bottle menacingly.

"I think I'm dying."

The dwarf shrugged. "So are we all. Immortality potions notwithstanding."

"No, I mean I'm sick. Poisoned. Can you help me?"

"Unlikely. Such cures are rare and costly."

Money, of course. Wasn't it always money? A sudden suction pulled her earthward. Dark wings crowded close to carry her away.

She fell.

The wings bore her up and out into a dark expanse.

She surfaced, briefly, into vortices of light and liquid pain.

Someone spoke, the words incomprehensible. Then the voice leaned close, and she could smell the traces of herb and powder that lived in his beard like exotic birds in a nest.

A few hours later, Mariya hurried east along the esplanade toward Buskers' Gate, good as new but perhaps no better off. The dwarf – Esbjorn –had seen to that.

The task is simple, really, he had said, twirling a slender vial in his fingers.

I'm listening.

Do you know of Camp Bloodfield?

Vaguely. It's that longhouse beyond the city, where the rangers meet.

The very same. Barbarians flock there, horsemen, gauchos, other feral types.

So what do I do when I get there?

Find a trapper named Yuril Dalshog and rob him.

You're right. Sounds simple.

Simple, maybe, but not easy.

Mariya reached the city walls. Through the gate trundled a carnival troupe in bright and motley wagons, beating tambourines and whistling wild tunes. One of them noticed her and called out: "M'lady – you are so fair the very sunset melts away in shame! Tell me you'll be my betrothed!" He clasped his hands to his heart and smiled like a knave.

Mariya ignored him. Presently, she passed through the gate into the shantytown beyond.

Yuril Dalshog is seven feet tall, with a beard like a forest fire. Can't miss him.

And?

He wears a ring. Black. Onyx. Cast in the shape of a wolf's jaw. I need that ring.

The job's hopeless! To nick a man's coin purse is one thing…but his ring – can't be done.

I'm sorry to hear you say that, Mari. May I call you Mari?

No.

Then I'll make sure to say Mariya when I call the foggers.

"Stand lively, missy!" someone shouted.

Mariya skipped back. A wolf team – the dogs big as ponies – surged into the gap, prodded on by a hatchet-faced kennel-master. One turned his great silver head to glance at her, smiling its lupine smile. Then they were past.

This was what Swordsporters called "tent-town," an ad hoc assemblage of structures housing every sort of transient. There were tents large and small, yurts, lean-tos, jacals built of scavenged wood, shanties of mud and dung, even miniature fortresses stacked up from blocks of baked clay like rude castles.

Its populace was lively to say the least. Mariya passed fur-draped hunters with ornaments of bone and woodsmen bearing cowl-staves lashed over with pelts. In a clearing, boys took turns hurling hatchets at tree stumps.

Everywhere people came and went, darting in and out of the colored tents, or leading their horses and travois and wagons along the muddy paths or squatting in drunken packs slurping ale by the roadside.

At the center of it all stood Camp Bloodfield.

It was a traditional longhouse, constructed of colossal cedar logs from the Gaunt Forest and held together by thick black pitch and spikes the length of a boy's arm. Four separate chimneys funneled smoke into the sky.

It was summer and the massive oaken doors were open wide to let in the cool night air. From the rock slab porch, Mariya smelled roasting pork and the unmistakable odor of honey mead.

She stepped inside.

The interior of the longhouse was a single room, vast and shadowy. She stood in the portal a moment and let her eyes adjust. Light came from dozens of bear-oil lamps; the air was greasy with animal fat. It was getting on in the evening and the place churned with activity. Dozens of customers, tough looking men along with a scattering of whores, sat around circular tables, drinking, gossiping, arguing, lolling stupefied. Benches lined the walls lengthwise, mostly unoccupied. At the center, dug into the earth, were the roasting pits, where boars and wild dogs turned on spits over roiling flames tended by men resembling blacksmiths more than cooks.

Sure you're up to this, lass? asked Nifkin from the corner of her mind.

"No," she said under her breath. "But I don't have much choice."

Better you than me.

"Some help you are."

"What's that?" asked a man in green leathers. "You say something?"

"Ah…no sir," she managed. "Not a thing."

He glared at her, taking her measure; then moved on, shaking his head.

Ha! He thinks you're daft! Nifkin chortled.

Shut up, old man. At least I'm still alive.

Nifkin's imaginary voice made no response which, perversely, annoyed her all the more.

Drunken voices broke her reverie. A trio of furriers assayed a popular drinking song – "Inshanta Loves Her Hunters Merry" – allegedly an ode to the lovely Inshanta, Swordsport's Chief Huntswoman. But the rendition was unfaithful: by the second verse it had descended into a parody where every line rhymed with 'ale' or 'breasts.'

Someone stumbled into Mariya, splashing mead on her blouse.

She spun around, anger stenciled on her cheeks, but the two drunks didn't notice – they ambled right on by, stinking like something long-fermented in the heart of some dismal wood. Fists balled, Mariya forced herself to take a deep, calming inhalation. This was no time to lose her temper. She had to see this through.

Then the crowd parted and she spotted her quarry: Yuril Dalshog, all seven feet and three hundred pounds of him.

Smothering an instinct to flee while she could, she selected a seat that offered favorable vantage and studied this man she was supposed to rob. Nifkin had offered his views on the subject to her more than once:

"Sizing up a mark is just like making love," her old mentor had said. "You go slowly at first, touching, feeling. Then, when you sense the time is right, you whisper a prayer and go for broke."

Mariya wasn't sure if she concurred: close-range larceny always strung her nerves, and gave her a vicious bellyache afterwards to boot – there was nothing pleasant about the build-up.

The payoff, however…perhaps she could concede some similarity there.

Enough waiting.

Concentrate, she admonished herself. *Play the part.*

Yuril Dalshog sat in the corner, drinking and boasting with half a dozen brutish cronies. Up close, he looked even more formidable. His body seemed formed from iron. The hair on his head and arms and his long tangled beard were rust red. A brass bracer encircled each wrist, and the backs of his broad hands were tattooed with druidic runes from the Weir Wood.

He wore only a single ring, on the third finger of his right hand – the onyx band Esbjorn had described. His fingernails were dirty crescents.

Want to tell me how you plan on making off with that thing, lass?

Mariya ignored him. The plan had come spontaneously, audacious yet repulsive – but this was no line of work for the fastidious.

So she slung some sashay into her hips and flounced forward. The men stopped talking at once. She felt the pressure of their interest everywhere on her body. With all the gusto she could manage, Mariya cried: "I've come to speak with the cur who calls himself Yuril Dalshog!"

Men gawked. A few stifled chuckles.

"Cur?" Dalshog growled. He stiffened in his seat.

"Aye, that's what I said." Mariya faced him now, hands akimbo, trying her best to look brave. "For only a cur would hide in a corner amongst these sweat-stinking hogs to avoid a woman's true love."

Dalshog, clearly taken aback, wiped spittle from his lips. "Do I know you, wench?"

57

Mariya stepped closer still, leaning forward till they were face to face. "Do you know me? Do you know me? Why, Yuril Dalshog – you lecherous ogre! Were you so drunk you don't remember?"

Dalshog, now clearly flummoxed, could only shake his head. "Well…" he began, "it's just that I…"

"Just that you what?"

The other men were grinning now. They could see that this hellcat had their friend on the run and they intended to enjoy the show.

Mariya pressed her advantage. "Let me see if I can get through to your mead-fogged brain, my dear Yuril. You know the Iron Antler?"

Dalshog nodded.

"You were there of late, last time you came to town?"

"Uh . . . I think so. Was I?"

"Do you meet so many women at the Antler that you don't even recall your dear Bonnie?" She poked him hard in the chest. It was like hitting a wall. She scowled at him fiercely. "How many, Yuril? How many?"

Dalshog now had the manner of a whipped dog. "None, none at all, no one – not a single one but you."

She took his enormous palm and set it on her heaving breast. "Do you feel that, m'lord? Do you feel my poor tattered heart down there? Do you?"

He swallowed heavily. "Aye."

"Does it feel broken? Can you feel the shards? Cut you, they will!"

The big man's face twisted wretchedly; he was spitted surely as the pigs over the cookfires. "I'm sorry, please! I'll make it up to you, I swear on my sword!"

Mariya grinned crookedly and leaned in between his thighs. "It's your sword what got you into trouble in the first place."

The men laughed. Dalshog scowled at them, but they only laughed harder.

Mariya kissed his hand. "You'll make it up to me?" she said, her voice honey-sweet.

"Yes, gods, yes, or I'll bloody well die trying!"

"You promise?" Again she kissed his hand, keeping her eyes locked on his.

"It is my most solemn vow as a man." He sounded as if he meant it.

Mariya favored him with a coquettish smile. Then she took his third finger into her mouth, swirled her tongue expertly, and extracted it. Slowly.

Dalshog inhaled a long ragged breath.

"Come to me at the Iron Antler at midnight."

He nodded. He was beyond words.

"And as for the rest of you trolls," she growled, "you'd do well to get yourselves out of this cesspool and home to your womenfolk. Do I make myself clear?"

They mumbled that they would.

"And now I must go. But you, dear Yuril, can look forward to a more thorough punishment anon."

He lowered his head, but grinned like a boy.

Mariya turned and strode away, fighting the urge to run. The trek across the longhouse seemed eternal, but soon she was outside under glittering stars. Night air never tasted fresher.

She spit the ring into her palm and ran for the city gates.

"Damn my eyes," crowed Esbjorn. "How did you do you it?"

Mariya didn't look at him. She retied the laces on her boots, jerking the strings tightly. "My methods are my own. You have the ring. That was our deal."

"Yes, so I do. Still, I'd like to know..."

She shook her head. "A secret of the trade."

He nodded. "That I can understand. I have a few of my own."

"I trust our relationship is concluded?"

Esbjorn shrugged. "For now."

"Meaning?"

"Meaning I may have work for you in the future."

"I doubt I will be interested."

"Don't be too sure. Here, take this for your troubles."

She caught the small velvet bag, poured out the contents into a cupped palm. A constellation of opals shimmered within. Her breath caught in her throat.

With some effort Mariya composed herself. "That ring. It must be very valuable."

Again Esbjorn shrugged. "Not so much as you imagine. Just remember what I said about opportunities."

She stowed the bag in the folds of her jerkin. "I will consider it. I suppose you could send for me if something comes up."

Nifkin's warning sounded in a corner of her mind: *Don't be a fool! He's up to something.*

"Where can I find you?" Esbjorn asked.

"Ask around. I might be anywhere." Mariya paused in the doorway. "Except the Iron Antler." She wrinkled her nose in distaste, and then she was gone.

For a time silence prevailed. Then Esbjorn spoke to the empty room. "Surprised you, didn't I?"

Yuril Dalshog stepped from behind a curtain. "So you did," he said gravely.

"I only wish I could have witnessed her in the act."

"You are a pervert," said Dalshog with an air of certainty, and scratched his beard. "All in all it was a fine trick. I didn't suspect a thing until she was well out the door."

"So she'll suffice, you think?"

Dalshog nodded. "She'd better – those were my opals you gave her."

Esbjorn laughed, a sound like wind blowing through reeds. "Ah, my friend, you will see. Our schemes will bear fruit yet. This is only the beginning."

"Let's hope the next pawn in this game comes more cheaply."

Esbjorn's laughter came up short. Several of his vials were missing, along with the coin pouch he usually kept in his belt. He ran past Dalshog, threw open the door, and shouted: "Mariya!"

But there was no reply.

Badlands

Del Beaudry

ll in all I suppose I should have noticed something. But, truth is, I didn't – it was just a shit run like any other. Went down to the hole, dumped the pots, loaded the empties onto the sledge, headed back to town. That was it. Same as always.

At dawn I led the others into the desert. Crossing takes nine days, with luck. We didn't have any.

Three days in the big bay pulled up lame. I hooked the traces under the bench and hopped down to have a look. He fussed some, but I rubbed his flanks and whispered to him until he let me examine the hoof.

It was a mess – yellow puss oozed from a jumble of cracks. "Quiltor," I told them. "A bad one. He's finished." The bay snuffled my shoulder.

There was some grumbling. None of them knew horseflesh, but everyone had to have a look just the same. Excepting the friar, that is, but he could barely move anyways. We'd laid him in with the cargo, his magnificent bulk slopped over the fat burlap sacks like some colossal capon served up on a bed of onions.

He slept for the most part, which was just as well, but the jostling had wakened him and by a prodigious feat of effort he now wriggled himself upright to inspect his surroundings. He must have liked what he saw for his expression brightened and he began to sing – an obscene ballad.

Ahead, the sun squatted on the western horizon like a fat red canker, wobbling fiercely beneath the heat flux. Beyond: the blue shadow of mountains.

"Not another song about whores," groused Dulcet. "Don't them mendicants think about nothin' else?" She grimaced, rat-like face the more so now, soot-blackened against the glare.

"What you got against whores?" chirped Besk with a grin. "Whores is nice company. Could teach you a trick or two, I'll wager. Get ye some more custom. Improve yer attitude and whatnot." He grinned, lips rolled back to display blackened teeth.

"Nice is as nice does," agreed Kerlin.

Dulcet spat into the dust. "Well, y'all must know from whores," she said. "What with being birthed by 'em and such."

Now neither of the footmen smiled. In the quiet you could hear the horses suck at the stale air. I peeled off my hat, mopped my brow with a filthy handkerchief, and wondered if I would have to do something. Fortunately, the young wizard intervened.

"How do you propose to proceed, Mister Sjorenssen?" I looked past his fine earnest face into the desert.

"You mean about the horse, sieur? Or the friar?"

"The horse."

I took out a pocketknife and pried pebbles from under my boot heel: a calculated show of deliberation. Aristocrats expect to be taken seriously, even when they ask dumb questions.

"We'll have to slaughter him."

"Is that really necessary?" He seemed genuinely pained.

"Afraid so, sieur. Otherwise he'll follow us along as best he's able. Likely to draw trouble."

The boy nodded gravely.

"Don't worry your pretty head, Pau," hooted Kerlin. "No one's expectin' you to do the deed."

"Shut up, shithead," called Dulcet.

While we'd been talking, she had loosed the bay's traces and led it off to one side. Something bright flashed. With a wheeze the bay toppled, its legs folding inward like a burned spider. Lifeblood ran in bloody streams more crimson than the sun.

Night. We camped on the floor of a dead sea and roasted conies over mesquite. Above the stars burned blue and green and lilac and hot jacinth. Dulcet broke out a wineskin and passed it round. We drank.

When his turn came Pausanius gagged and coughed wine and wine-dark spittle onto his ratty robe. Everyone laughed. The two footmen teased him, but without malice. Evening's cool had washed away their rancor. Everyone was happy again, and why not? Soon we would be obscenely rich.

Six days to the river. Then a barge to Aberdeen, with its bustling wharves and sleek-headed merchants, grown fat on upcountry loot.

Since I was hired help, mine would be a quarter share only. But so what? The cart bulged with glittering spoils. Even allowing that they meant to cadge me – shorting the guide is standard practice – I could still look forward to wealth beyond reckoning.

After the others retired I sat with Dulcet and tended the fire.

"There any more wine?"

She shook her head. "Besk took it to bed with him."

"Figures," I muttered.

"Getting uppity already, huh?" she smirked. "Grown to resent Goodman Besk, have ye?"

"I like him fine. I like all of you fine so long as you pay me."

She fished a little flask from under her coat, passed it over. I took a pull, hacked. Fennish moonshine.

"That's good," I said.

"The fuck it is."

We drank in silence. We seemed to be getting on, so I decided to see if she wanted to talk. Sometimes life depends on a single scrap of information. That sounds like a proverb. Someone must have said that to me once.

"What happened down there, anyway? In the Piles, I mean."

She flashed me a wary look. "That's charter business. You know that."

I nodded. The flask was done, so I broke out some chew, passed her a piece. For a while we just chewed, spitting juice into the fire, watching it sizzle and flash.

"Look," I said. "Monmouth is small town. When a party heads down, everyone knows. When they come back up – which is a lot less often – you know that, too. It's what's in-between that folks wonder about."

Dulcet leaned back against her gear. "That so?"

"It is. Take your bunch, for instance. Fourteen to start. You all, the dwarf, and a couple others whom I reckon to be charter. Plus six hired hands – Quorranian jackknifers."

66

"Uh huh."

"Only five come up."

In the firelight her eyes shone like polished agates. "You been down?"

The urge to lie was overpowering – it took all I had not to succumb.

"Just once," I admitted finally. "Years ago." The touch of her pity on me was rancid honey, viscous and hateful. But at least she kept talking.

"It was supposed to be a quick-hitter. We had a map – shortcut through the catacombs. Straight to the vault. Pau opens it with his spells. Then we load out and head back up. Simple, right?"

"Sure."

"Sure." She clucked sardonically. "Trogs were waiting for us at Bunker Crossing. Caught us in a crossfire. Killed Nax and three of the jackknifers right off. Drove the rest of us into the warrens. Six days we was down there. Spores got Preja and two more jackknifers; last one lit out first chance he got."

"So how'd you get back up?"

"Pau dowsed us a path. Slow going, and mostly blind, since we was all but done for torches. On the last day, tramped right into a scorpion nest. Blue Giants. That's how Friar Klotz come to be stung."

I nodded. "It was decent of you to bring him along. He'd have died back in Monmouth, for sure."

Dulcet stood up. "Charter looks after its own," she said. "That's how it's done." Her voice was rough. Some fugitive emotion I couldn't place.

The liquor had left me good and drunk and not at all tired. So I lay back and watched the florid desert stars frisk across the sky and waited to fall asleep.

And dreamed. Grandly. Of gilded specie and splendid gems prized from Earth's drear grottoes by sword and guile and magic words. Of wolfen ghouls that sup on toothsome virgins and barrow-wraiths at slender feasting tables who drink from accursed grails an antique brew decocted of human souls and graveyard dust. Of fractured dragon eggs that rocked and hove like balky cradles. Of larval demons a-writhe in the offal of dead gods.

What a thing! To go down into the long night beneath the world and return, treasure-laden. In the dream it was like a benediction, to be sanctified in gold dust poured forth like blood from a sacred vessel.

Angry shouts woke me. They were gathered round the wagon bed where the friar lay – face down and heaving – amid a wallow of glittering coin.

I sat up, wrapped the blanket around my shoulders, then I rubbed temples. My head hurt like hell. "Is he alive?" I asked.

Dulcet nodded.

"Not for long," rumbled Besk. "I'm fittin' to cutthroat the pig-fucker momentarily."

There was no need to ask why. Water still dribbled down the slats to darken the sand below. Damp sackcloth lay strewn atop the treasure.

"What's left?" I asked Kerlin.

"One barrel and part of another. What that didn't run out the bunghole. A couple skins, too."

Not enough. Not nearly.

Everyone looked at me. I suppose they must have wanted be say it straight out. To confirm what they already knew. Because I'd been across the Badlands before; because it was me they hired to bring them across.

But it was already getting hot and I felt like shit. Let them wait. I pulled the blanket over my head and let myself fall back onto the sand.

For an instant there was only must, dark and blessed silence. Then the shouting started back up. "Is there any coffee brewed?" I asked from under the blanket. I sure as fuck hoped so.

The argument took most of the morning. When we finally got underway it was close on noon. In the end, they did what I told them: we turned north and made for an oasis called Potter's Dip.

It was a lousy plan. Nobody liked it, least of all me. There's all kinds of reasons to stay clear of the waterholes. They're popular, for one. But we were out of good options – Klotz had seen to that.

He had gotten worse. Clammy skin, weak pulse – a milky film on the eyes. He would thrash around and talk nonsense. Finally, Kerlin bound him hand and foot.

"No more mischief that way." He wanted to gag him, too, but Dulcet would not permit it.

"You'll choke him," she said. She was right, though by the look of him that might have been a mercy.

We were well out on the playa now, green clay under our boots, the sun overhead red and swollen, the sky beyond a fearful blue. We went on through the heat of the day and into the quickening twilight until the air against our faces cooled and the ground was hotter than the sky.

Into the night, me on point, reckoning by the stars, the others stretched out behind in single file. The evening cool seemed to revive Klotz He became alert, almost avid, scanning the starlit landscape with fascination. Whatever he saw seemed to please him.

"A song!" he cried, and sang. It was a plague song of the Old North, set to a tune already ancient when the ships of men first made landfall on this Godforsaken continent:

Oh! The Black Fiend marched a trail of woe with carcasses for his train,
whilst up ahead all the populace fled and the war dogs made a buffet.
And beneath the stampede was done dreadful deed on those not so nimble afoot.
On whom do they tread? Oh it's clear, never fear: why, none but the old
and the slow and the children — quite so! — now ground down to aspic for pie!

While up in the van cried the hangman: "Behold! Who has seen such a fine holiday?
When lovely black boils preempt all our toils and the gibbet rope sports like a cur?
Oh! Let man and child and woman beguiled cry hip-hip-a-hippy-hi-hey!
Today even nooses shall need no excuses to stop and enjoy the parade!

There were dozens of verses. After a while we gave up trying to silence him and simply marched to the rhythm like soldiers.

We came to the oasis in the half-light of dawn, a thicket of brambles below an umbrella of date palms. Somewhere beyond: the movement of light upon water.

There was no pretense at stealth. We struck the game path and made straight for the waterhole. It was crowded. Zebra clustered by the rim but gave way as we approached. Further on, at the edge of the bush, the lions — a huge male and his harem — were taking their ease, muzzles stained with blood. Close by, a trio of cubs played peek-a-boo around a striped carcass.

The horses didn't like it — the palomino nickered his distress. "It's alright, boy" I told him. "They don't care about us." Which was true enough, though it took a while to convince the horses.

Finally, when I had them calm enough to unhitch, I led them down to the water and they drank. The lions watched this procedure with regal disinterest, lazily blinking their enormous yellow eyes, until one by one they fell asleep. Sprawled backwards, bellies distended, they seemed gentle as housecats. I'm sure I could have strolled over and scratched one behind the ears.

"The friar's dead," said Pau.

"What?" I asked, stupid with fatigue. His words had somehow ceased to convey meaning.

"He's dead. He died in the night."

We divvied up the chores. Dulcet rubbed down the horses; Pau filled the casks while me, Besk and Kerlin gathered stones for a cairn. It was dirty, miserable work. Good sized stones proved scarce and what we could find we had to dig out of the clay and haul over to the pile. At length, I found a decent cache and we set to work properly, Besk digging while Kerlin and I ferried stones.

We were carrying a big jagged one – huffing and swearing – when Besk shouted the alarm. "Raiders!"

I am still fuzzy about what happened next. Someone lost his grip – maybe me, maybe Kerlin, maybe both of us – and the rock came free. Then I heard a wet crunch.

And there lay Kerlin, twitching, the rock atop his leg. I heaved, got it off and a bloody gusher caught me full in the face. When I had the blood out of my eyes, I examined the ruin of bone and ligament that used to be Kerlin's knee.

"Cocksucker," he hissed. "You want me dead."

It was Besk that got us through their perimeter. It was neat work: He set fire to the scrub and flushed the lions directly into their lines and their birds scattered in panic. Then we cut straight through the gap and back out onto the playa.

That's one reason I never use ostriches myself. Damned skittish animals. And they hate fire. Also, lions. Still, it didn't take them long to round up their birds and pick up our trail.

The rest of the day was cat and mouse, with us the mice. They tracked us on three sides, staying well beyond bowshot. There were a lot of them.

Now, anytime you head out into the Badlands, you have to worry about raiders. They're a constant hazard. But all things being equal, it's the small party that's most at risk. Like any smart predator, raiders tend to avoid tough quarry. They much prefer to make a living picking off stragglers – easier to hunt, easier to kill. That's why sensible travelers will pay so dearly to ride with the big caravans. It's a hell of a lot safer.

We had discussed all this back in Monmouth. "That's why we stay off the caravan routes, skip the oases, carry our own water." Everyone nodded at me like they understood. "Good. Still, I'd feel better if we had a few more spears. Don't suppose you've reconsidered 'bout Spence 'n the others. Good men. Handy in a pinch."

"No one else." Dulcet said with finality. "Just us." And that was how it was.

It's a hard thing to figure, why she would listen to me with one ear yet ignore me with the other. It certainly wasn't because she was foolish. Whatever else, Dulcet was nobody's fool. And I don't think it was because she distrusted me or doubted my judgment.

Take the horses. She'd given me a free hand, and money was no object. Good horses are always in demand and to get the team I wanted I had to pay triple – I swear that camel-fucker Zool could *smell* specie. Still, they were the best in town and Dulcet didn't bat an eye at the price.

The way I reckon, it comes down to this: when someone hires you, they think they own you. And they treat you like it. Soldier, surveyor, witch – the occupation doesn't matter. Neither does expertise or accomplishments or plain old common sense. None of it counts for shit because in the end you're just the fucking hired help.

That's the essence of commerce: what you buy is your possession. What you do with it your own business.

That's how I came to think of it, anyways.

We had fallen back to the wagon. I drove the team while the others crouched in the wagon bed. For cover, they had wedged Klotz's swollen body against the tailgate like a sandbag. It stank like you wouldn't believe.

No one spoke. What to say? When evening came they would close in and kill us. We all knew it. We watched the sun make its inexorable transit. I did my best not to kill the horses. Behind, our shadows grew long and black and stretched away into the trail dust like a funeral train.

"Gotta make a stand." That was Besk.

Dulcet shook her head. "Nowhere to make a stand from. No cover. No high ground."

I knew she was right, but reflexively I scanned the empty landscape. Nothing but hard-baked clay in all directions. Ahead, at the border of vision, the blue wall of the mountains, darkening fast beneath gathering clouds.

Pau caught my eye. "What are those?" he asked, pointing west.

"Thunderheads. But they're a way off yet."

"But they're coming." His voice held a note of triumph. "They *are* coming."

I don't know much about sorcery. Not that I'm not curious, but I've had lousy sources. Shithole towns like Monmouth don't have wizards. They do come through occasionally on their way to the Piles but they don't share their secrets with the local riffraff. So Pau's spell took me by surprise.

He'd been rehearsing all the way from Potter's Dip, going over it in his head to make sure he had it just right. We never even noticed. It was all a matter of *imagining*, he told me later. He used that exact word. That's how it works — imagine it perfectly and it comes true.

Pau's storm arrived at sunset. It was glorious. Green fire danced on our spearheads; lightning whickered from cloud to cloud like serpent's tongues. Thunderclaps made the playa toll like some titanic gong until we covered our ears lest we go deaf.

But that was just so much cosmic theatre. Ominous and grand, but inconsequential. It scared the raiders but didn't hurt them. They still would have gotten round to killing us; it just would have taken longer.

It was the tornadoes that saved us.

Seen from a distance, haloed in sand and dust, they might have been a cavalry charge. But no horse runs so fast – they covered ten leagues while I watched. For a few magnificent instants, while they closed, I could make out individual columns. There must have been hundreds, some no bigger than dogs, some tall as church-towers. Scudding across each other's paths, hopscotching along, they had the heedless ballistic genius of schooling fish.

I watched as long as I could – which was not long – then shut my eyes against the stinging sand, held on, listened. I will never forget that sound: an awful humming like giant wasps going to war. Then the shockwave hits, the suction pops me from my seat like a champagne cork and I'm airborne, clinging to the traces for dear life. And the storm breaks around us like water on rock.

By the time I could check the team and take a look back, the show was mostly over. What's left is the litter. Ostrich feathers strewn over the playa like barley chaff in the field when threshing is finished.

"Jesus," Besk, says, low and reverent. "Sweet fuckin' Jesus."

That night we celebrated. We built a bonfire and cut cubesteaks and roasted them on sticks over the open fire. Besk raked some coals to the side for more subtle work. There Dulcet stewed ostrich livers in the juice of the *nopal* and poached brains delicate as egg whites. Afterward, we sat around and patted our bellies and picked our teeth and congratulated ourselves on our escape. Everyone was merry, even Kerlin, despite the leg.

"To Pau!" he shouted and the fire growled its approval and blew sparks into the night like a beacon.

"Pau!" we cried, and raised cups to our savior, though now we had only water left to drink.

Again there was talk of the gold, what it would buy. Each presented his vision. Besk would buy up riverboats by the dozens and so corner the down-country trade in otter pelts. Monopoly would multiply his riches and he would not bother to conceal the fact.

"It's not as if we wants to put on airs," he explained earnestly. "But if ye want proper folks to pay us mind, we'd best look the part. That's the way of the world – sharp dress marks the gentleman, so the saying goes." He went on to describe in detail a costume he thought fitting: A rakish cap of royal blue with cardinal feather tassels; a surcoat of the same shade, with his crest emblazoned thereon in thread of gold; tunic and breeches of yellow Cathay silk with pearl buttons; and boots of crocodile scale, fitted with platinum buckles.

Yet he also affirmed the virtues of philanthropy. He vowed that in his later years he would become a charitarian, giving generously to the poor, the maimed, and imbeciles.

When his turn came, Pau spoke with uncommon ardor, and the thrust of his remarks exposed a deeply rooted idealism. "Consider for a moment, my friends, the human drive to know. Is it not a wondrous thing? To hunt wisdom – to chase her down as the hound courses the hare – what nobler impulse inheres to man? Here is the scholar's calling: to follow wisdom wherever she may lead. But how few are free to follow the scent! How often will the trail be sullied by crass necessity!"

He spoke of the scholars coming up, of their many talents, which university life would so thoroughly squander. "They arrive," he told us, "shiny with

76

promise. But by the time the tassel turns and the prentice becomes adept, nothing remains to him save recrimination and vast arrears. Imagine what could be accomplished without the shackles of debt, how much of the unknown gloriously revealed."

So Pau proposed to aid them – to pay students' tuition, build laboratories and libraries, to endow faculty chairs and fund expeditions and by this renaissance elevate the world – and we could not help but be captured by his fervor. When he was finished everyone applauded and we saluted his generosity and called him a great humanitarian.

And, indeed, while his speech remains with me, still moves me, I wonder whether I understood it so well as I thought at the time. To become a sorcerer, I have learned, takes more than money, and the aspiring wizard will often accrue subtler debts, especially difficult to discharge.

But I hate to doubt Pau. I liked him best.

Kerlin's ambitions were more straightforward. He confessed an interest in visiting the Old North, despite the many perils of such a voyage. "I'd like to see them big old forts high up in the mountains that's a thousand years old. And the big valleys where there's a hundred horses for every man and ten times that many cattle. Maybe even sail to Cathay."

Then they asked me about my own plans and I lied and told them I hadn't thought about it but when they pressed, I said: "Maybe buy a little boat. Sail around the cape, go on down and see some of that good island life."

"Lots of pretty girls thereabouts," mocked Dulcet, and spat in the fire. "Might even find one that'd take to an ugly fuck like you, what with all that coin you'll have. Hell, might even turn yourself into a respectable sonabitch." She had my eye; this time I met it. She smiled her rat-smile, and I smiled back.

I said: "What about you?"

"Me? Likely blow it at the wheel and wind up back at digging." That sounded like bullshit to me but I didn't object.

"Anyway, I've had it with your fairy-tale circle jerk. There's business but needs doin'. Father Klotz deserves a proper burial. On account of him being a God-fearing man and such."

"Who the fuck cares?" Besk groused. "Dead is dead – he ain't gonna know the difference."

"I care, you cum-drunk faggot!" snarled Dulcet. "He's Company. Or have you forgotten –"

Besk was abashed. "No. Of course not," he said. He was quiet a minute. I could tell he was trying to pick his next words carefully. An unfamiliar task.

"Just that – well, I ain't never been baptized. Just couldn't go in for that Jesus shit."

"Neither could I," said Dulcet. "That's not the point."

No one explained what the point was; everyone just got all quiet and went to their blankets and acted like they'd gone to sleep.

Me and Besk were up before dawn to dig. While we worked the sky brightened: from charcoal to the blue-black of frozen flesh to glorious indigo and at last to fiercest desert blue.

"Don't care much for pits," says he. I nodded, hoping he would shut up. But he went on. "Fuck of a way to shove off." He glanced at me for confirmation. "What about you, drover? You object to dying in a hole?"

I was in no mood to discuss metaphysics; I just wanted to get the job done. It wasn't hot yet, but would be soon. "Dead is dead. Your own words. So what's the fucking difference?"

He grunted, then expelled a wetly burbling fart. I covered my nose with my shirt.

"Ain't nothin' particular. All things being equal, I'd prefer a proper tomb is all."

That was more bullshit, of course. Seemed like an awful lot of it was piling up. Still, I kept my peace, kept to the digging. For the life of me I can't explain why.

We held the funeral after breakfast. Pau gave the eulogy. He claimed to be agnostic but he seemed to know his Scripture well enough. Anyway, he was very eloquent and his delivery was impeccable.

When it was done we dropped Klotz in the hole and filled it back up with sand and clay. Dulcet cried, which surprised me, but I didn't ask her about it. Then we went on.

We made good time. By midday I could pick out individual peaks amid the blue haze of the mountains. Kerlin got worse, though. The infection had spawned a fever and he lost his senses, drifting in and out of consciousness. While awake he babbled madly. Pau tried to get him to drink but he fought and Besk had to put him in a bear hug so Pau could pour water down his throat.

In the afternoon we arrived at the edge of the playa. Here the land rose steeply to the coastline and the ascent was too sheer for the wagon. So I took us south along the shore until we found a coulee that once had fed the vanished sea. It seemed suitable. The grade was gentle enough but the course was strewn with stones – good place to break an axle – so I dismounted and led the team, picking our path cautiously.

It was slow going and for a while I thought we might have to turn back and find another route. But a few hundred yards upstream we struck an old trail that cut across the river's path, leading up to the foothills. Getting the wagon out of the wash and onto the trail took some doing – nasty, brutal work – but once we made it we had solid ground underfoot and made good time.

We were in the hill country now. It was tough, desolate land, but I liked it better than the playa, maybe because it was more alive. Bristlecone pines clung to the slopes, wedged into the butts of the rocks, and the air carried the tang of distant water.

Up we went, following the switchbacks, until the sun slipped behind the mountains and daylight abandoned us and we walked in shadow. We camped in the hollow of a hill. There was lots of deadwood here, so we built a big fire and were soon glad of it, for the evening grew chill.

As the night went on we fed the fire, adding thick logs so it burned high and bright. This was not so much for warmth as for safety. Game abounds in the hills – antelope and wild pig and bighorn sheep – and their predators dwell here, too. Thus it was not long before they noted our intrusion and came round for a closer look.

All night, lean things slinked about the shifting fringe of the firelight, though I never got a clear look at even one. Yet by their calls they announced themselves quite clearly, just as a rich man's slave will walk ahead and cry his master's rank and name. So it was with the howling wolves and barking jackals and the hyenas who laughed like drunken soldiers.

Perhaps there was a kind of witchcraft in the animals' cries, or perhaps we were simply glad to be done with the desert, but something fey came over us that night. We had no liquor yet we behaved as drunkards. We laughed, danced, made merry like wild men. And we gambled – which we had not done before – strewing sacks of gold and pouches of jewels about the camp like so much rubbish. Everyone played, even Pau, who said he despised fortune. (His voice cracked when he called out his bets.) Kerlin played too, so well as he could, though I doubt he understood much of what transpired.

The stakes were absurd. Three times I lost a king's ransom on the roll of the bones. But I won it all back, and more. Dulcet lost and lost until she had nothing left to wager but her body and I won that too, and made her swear to be my slave and this she did and my cock grew so fat with blood that it wedged against my belt and throbbed as though cut by shears.

When the game was over we huddled side by side on our billets. I should have fucked her then, but Besk was still awake, sitting by the fire, and I didn't want him to watch. So we diddled each other under the blankets like clumsy teenagers and got no relief.

I must have dreamed that night, though I remember only a little of it. Somehow I had fallen fell into a hole filled with a strange substance, sticky and vile, that clung to me like honey but it smelled of the slaughterhouse and I was ashamed and didn't know why.

Pau shook me awake. "The horses are gone. Someone cut the traces." There was genuine terror in his voice.

I glanced around. The cart was still there, and the loot. But no horses.

There was more trouble. Besk and Dulcet faced each other across the ashes of the fire, fingering knife handles, with murder in their eyes. Kerlin lay where we had set him, wrapped in swaddling.

"Fuck," I said, "this is getting bad."

Coffee had to wait. Pau had his hands full with Besk and Dulcet. They stood balanced on the verge: Once the knives came out things could only end in blood. So Pau crouched between them and preached sweet reason and begged them to honor their oaths, and I went off to see what had happened to the horses.

Which didn't take long to sort out. The thief had made no effort to cover his trail. When I got back, I explained it to them. "He's been following us for days, hiding his tracks in ours. But last night he didn't bother. Must have figured this was the right time to take the horses. He's led them up there." I pointed into the hills. Then I scanned their faces. "Now who's going to tell me who that fucker is and why he's after us?"

None of them said shit, but they were easy enough to read. Pau fiddled with his amulet and avoided my gaze; Dulcet blushed like some fairy tale princess who's gotten her first look at horsecock. I didn't even bother with Besk. I just stared at them, daring them to keep on lying.

It was Pau who broke the silence. "Why do you think we would know?" he asked, and sounded so much like he meant it that I found myself momentarily speechless. I mean, what do you say to that? It was so Goddamned brazen – yet I still wanted to believe him, even then. He had that effect on me.

So I let it go. "Forget it," I told him. "All that matters now is getting to the river. Nothing else."

But we went nowhere. Not for hours. Because first, they had to have another long argument. Besk wanted to split up – he would stay and guard the wagon and see to Kerlin while the rest of us went for help. Of course Dulcet wouldn't hear of it. While they fought, I made coffee and ate breakfast.

Eventually the smell of salt bacon and ostrich egg got to them and they shut up long enough to eat. Then they argued some more. Finally, predictably, Dulcet prevailed.

So it was late morning when we at last got down to business. First, we buried the treasure, which took longer than it should have because I was the only one who'd had the sense to pack tools. Then we burned the wagon and followed the tracks up into the bluffs.

The trail cut a steep path between the sandstone buttes, snaking among the gulches. In a few spots it was so narrow that I doubted we could even have gotten the wagon through. There was no small talk. We just hiked, sucking in dust while, high above, vultures kept pace, tracing lazy spirals in the transparent ocean of the air.

Night comes quickly in the high country. Once the sun gets below the canyon walls you only have a few moments of purple twilight before the blindness of full dark. So when, late in the day, Besk spotted a usable campsite we called a halt and took what we could get.

The spot was a shallow cave nestled high up on the canyon wall. We had to climb to get there. Which we did one by one, freehand. No one even suggested using rope. Who could you trust now to set the line?

Besk made the ascent with Kerlin strapped across his shoulders like a gutted buck. It may have been the greatest feat of strength I have ever witnessed.

The cave was shallower than it had looked from below, not much more than a hollow in the rock, really. Nonetheless each of us endeavored to sit as far away the others as physically possible. Of course we built no fire – it would've been visible for miles.

I don't suppose I slept much. Doubt any of us did, given the circumstances. But maybe I dozed some.

Anyway, for the record – that's assuming anyone winds up reading this – I want to make one thing crystal clear: That night I neither heard nor saw anything remarkable. Nothing at all.

Still, I can't say that I was surprised when dawn came and I glanced over at Kerlin and beheld what had become of him. Jaw slack, skin dark. And his eyes. Though wide open and paralyzed in a semblance of attention, it was all too clear that they looked out at nothing at all.

This time there was no talk of burial. We just left him in the cave. By the time we had all climbed back down, the vultures were thick as picnic ants. I could make out no trace of the carcass.

Up we marched. We could see the pass well enough but it took all morning to get close. The ascent wound between sandstone causeways, doubling back again and again. At last, we found ourselves at the base of a narrow chute that rose sharply upward, guarding the final approach.

By now everyone was exhausted so I called a halt before the final push. We were maybe a hundred yards below the summit. No one was talking. I sat in the dust and sucked water from a skin. Dulcet was beside me. Her dirt-crusted face looked like a horror mask. Our eyes met. Something bright stirred within but I can't say what it was. I offered her the water-skin but she didn't take it. She was looking up toward the pass.

And something tickled my spine. It started where my hipbones met the road and got stronger as it went up. When it hit the base of my skull, my teeth clattered like a roulette wheel and I wanted to shout a warning but somehow had forgotten how to speak.

But it was much too late. Through the gap and down the slope charged the horses, the palomino – wall-eyed in terror – in the lead. I did nothing.

No, that's not quite right. I did do one thing: I tried to save my hide. But that was just instinct. Roll up. Put your head between your knees, cover your neck with your hands. Shut your eyes tight. I might as well have been a possum.

Mostly I credit the palomino. Maybe it's sentimental, but I like to think he recognized me, didn't want to squash me flat. Some folks will say that horses – aside from warhorses anyways – are basically nice and don't want to step on nobody. But that's wrong. Truth is, they will do whatever they can to avoid a fall. Because that could mean a broken leg, which is a death sentence for a horse. They're sensible creatures, all in all. Out for themselves like anyone else.

Fact remains, though: I didn't get trampled. And I only broke the ribs when Besk landed right on top of me. Compared to what happened to the others, it was a fucking miracle.

Besk, he was dead for sure – I had his brains all through my hair. As for Dulcet, I can't say for sure 'cuz I never got a good look. She wasn't movin', though, and given the circumstances you have to assume the worst.

I ran. Or, more exactly, I slid, scrambled, stumbled, hustled, bounced on my ass, did anything I could to get down the slope fast. When I hit level ground, I sneaked one look back at him.

Short as he was, he handled that big ol' crossbow smooth as you could imagine. Pau was still alive at that point – I think he was trying to sit up. But that dwarf was fucking deadeye – he put the quarrel right in the soft spot above the breastbone. I didn't need to see nothing else.

I ran until I found a wash that sheared south from the track. For a while it wasn't so bad. Where the dirt was loose, I could slide along and I made a little time. But once I was over and into the next canyon, the path got steeper and the pain really set in.

I'm not sure how long I kept going. I crossed four canyons, maybe more. But by afternoon I could barely crawl and I knew I wouldn't make it up the next one. So I slid down an arroyo, cutting myself in the brambles, and found myself in a small valley. I could hear the gentle rumble of the river.

The spot was on a little headland backed on three sides by rock. The river lay over the western verge. Across its midsection was a girdle of low mounds, overgrown with wild rye and sourgrass.

It was a sorry excuse for a graveyard. What markers remained had toppled and the names of the fallen had been defaced by wind and rain and time. I dragged myself as far as I could from the wash, toward the sound of the water. Every breath brought white-hot pain.

I heard him long before I saw him. He was humming a walking song and the canyon's chutes amplified the tune like an alphorn, sending basso notes caroming from the valley wash.

He came over the rise, leading his mule, and picked his way down the arroyo and onto level ground. Then he unsaddled the mule, tied the traces around a rock, and left it to graze. He got out the crossbow, cranked it open, set a quarrel, tested the fit. The he came toward me, crossbow leveled.

He stopped maybe ten paces away. This was my first good look at him.

He had the head and torso of a big man, and a thick beard, but his legs and arms, though heavyset, were short as a child's. An iron skullcap sat on his head. Crusted shit and mud clung to his clothes and sprackled his boots. He stunk horribly.

He looked me over, spat. "Bet them ribs hurt."

I said nothing to that. We both knew they did.

"You a townie? You hire on in that shit town?"

I nodded. "Yeah. In Monmouth. I was the guide."

"Monmouth!" he hooted, and stamped his feet for joy. "That's the name of that fucking place! I had plumb forgotten! Thank ye, townie, for remindin' me. A man ought to know by name the spot where he was left for dead, I reckon." He grinned at me crookedly. "Ain't that so?"

"Sure," I said. "Ought to know."

"What about that place where they dumped me – that got its own name, too?"

I shook my head. "Folks just call it the hole."

He seemed disappointed. "The hole – nothin' more?"

"Just the hole."

That didn't agree with him. He set down on a rock, crossbow on his lap, and pursed his lips. "Don't seem fitting."

I shrugged, then wished I hadn't – hot wire cut straight through my lungs. I nearly fell over.

The dwarf reached into his vest, produced a wad, bit some off, tossed some more to me. "Ye chew, I reckon."

I nodded, then tried to maneuver the chew into my mouth with an absolute minimum of motion. Chewing hurt, but it was worth it. God was it good. For a few lovely minutes, he shut up and let me enjoy my chew.

"What'd they promise?" he asked.

I drooled tobacco juice onto the rocks before I answered. "Quarter share."

He nodded. "Standard."

"Uh-huh."

He looked me up and down. Seemed to be taking my measure. "I suppose now yer gonna tell me that you knowed nothin' of what they done. That you're innocent and therefore rightly deserve to live."

I shook my head. "I didn't know, not then. But that doesn't make me innocent."

"Suppose not," the dwarf agreed.

He stood up. "Time to finish your chew."

He ordered me to turn out my pockets. When he found nothing there, he made me drop my drawers and strip off my shirt. Managing the latter cost me grievously. When my screaming got loud, he gave me a stick to chew. Still nothing. Then he told me to take off my boots.

I tried, but I couldn't bend over without screaming. He promised to gut me then and there, so I tried again until I nearly blacked out. But the act was beyond me and he recognized that now.

Instead, he had me lie on my back with my hands above my head – which was almost as bad – while he cut away my bootlaces with a bowie knife. Then he shook the boots out and banged 'em against the rocks. All he got for his trouble was sand and crusted clay.

He set them aside. "Get up," he demanded. I got up.

"Pull up yer drawers." I pulled them up. "Hands on yer head. Turn round. March."

He marched me right to the edge of the cliff. Below, the brown water sloughed lazily in its course. A long way down.

Rough hands reached beneath my shit-stained drawers, palmed my ass. "Bend over now, nice and easy. Just one last spot to check."

I bent deeply at the knees, almost squatting, then kicked away hard as I could. For an instant I dangled over the sallow water, suspended by worn cotton. Then, with a dreadful sound, the weft tore through and my weight came free and I tumbled headfirst and howling into the river.

That's about it. I made it downriver alive despite the ribs. I got a little lucky – the details are unimportant. When in Aberdeen I sold the diamonds I had stuck up my asshole they didn't amount to no king's ransom, but they were still worth the trip. I made out alright all in all. Got nothing to complain about.

I live offshore these days. Bought a fishing boat. Can't say where. Somewhere pleasant and quiet where that fucking dwarf won't find me.

I try to take it seriously, the fishing, I mean. It's a job like any other and I want to be a decent hand at it, even though I wasn't raised to the trade. But concentrating is hard. Fishing means a lot of sitting around waiting for something to happen. And if the fish won't bite, well there's not much else. Not much happens here. Allows lots of time to recollect. To consider.

Most days, after breakfast, I take a walk down to the water and think about Dulcet. Imagine what she would have bought with her share. Best I can remember, she wouldn't say, but I think on it it anyway.

Afterwards, I make for the docks, climb onto my little boat, cast off and see how I can do with respect to fishing – which is for the most part poorly, I'll admit.

But sometimes I don't even bother. Some days I just hang around portside and watch for the mainland packet, to see if any strangers will come ashore.

Bitter Honey

Julie Frost

nother of our clan's children starved to death in the night.

Ours was a grim gathering in the abandoned badger sett where we made our winter home. My husband Ceallach pounded his hands weakly on the dried mushroom that served as a table, and buzzed his wings. "We must invade the bees' colony. Otherwise we all starve."

Keriam, a senior member of the Council, shook her head. "The bees are more dangerous than starvation. They are many, and we are few. One sting, and we die writhing. Or had you forgotten?"

Slouched in a seat of dried moss, I let the argument wash over me. The previous spring had been arid; winter had brought frigid cold but little snow. We'd gathered what food we could through the summer and autumn, but it hadn't been enough.

I surveyed the group. Already, hunger had marked us. Antennae drooped above gaunt faces. Bones stood out in livid detail. Many no longer had the strength to fly. In our sorry state, an attack on the colony verged on suicide.

When I spoke up, it was not on my own behalf nor even for Ceallach. I was pregnant. And though we had had told no one, I still held hope that our child might live.

"Sitting here and dying slowly holds little appeal," I said. "If we must die, let it be in battle, not puling in our holes like dung beetles."

"Easy for you to say," sneered Keriam. "Your father would never allow his little princess to take such risks."

I sat up straighter, exhaustion forgotten. "Are you challenging me?"

Keriam dropped her eyes. "No, Olwyna."

"If you haven't the courage for the endeavor, no one will force you to go." I crossed my arms. "As for me, the choice is mine not my father's, and I choose to fight. He does not compel my obedience in such matters."

"That is true enough," my father said from the head of the table, with wry amusement.

The sour mood broken, we made our plans.

That night we flew, Ceallach leading, to the tree where the bees had their hive. Eighteen of us had strength for the journey. Eighteen. To battle hundreds, or thousands, of insects. Our only advantage was that bees slept at night, whereas we were equally comfortable in darkness or daylight.

Scouts were not an option. The bees would kill any who transgressed their nest. That we were driven to try such a scheme was a mark of our desperation. Our fire-hardened hawthorn swords gave us longer reach, but not by much, and they had us hugely outnumbered.

Ceallach drew me aside. "Your father asked that I keep you in the rearguard. If the battle goes badly, your responsibility will be to get out as many as you can."

I cast my eyes downward. "All right," I snarled. I was doing my best to sound angry although, truth to tell, I was more feeble than I let on. And there was the child to consider.

He lifted my chin and planted a burning kiss on my lips. "Brave Olwyna. When this night is over our bards will sing of you. Keriam will eat her words, along with the honey we bring back."

He turned and summoned a will-o'-the-wisp to give us light in the darkness of the hive. I blinked back sudden tears – it would not do to let him see me cry.

Soon we were deep inside the hollow tree. So far we had encountered no bees. I shivered, though not from the cold. Though we laired in burrows in wintertime, were are by nature creatures of the air. Our kind dislikes confinement, and here the walls were very close, and the shadows strange. .

Some of the youngsters murmured, made warding signs. One or two looked as if they wanted to go back. I glared. "Are you turning tail now, Anwar? You were as keen as any of us to come." He mumbled something, not looking at me. "What?" I said. "I can't hear you."

"I hadn't realized the tree would be so –" Anwar gestured. "Confining."

"Be grateful they nest in a hollow tree rather than a paper hive," Ceallach's brother Gwylym snapped, clouting him above the ear. Anwar subsided with tight lips, gripping his sword tighter, and we continued on.

We finally entered the central chamber, and my heart fell.

One tiny, pitiful comb of honey was all that remained. The bees were in as dire straits as we.

The hive had been decimated. Perhaps only two hundred bees huddled sleeping where thousands should have clustered. But although this meant we were outnumbered only ten to one – rather than a hundred to one – we were still badly outmatched. I had never been so afraid.

91

Then, with a cry, Ceallach led the assault. Those who had strength threw fireballs. At full power, we could have burned out the hive and taken the honey at leisure. But now our fire was colorless and cold and would not catch. But it woke them. They attacked.

Three warriors dropped from the air, buried in bees. Screams filled our ears as stingers found their way between joints in their armor. Their assailants died with them, barbed stingers ripped from thoraxes, venom sacs suppurating horribly.

The hollow tree hummed with the sound of wings: ours bright and sweet as chimes; theirs a dark vibrato. The tight space favored the bees – it compromised our superior agility – and I twice blundered into a wall before I got the hang of flying in these dark quarters.

I struck the head off one bee, but two others buzzed into the breach. I fended them off with my sword. A third landed on my back, dragging me down. Its stinger scratched at my armor, seeking ingress.

Panic clawed at my lungs. I shrieked, twisting, trying to get it off before we crashed – or before I was impaled.

Two of my dragonfly-winged sisters sped past me and entrails fell like rain. Something heavy jostled us; the bee lost its hold. That was all needed to spear it through the abdomen. It landed amid a growing heap of dying and dead. Shaking with fear and rage, I hummed up to rejoin the fray.

For the moment we held the advantage. We had broken their initial assault, wounded or killed dozens of workers. But a detachment had waited in reserve, to guard the queen and her honey. We had to scatter them at once. There would not be another chance.

"To the honey!" I shouted, and we came together to make a wedge, Gwylym at the point. Only eight of us remained. Ceallach was among the missing. My guts churned with horror. But there was no time to indulge my grief.

"Briallin! Morthwyl! You get the honey. The rest of us will hold off the bees." So saying we flew hard at their right flank, slashing with swords, stabbing with lances.

The bees came at us in clusters now, their tactics changed. Five surrounded Anwar, vibrating their wings to create heat. He howled in terror and pain, begging us to save him. But we could do nothing and in a matter of seconds, he was roasted alive in his armor.

Briallin and Morthwyl worked to wrench free the honeycomb and fluttered away, bearing it between them. But it was too heavy; their flight grew erratic. A squadron of bees flew overhead to close with them. Briallin and Morthwyl hovered clumsily, surrounded and at bay.

I whizzed to their aid, spearing bees left and right. But too late for Briallin, who was overwhelmed and borne down, shrieking, to join the dead below.

Now Morthwyl struggled to bear the weight of the honey, shifting it this way and that. A section broke away to wedge amidst the fallen.

I stooped to retrieve it, but Gwylym pulled me away. "If they have some left, they may not come after us," he gasped. "Go with Morthwyl; we will take rear guard."

I looked longingly at the honey, which represented many days' worth of food, but he was right. I turned to follow Morthwyl –

And a bee hit me in the back and latched on.

I twisted and spun as I fell, trying to dislodge it. Its mandibles clacked in my ears, and I could feel its abdomen working, hunting for a weak spot in my armor. I tried stabbing behind me, but could not find my mark. In desperation I gripped one of its legs in my free hand and tore it loose, but still the bee hung on.

Its stinger slid towards the gap in my armor for my wings, and even as I grasped another leg, I thought: *I'm going to die in this place. What a foolish way to*

go after we captured what we came for. At least I will join Ceallach in the Hall of the Faerie King, along with –

A sword whistled close by and severed the bee's neck before its stinger plunged home. My relief was short-lived; as it dropped the bee caught on my left wing, shredding the membrane. A hiss of pain escaped my lips, and then Gwylym was at my side, bearing me up.

A few more bees made desultory attempts to harry us, but Gwylym was able to hold them at bay. We burst out of the tree into cold moonlight, breathing hard.

Morthwyl was a distant blur, fluttering erratically westward toward our badger sett with his burden of honey. He was the only other survivor. Gwylym and I exchanged sorrowful glances and flew home on unsteady wings.

We were greeted as heroes. Even Keriam forced a tight smile. I didn't feel much like one. Fifteen were dead. Nothing could assuage my sense of guilt. Grieving widows, stoic husbands, and uncomprehending babes: their every look hammered at my conscience. We had lost far too much.

But the honey would sustain those who remained through the winter.

I retired to the back of the sett and collapsed on a bed of moss. Now that the battle was over, there was no place to hide from my grief. I buried my face in my arms and let the tears come.

A little while later, a gentle hand caressed my hair. "Ceallach would have deemed his sacrifice worthy, as would the others. They knew well what lay ahead." My father's voice was gentle and sad

I looked up. Our clan's few remaining children were curled up in a pile on the floor, content and well-stuffed with honey. "It doesn't make me miss him any less."

"I know. But our clan will survive."

Was that enough? It would have to be, I told myself, hands on my abdomen. "Your father died a Champion, little one," I whispered to the unborn babe. "And we shall sing of him for generations."

Terms of Use

Eric J. Juneau

```
Logging in to server......

Parsing protocol.......

Client XTP:1020//:4545......loading

Logged in!
```

yril was standing in the marketplace, weighing the respective merits of a Frost Dagger and Harbinger Leggings of Strength, when his player logged in. The sharp jolt made him grit his teeth. Then he smiled pastily.

"Hello, player," Cyril said. "Welcome back to Izzi San'Yattrib. The world time is 3:11, and you have no new messages." Every single time, he had to say that. It was like being a Non-Playable Character again, back when all he did was point out how many years it had been since the Thuggian fields were plagued by Razor-Clawed Rats.

"Where are we going today?" Cyril asked. There was no immediate response. Either there was some lag, or his player was taking his sweet time. "Hey, hello? I'm standing here, looking pretty. What are we going to do today? I hope you didn't log on just to admire my armor. Hint, hint."

Cyril's armor consisted mostly of things he wore when he was still Level 11. The best thing he had was a golden chestplate he'd received as a rare drop from a Murfeter Ox. Clerics didn't get a very high armor class, and it was the only thing that kept him out of newbie missions.

"Hey, how about we check some Clan boards. Maybe join one?" No response. "Or we could harvest some Thysil Greens?" No response. "Hey, it's your credit card. Or your parents'. Waste your time – see if I care."

Then Cyril received an answer.

"What? Oh, not the Serpent Dragon. Come on, I don't feel like fighting today. Yes, I know we have all the requirements, but that doesn't mean – "

His player headed him towards the Flagpole to look for a party.

"You sure? Don't you want to look for some new armor first? No? All right."

He heard the ambient noise of the crowd before he saw it. Sound loaded faster than objects. Then the rest of the world formed around him.

A medieval pig-man walked by, snorting through the gold ring in his nose and holding a sticking-spear. A pale-skinned Unicornian with six arms shook a carpet out his window. Elves, centaurs, gargoyles, and dwarves passed him on their way to the fields.

The streets never used to be this crowded, but a lot of avatars' players had become bored and never logged back in. Without a player, avatars were limited to safe zones. It was an old world, and Cyril was glad his player was still active, even though he obviously hadn't read a single FAQ.

"Birdoco license! Get a Birdoco License!" a shopkeeper shouted.

Cyril looked over. "Birdoco license? We could train a Birdoco. That way I wouldn't have to walk everywhere. It would take less time to get places."

He was ignored.

In the center of the marketplace, a large crowd had gathered, all focused on a central point. "Hey, what's this?" Cyril said. "Let's check it out." Thankfully, his player obeyed his request and steered him towards the thick mass.

There were too many tall races in the back to see what was going on. He could hear swords swinging and muffled magical explosions..

"Why is there a battle going on in the middle of town?" Cyril asked. He jumped up and down, trying to find a space between two Mammothites.

"Cyril! What ho!"

Cyril looked towards the voice. A giant man with an axe on his back and wild cinnamon hair waved at him.

"Oh geez, Bolbadir," Cyril covered his face with his hand and looked away. "Don't connect with him, please?" Cyril asked. But it was too late.

Bolbadir raised his axe and pointed, "Cyril! A battle! Doth it not excite the blood?" He pointed over the heads of others. "Come hither. Methinks here be the best view for thee."

Cyril sighed and trudged over to Bolbadir. He still had that obnoxious AuthenticSpeak mod installed, but at least there was a vacant spot by him.

The Barbarian clapped a beefy hand on his shoulder. If it wasn't for his armor, Cyril would have lost 5 HP. "How doth the morrow find you, yon Cyril?" he asked.

"I'm fine, dude. You don't need to talk like that."

"In what manner of speech dost my friend protesteth?"

Cyril slumped his shoulders. "Never mind."

Two knights stood facing each other in a circle, casting magic spells and skillchain attacks. A white ring encircled them, marking off the boundaries of the arena.

"It's a Player vs. Player fight?" Cyril said. "In the middle of Jastok square? What's going on?"

"Well, the gladiator in the guise of silver yonder hath pooched the other of a Reggai Mirror, that which hath come from hours of grinding in the stygian depths of the Garuda Plains. Yonder truth-seeker with the blade of vermilion decries this. The Game Judge wrought his decision that the avatars shall hold contest to render verdict."

A Game Judge stood stiff in the corner, watching the two. His hands rested on a long cleaver-like sword plunged in the dirt. He was dressed in thick cast-iron armor, covering every bit of skin. A knee-high mirror with gold trim sat at his feet.

Cyril said, "So you're saying one of those guys tried to scam an item from the other. And the Game Judge is having them duke it out?"

"For sooth!" Bolbadir said.

"You get all that?" Cyril asked his player, who confirmed that he did.

The black knight held out his hand and a white protective dome appeared over his head. The silver knight took the opportunity to strike a blow, but it wasn't very effective.

Cyril asked, "Why is the Judge having them fight about it instead of just making a judgment?"

Bolbadir shrugged his heaving shoulders. "'Tis knowledge unbeknownst to me. Perhaps he was vexed earlier, and wishes to project his wrath. Who knoweth if the Judges have players any longer? They may be no more than lost souls wandering the landscapes, hoisting their own brand of justice upon the unfortunate."

The black knight lifted his sword overhead and brought it down. It passed through the other knight's body, and the number 2456 appeared over his head. A basic, but strong attack.

100

The defender stretched his purple blade into the air and a white wind full of sparkling fairies swirled around him. The number 1435 appeared in green, then faded away.

Bolbadir nudged Cyril. "Yonder black knight hath been proving his mettle for some time now. All the gray-clad warrior may do is heal a score as much as strike."

"What?"

No sooner had he said that than the black knight brought down his sword like he was chopping wood. The silver knight dropped to his knees and collapsed in the dirt as soon as the white numbers of doom blinked over his forehead. Some avatars clapped their hands in courtesy.

The black knight turned to the Game Judge and said, "All right, I won. Give me the mirror."

The Game Judge remained motionless. "Aye, you have. Judgment is rendered fair to you." His tone sounded stilted and emotionless under the metal.

The Game Judge picked up the mirror, tucked it under the crook of his arm, and walked away to the edge of the crowd.

"Hey!" the black knight called back. "Don't I get my mirror back?"

The judge turned around. "The battle was to decide justice, not reward. There is no reward for liars, and stupidity is its own punishment. Do I make myself clear?"

"What? You can't do that. I earned that mirror."

The Game Judge pointed his saber at him, raising it as slowly and menacingly as possible. "All judgments rendered by the Game Judge are final," he said, quoting the sacred Terms of Use. "Or would you receive a different judgment?"

The black knight stood motionless for a moment, clenching his fists, trying to find words. The audience held their breath.

No one had ever seen an avatar take on a Game Judge. In fact, the Terms of Use considered that to be illegal. Those who spread rumors about such an event were dismissed as having been on the losing end of one of their decisions. Would the rules be broken this time?

The knight huffed and walked back into the crowd. This instance would not be different.

The Game Judge walked back into the market and the crowd dispersed.

Bolbadir said, "'Twas a fine match. Nothing like a bit of spectacle before a day's work." He breathed in and out. "So Cyril, what news? For what reason dost thou partake of the market?"

Cyril didn't respond for a second. "Hang on, my player's trying to make me wave, but he keeps opening the system menu." Cyril waved his arm back and forth outlandishly. "Ah, there we go. I'm going to the Flag to raise a group for the Serpent Dragon today."

"The white wyvern of Rofitunia? Ooh, 'tis many a fellow who's gone to the graveyard thanks to that beastie. Ye'd best stay clear, for his aggression meter speaketh of gross exuberance."

"I just need a Topaz Gem. I'm probably the only person in the world who's trying to get it without buying it."

"Ye have enough Thalassian Elfgrass, I'd wager?"

"Yep."

"And ye've paid your tribute to the Phoenix Woman? Shown her your title and deed?"

"Yeah, did that."

"Thou art well met. For this journey I shall accompany you, for no doubt a strong hand with an axe in your corner shall pull the victory for you, and earn you your just reward." He pulled his rune axe out of the scabbard on his back and held it to the sun so the razor-thin blade sparkled.

"Fantastic," Cyril monotoned. "Well, you can be a damage-dealer."

"Zounds, 'tis the role I was born for. Naught but a healer dost we require now, and we mayest be on our way. Though finding one may takest time."

Cyril smiled and looked over Bolbadir's spiked shoulder. "Don't worry, I think I see one on the way." He waved at the oncomer. Bolbadir looked puzzled for a split second longer than a smarter avatar would, then turned around.

"By the surly beard of Mrifk!"

Her head was covered in a shiny chitin carapace, hiding her hair, if she had any. She barely looked human with her bulging red eyes, purple skin, and body armor that was more organic than metallic. Thick wooly hair grew on her shins. When she opened her mouth, two top teeth clicked back and forth like mandibles. She looked like an aborted fetus that had grown up and merged with a black widow spider.

"Hey, Cyril," it waved.

Bolbadir's hand went to his axe as he darted in front of Cyril. "A venomous monster in a safe town! What vile abomination did ye crawl from? Get thee behind me, demon!"

"Dude." Cyril elbowed Bolbadir in the ribs. "It's cool, I know her. She's one of us."

The monster said, "Hey, I didn't choose to be an Arachneborg. My player's kid brother mashed the keys when she was picking an avatar, so I got confirmed as her choice. She wanted one of those unicorn people, so thanks for your consideration."

"Sorry about that," Cyril said.

"Yes, I mourn deeply for your condition," added Bolbadir.

Cyril elbowed him again.

"I mean, my reaction," Bolbadir said.

"Your reaction!?" she said, "My player's a twelve-year-old blonde girl from upstate New York. She named me 'Peachbutt'. How do you think I reacted to that?"

Bolbadir snickered. Cyril resisted the temptation to smack him over the head, which might have provoked a PvP. "It's cool, okay? She's a good healer. I've been in a few dungeon crawls with her before."

Bolbadir cleared his throat and regained a serious countenance. "Any allies of yours are allies of mine."

Peachbutt said, "I heard you were going to take on the Serpent Dragon. We're trying to get the Quest Completion reward. My player gets a trophy in our Save House if she gets ten quests in a day." She sighed, rolling her eyes. "She tells me to tell you it's 'sparkly and glittery'. Also, she desperately wants to do your hair," she pointed at Bolbadir.

He looked startled and touched his beard. "What? My curly locks?"

Cyril rolled his eyes and asked Peachbutt, "Do you have any white magic?"

She laughed. "I pick up nothing but white spells. I've got enough items to heal an army."

"All right, that's good. Let's get going." Cyril took off towards the Serpent Dragon's cavern.

"Wait," Peachbutt said, "We're walking? Don't you have a Birdoco License or an Airship Ticket?"

"Talk to my cheap player," Cyril replied.

The journey to the Ignatius Cavern took ten real-time minutes on foot. They expected to see an empty cave on a hill, leading into the Serpent Dragon's lair, but when they arrived they saw a group of rigid avatars standing in formation. They were all dressed in a stylized version of samurai armor – plated vermilion tunics drawn down around the leggings. Shogun helmets trimmed with bronze completed the garb.

"Blood Knights? What are they doing here?"

"For sooth! Doth my eyes deceive me? Be all ten of them staking a claim?" Bolbadir said.

"But they're all the same class," Cyril said. "You'd need a party with a lot more variety than that to defeat the Serpent Dragon."

"Are they NPCs?" Peachbutt asked.

"I think not," Bolbadir said. "Why doth they stand like that? Art they guarding the cave?"

"Oh no," Cyril said. "Their sigs all match."

"What does that mean?" Peachbutt asked.

"They're RMTs."

"What?"

"You don't know what RMTs are?"

"*I* know what they are. She doesn't." She pointed to the sky.

"RMT stands for Real Money Traders. They're usually people in Korea or China, sweating over computers twenty hours a day. They camp in front of rare monsters, wait for them to respawn, and kill them for their items. Then they sell you the item in real life and give it to you here."

Bolbadir added, "None may pass where they set stakes, for their strength is unmatched from grinding day upon day."

Peachbutt paused to roll her eyes. "My player wants you to know that they sound like real meanies."

"Yeah," Cyril said. "Dammit, do you know how many bunyips I had to kill to get the Wolf Key?" Cyril felt a sudden series of jolts. "Hey, hey, don't pound the keyboard. You'll overload me. We're all frustrated down here."

"A pox!" Bolbadir said. "A pox on those parasites on the boils of society. Their grim countenances shall be – "

"Yeah, yeah," Cyril nodded. "You don't need to get all melodramatic on us."

"This land is not owned by them," Bolbadir yelled and hoisted his axe. "It belongs to all of us. For is not fairness of the trade our right and task?"

"Are you gonna tell that to them?" Cyril said.

Even a seven-foot man with an ogre-killing axe couldn't win a battle with ten maxed-out warriors. Bolbadir plunged his handle into the dirt and grunted in frustration.

"This lawless world brings forth the rage in my blood," Bolbadir said.

Peachbutt said, "I'm so sick of this. I get messages saying they're banning accounts, I get updated and patched till I can't tell where my original code is anymore, and then we still have this crap."

"Life is far from fair," Bolbadir said.

"I'm not asking life to be fair, I'm asking the game to be fair." Cyril sighed and waited for instructions. "Guess we gotta go back," he said. "Maybe we can buy a Topaz Gem in the marketplace. We could sell the Thalassian Grass and Phoenix Woman's contract – hey!"

Cyril didn't even realize the override had been engaged when his legs started up the hill.

106

Bolbadir called out, "Cyril? What vexes thee?"

Cyril cried out, "What are you doing, player? I don't want to talk to them."

It looked like his player intended to walk past the RMTs. Maybe they wouldn't do anything at all. Maybe they were just bots.

Cyril made it within a foot of the cavern before the nearest one pulled out a pole arm and held it to the side, blocking the path.

Cyril bounced against it and pawed it away, eyeing the RMT.

"We have a claim," the Blood Knight said stiffly, as if a translator was doing the talking.

"No," Cyril spat back. "You guys are just camping here. Why don't you give someone else a chance?"

"Do you want a Topaz Gem? We can sell it to you for twenty-five American dollars. Go to w-w-w-" he said.

"No. I don't want to buy it. I want to earn it. I did the work to get to this monster. I did the leveling to fight it and win."

"Do you want a Topaz Gem? We can sell it to you for twenty-five American dollars. Go to – "

"I'm not buying anything from you – "

A white beam of light shot out of the ground in front of Cyril, divided, and spun around them, creating a circle around the two.

Cyril shouted to his player, "What are you doing? You're starting a PvP? Are you insane?"

"I detect an insult. Aggressive behavior will not be tolerated," the RMT said. He stepped forward, holding his polearm across his chest.

Cyril didn't see too many options any more. Escape was impossible in PvPs, and the arena ring was impenetrable by outside or inside forces. He had no choice but to attack. Fortunately, his Cleric speed gave him the initiative.

Cyril drew his dagger and shouted "Winding Thrust!" Winding Thrust was a new ability that combined magic and strength. It was so powerful he could only do it once a day.

Pools of pinkish magic energy sparked around Cyril as he darted to the left and dove forward. He held the dagger over his head like an axe, then sliced it across the RMT's chest. It made 188 points of damage. Cyril smiled, thinking that was a pretty good hit.

The Blood Knight held his lance to the sky. A spiral of effervescent magic power absorbed into the tip. The RMT thrust the spear forward with a burst of yellow energy. The last thing Cyril saw before everything went black was the number 3,846.

When he came to, he was back in bed in his Save House, staring up at the ceiling. He felt tired, a little weaker, but mostly embarrassed.

"Jeez, what happened?" Cyril asked.

"Dude, you took on an RMT. What did you expect?"

Peachbutt and Bolbadir were hovering over his bed.

"I'm not in the graveyard?"

"I gave you a Phaedra Tail," Peachbutt said. "Had to warp you out of there before you croaked. My player says you look really cute sleeping."

Bolbadir said, "Had our irons been forged to the strength of our hearts, we would have conquered our foes. I personally wouldst have sliced them from gizzard to gullet."

"Thanks, Bolbadir." Cyril sat up and checked his stats. "Where's my chestplate?"

"Your foe seized it as reward," Bolbadir said.

Cyril grunted. An RMT could sell it for fifty bucks. "Damn."

He swung his legs out of the bed and rubbed his face. His health was full, but there was no item to heal his ego.

"Player, contact a Game Judge," Cyril said. He received an acknowledgement and felt the message go through.

"Be that wise?" Bolbadir asked. "They do not seem to be in a merry mood these days."

"I don't care. This is something they're supposed to take care of. This is supposed to be a fair game." He got off the bed. "Meanwhile, I've got to find something to replace my armor. Wanna go to the marketplace?"

Peachbutt said, "Sounds good. My player can't get enough shopping."

Cyril opened the door and saw a giant black-armored knight standing in his doorway – the Game Judge. He stood with his hands on his hips.

"Hail, avatar," he said. "A fine day to you, blah, blah, blah. What do you want?"

"Uh…uh…" Cyril couldn't think for a minute. Staring face to face with an overpowered warrior, holding a sword as big as his body, made him forget what he wanted in the first place. "How'd you get here so fast?"

"Apparently, you don't know what the term 'Game Judge' means. Game Judge means I have total power. If I want to give you purple spots, I can do that. If I want to switch your arms and legs around, I can do that too. Now what's the problem?"

"Uh, there…oh, there are RMTs at the cave of the Serpent Dragon."

"Yeah. And?"

"And…are you going to do something about it?"

"What for?"

Cyril scowled at him. "They're ruining the game for everyone else. They're breaking the rules. They're blocking anyone on an ordinary quest from getting to the Serpent Dragon."

The Game Judge shrugged. "The Serpent Dragon? You haven't fought him yet?"

"I'm trying to get a Topaz Gem."

The judge scoffed, "Just buy one."

"I don't want to buy one. I want to earn one fairly."

"Look, do you really want to annoy someone like me with your petty problems?" the Game Judge said.

Cyril didn't know which response would keep his neck and head together. "But you're a Game Judge. You're supposed to enforce the rules. Isn't this against the rules?"

"What rule are they breaking? It's not illegal to stay in one place for a long time. Not illegal for anyone to want to defeat a Serpent Dragon."

"They're camping! The Serpent Dragon's no match for someone at Level 75."

"There ain't no law against running over an ant with a steamroller," the Game Judge scoffed.

Cyril said, "You know they're just trying to harvest items to sell."

"That's the real world's problem. Not mine."

"They're making the game unfair. That's why there are so many wandering avatars these days. Their players never logged back in because it wasn't fun anymore. Because of things like this."

"Look son, there's always gonna be RMTs. We kill a hundred, they come back with a thousand. As long as there're assholes who don't want to wait for anything in life, there'll be someone to sell to them. We could wipe a thousand avatars, they'll still come back with new ones. 'Nuff said. Anything else you want to complain about, or do you want to get fed to a dragon?"

Cyril opened his mouth, struggling for something to say. But he'd used up all his arguments and just shook his head.

The Game Judge nodded. "Next time, don't bug us Judges. It's just a game – lighten up." He disappeared in a flash of light.

Cyril closed the door to his house.

Peachbutt said, "Wow, that was harsh."

Cyril said, "I hate this. I feel like I'm an NPC again – no power to do anything. And I'm sick of it. If only someone could kill those guys."

Bolbadir looked puzzled. "Cyril, those are words of courage, but their truth is fallacy."

Peachbutt said, "Those RMTs might as well be invulnerable. They've got the best armor, the best weapons. Just like," she sighed, "Just like Chrissy at school, who's apparently very proud of her Prada backpack."

"Isn't Prada the potion-maker in Gahennasburg?" Bolbadir asked.

"Look," Cyril turned up to his player, "If the Game Judge can't do anything about it, then let's just buy a Topaz Gem. I mean, really, what were you doing, engaging a RMT in PvP? Their stats are maxed-out and they have Crystal Spears and Relic Armor. You'd need a party of a hundred to take on all those guys."

"I can't believe you got a party of a hundred people," Peachbutt said.

"I know. It took my player ten straight days, 270 e-mails, and three sacrificed dinners. He talked to people from Indonesia, South Africa, Germany, and Saudi Arabia. He e-mailed everyone in the school directory, including parents and teachers. Plus he got in an argument with his parents that almost got his account cancelled."

Cyril had never seen so many avatars at the Flagpole. They mulled about as if at a cocktail party, sharing tips, bragging about their latest menial accomplishments, level raises, or spells obtained.

"I have counteth fewer than a hundred," Bolbadir said, at his side. "Be that enough?"

Cyril sighed. "It better be. We've got some high-levels here looking for a challenge, so that's good. Oh god, no."

"What?" Peachbutt said.

"My player wants me to make a speech. You've got to be kidding me," he mumbled as he hoisted himself up on a tree stump.

"Attention everyone!" he shouted and waved his arms. "Thank you all for coming! I hope you're all prepped and ready."

A collection of fists pumped in the air and shouted, encouraging Cyril to keep going.

"Today we're going to make a stand for all players over the world. That we're not going to take abuse of the system lying down. This is a world for everyone. A world where we all work together to build a community. And it should be fair. If some people – "

"Um, Cyril."

Cyril looked down at Peachbutt. "What?"

"I have to go. My player says her parents are telling her to get off the computer."

"What? But you're one of our primary healers!"

"I know, but last time, they took away her TV for a week, and she couldn't watch *Jazzy Girls*."

"You're passing up the battle of the century for *Jazzy Girls*?"

"Sorry." Peachbutt walked away, heading back into the forest. Cyril turned back to the crowd, deflated. "Let's go do this!" He jumped off the stump and headed in the direction of the cave, with an army of soldiers behind him.

The same ten RMTs were standing at the cave mouth like royal guards. They did not react to the sight of a horde of rebels riding over the hill.

"Split up! Remember your assignments. Engage the enemy!" Cyril shouted.

The set of ninety-odd players divided among the ten targets. Every group had at least three times as many members as a basic party needed. Each could probably take out a final boss in five minutes, but these opponents were way beyond that.

Each of the RMTs responded in synchronization. They were caught unaware, but not unprepared, and unleashed their strongest attacks first. Cyril saw a Level 10 Knave disintegrate in one cast of Moon Bonanza.

Cyril called out. "Cast Resurrection! Someone cast Resurrection on him." Before he could finish the phrase, someone did.

Cyril was shocked. People were listening to him.

"Man down in Group Three," someone said.

"I'm on it. Use that Amulet of Zovirax. Cast wide area Carapace."

"Got it. Sending. I'm generating a buff for group nine."

As Cyril hacked away at his opponent, his consciousness flooded with status updates and messages. When someone needed to be healed, he got someone to do it. When someone had been poisoned, he found someone with an antidote. When an avatar was fatigued, he told someone to step up.

They had been locked in combat for twenty full minutes, and no one had been killed yet, which was an accomplishment itself. He couldn't tell if they were winning, but they were holding their own.

"We got one!" a Mage-Rogue said.

Cyril saw the black light of an avatar death shoot over the heads of nine people. He held his breath. If one of the other Blood Knights was going to resurrect him, he had thirty seconds to do so before he would be warped to the graveyard.

Thirty seconds went by and the prone body disappeared. Of course, Blood Knights were meant for a single purpose – attacking. They had no healing items, not magic spells. Not only that, but they didn't care enough about each other to help. They were too focused on their own battles.

However, the death brought the RMTs to their senses and they started fighting like they meant it. They switched to more suitable weapons and armor for fighting avatars and cast defensive spells instead of relying solely on aggressive might.

"We're losing more men," Cyril heard. The party member stats started to decline. They couldn't heal fast enough to do damage without being overpowered.

The RMT Cyril was fighting unsheathed a glowing yellow sword and swiped it horizontally. Cyril jumped back, but it slashed through the Mercenary nearest him for instant death. No one could heal him before he fell to his knees and disappeared. Now, instead of fighting to win, they were just trying to stay alive.

"Hold together, people. We can still do this!" Cyril said.

Even Cyril couldn't believe his words, and he silently cursed his player for bringing him into this. Blood Knights were still dying, but for every one they killed, six fell from their own ranks.

"I'm out of items."

"Me too! We'll have to ignore healing if we're going to get them."

Cyril thought this would be a slaughter, but not on both sides. If even one RMT was left, they would have failed. "Then that's what we do," he said to the others, "Fight! Keep fighting! Don't worry about healing! We've got their backs against the wall. Don't let up."

Cyril caught the sword coming at him out of the corner of his eye, and held up his dagger to block. While pushing against the blade, he looked behind him to scope the situation.

The RMT being attacked by Bolbadir's party, the only other remaining, raised his spear, charging up a special attack.

"Look out, it's an AOE!" Cyril shouted.

Bolbadir heard the warning and lumbered away as the wave of magic spread out in a runic circle. The eight others surrounding him collapsed from the area effect.

"Foul beast! Taste my steel!" Bolbadir lunged forward with a speedy special technique, plunging his axe into his foe. The RMT sagged back, defeated.

Cyril's foe brought his weapon around and targeted the dwarven warrior behind him. With a sharp poke, he fell into a heap. It was just him and Bolbadir left to defeat this last RMT.

Cyril dodged the next attack. His HP was so low that a normal blow might kill him, let alone any special attack.

Bolbadir shouted, "Yonder Cyril! Fearless leader! Where art thou?"

"Over here!" Cyril shouted.

Given his current resources, Cyril could never finish him one-on-one. He didn't have enough health left to endure more than one blow. But the two of them together could do it.

"I'm coming, squire." Bolbadir scraped up his axe. Energy glowed around him as he hoisted the weapon high over his head, glinting off the artificial sun.

Cyril smiled. If he could let Bolbadir charge an attack, that would be enough to finish the last RMT.

Cyril danced around with his dagger, using his cleric speed to avoid being hit. Bolbadir hurtled forward like a Viking berserker, primal savagery in his eyes.

The RMT heard the roars behind him and saw a maniac rushing down the hill with a gigantic axe.

"I will bathe in the blood of my enemies! My axe will rain blows unto your skull, and release you to a land beyond human suffering, dishonorable scum!"

Cyril liked to think the RMT's eyes widened in surprise and fear, but the helmet obscured his face. He couldn't believe they were actually going to win.

"Your days of terror are at an end. None shall pass before my bl – "

Bolbadir paused in mid-step, his axe above his head. Frozen. Did someone cast a spell on him?

His body became a vapid blue outline, a blink of snowy static, then winked out of existence.

-Bolbadir has disconnected from the game-

"Oh, crap," Cyril muttered and turned back to the RMT. He raised his pole arm over his head and gathered magic energy into it.

Cyril held up his arm, waiting for the impending blow. He hoped they wouldn't recycle him into an NPC stable-cleaner.

"Hey, hey, hey, what the hell is going on here?'

The Blood Knight and Cyril stopped and looked the cave's mouth for the source of the voice. A Game Judge walked out.

"Jesus Christ, you're slowing all our servers down. There must be, like, a hundred people in the same area. Do you know how much lag you're making?"

Cyril didn't know what to say, but the Blood Knight turned away from him and moved towards the Game Judge.

"What's this? A Level 75 Blood Knight with complete armor? That's awful suspicious, don't you think, Mr. Dret49585849. Shucky-darns, you wouldn't happen to be an RMT, would you?"

Cyril said, "See, I told you."

"Shut up, kid," the judge said.

The Blood Knight brought out a Mega-Life Juice and drank it. It was a rare item that restored all his HP instantly. Then he pointed his spear at the Game Judge.

"We have a claim. Aggressive behavior will not be tolerated."

The Game Judge laughed in his hollow armor. "Oh, that's cute. You're challenging me? I like that." He snapped his fingers. "Serpy, if you please."

SNAP! A white blur came down on the RMT's upper body and snatched him up like a fish on a line. Cyril uttered a girlish shriek and crab-crawled away. The Serpent Dragon shook the body in its jaws like a doll, then with a whip of its snake-like neck spit him back out, slamming him on the ground. The RMT bounced like a ball.

The number 58,579 appeared in white over his corpse, which promptly vanished.

"Holy mackerel," Cyril said.

The Serpent Dragon lowered its opal head closer to the ground and stared at him with beady sapphire eyes. Its snout was wide and flat like a wyvern, with two tiny nostrils expanding and contracting with breath. The rest of his body was burrowed within its grotto.

"Not bad, kid," the judge said. "You took on all those goldsellers and lived. Someday, you will earn this Topaz Gem," he patted the wyvern's cheek. "But it won't be today."

The dragon retracted its long scaled neck back into the darkness of the cave and disappeared.

The judge said, "Go home, kid. Get some rest."

Cyril said, "No problem there. My player's been online since four in the morning."

The Game Judge snapped his head back, startled.

"Four in the morning? Jeez, kid, get a life. It's only a video game."

-.....Logged out-

The Jewel Below

Michael D. Turner

here is a treasure hidden beneath the city," the dirty beggar-boy declared. "I swear it is true! Abar the Golden, grand-father to Ilkan the Munificent — may he live in glory for a thousand years — who is our Sultan now, sealed all the ways into the ancient under-city and hid a great treasure there."

Al-San the poet was dubious. "It seems more likely to me that the mighty Sultan, wise in the ways of the world and possessing many vaults and chambers right in his own palace, sealed the passages to curtail their use by thieves and other miscreants."

From the shaded porch of Beba the wine merchant Al-San contemplated the boy squatting on the sun-baked bricks below the latticed rail. The rag-clad youth was not so thin as to be starving. A thief, perhaps, who spun out his tale so he that he might draw close enough to lift Al-San's purse.

He drained his cup, waved it. The girl that Beba had assigned to the porch hurried over, water-chilled pitcher balanced on her shoulder, and poured more wine. Al-San eyed the boy cautiously during the procedure.

When the girl was gone, he continued: "Indeed! The wisdom of the Golden Sultan is legend. But crime is ineradicable, is it not? Many thieves were hanged during his reign — but did anyone complain that the marketplace was short of thieves?"

The point had a point, reflected Al-San. The notion was unthinkable.

"What cares a Sultan for thieves in any case? What ruler's coffers are so full of gold that he will squander a fortune to inconvenience desperate men with empty bellies?" The boy shook his head. "Confounding thieves was only a happy coincidence of the Sultan's plan. It had a greater purpose." Here he paused dramatically. Al-San waited for him to continue, but the boy remained silent.

"What was it?" Al-San asked with a sigh.

The boy held out his bowl. "A coin, Master, for the tale? A mere *bezati* – that I'll not starve – to hear the full of it?"

Al-San sipped cool wine and considered. He drew a nut-shaped copper coin scored by a hundred merchants' teeth from his fat purse, tossed it down. The boy caught it out of the air and it vanished into his rags.

"A blessing on your house, Master."

"The tale," demanded Al-San.

"Sultan Abar sealed the undercity to hide a treasure too valuable to risk losing, yet too dangerous to keep in his own palace. A thing of wonder, wrested by a mighty hero from the tower of a black sorcerer. A thing of magnificent beauty and great power – ah! – but also hard to control. What to do with such a thing? Too precious to relinquish, too threatening to keep close at hand."

"So he sealed it under the city."

"The Catacombs of Jubah have great renown! Cunning mazes, tunnels that twist this way and that, great vaulted chambers built by kings long forgotten. A haven not only for thieves, but others, too: black sorcerers and the mad followers of false gods. And so the Sultan – wise beyond measure! – conceived a way to kill two birds with one stone. The catacombs would guard his treasure, while the treasure would guard the catacombs."

Al-San fingered the hilt of his jeweled scimitar. "What was this treasure, this object of wonder and peril?"

"Some said it was a wondrous jewel, others a magnificent statue. Still others claimed that it was an oracle, a font of mystic lore. But all this happened long ago, when Abar the Golden was still a young man in the fullness of his strength, while today his grandson, our own beloved Ilkan– may he bask in the glory of God forever – shows a beard more white than gray. After so long, who can say for sure what the great treasure was?"

A cunning gleam had now come into the beggar's eyes. "Only one. I and I alone know what the Golden Sultan sealed beneath the city, Master. For I have seen it with my own eyes."

"Speak then," Al-San sneered. "What is this mysterious treasure, and how did you come to find it? And, while you are at, you may explain why one who knows such a priceless secret must perforce beg for his supper on the streets of Jubah!"

The boy bowed his head courteously. "I shall explain all, Master." He glanced up at the sky. "But see how the hour grows late – I have taken up too much of your time already. I will return tomorrow and finish the tale. The delay will add relish. " He made to depart.

Al-San tossed him another copper. "That is all you will get. Now finish, or I will have you whipped."

"May God bless your charity, master!" The boy settled back into his spot. "In order that you will comprehend how I came by my discovery I must, with your leave, report a few details of my own sordid condition, which I pray will give no offense."

Al-San nodded acquiescence.

"Due to the lowliness of my station and the cruel vagaries that come with it, I must be especially careful where I spend the night. As a rule, I never sleep in the same place two nights running, nor any place more than thrice in a single month. For it is the sad truth that men will rob even a poor beggar.

Each night I must hid myself anew lest someone accost me while I sleep and slit my throat for whatever paltry *bezati* I have in my robe."

"Truly, life is a hard thing for all concerned," Al-San said, picking a burr from his robe.

The boy nodded with equanimity. "Every trade has its draw-backs, so they say. For myself, I shall never face death on the battlefield beneath a cloud of arrows on the battlefield; yet neither shall I ever know a peaceful night's sleep. In any case, it is my habit to keep an eye open for any such nook as may provide, under night's bejeweled cover, fair haven for my rest. On the night in question, the rains were severe."

"When was this?"

"Last year, during the monsoon. Such flooding! We've seen nothing like it in Juba since –"

"Yes, yes." With a wave Al-San cut off the digression. "I remember last year's rains. They flooded the plains and damaged many farms and bridges, including my own estates. On with the tale."

"As you wish. That night I found myself hard pressed for lodgings. My first choice was under water; a pair of cutthroats occupied the second. I wandered the back alleys, searching for someplace dry to pass the night. At last I took refuge in a stairwell adjoining an old culvert, curled up, and did my best to sleep. Presently, a disturbance awoke me. Some bricks had fallen from the wall, loosened no doubt by the rain. A modest opening lay revealed. Seeing a gap – and no rain beyond – I enlarged it, hoping to secure better shelter."

"Hoping to find your way into some merchant's house," Al-San conjectured, "to plunder his larder and pilfer his stock."

The beggar held up his hands before him, showing in the way of the market traders that he still had both and was, therefore, no thief. "I sought only to get out of the rain, master!

"In any event, the space beyond was no mere merchant's cellar. I reached as far as I could but my hands touched only air; I would be obliged to climb inside in order to explore it."

"And this you undertook…"

"Not then. As I said, the rain was very bad, and moreover I had no means for light. So I restored the bricks as best I could and vowed to return better prepared.

"And so I did, Master. My hopes were humble: I sought only a place to sleep in peace. Instead, I discovered a vast and fabulous realm, the famous under-city, so long sealed. With candle-stubs or tallow-soaked rags for torches, I wandered its depths, explored its ways. And then I found it, Master: the Great King's treasure. But alas, I am too lowly to profit from such a thing."

"How do you mean?"

"Consider for a moment, Master. No one looks after beggars. The instant I disclosed my secret, my fate would be sealed. I would be cheated, robbed, killed outright to ensure my silence. What I need, Master," the beggar said, clutching his hands as if in prayer, "is a patron, a person of wealth and position, who would know how to get the treasure's full value. A true nobleman who would act justly and reward his poor servant fittingly…"

Now Al-San saw which way the wind blew. He vacillated. Good sense recommended having no part of the scheme. After all, the beggar's story was at best improbable. Conceivably it could even be some kind of trap. Yet Al-San found himself intrigued. The prospect of wealth did not affect him; he had that already. But as a poet he was avid for wonder – it being the raw material of his craft.

He spoke guardedly. "The Sultan's wish – any Sultan's – is tantamount to law. How should I, a nobleman and an army officer, subvert his will?"

"There is no edict," declared the beggar. "You did not break the seal. The way stands unlocked, unguarded. It is now simply treasure. "

"And the first rule of treasure…"

"Is finders keepers."

"There, Master," said the boy, pointing. "Behind those stairs – that's where the brick fell away during the rains. That is the way in."

The pair stood in a narrow twisty alley lined with windowless mud-brick buildings. Al-San looked around cautiously, fingering the jeweled hilt of his sword. The alley looked deserted.

"I see no space."

"I replaced the fallen bricks," the boy reminded him as he poked the wall with a finger. "Only dust holds them now." He worked swiftly. Out came one brick, then two more. The hole grew.

Now there was space to admit even so broad-shouldered a man as Al-San. The beggar reached inside and plucked out a stout stick to which a rope had been securely tied. He braced the stick across the hole and let the rope trail into blackness.

"It is not so far a climb, Master. Two man-lengths, no more."

Al-San checked the boy's handiwork. Satisfied, he drew a lantern from the sack draped over his shoulder, trimmed the wick, and lit it, then handed it to the boy.

"You go first," Al San said firmly, "to light the way."

"Of course, Master."

"If all is as you say, you shall have your fair share: one half."

The boy shook his dirty head. "A third, Master. No more. Even if I dared touch the great jewel, it is far too large for me to carry. And if I should

124

somehow manage to bring it out, I could not sell it. A humble beggar with such a thing? It would be seized by the first guardsman I encountered, and I would be slain as a thief. " With that he lowered himself into the hole, lantern-stem clutched in his teeth.

Al-San watched him descend, reach bottom. It was not far. The lantern cast a flickering yellow glow some yards in every direction. With care Al-San scanned the margins: no ambush offered itself. If he was going to turn back, now was the time.

He paused momentarily to settle his nerves, sucked in a deep breath, exhaled. Then, gingerly, he slid down to join the boy.

They were perched on a pile of dirt and tumble-down brick that shifted underfoot. "That way," the boy said, gesturing. To the left was a low passage that ran beneath the building's foundations. He would have to crawl.

Al-San asked: "What is your name, beggar-of-the-marketplace?"

"I am Dakkam, Master."

"Well, Dakkam, it seems I am to place my life in your hands. Swear to me by our God's name and your own that you will lead me well and true, that you will not forsake me in the dark maze below the city, but will lead me safely to this treasure and guide me out again."

"Master, I swear it. By my name and all I hold holy, I swear it to you."

"Very well, Dakkam. And this I swear to you: That I, Hakim ibn Hassan ibn Akbar Dar Al-San, God willing, shall reward your service deed for deed – loyalty with riches, betrayal with vengeance. Such is my oath. Now, lead the way."

On all fours, like penitents seeking salvation, they entered the labyrinth.

They crawled for a good while. The first few tunnels were all the same, built up from rough-hewn river stone, rudely stacked, narrow and low-ceilinged and wet and clogged with stinking rubbish. Al-San's silken robes were soon smeared with filth. But in due course the passage expanded and they were able to walk upright. "Be careful of the footing here, Master," Dakkam spoke from the shadows ahead. "The way slopes, and it is wet."

"It still stinks," groused the poet. He hated to be dirty.

"Not so bad as before, Master. The way ahead is more comfortable, and the air dry and clear."

And so it was. They shimmied sidewise through a fault in the stone and emerged into a wide hall supported by pillars, cunningly engineered. The walls were tiled in muted colors – ochre, somber blue, funerary charcoal. Al-San took the lantern and walked back and forth, inspecting the passage, boot heels clicking on the flagstones.

For a time they walked in silence through high empty halls. At each intersection, Dakkam moved with decision, leading first one direction, then another, never slowing his pace. Al-San was caught up in wonder. Here was a forgotten world, a shadow-city to rival the one above.

"How did you come to learn your way here?" asked the poet at length.

"It was not difficult, Master," replied the boy modestly. "Notice the footprints we make in the dust. With light one need only follow them back to return whence once came."

"And without light?"

The youth hunched his shoulder as if from a lash. "It is better to have a light."

The answer did not satisfy Al-San completely. "Well enough the first time through. Still, you must distinguish one passage from another somehow, if only to remind yourself where you've been."

The boy nodded. "You are wise indeed, master. We street-folk employ a system of subtle marks, signs known only to ourselves. Thus do gangs mark their territory, beggars lay claim to a pitch, streetwalking whores warn off their competition." They came to an intersection and he held up his hand. "Observe: there, at the height of my shoulder, do you see it? I swiped four fingers on the tile. The mark yet remains."

"So, as you explored each way…"

"I would wipe the marks from dead-end routes, or mark them differently to tell where they went. Now I have guideposts throughout, and make my journeys with ease."

"Very clever, Dakkam." The boy smiled.

After a period they came to a wide stair, ascended, and arrived in a vaulted hall of monumental scale, built from great blocks of polished stone and decorated in porphyry and jasper and chert.

"My own home is not constructed so finely," Al-San declared. "How could the Golden Sultan allow such a place to be abandoned?"

"Not abandoned, Master," Dakkam replied. "Forbidden."

For Al-San the word was like a lance. It punctured the bubble of wonder; fear came hissing in. "How much farther to this jewel of yours?"

"It is near, Master." Dakkam raised the lantern and pointed into the gloom. "The third chamber on the left, past the portico. You can see my footprints in the dust."

But Al-San could not; the spot was lost in shadow. The beggar tugged at his leave, urging him forward.

The gesture was only mildly presumptuous, but in this dismal place it gave Al-San a pretext for relief, and the alchemy of caste replaced his fear with contempt. Smirking, he batted the hand away and strode forward, the boy at his heels.

Something fiery flickered beyond the portico, brightening as they drew near. Al-San stood in the doorway and gaped.

The fire was their own lantern light, reflected and multiplied a thousand-fold by the magnificent object within, so that on every surface – walls, ceiling, floor – flickered a dazzling net of fireflies, fierce and bright and remote as the light from heaven's stars.

Dakkam's magnificent jewel was an amber statue of monstrous form. It was man-sized and bipedal, but the body was ape-like and grotesquely muscular. For feet it had hooves, and its hands were massive lions' paws.

But it was the face – that of a beautiful woman, eyes shut in repose – that captured Al-San's gaze. Something in its tranquil expression hinted of amusement or even joy. It might even have been called beguiling – save for the dozen curling goat-horns sprouting from her brow in place of hair.

Dakkam spoke, interrupting his thoughts. "You see, Master, I spoke only truth. A great jewel, a statue of surpassing beauty. Too precious for me to hazard alone!"

Al-San circled the thing, examining it from every angle. "It is certainly magnificent! But hardly beautiful. It is a masterpiece, yes, but it's hideous! Carved for the temple of some false god, no doubt.

"You are shrewd, Dakkam. To get good value from such a thing will take some subtlety. One cannot simply haul it into the marketplace. But you're wrong about what would have happened had you tried: you wouldn't have been hanged for a thief – you would have been burned alive as an apostate.

"Even getting it out will prove difficult. It is too wide for the way we came. We'll have to scout out a different route. It would be a shame to break it, but it is so large! Amber is not heavy, though. I may be able to lift it."

So saying, Al-San stretched out a hand and laid it upon the jewel. To his shock, it was warm as living flesh. He tried to pull away, but discovered a muscular arm around his waist.

The statue inclined its head. Its eyes opened. The pretty face looked down at him. Something wet splashed his abdomen.

Then watered steel flashed forth from Al-San's scabbard, striking twice like forked lightning. Once, twice, the blows rang like tolling bells, sparks flashed beneath his blade, but no mark marred the horrid thing's tawny surface. For Al-San, it was if he'd struck an anvil. The sword wriggled from his nerveless grip and clattered away.

The thing lifted Al-San into the air, then broke him over its knee, the way a man will break a branch for firewood. Then it cast him aside.

Al-San lay against the wall. There was a dagger in his sash, but he no longer had the strength to draw it. He knew then that he would die soon. All that was left was to watch.

The statue, red with his own blood, resumed its station in the center of the room. Its movements grew languid. From it came a sanguine glow that eclipsed the light of the lantern.

Al-San felt a tug at his belt. Dakkam smiled down at him. Then he took Al-San's purse, still fat with coin, and his bejeweled dagger and moved away.

"Dakkam!" Al-San called after him, his voice cracking with the effort. The boy looked back and put a finger over his lips to signal silence.

Then, on hands and needs, Dakkam crawled forward and abased himself before the idol. "Noble blood you have tasted, now will answers you reveal."

The thing replied in a soprano voice of surpassing loveliness. "Three times have you fed me, three questions have I answered. For a beggar's blood I told you my purpose, for the blood of a thief I taught you the charm of beguilement, for the blood of a merchant I gave you the charm of seeming. Now I drink noble blood. Ask what you will."

"Teach the spell that summons the spirits of the dead," the boy demanded.

"Dry the root of the *abasi* weed, which grows on the graves of infidels. Grind it into powder. Soak it in the blood of a gibbet-crow. Take the mixture and make the mark as follows…"

Al-San watched as Dakkam, no longer a beggar-boy but a vole-faced man, tore strips of rag from his own raiment. Dipping his finger into the spreading pool of Al-San's lifeblood, he hastily recorded the knowledge of dark sorcery the statue revealed.

The poet's eyes dimmed. With his dying breath, Al-San cursed himself for a fool.

On the Border

Tracie McBride

lthough he had only served the Book for three years, the Bearer had already forgotten his own name. He knew every detail of its maps – every contour was seared into his mind like a branding mark. Yet he could not say which page represented his place of birth, nor could he recall the family from whom he had been taken.

An iron chain riveted to the Book's spine depended from a collar around his neck. He dared not let it dangle for fear of crippling himself, so he clasped the Book tightly to his chest. He shuffled forward as if blinded, and in a way, he was. The constant presence of the Book had skewed his perceptions. The contours of the land showed themselves to him in surreal, giddying colours, at distances ten times greater than other mortals might perceive. But he could no longer see sky or stars at all, and everything else was but a blur.

Right now he knew himself to be situated on the Khalgin Sand, a narrow spit of desert running east-west along the border. It glowed a vicious shade of vermillion only he could see. But he had to infer the presence of the thousands all about him from indistinct columns of light, flickering with vitality – and of course from their voices, which muttered, japed, and swore.

"This way, Bearer," came a man's voice at his shoulder. He turned and followed. His boots dragged through the sand and he stumbled to his knees. His guide dared not touch him – only he could bear the burden of the Book

– so he laboriously pushed himself back to his feet, swaying in the mid-morning heat. The guide directed him to a small tent, and, holding back the flap, ushered him inside.

With the landscape hidden by tent-cloth ordinary sight returned. The Bearer looked around. The tent was furnished with a long table on which sat a full inkwell and quill, and a single chair. With utmost care he set the Book on the table. Then he slumped into the chair and waited.

From their respective positions, the leaders of the two armies watched the Bearer enter the tent. Each rode to the front of their line, dismounted. They approached each other with ceremonial slowness.

One faced the other, their expressions studiously impassive. Then, in unison, they strode to the tent, shoulder-to-shoulder, like marchers in a parade. They went in together, too: for one to follow behind implied submission. It was an awkward fit.

Inside, the leader from the North lifted off his helmet and stripped his gauntlets, setting these neatly aside. He ran his hands through his shaggy white-blond hair, armor clanking as he moved. The leader from the South, whose only bodily protection besides her leather battle-dress were the talismanic tattoos on her broad brown cheeks, flashed a vulpine smile.

"Comrade," said the man.

"Brother," said the woman.

They pressed their right palms and forearms together in the manner of the North, then pressed their foreheads and noses together in the manner of the South. Then they stepped apart, ritual salutations complete. They gazed at one another with expressions approaching fondness.

"It would be a great tragedy to see the blood of so many fine warriors shed needlessly today," said the man.

"Indeed," said the woman amiably. "Although your losses would surely be greater than mine."

The man scowled, his jaw tightening – then abruptly laughed. "You have not changed, Maeve."

"But you have, Sacha," she said. "You've become harder to bait."

They took stock of the Bearer. He was a slightly built young man – barely past twenty, Maeve guessed – though his position had prematurely aged him. Worry lines cut his visage deeply; his brown hair had thinned, and he trembled like an old man, or a drunk. Maeve wrinkled her nose in distaste. Were it not for the Book, she would have judged him a half-wit.

"Open it," she said. "Show us the Borderlands."

He complied with sudden dexterity, his fingers skipping effortlessly to the correct page. Maeve and Sacha bent over the Book. It showed a five hundred square mile area straddling the border between their respective homelands, stretching from one coast to the other.

The vibrancy of its depiction took them aback. To the west: a miniature of the Cerulean Cliffs, their distinctive blue replicated perfectly. Near the northern edge: the Armatic Forest, painted presently in shades of lush green and autumnal brown, the odor of wood spice wafting up from the leaves. A thin blue line representing the Yacto River snaked through the forest and across the page to the Eastern border where it widened into the Oro Delta and at last joined the sea. Clustered along either side were tiny houses denoting human settlement.

"I never thought it would be so beautiful," said Maeve huskily. Yet she drew back, nostrils flared, as if she smelled something offensive.

"Yes…" breathed Sacha. "So beautiful…" His eyes took on an unhealthy sheen; his hand hovered over the page, then drew closer.

"No!" the Bearer shouted. Quick as a snake, he smacked Sacha's hand away. Sacha shook himself like a dog and took three deep, shuddering breaths. His bewildered expression gave way to one of fury, and he drew back his fist.

"Only I may touch the Book," the Bearer said hastily. "Your hands court sheer death. I acted only to protect you. No one else may touch it. But it will try to draw you in. It yearns for your life force."

Sacha edged away, rubbing his hands together as if to reassure himself that they were still attached to his body.

"Then we had best get this over with quickly," Maeve growled. "My sovereign has sent me to take possession of the port here" – she pointed – "and the farmland to its south. We are prepared to go to war if need be, but we would prefer to compromise, and so spare both our nations bloodshed."

The Bearer gave a short, barking laugh that rattled his chains. "Fools! There is no bloodless way to carve up the land. The Book will not allow it. The Book…"

Maeve touched her dagger to the back of his neck. "If you don't shut up," she said through gritted teeth, "yours will be the first blood the Book tastes today."

The Bearer said no more. Maeve sheathed her blade.

"In return," she said, turning back to Sacha, "we will cede to you full possession of the Armatic Forest, this stretch of coastline from here to here, and the Kamankayan plains immediately inland."

"The plains?" asked Sacha softly.

Maeve coughed into her fist. "Yes. Its wild horses are famous for their speed and agility, and we all know how your queen values good horseflesh."

"But those plains are your birthplace, Maeve. Surely he is not asking you to hand them over."

She shrugged. "Do I look like a sentimental fool? He is my king." Her tone was light enough, but she turned away for a moment.

When she turned back her face was again an impassive mask. "Do we have an agreement, or not?"

"Almost. I also want this village - Wesk." Sacha indicated a symbol on the map, little more than a smudge.

Maeve frowned. "Am I missing something? It has no strategic or economic value as far as I know."

"No, but it seems that one of us is a sentimental fool."

Maeve's frown deepened with incomprehension.

"I fell in love there once."

Maeve's mouth formed a silent o, but repressed the subsequent smirk. "It's yours. Bearer, you may formalize our accord. Make the marks."

The Bearer, trembling already, now shook with such ferocity that Maeve feared he would collapse into a fit at any moment.

"Do you know what you ask me to do? There will be consequences. The Book will demand them."

Maeve bent down and whispered in his ear like a lover. "Tell me, little man. Tell me what will happen."

"I…I don't know…"

"Then let's find out."

The Bearer shook so badly he could barely grasp the quill, but the Book took hold of him. His grip steadied and the nib descended smoothly towards the page. He watched in horror as his hand drew ink across the map, leaving in its wake a clean, impeccable line dividing the land in two.

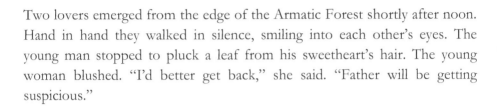

Two lovers emerged from the edge of the Armatic Forest shortly after noon. Hand in hand they walked in silence, smiling into each other's eyes. The young man stopped to pluck a leaf from his sweetheart's hair. The young woman blushed. "I'd better get back," she said. "Father will be getting suspicious."

She took a reluctant step away, arm outstretched, her fingertips still brushing his. She saw his lips move in reply but a sudden roar swallowed his words. The earth bellowed; the ground shook. A wall of rock and earth rose between them and rushed skyward.

For a time the young man lay senseless. Presently, he rose and flung his battered body against the barrier, calling her name. Eventually his tongue grew so caked in dust that he could no longer speak. He leaned against the wall and wept.

Out on the Kamankayan Plains a mountain rose where none had ever stood. A herd of wild horses stamped and whinnied as the ground under their hooves transformed. A piebald stallion reared in fury. What had become of his harem? A mare galloped in circles, her call shrill and desperate, while her foal stood shivering and alone on the other side of the wall.

In a western hamlet, fishermen woke from midday naps to see their moored boats buried under rubble. On the south shore of the Yacto River lay an old woman, wailing. A stockade of flint and quartz had erupted on the other side, obliterating the cottage where she had lived her whole life and where her baby grandson had, moments before, been sleeping soundly.

The Bearer sat, precariously balanced but unharmed, on top of the newborn mountain. Far below, hardened soldiers – their leaders entombed within rubble - panicked or flung themselves to the ground, whimpering as the broken earth gouted flame.

The Bearer hugged the Book ever tighter to his chest and wept.

Between Honor and Glory

Mark Finnemore

artyn rounded the corner and nearly got run down by a plump boy driving a mule-drawn cart. He grabbed the back, heaved himself into its bed, and lay down flat, hoping his pursuers wouldn't see him. They didn't: the men rushed right by, hollering and brandishing their truncheons. The cart turned another corner and the men slid from view. Martyn sat up.

"What in all the bloody hells are you doing in my wagon?"

Shocked by the bellowing voice, Martyn turned and saw it wasn't a boy at all, but a short stocky man with a waist-length red beard.

"You...you're a dwarf!" Martyn gasped.

"And yer a damned highwayman!" The dwarf dropped the reins and picked up an axe. "Defend yerself!"

"Whoa!" Martyn held up his hands. "I'm no highwayman; I'm just – um –"

The dwarf studied the stowaway, a skinny young man with a stubbly beard akin to a dwarven maiden's. "What do ye want, then?"

Martyn sat on a bag of oats and extended his hand. "Martyn's the name."

The dwarf ignored Martyn's hand. "Why're ye running from that gang?"

"Well…" Martyn cast about for a convincing excuse, but nothing came to mind. The truth would have to do. "I got involved with the Reeve's daughter. She practically threw herself at me – a fellow like you must know how it is! – and one thing led to another…" Martyn paused. "Now she's pregnant, and, well, you understand."

The dwarf nodded. "Oh, I understand, all right."

Martyn let out a relieved sigh.

"Have ye no honor at all?"

"Honor?" Martyn said. "Where's the honor in changing diapers? I'd rather be out changing the world!"

The dwarf snorted. "Ha! You've already changed the world, boy! You're just too dense to see it." He shook his head sadly. "Where's the honor in running from responsibility?"

Martyn began an indignant reply, but the dwarf held up his hand. "Save yer bluster fer someone who might actually believe it. I'm not one of yer goat-brained chums from the pig-sty or dirt farm or wherever it is ye hail from. What matters is – do ye love this woman?"

A jug of ale lay stuffed between sacks. Martyn nodded toward it. The dwarf shrugged, so he popped the cork, took a long pull, and lowered it with a belch. He had another before answering. "I do love Ashby – that's her name – and she loves me, or she says she does at least. The problem is her father the Reeve – he says she can do better. I 'lack both money and prospects' were his words, as I recall. Now I have to get out of town or have my legs broken."

The dwarf nodded. "So – yer not good enough for his daughter? Well, no man ever is. But ye won't impress him by running away. So, what do ye plan to do?"

"Do?" Martyn shrugged. He hadn't given the matter much thought. "I guess I have to find a way to earn some money. Perhaps then the Reeve will think I'm worthy. Anyway, what're you doing here – are you on your Gallivant?"

"What do you – a *human* – know of Gallivant?" He spat when he said 'human,' as if the word had its own flavor, one he found sickening. Then the dwarf grabbed the jug and took his own swig.

Martyn tried to affect an air of ease. "Despite my ignorance about women, I am a man of some education."

"Is that so?" The dwarf rubbed his beard, nodding, and examined Martyn anew. He took another swig of ale. "I'm Bizlow of the Ironbones clan," he announced, "twenty-seventh son of Genbar the Giant-slayer. My quest is the life of Sisspahn, the White Drake of the North."

Martyn strove to hold back laughter. His face reddened.

Bizlow noted his expression. "I'd heard humans were a cruel lot." His tone was more sad than disgruntled.

"*Me* cruel? I'm not the one off to murder a dragon!"

"Dragons are vile, gem-hoarding beasts."

"I've heard the same said about dwarves."

Bizlow set aside the empty jug. "Humans – yer humor is as weak as yer ale!"

Martyn ignored the jibe. "They say ice drakes are big as longships, with teeth and claws like frozen swords and breath like a blizzard. Slaying one can't be easy. How will you pull it off?"

Bizlow pulled a roll of oiled canvas from under his seat, unrolled it, and held up a crossbow bolt. "With this!"

The bolt looked ordinary enough. Someone had scratched a few mystic-looking runes into the shaft, but that proved nothing. Hawkers down at the market practiced this trick every day, hoping to pass off second-rate goods as precious relics. Was Bizlow a rube? Martyn chuckled. "You intend to slay an ice drake with that — tavern dart?"

"It's a dragon-slaying bolt," Bizlow said with dignity, "sneaked most cleverly from the clan vault."

"Stolen, you mean! And you call *me* a highwayman!"

"All right; that's enough! Gallivant is serious business — I've got no time for yer foolishness. Out of me wagon!" Bizlow looked around for the ax.

"Wait!" Martyn looked back to make sure Ashby's father and his men weren't following. He couldn't see them, but that didn't mean they weren't there. "Please, let me ride with you a little longer. I promise I'll be quiet."

Bizlow scratched his beard and considered. "Did ye learn to write, gettin' that 'education'?"

"Yes." Martyn nodded proudly. "But that won't help with dragon-slaying, I'm afraid, so if you'll please just take me as far as Buddleby, I'll —"

Bizlow coughed out a gruff laugh. "Oh, I don't need any help fighting, boy. I need you to chronicle me deeds! There's treasure to be won — enough to impress that girl, I'll warrant. And maybe you'll learn something about honor along the way."

They rode north along the base of the Iron Cliffs into a region called the Broken Lands, reputedly home to dragons. It was a rocky lifeless place strewn with enormous boulders. Legend held they had been dropped by careless gods.

Martyn had intended to slip away earlier – he certainly had no interest in following Bizlow to his death – but then he realized that Bizlow's quest was the answer to his own troubles after all. Trying to steal from a dragon's hoard was about as foolish as fighting one, as Martyn reckoned it, but firsthand accounts of dragon-slaying brought sure income. Chronicling Bizlow's quest would earn him the money to prove his worth to Ashby's father!

True, the dragon would almost certainly kill and devour Bizlow at the end of the story, and that would be tragic; but tragedies *were* more popular than ever these days. And Bizlow's mind was obviously set – who was Martyn to talk him out of his destiny?

From his pouch he produced vellum and a spike of hard charcoal. He licked the end thoughtfully. This was an altogether new undertaking. How to begin? He needed to start thinking like a saga-writer. The first thing was to establish Bizlow's motivation.

"So, why do you want to slay this dragon? Did it raze your crops and eat your herds?"

Bizlow grunted. The dwarf, Martyn had already learned, employed a whole spectrum of grunts. This one signaled a negative response.

"Did it burn your village?"

Again the grunt.

"Then why?"

"My first brother attempted to swim the Tyver River. But dwarves are not strong swimmers, and he was carried over the falls to his death." Bizlow held up his hand to forestall Martyn's regret. "He died seventy-two years before my birth. He was a fool. And my next seven brothers were even greater fools."

Martyn was astounded. "You mean eight of your brothers were swept over the falls?"

Bizlow nodded. "The ninth succeeded and thereby ascended to high rank among the Ironbones. But that was long ago. Swimming the river is no longer enough. Each dwarf must outdo his predecessors."

After a moment's silence Bizlow continued. "Six more brothers died trying to survive a plunge *over* the falls. My sixteenth brother – now famous for his cunning – succeeded. He went over inside an ale cask stuffed with furs. Now our young bucks ride the falls for sport, though many die or become maimed in the process."

Bizlow unstoppered a new jug of ale, drank, passed it to Martyn. "My brother Ryhaab – of whom I was fond – set out for Sisspahn's lair a year ago. He never returned." Bizlow held up the bolt. "But Ryhaab didn't have this!"

Martyn looked at the bolt. It seemed too slender a shaft to hold all Bizlow's hopes.

"So, how many sons does your father have now?" Martyn asked.

"Four," Bizlow said. "My younger brother has yet to set forth."

"Four! Out of twenty-eight!" Martyn shook his head, appalled. "And soon your younger brother will throw his life away, too. Then your father will have only two sons to carry on the line."

Bizlow scowled. "What of it? Cowards win no honor for the clan: my father knows the saying well. He taught it to me. And, besides, who are ye to preach on life's sanctity? Your son will have no father at all!"

"Well, at least I –" Martyn's stopped short. Something big swept by overhead, its shadow blotting out the sun. A dragon.

It soared away, then turned – a graceful tangent – and made right for them.

Bizlow grabbed the crossbow, clumsily fit the bolt in place, and raised it with trembling hands.

"Shoot!" Martyn yelled.

Bizlow's finger jerked, sending the bolt sizzling through the air. It arced below the diving beast to shatter against a boulder.

Martyn's gut wrenched as they scrambled from the wagon and took cover behind another great stone. Bizlow drew his axe. "Looks like we do this the old fashioned way," he growled.

The dragon alighted on a nearby rock, sending tremors through the earth. Despite Martyn's fears it seemed in no particular hurry to devour them.

The dragon wasn't as big as a longboat, but it was plenty intimidating – four times the size of a horse, plus the tail and long neck. Its head was about the size of a coffin and wedge-shaped. The scales were magnificent: ten thousand tiny shimmerings of copper and amber and lilac and gold, the colors changing in liquid ripples as it moved.

"Ye shouldn't have yelled," complained Bizlow. "Ye made me fire too soon!"

"You should've let me have the bow," Martyn countered. "My aim is better."

"The quest is mine. As was the bolt."

"*Miertzryke!*" The dragon's voice was horrified. "A dragon-slayer? I smelled magic, but…you tried to kill me!"

It took Martyn a moment to realize that he heard the dragon's words not with his ears but his mind. He cocked his head at Bizlow. "It really was a dragon-slayer?"

"Of course. I said so, didn't I? But how did the beast know?"

A head like a huge ocean pike's seemed to glide around the corner of their makeshift redoubt. It peered at them. "Surely you know dragons can read men's minds? Comes from eating their brains!"

Martyn jumped backwards into Bizlow and knocked them both to the ground. As they fell he could sense the creature's amusement.

"Forgive me! You two are obviously in no mood for jest. As to your question, dwarf, I knew it was *Miertzryke* because you did. I saw it in your mind and I felt the magic – natural talents that all dragons share."

"Don't toy with us, beast," Bizlow snarled. "Eat us and be done with it."

"Thank you, but I've already eaten," it said primly. "Besides, I dislike man-flesh: it's rather gamy. Also, my name is not 'beast', but Mooralum. But let us address the central issue: why did you try to kill me?"

Martyn rose and brushed the dirt from his clothes. "He wasn't trying to kill you in particular. He seeks the dragon Sisspahn."

"Sisspahn is old and shrewd and vicious. He is ten times my size and cruel beyond reckoning. With the *Miertzryke* you had a slim chance; without it you have none. It is a fool's errand. Why throw away your lives?"

"For honor," Bizlow said.

Something like a sigh filled their minds. "What you seek is glory, not honor," said the dragon. "And what you will find is your graves."

They continued north. Neither of them spoke much, and Martyn had lost heart for working on the chronicle. The run-in with Mooralum had proved one thing to him: Bizlow was not going to cut it as a dragon-slayer. And now that he knew the dwarf's death was certain, Martyn found he had no stomach to watch, let alone profit from it – not even for Ashby's sake.

Bizlow seemed to be reconsidering as well, but then they encountered a party of dwarves from the Red Hammer clan. The groups passed without a word.

Martyn assumed that he caused the dwarves' icy response, but Bizlow shook his head.

"What then?" Martyn asked.

"You saw the device on their shields?"

Martyn nodded.

"You see this?" He slapped his own shield, a plain round buckler devoid of sigil. "They had no idea I was of the Ironbones, or any other clan. Nor would they have cared if I had told them. I was beneath their notice – insignificant. I am without family, without honor, unworthy of greeting whether amicable or hostile. To them, or any other dwarf, I am *nothing!*"

The weather turned foul as Bizlow's mood soon thereafter. A wet clinging snow fell, and icy winds clawed through Martyn's drenched clothes.

They found the cave and went inside. It was good to have shelter, even at the entrance to Sisspahn's lair. But the feeble fire they scraped together brought little warmth: the wind slithered in, wrapping them in its chilly coils. Martyn shivered.

Mementos of would-be dragon-slayers littered the cave – bones and slop, ashes, last words scratched into stone. Some were boasts, others expressed regret or indecision or fear. Some had the form of letters to a loved one.

Martyn drew his dagger and carved *Ashby, I'm sorry* into the frozen stone.

"I go on alone from here," Bizlow announced.

"But…your deed."

"I'll tell you about if I come back. If not…"

Martyn drew a slow frigid breath. The dwarf was giving him a way out. He ought to do the same. "You don't have to do this. It's not worth it."

"Honor cannot be bought cheaply," Bizlow said. "I don't want to live out my years like you – a man without honor or family."

Martyn watched Bizlow head down the passage with lantern in hand. He shook his head and shouted after the dwarf: "Better without honor than without *life*!" But he fell into miserable silence as his words echoed down the passage. He didn't believe that any longer, if he ever truly had.

The wind sighed through the cave as darkness gradually swallowed the light of Bizlow's lantern. Martyn blew out a frosty breath and lit a pine torch. He couldn't let Bizlow go on alone, not without knowing he'd never be worthy of Ashby no matter how much money he acquired. Damn Bizlow and his incessant talk of honor!

Martyn grabbed the crossbow and headed down the passage, falling several times on the icy floor. He chuckled bitterly through numb lips; he hadn't even seen the dragon yet and already he was bruised and aching!

He found Bizlow at the foot of a steep icy incline trying to claw his way up. The dwarf could get only a few yards before sliding back down. "Lend a hand if yer coming," he growled. "But stay back when we find the beast. Yer job is to witness my deed, not to die trying to be a hero!"

Martyn snorted out a plume of frost. "You needn't worry about that!"

For a time they debated the best way up the slope, then put their ideas into practice. The task was challenging, but after several failures they struck upon a workable scheme: chip shallow steps into the ice for their feet and drive crossbow bolts in for handholds. It was slow, painstaking work, but at length they gained the summit and rested there a few minutes to catch their breath.

Martyn slipped the last bolt into his quiver – the rest sprouted from the frozen slope like stunted little pines.

One bolt. Not much to work with, not unless by some miracle it was another *Miertzryke*. He chuckled at his own wishful thinking, but pulled the bolt back out to check nonetheless. No such luck. It was altogether ordinary.

All at once Martyn was struck by the absurdity of their enterprise. It was all so preposterous. Maybe no one had ever managed to kill a dragon at all. Martyn wondered that he'd never questioned the tales of dragon-slaying he'd heard as a youth. The dragon was always as big as a gold-lender's house, with claws like scythes and breath like the furnaces of hell, yet somehow the hero would still slay it with a well-placed stroke of his magic sword or by spearing it just so with his lance, and it would not occur once to even one of the listeners – himself included – to call it what it so patently was: nonsense. Pure fantasy.

You could just as soon sink a ship with a sling stone.

The passage ended at a narrow ledge. They crawled to the edge and peered over. They crouched, blinking at the sudden brightness. The lair opened before them, a glittering sunlit vastness that dazzled the eye but also appeared to be, for the present at least, mercifully empty of dragons.

The light came from an enormous hole in the mountain far overhead. Below, icy heaps of coin and treasure carpeted the cavern, reflecting the sunlight like the open sea at daybreak. Bones littered the floor as well, of elephants and huge fish and bears and many others, and the bones of men, too, some still encased in their useless armor.

"I'm going down."

Bizlow's whisper stopped Martyn's heart for an instant. He took a deep breath to settle his squirming gut, but the slaughterhouse stench of the lair surged into his nostrils. He choked down vomit, then took a moment to regain his composure. Then he unslung the crossbow and loaded the last bolt. He nodded to the dwarf. Bizlow slid down the icy slope on his rump. Gaining the cavern's floor, the dwarf began to explore, poking here and there among the gold and rubbish and ice.

"My mother's beard!" he cried, squatting before a suit of plate armor. "It's Ryhaab! My brother! I'd know that armor anywhere – father gave it to him at the farewell ceremony."

Bizlow rummaged around some more, then rose triumphantly brandishing a broad-headed maul in his hands. "Blood of the Earth! *Thunderhead!* Thunian's hammer itself!" He inspected it from every angle in reverent wonder. "I'd heard rumors Ryhaab had filched it from the armory, but – "

Martyn cut in. "Then we'd best leave now and return it to Thunian."

"Yer a goat-headed fool!" Bizlow scowled. "Thunian is the God of Storms – he lent this hammer to Grusk, forefather of our clan, a thousand years past. And he don't need it to do his business anyhow, any more than an ogre needs a mirror to know it's ugly!

"Besides, I can't leave Ryhaab lying here in all this filth. Got to bring him home, put his bones in a proper crypt."

Martyn sighed. There was no arguing with the dwarf when his mind was made up. Bizlow kicked over a trunk, spilling gold and silver coins on the dirty ice, and packed in his brother's remains. Shivering and silent, Martyn watched the grisly family reunion. He wished Bizlow would hurry: Sisspahn could be back at any moment.

Bizlow closed the latch, patted the trunk affectionately. "A hard death," he said, "but one that soon will be avenged." He seized the hammer in both hands, raised it high, then brought it down hard on a pony-sized boulder. There was a resounding boom; the rock split in two.

"So it will be with Sisspahn's bones! Thunderhead is our foremost relic, the mightiest weapon in the Ironbones' armory. Why, I wouldn't trade her for a hundred dragon-slaying arrows, even if they came with a company of elf archers to do the shooting!"

"Forgive me for saying so," said Martyn, "but Ryhaab had the hammer, and his bones sit packed in that box."

"He must have been caught unawares. Thunderhead has far greater power than ye know. Look." He grasped the base of the haft in both hands and began to spin, going easy at first but soon increasing his tempo.

After several revolutions Bizlow let out a roar of exertion and let fly, stumbling to the ground as he released his grip. The hammer sizzled through the air like lightning to strike high on the cavern wall with a thunderous crack. Chunks of stone rained down as Thunderhead flew back to Bizlow's hand. "You see, Martyn, no dragon could withstand —"

An impossible roar drowned Bizlow's voice. Something enormous swooped down through the hole above.

The dragon was on the ground before Martyn could move. The wind of its wings sent coins and jewels airborne, pelting Bizlow like lead shot.

Mooralum had judged Sisspahn's size ten times his own. It was no exaggeration: if Mooralum was a salamander, Sisspahn was a crocodile. The monster before them had a ridge of spikes along its back, blue like glacial ice, while its scales were almost clear, sharp and severe as frozen diamonds.

Dark laughter invaded their minds, and then a sinister hissing like hot coals doused with water. "Did you know an enemy is most vulnerable when he turns to flee? But alas, you can't be blamed. They all run."

Its rhythmic, slithering pace mesmerized as it stalked closer.

"Your brother ran, dwarf. I seem to recall he was quite fast, for such a stumpy little squirrel. And quite tasty too!"

151

"Then you'll remember this," Bizlow roared as he once again hurled the hammer. But in the urgency of the moment Bizlow neglected to spin before throwing, and the hammer did not hiss through the air as before, though it still struck Sisspahn a shuddering blow that buckled the dragon's legs.

Bizlow stepped forward to engage the monster even as Thunderhead circled back, but his boots slid on black ice. As he scrambled to keep his footing the returning sledge knocked Bizlow into a wall, and hammer and dwarf dropped to the cavern floor together.

Sisspahn shook off its daze. Its scaly jaws twisted into a sneer of contempt as it resumed its stalking.

Martyn ducked back under the ledge. Had the dragon noticed him? Perhaps not. Instinctively, he wriggled backwards toward the passageway, toward escape, but then he stopped. Was he really prepared to abandon Bizlow now? No – but what could he do to save him?

Martyn wracked his brain for an idea, any idea. Mooralum's words returned to him: *I knew it was Miertzryke because you did. I saw it in your mind and I felt the magic – natural talents that all dragons share.*

A plan took shape. Martyn lifted the crossbow's butt to his shoulder and roared with all the authority he could muster.

"Hold or die! This quarrel is *Miertzryke* – a dragon-slayer!"

At the word *Miertzryke*, the dragon curled its long neck round to face Martyn. Its yellow eyes narrowed. "So. Another mouse in the cheese house."

It inspected him, the great spiked head pivoting smoothly. Eyes like molten gold sought his own. Martyn knew better than to meet that gaze.

"The *Miertzryke* is a serious matter. If you do in fact possess it. But human-folk are famous liars. How do I know your bolt is *Miertzryke*?"

Cautiously, very cautiously, Martyn slipped the quiver from his shoulder, let it drop, and kicked it down the slope, never once removing his finger from the crossbow's trigger. "The quiver is empty. See for yourself. Why would I carry only one bolt unless that was all I needed?"

Sisspahn's consciousness slithered through his skull, prying at his memories. Martyn imagined again the stories he had so loved as a boy, but with a difference. He pictured himself and Bizlow as the mighty heroes, riding from land to land, murdering poor Mooralum along with a whole host of other, imaginary dragons, each shot dead on the first try with a Miertzryke bolt.

Sisspahn puffed out its scaly chest. "So you two are famous dragon-hunters. A likely story. Shoot, then: I will be your greatest prize."

Martyn shrugged. "Truth is, the dwarf has better aim. I'm afraid I might miss you from here, and then I'm done for. But I'm certain I'd hit you dead on if you'd just be so kind as to take another step forward."

Sisspahn lifted a leg – and then paused. "You may live. Depart at once."

"The dwarf comes, too. You keep your treasure and your life. Now: enough talk. You have 'til I count three to back away. Or we take our chances with my aim."

Martyn took a calming breath. "One!" he shouted.

The dragon watched him. It did not move.

"Two!" Martyn remembered Mooralum's horror upon realizing the earlier bolt *was* a real dragon-slayer. With all his will he seized on that feeling, letting it flood his consciousness.

As Martyn opened his mouth to say 'three', Sisspahn spat frost. "Very well. A scrawny human and a gristly dwarf – you're not worth the risk. If you take anything besides your friend I will kill you on the spot, dragon-slayer or no. Now begone!" The dragon slunk back into the shadows of the cavern, hissing and muttering as he went.

Martyn slid down the ramp, hustled over to the dwarf, nudged him with his foot. Nothing. Again. Bizlow groaned miserably. He looked up at Martyn like a drunk woken from a stupor.

"What happened?"

"Some of your damn talk about honor must've sunk in," said Martyn, and he steered Bizlow up the path.

They crouched on the brink of the icy slope. Below were the crossbow bolts, neat as pegs in a tree. "I must go back," Bizlow said.

Martyn could not believe what he what he was hearing. "You really do have a deathwish."

Bizlow chuckled and shook his head. "You still don't understand…"

"Fine," Martyn growled. "Then I'll go back too. I fetched you once and I can do it again. I'll prove to Ashby that I love her, and prove to her father that I'm worthy –"

Bizlow shoved him over the brink. Martyn tumbled down, fumbling for a grip, snapping the bolts as he fell. He landed hard on his rump.

"Don't worry about her father, lad," Bizlow called down from the top. "You've already proved to yerself that yer worthy. Now that you know it, he'll know it too."

"I'll tell you what I know," Martyn said. "I know you're a pig-headed fool who cares nothing for life – your own or anyone else's!"

"But I do care. That's why you're down there."

"I'm not talking about *my* life, you dolt! Suppose you do manage to kill the dragon somehow – what then? What do you think your younger brother will have to do for his Gallivant – pull the sun from the sky with his bare hands?

Young dwarves will be killing themselves for decades trying to best your performance. Put a stop to this senseless practice now – that's the most honorable deed you could ever accomplish!"

For a moment there was silence. Bizlow looked down at Martyn, whether in disdain or contemplation Martyn couldn't tell. Then he turned and headed back up the passage to Sisspahn's lair.

Martyn jumped up onto the sharp icy rise, trying to pull himself back over its lip by sheer will, but it was no use. Shoulders sagging, he took the first slow steps of his long journey home.

A knock at the door woke him. Martyn rose to answer, careful not to wake Ashby or the infant asleep at his side. His own rest had not been peaceful, wracked not for the first time by nightmares of Sisspahn and guilt over Bizlow's fate. He hadn't tried to sell his story, hadn't even bothered writing it. It didn't seem honorable to profit from Bizlow's death. But he hadn't come home empty-handed either – he'd returned with the confidence to stand up to the Reeve, claim Ashby's hand, and witness his son's birth.

"Package for you, sir."

Martyn accepted the package and shut the door. He unwrapped it and found Bizlow's plain wooden buckler inside.

There was a note as well; Martyn could hear the dwarf's voice speaking the words as he read it. "Thank ye for helping me see that killing the dragon might've brought me glory, but would not prove my honor. Your words made me realize that before I made it back to Sisspahn's lair. I waited until he flew away, and then got me brother Ryhaab's bones and brought them home.

"I no longer have need of this shield, since bearing Ryhaab – and Thunderhead – back to the Ironbones earned me a new one. Perhaps you can paint your family crest upon it, and teach your own child the difference between honor and glory."

God of Blood and Rain

Raven Daegmorgan

atience had never been one of his virtues.

He let the fine, dusty red sand sift through his fingers to blow away in the inconstant breeze. The black sun hung above him – a quarter of its journey yet to go to the blazing, dry heat of noon – sucking every vestige of moisture from air and soil, eating the pale sky in its endless, cyclical fury.

His high priest approached him carrying a silk-wrapped staff of dark ash, polished smooth with age. The shaft – ornamented in bloodstone arabesques – was crowned by a single emerald, the size of a child's fist. He took it up and flourished it, intoning: "Bring forth the sacrifices!"

The slaves followed: dozens, perhaps hundreds, prodded along by strong, silent men carrying obsidian-tipped spears. Men, women, children, elders, infants clasped to their mothers' breasts: they came wide-eyed and terrified, sobbing and wailing, ill-clothed and dirty.

The high priest receded silently, bowing. Behind him the slaves were prodded and beaten into place. As he clutched the staff and beheld the throng, he dreamed of future glory. He cried out words of power that had once commanded the whole universe to obey, even made life from death; then slammed the staff's base into dusty red soil – sterile and dead a thousand years – and raised a puff of orange dust. The earth and sky shuddered as if wounded.

The land groaned.

The sacrifices screamed, generations crying out in terror. Crimson mist rose from their sloughing flesh and clattering bone, swirling and spreading upwards to create a red canopy over the sky. Down flashed blue-white lightning to curl about his staff, while below his feet energy surged in gold-green waves across the barren earth. The earth churned uneasily. Thunder boomed in the sky above, not weak and distant but strong and loud, and his men cowered.

Then from the sky water fell, pale and bloody, a moisture unknown to these desert stones since before the gods had come from lost Urth across the cold darkness and shaped the world.

He shone with power, brighter than the everburning sun, and all averted their eyes. Wherever he swept his hand, green energies flowed, bringing new life to the dead soil to be nourished by drops of red rain. In its wake: warm wind, swaying grasses, black earth.

"Behold, I am the God of Blood and Rain" – he gestured to the new thing he had named, the water that fell from the sky. "I bring life to the dead wastes! I bring salvation to the earth!" In the depths of the sun-struck wastes, he had created an oasis of life – from nothing!

Priests and warriors threw themselves down onto the quickening earth, chanting his name, praising his greatness. Their worship roared through the thickening air, rolling out across the lifeless red sands like the lusty scream of a newborn saved from its dead mother, or the thunder of a marching army upon the horizon.

They would not go quietly into the dust of history, not his children, not now. Blood would flow like water across the red sands. Some had said it would take careful cultivation to restore the world to the glories the gods had once brought it, careful tending of what they had left; but patience had never been a virtue – not for him.

Remember When

Melissa Cuevas

 emember when, Sean? Remember when…machines cleaned? Vacuum cleaners, washing machines, dishwashers, oh my! Remember when toilets flushed and light bulbs lit? Remember when ketchup came in little packets…remember when there was ketchup?

Ketchup. French fries. My mind wandered, fueled by the inevitable hunger after the marijuana binge I was still coming down from. There was silence for a long moment. Obviously Sean was not in the mood for remember when, and I rested my forehead against the wall. He had to answer. He had to…

"Funny," he finally mused in a clear baritone. "The walls really *are* padded…"

Oh, hell, no. Not that. Anything but that…I counted on Sean for the true answers, and if he thought that, then I was truly doomed. "Sean…" I clung to him, fighting the tremble in my arms. I could hear Garrett far, far away, the unfaltering cadence of his yells tending towards profanity rather than pain. They weren't hurting him – yet.

"Birchling." Sean's voice was strident, composed. "This is an institution."

Like I didn't already *know* that! All those years of threats, and it had finally come to pass. I huddled tighter around Sean, planting my forehead against my knees. I was helpless, the Garand gone, the long Bowie, gone, the bow, gone. All I had left were the weapons God gave me…I fought a laughing

159

sob. Blunt teeth and gnawed nails were all that He had ever bothered to grant me…even when He bothered to grant those around me an astounding array of claws and fangs, horns and spikes. And I was being *watched*, like an animal in a cage. Hell, I was an animal in a cage. Who was I fooling to think otherwise?

"Eat, Birchling." Sean advised. "They expect crazy. Give them sane. Stand up. Eat. Look normal."

Were they fools enough to fall for that? I rolled to my knees, feeling the interest of the watcher heighten. There was a tray close by…not much of a weapon, and I dismissed it almost instantly as such…but it had food. Probably poisoned…

"If they wanted to kill you, they could have shot you hours ago."

Damn Sean. Sometimes I hated him, usually when he made the most sense. I picked up the tray and scrutinized it – all finger food. Obviously they were not fool enough to give me even a plastic spork, but it looked good. Probably drugged…

"That is a possibility." Sean finally granted. "What do you know to tell them?"

Nothing. All of my intelligence was six weeks old, which made it more than five weeks out of date. High Command would have moved just hours after their last contact, six weeks ago. The Cabinet, likewise. As a source of information, I lacked. Had they caught me six, seven weeks ago, I could have been a breach. Now, I was yesterday's news. I couldn't be a breach. And damn, I was hungry.

"Then eat, Birchling." Sean sighed, and after a long and wary moment, I complied. I knew fairly quickly that I had been right: the food was drugged.

Remember when? Remember when we were all together that fall, in Kentucky? The fox grapes hung like black pearls off their bare tendrils and stained my fingers bright red purple. The mosquitoes were fierce, but the laughter of friends helped me brave them. So many friends back then, readying to go to ground for the upcoming winter. So many good people, gone.

Sean, I don't want to play this remember when.

We were good people then, even I was. Speechless' booming laughter, the weight of his forearm over my shoulder before he turned back to his true love. That was fine; I had my Garrett...my eyes found him. He was tall – almost clean even, with heavy unruly ginger hair – and a smile just for me.

Sean, I don't want to play this remember when!

I clipped another tiny bundle of grapes from the vine, my own voice lilting and highly pitched with laughter. I was home. I was with friends who would bleed and die for me. It was early in the war; the children were still children, turning strings of leatherback beans under Glory's watchful eyes. Laine's kids were adults now, or dead. Was this three years in? Four? I had forgotten. But it was a magical time, before the hell grind had finally worn through us. Back then we still thought we could win this...

Sean?

When did we die? When did we stop being good people? When did the children stop being precious and turn into cannon fodder? I was lucky – there had never been any of my own – but I'd helped hurry things along, given my quota of young every spring, when the war season kicked up again. If they lived, good. If they didn't...there'd be more next spring. When did we stop being the ones who fought when we didn't have a hope of winning, and become just one more part of the hell?

I do not want to play this game anymore.

Was it remember when I didn't want to play anymore?

161

No. I'm tired. I want to die. I want to sleep. I want to quit. I want to give up.

There were hands on me, outside the drug-induced ramble in my head, and I shifted.

"Is that what you *really* want?" Another voice. Not Sean's. Not my own. Nor any I knew. Was that what I really wanted? I wanted things I couldn't have, and was wise enough to avoid tearing myself up for them.

"Come talk to me, Birch Lawson. And we'll work out what you really want."

Fool. I blinked – and I stood….in a McDonald's. The floor was just like every one I'd ever been in, the same faux terra cotta floor laid in haste. It was bright, as was the sun outside. The parking lot dripped noon, or…no… earlier. The angle of the sun was wrong. It was morning. Nine or ten. There were cars out there, whole and upright. People…why?

"This is where *you* chose to meet me, General Lawson."

General. I fought down a laugh. No one had bothered to paint me that since….well, close to a time with that autumn. The President had…there'd been a medal on a sky blue ribbon, with white stars. General Lawson. I sought out the speaker…unlike the people wandering aimlessly in this vision; he was sharply delineated, perfectly in focus. Unlike them, he was real. Male, dressed completely in black, almost ecclesiastical in its severity. He was clean…spotlessly so, an odd mix of reserved good manners and blunt truth. "I chose to meet you, whoever you are, in a McDonald's?"

He shifted in the pressed plastic seat and shrugged. "It is perhaps what you were thinking of when you woke. You were thinking of food, I believe?"

Ketchup and french fries. I sat beyond him…out of his reach. Too bad, too. He was fine looking, but he couldn't have what he hadn't paid for. I'd make it cheap, though…

He frowned pensively, and I watched him. "No, *General* Lawson." He stressed the honorific and I dropped my gaze to the table top. "I'm not here to *buy* you. I'm here to offer you the same as we've offered so many of what your mind calls the good people. I've listened to you and Sean. Listened to them think of you, speak of you…to see if you are salvageable."

I wasn't. Too many years…decades…had passed for that. I hadn't even been sane when the war *started*. Sean's blood coursing down my forearms… die…die…the weight of his body as I leveraged it into the dumpster. And every step since then, the reassuring weight of him as I took him with me. He would never leave. I wouldn't let him. He was mine.

"Good people, General Lawson. You still are one."

"I'm not a general anymore." I stated mutinously. If I was, I'd be on High Command, not left to be picked off in the wilds of Arkansas.

"High Command is not our best." Bradshawer's voice was mocking, grinding. *"If it was, it'd have Lawson on it."* Again, prime remember when, I'd stay there more often, but the results still hurt.

"Lawson is too unbalanced to be with High Command. She talks to a skull. And she thinks it answers her."

"Maybe it does." Israel Bradshawer had been serving as President Cartwright's Secretary of State then. There was another good one gone, the President. Slaughtered at Memphis….

The man said nothing, just pondered the view out of the great plate windows. "High Command surrendered three weeks ago. Their actions were dishonorable and without merit. *You* are the highest ranking legitimate officer."

Legitimate. That was a new one. I'd never been accused of it before. "They sold me out." Sean had told me that, but I refused to believe him.

"They did." The man agreed easily enough, still staring outside. "And then fled the continent. They fear your wrath. But as we promised to protect them, we promise to protect you. Many made that a requirement before they agreed to anything. You, and you alone, were on every list. High Command. The President. Her cabinet. All capitulated in the understanding that we would not…how did she put it….put you down. That we would take care of you for the rest of your life."

"That could be a long time." I mumbled, staring at my fingers. I'd lost track, but I was certain that I had lived much longer than I should have. And not aged a day. I couldn't even get too damned *old* for this.

"I know."

"Who are you?" The very idea of a McDonald's made my mouth water, and breakfast meant those delectable little biscuits…

"My name is Tamaren." He stated, dragging his attention away from the parking lot and back to me. "It is my honor to be the one to try to reach you."

"Reach me?" Sean whispered: *psychologist, or worse.* "I'm less than a foot away from you, in a padded room." His were the hands on me, I was certain of that.

He smiled, and the idea of how much I would charge plummeted. He was so very nice…it had been a long time since I'd seen a man who looked anything like this. Ask nicely…a please would be enough…

His gaze sharpened, and he shook his head in denial. "No, General Lawson." The words were pleasantly sheathed steel. "As I said, I am here to reach you. To see if you are salvageable. If any of those we brought out of your cell are salvageable."

"Am I?" I knew the answer already. I'd been bugnuts *before* the war had started, and I had only gotten worse.

"Most certainly."

I frowned. Most did not think so. And those that did were arguably as crazy as I was. Bradshawer. Glory. Those that cared only wished me to be cared for the rest of my long, long life.

"You have not lost the most critical thing, General. Your…compatriot… perhaps has. But you…no. You still have everything you need for me to lead you back to yourself."

"You can't have Sean." *Give me the skull, Birch. We'll get rid of it. It'll be better that way…*

Tamaren raised his brows in vague disbelief. "I do not want Sean."

"Most shrinks do."

"I am not here to shrink anything. You need Sean. You must have him, until the day you can be led back."

Need. Must have. Finally, someone who understood. "Then what is it I must have to be brought back to myself?"

"You still remember when. You still remember what you see as good people. You mourn no longer being one of them. And you see that as a *loss*, something to be resurrected. In spite of everything, in spite of knowing that it hurts, you want it back. No matter what, you remained true to those you loved, even when they failed you. You love. You mourn. You despair for yourself. And you *remember*. The pieces can be put back together, as long as I have that glue to work with. As long as you haven't lost yourself."

"And Garrett?"

That question bothered him much more than any I'd asked about myself. He had answers for me – except maybe that one. "You tell me, General. Is Garrett Ludlow good people, anymore? Judge him – as the one he's fought beside, only you have that right."

"No." Garrett had not been one of the good people in so long…

Tamaren sighed, a noise that came close to surrender. "We will still give him the benefit of the doubt." He paused. "Perhaps we can bring him back. Perhaps not. Concerning you, however, I have no doubts. And because of that, he is no longer yours, and you are no longer his."

I let the condemning frown cross my face, and he caught it with a quick glance. "Eh," he murmured. "He drags you down, and I lift you up. You are the memory of your people...so remember for me. Do you believe he loves you? Or do you still remember what love is?"

I remembered love. Speechless had loved Laine, he would have died before he'd sold her as blithely as Garrett had sold me. And Julian had loved me once, before the flowing, seething chaos of Rolla. "I remember." Poor Julian. One of those good people, who should died in the opening moments of the war, not years later...

He'd called me beautiful in spite of it all.

"What is it you want from me?" He talked too much. He brought up things that should lie dead.

"You know what I am." He breathed, and I nodded. Of course I did. The moment I'd woken up in the nice padded room, I knew. They'd been after me for months.

"You are from the Empire." The new player in the game. The one left whole enough to come pick up the pieces. We'd ground ourselves into nothing against the League, and then they arrived.

"The League was winning." Sean chose that moment to insinuate himself into the discussion, and Tamaren glanced towards his bag. It was rude to leave him in the bag when he was speaking, so I removed him and rested him on the edge of the table, his empty eye orbits facing Tamaren. "They would have destroyed us all," he continued, and Tamaren nodded in gentle agreement.

"You hear him?" I asked, flabbergasted. It was a victory to just get people who believed. Some... Israel, Glory, made obvious acknowledgement when he spoke, but they were wretchedly few. When pressed, Israel commented that something changed in the air around me. Glory merely shrugged and stated his words were for me alone.

"As I hear you, I hear him." Tamaren stated. "He is correct. Your people had less than a year, General Lawson. You have fought until you cannot fight any longer. There is no shame, no dishonor, in that. Our offer does not change."

Honored enemy status…whatever the hell that meant. Already, they worked to replace an infrastructure shattered by decades of cataclysmic struggle. There was electricity in many of the encampments now. Resettlement. Food, clean water, medical attention…and indeed, psychiatric aid. "I don't know if I can stop fighting." What was I, then? Could I remember *that*? Memory of my people, indeed!

Tamaren reached under his severe black coat and removed something from its inner pockets before adorning Sean's skull dome with a sky blue ribbon spangled with stars, a bronze medal resting on the table. "Birch Lawson, last General of your people." He breathed, caressing the pale ivory rise of forehead. "Honored enemy of the Empire. You have fought for so long, suffered so much, for no other reason than an honest urge to protect your people. But you do not have the heart and soul of a warrior. You have the heart and soul of a mother…"

A mother with no children.

"…the heart and soul of a builder."

I looked down at the football, my fingers trembling. The blast radius would take down half of Memphis, so many of ours, was it worth it? The President's blood crusted black on my clothes…he was the last. His death be not in vain… "Do it. I snapped, ignoring Julian's startled and betrayed gaze.

Tamaren sighed again, reaching across the table to touch the space over the bridge of my nose with a fingertip.

The workshop was bright with spinning motes. A man with a rich baritone, Sean's baritone, chuckled. "Never you mind that, Birchling. They're always lopsided in the beginning. You have a good hand, and fine lungs. Try again." My father. My father had

167

Sean's voice…no, Sean had my father's voice. The man looked at me thru a fringe of dark hair, his eyes the same pure green as my own. He'd taught me to be a builder. An artisan.

"You are the memory of your people, General Lawson. It is all right there, in your grasp. While others pushed it away, you held it close. We can rebuild, but we cannot *remember* for them. Their history is not ours. This place…." He glanced around the McDonald's. "That…" he motioned out of the glass windows. "Is on the verge of being lost. Without you, your greatest fears will be realized. Your people will cease to be."

"Rather a portentous statement, isn't it?" I asked, and he flared his nostrils in distain.

"You doubt that a single soul can buttress a people against oblivion? After all you've seen? Or do you doubt that *you* could be it? You, shattered and camouflaged in insanity." He picked up Sean and stared into the dark orbits. "You *know* there is no Sean. You *know* Sean has been dead since you killed him. That is, after all, why you carry him. Not to ask him anything at all, but to remind yourself every moment that yes, he really is dead. You consigned him to oblivion decades ago. He is not an advisor. He is a *trophy*, the first kill of a great general."

He replaced Sean carefully on the table. "But nothing changes facts. If Sean is nothing but a trophy, then *you* are the great general. There is no Sean. You hear yourself, filtered through an external medium. Keep your trophy, General Lawson. You deserve it."

"What is it you want?" I growled, snatching Sean back from him. Oh, no. Absolutely not. If there was truly no Sean, then I had made all those decisions on my own. *I* had bombed Memphis. *I* had planned Rolla. *I* had left a string of desolation from Tennessee to Missouri to shame Sherman's legend.

Tamaren watched me warily, his eyes contemplative and sorrowful. "Like it or not, General Lawson, you are now a subject of the Empire. You have led your people through the unimaginable…and even now, after everything that's happened, you're willing to fight *us.*"

I glared at him. Of course I was willing to fight the next pig at my people's trough. The only problem seemed to be that not many shared that conviction. Feed them, clothe them, make them warm again, and they fell like dominoes. I could not fight without support, and I wasn't getting it. "And we prize that determination. You were willing to lead your people through that, and we're asking you to lead them a little bit farther. If you do not…if you and their other leaders do not…." He shook his head, "Then they are truly doomed. McMillan and Bradshawer have paid lip service to capitulation only. They play wait and see. That will not work, General. If we are to commit to your people, we need support."

"You're asking me to sell out." If I did, the concussion would rock the surviving freedom cells.

"Why do you fight?" he asked, his voice small.

"There was no other choice." Sean answered, and he glanced at the skull. "They would have destroyed us without a fight. Obliterated us." I continued. "If it's a choice between lying down and dying, or fighting and dying, I choose the latter. Take as many with us as I could. Make them pay for each and every one of us they killed."

He nodded, his eyes again on the parking lot. Such a mundane vista to generate such interest. But I guess it wasn't mundane anymore. So many of my own people had never seen an asphalt parking lot basking in sunlight, filled with people walking in the open, a woman pushing a stroller, cars flashing by, the orderly change of traffic lights.

"So you do not fight to preserve your true people…" Again, he touched the bridge of my nose. "Only to preserve their flesh and blood bodies and avenge their deaths?"

"I can't…." I stared at the parking lot. "That will never be again."

"Perhaps not." He sighed, shaking his head. "General Lawson, your people stand on the brink. They have lost so much that they do not remember who or what they are. Right now, the only thing keeping them safe is that they have people like you, like McMillan and Bradshawer, who are considered honored enemies by the Light of Heaven. If those we respect do not rise to lead, then by this you signal that you do not consider them your people any more. If they lose that, they become merely subjects of the Empire. All our subjects are beloved, and protected, but it will take them decades to rise beyond that. They will never remember anything but what we tell them, because we do not have access to that." He waved at the window. "I have looked into others' minds. Time, horror…has all worn it away. Their memories are mostly pale shadows of even your fleeting surface recollections. *You* are the one with the standing in the Emperor's eyes to rise above this. You are the one closest to what you were before. You remember. You are the last surviving officer of the last legally declared leader of your people. Take your position as honored enemy, ride it to citizenship, and bring your people out of this. You can do what you have dreamed of, fought for, for the past eight decades. They won't be the same, but they can still *be*, as long as you….remember when."

I pulled the medal from Sean and studied it. Give up?

"It's time to stop fighting, Birchling." Sean sighed, in my father's voice. It was creepy now that I had definitely placed it, but he seemed unperturbed when I stared at him. "We can't win. Now, we just mitigate. Are we strong enough to stop beating our brains out?"

"I…don't know." If I did this, I would lose Garrett….

"Pffft." Sean hissed. "Julian was a better man."

Probably, definitely, but Julian was dead at Rolla. But Sean was right: I needed to get away from Garrett if I was going to make sense out of this. I would lose…well, there were precious few left *to* lose. I suddenly felt more alone than ever…even Sean wasn't company anymore, if he was just me. I'd been talking to myself, only *myself*, for eighty years. That suddenly seemed even more pathetic than I'd thought before, and the parking lot blurred in front of me. At first I thought I was losing the remember when, but the scene cleared with the fall of the first big tear. I was crying.

When was the last time I'd done that?

"Cry it out." Tamaren pulled me into his arms. "It's been a long time coming."

He was correct. It had been a long time coming.

"What do I tell the Light of Heaven?" He asked carefully when I was silent. "Do you stand for your people?"

"Tell the Emperor… I do, yes. Tell him… I remember when."

Eyes of the Spider

John Hitchens

r'ivn noc Kthath, pillager, freebooter, sometime mercenary and full-time opportunist, surveyed the temple of Azoth from his rooftop perch on the City Magistrate's building. The temporal and the spiritual edifices stared uneasily at each other across the length of an easy bowshot. The temple crouched in the gloom, its vast bulk a blacker blot set in the center of the dark port city of Kheled. From his vantage it looked to Dr'ivn like a malignant spider ready to trap unwary travelers. It was probably no accident of design, he thought. He searched the temple roof for details. Manitor, the brightest of the three moons, had already begun its descent, and its wan rays found scant reflection off the surface of the temple's basalt walls. He would have to trust the priest.

"Are you certain your plan will work?"

"Certain? No," hissed the purple-robed priest in the same low tone. "Nothing is certain – the eyes of the spider see much, but not all. We may have to fight a few spiders, but once we have breached the defenses, it is a clear path to the Spider God's fane. Eight eyes has the God, each a pure sapphire larger than a handspan. With the group you have assembled, it will be short work prying them out. Meanwhile, I will kill the high priest, Myrklum of the Seventh Robe, and all organized resistance will crumble. And I, Jakar of the Sixth Robe, will have my revenge."

Dr'ivn nodded. He had heard the plan the night before, half-drunk on Kheled wine. His reputation had preceded him, and he had been sought out to hear the proposal. It had sounded like a good idea then. Now, sober and shivering in the moonlight, he was not so sure. Yet Dr'ivn had never been one to hesitate. He turned to the party behind him and raised his hand.

Four strings thrummed, and four ropes of finest spider silk sped into the distance, launched from as many crossbows. A heartbeat later, Dr'ivn heard the bolts strike the curved roof of the temple – and stick, holding when the lines went taut. The spider silk with which the priest had coated the arrow heads had done its job.

The near ends of the ropes were tied off to the crenellations, and a tenuous pathway, four strands wide, lay ready to be traversed. Dr'ivn grabbed a rope with his left hand, then looked at the street four stories below.

"Remember, if you fall, fall silently," he said, then leaped over the edge. He started off hand over hand, dangling from the rope overhead. Beside and behind him, the others followed, two to a rope. The spider priest, Jakar, came behind him, while the other ropes were swarming with the Fellowship of the Purloined Purse, the most notorious gang of thieves in the entire swampy province. Jendra and Nestra, the red-headed twins, had the rope to his left. Although they were wrapped in black like everybody else, he could easily tell them by their slight bodies. Their pale skin and freckled faces had marked them as northerners, and he thought he had detected more than normal interest from Nestra last night. Dr'ivn made a mental note to pursue her after the raid. The other four were more typical of the region: slender, medium height, with black hair and eyes and a casual wariness only the finest warriors ever attained. He knew Dassad for a hothead, and that Renner, the leader, was greedy, but Sopos and Heler were ciphers. He would have to take their measure as the raid progressed.

The temple roof was close now, maybe twelve arm lengths away. One of the twins inhaled sharply. Dr'ivn looked up and saw the cause of their distress – two – no, three spiders, each the size of a steppenwolf, scrambling over the roof towards the ropes. Hand over hand they raced for the other side, but before they could reach the roof the spiders were advancing on them over the clear highway made by the ropes.

Heler hung on one-handed while he drew his sword, but before he could bring it to bear he was bitten. He started to scream. Dr'ivn unslung his sword and slashed right, slicing Heler's throat and silencing his cries.

Dr'ivn had no time to watch him fall – he had his own spider to deal with. He pumped the rope with his left hand, elevating his body to waist height. As the scuttling arachnid snatched at his left arm, Dr'ivn released the rope, snatching his arm back out of reach while spinning around, long blade stretched to maximum extension. The whipcord power of his blow drove the sword halfway through the spider's head. Then, at the very last second, Dr'ivn's left hand caught the rope once more. The spider plunged to join Heler in the street below.

Behind him the twins devised their own method. One laid herself across two ropes like a platform while the other sprang up to crouch atop her, aiming a crossbow. The string twanged and a second spider fell. That left only one arachnid, advancing on the petrified Sopos. As it passed, Jakar flung a handful of powder at its head. The spider stopped; its color changed to grey as it turned to stone. It fell to the street with a mighty crash.

Dr'ivn swore. "Too much noise. Hurry."

They reached the roof of the temple without further incident. Sopos crawled frantically across the sloping roof towards Dr'ivn.

"You killed Heler" he said, seething.

"He was already dead", Dr'ivn said. "There is no cure for the spiders' poison." He saw the priest open his mouth to say something, and Dr'ivn cut him off before he could contradict.

"That powder you used – why didn't you tell us you had it? And why didn't you share it? "

"Not enough to go around, my friend. We are lucky I managed to preserve this little handful when I fled the temple."

The man's tone grated on Dr'ivn, but their need of the priest was great. He turned back to Sopos. "We all knew the risks when we started. Think of the greater share of the treasure you will now receive. Now let's stop arguing and get off this roof. Jendra, Nestra – let's find that chimney." Balanced like a great cat, he continued in a crouch up the curving roof, following the twins.

Behind him, Sopos spat, and Dr'ivn felt wet spittle land on the back of his head, followed by "Barbarian pig!"

Dr'ivn paused, then shrugged. He would kill Sopos later.

Clothor, curate of the crimson Third Robe and current leader of the upper guard, walked the black stone balcony that circled the inner sanctum of the temple. The walkway, made of massive stone slabs laid onto ponderous trestles angling from the inner walls, overlooked the general seating, the sacred altar, and the grotesque statue of the Spider God himself. Half again as large as the fabled pachyderms of Nibia, it dominated the room, its eight great glittering eyes surveying its realm with a predatory gleam. Clothor had been told that each eye, a single sapphire transported from deep within the jungles of Sathir, was worth more gold than the entire treasury of Kheled.

Nobody would be foolish enough to try to steal them. Their existence was a secret known only to the priests, and any intruders would be killed long before they caught sight of the statue. Still, a familiar fear, one that he could never shake, seemed to stalk him.

It was not the three-story drop that bothered him, even though there was no railing to prevent accidental falls. In any given month, they seldom lost more than one acolyte to that peril. After all, the pathway was wide enough for two to walk abreast. It was not the burden of duty that bothered him either: only the highest-ranking robes were allowed access to the chambers on this floor, and the last enemy incursion had been fifty years ago, when the Serpent priests had mounted one last desperate attack against them.

No. What was bothering him was that after five years of service, he was still afraid of spiders.

He had to keep his secret from his fellow priests lest it be exploited. He had originally joined the temple to evade the hangman, but some nights as he dreamed fevered dreams of fangs and poison, he wondered if he had made the right choice. Surely he had a right to be scared! He could die from a spider bite as easily as any man; membership in the priesthood did not bring any extra protection. The temple's walls and ceilings crawled with spiders of every size, small cat-sized ones to horse-sized giants. And all of them watched him with eight glittering, hungry eyes, waiting to pump him full of venom that would turn his insides to jelly.

There was only one power that allowed such as he to dwell here – the protective amulets all acolytes were issued when they first joined the temple. He fingered the gold-filigreed pendant that dangled from his neck, keeping the spiders at bay. While he wore it – and he never took it off, even when bathing – no spider could come within a few paces. It was rumored that priests of the Sixth and Seventh Robe could command all arachnids, and did not need the amulets, but speculation about such powers was discouraged. The last two to wonder openly had lived for three days, dangling paralyzed in webbed cocoons over the altar, slowly consumed by myriads of baby spiders. He shuddered, remembering cleanup duty.

His eyes followed their habitual pattern of checking – doorways – a glance at his counterpart opposite – the walls teeming with spiders, scrambling away as he approached – the two great skylights slanting down from the inaccessible roof, kept clear by whatever strange sorcery powered the amulets. As he reached the part of the walkway directly beneath them, he glanced up as he always did to see what stars might be showing.

All he could see was a dark blot: the skies must be cloudy tonight. Wait - was the blot moving? Surely it was coming closer. It was falling on him!

Clothor threw up his hands in terror just before his neck snapped.

Dr'ivn swore as he landed atop the priest. His right knee had taken the brunt of the fall, connecting painfully with the priest's hard skull before his considerable weight broke the man's neck. He had wanted to come down more slowly, but the priest had been about to spot him, and he had been forced to drop the final distance while he was still twice his height from the floor. As he gathered his wits, the twins landed lightly behind him. He knew the others would be descending more carefully – but all thoughts of his team vanished as he spotted the other guard, thirty paces away with gaping mouth, on the other side of the opening.

"Nestra," he whispered, pointing.

With a speed and nonchalance he was not sure even he could match, Nestra unslung the small crossbow from her back and, one-handed, shot the guard in the chest up near the right shoulder. A moment later Jendra, aiming with greater care, killed the staggering priest with a bolt through his breastbone. He fell back with a thud on the thick stone. Dr'ivn held his breath and listened. One. Two. Three. Four. Five. Nothing. No alarm had sounded, and now the others had joined them. He let out his breath. Dr'ivn felt uncomfortable here, exposed on a cleared platform, while spiders silently watched them from a short distance away.

"Jakar. Why do the spiders not attack?"

In answer, the renegade priest reached over the body of the red-robe and ripped a chain from around his neck. He dangled the pendant from his hand. "These amulets prevent any spider from coming within two paces. All the lower level Robes wear them. You may wish to put it on." Jakar dropped the talisman into Dr'ivn's hands.

"Shouldn't you be wearing it?" asked Dr'ivn, looking with mistrust at the amulet in his hand. He hated to rely on magic.

"I won't be needing it. I have…sufficient abilities in that regard. Now I have my own business to attend to, and you had better start prying out those gems. I estimate you have five minutes before our incursion is noticed."

Jakar strode away. As Dr'ivn stared after him, he saw the priest's body ripple, then distort into a hideous purple spider larger than a cart horse, with black flecked hair spiking out in all directions. Beside him he heard Dassad retching, and Renner mumbling prayers to some unknown god. Dr'ivn stared until the priest-turned-spider had disappeared down a dark passage. Trying to disguise his unease, he shrugged and turned to the others.

"Let's grab those gems."

Jakar stalked down the walkway in spider form, laughing inwardly. It was a spiteful chuckle, containing neither mirth nor mercy. No spider dared approach him, and those that found themselves in his way quickly scattered out of range. Jakar knew what most humans would never know, that spiders rarely fought each other unless forced to by outside agencies. Occasionally a large spider might kill and eat a smaller one if it was unlucky enough to be caught in its web, but that was about it. Injured spiders could not heal, so there was no point in risking a fight unless you outclassed your prey in both mobility and size. He spared one thought for the group left behind. The fools had no idea what they were in for. They would find out soon enough.

He took the familiar passageway leading to the rooms of the Sixth and Seventh Robes. The floor of the octagonal tunnels, hewn from demon-spawned basalt over two millennia ago, was cold and smooth under the pads of his feet. Teakwood doorways stood recessed into the walls at irregular intervals.

There were three members of the Sixth Robe, assuming he had been replaced already, and one of the Seventh. An impulse to check his old door was quickly stifled; this was no time to get sidetracked. It was probably that toe-licker Flabia who had traded her vermillion robe for his purple, but he had his sights set on the ultimate prize – the black robe of the Seventh. He padded silently down the ancient twisting corridor to stop a few spider-strides from the last door. Myrklum's door.

He paused to review. The doors were too strong for spiders to break, and were reinforced with wards that would slay any human of insufficient rank who tried to pass. Unfortunately, only Myrklum was attuned to wards of the Seventh Robe, and if Jakar managed to pass through his door, his magic was not sufficient to overwhelm that of the High Priest. Fortunately, he was neither wholly spider nor wholly human.

Jakar shifted back to human form and drew the last of his precious magical treasures from his sash. He stared at the iron ball in his hand. It had taken all his remaining cash and some stolen temple jewelry to purchase, but if his information was accurate, it was the key to his ascension. He glanced behind him. Good – no spiders in sight. He retreated a prudent distance, then rolled the iron ball towards the door.

"Knock knock," he muttered, a grin breaking out on his face.

As the ball neared contact, he transformed back to his giant spider form, then scuttled around the corner. He was just in time. A giant explosion shattered the silence and the corridor flared with blinding light. When it subsided Jakar dared a look around the corner.

The high priest's door was utterly destroyed, fragments of smoking wood tottering from thick hinges. Jakar wasted not a moment. His eight legs propelled him quickly through the smoke, and he crashed through the wards. They sparkled briefly, tracing translucent golden sigils in the air, but they failed to stop him – being set only for humans.

Then Jakar came face to face with Myrklum, priest of the Seventh Robe. He was sitting up in bed, trying to get his bearings. He wore black silk pajamas with white spiderweb designs, and Jakar thought he looked ridiculous. He also looked extremely vulnerable. His eyes widened in terror as he saw the huge purple spider bearing down on him.

Myrklum thrust his arm towards Jakar and barked the words of spider abjuration. They could command any spider so addressed – but Jakar was not wholly a spider. He had counted on Myrklum misreading the situation. Had he been in human form, surely the high priest would have used a deadly spell on the hated rival he thought he had dealt with for good. But a spider charm would not do the trick, not this time.

Jakar's spider side battled the spell for less than a heartbeat before his disciplined human mind took control. He blasted through the charm, his four great forelegs gripping the high priest's body. Then, with deliberate precision, he sank his two fangs into his adversary's neck.

A spider has a limited supply of poison in its sac, and can choose how much, if any, to inject into its prey. It takes the spider time and energy to regenerate it, so the amount used is judged carefully, based on the size of the prey and the spider's need. But Jakar didn't bother with such niceties – he used it all.

The high priest gurgled, jerked, and choked as a deluge of venom coursed into his veins. The results were immediate, and Jakar withdrew his fangs and backed away, allowing the dead leader to collapse on his bedspread in a pool of blood and foam. Myrklum, high priest of the Temple of Azoth was dead, and by right of conquest and custom, Jakar was now the High Priest. He transformed back to his human form and stripped off his purple robe. Naked, he walked to the dead priest's dresser, yanked open the drawer, and withdrew a black robe.

Sopos glared at Dr'ivn's broad, muscled back. The westerner was standing at ease, sword in hand as he kept watch. He seemed to Sopos to have no conscience: he had slain Heled as one puts down an injured horse! No remorse; no regret. Perhaps the priest could have saved him. Maybe Dr'ivn did not know how it felt to lose a lover. It did not matter: Sopos would have his revenge.

He glanced around at the rest of the group. Dassad and Renner were on the floor, anchoring ropes for the task at hand. Hand over hand they paid them

181

out with mechanical precision. Beyond the edge of the walkway and some ways below, Jendra and Nestra dangled precariously over the courtyard, waiting to be lowered onto the Spider God's statue.

Sopos peered over the ledge. The statue was made of polished black stone, with relief work so lifelike he could see hairs covering the body and legs. The accuracy of its design was so uncanny that for a moment he fancied it alive, a colossal spider frozen in time, that one day would come back to life and consume the world.

Then his eyes were drawn to the beast's head. There they were – the sapphires of Sathir, each larger than his fist. No, two fists. In these dim surroundings they usually looked grey, but occasionally one would flash a brilliant blue as torchlight or moonlight struck it at a particular angle. Just a single gem would allow him to live out his life in luxury. He would buy a palace, complete with eunuchs and a harem. He would obtain twin boys for his own pleasure, and import the finest opiates, liquor, and comestibles that one could purchase. Fountains would splash in his courtyard, and every room would have a servant waving bango-leaf fans to keep it cool.

In time he might even forget Heler.

He glanced again at Dr'ivn. The twins were down now, knives out, scrambling over the statue towards the gemstone eyes. They would have them pried out in minutes. Then it would be a quick trip up the skylight and back over the rooftop and ropes, and a clean escape. They had no need now of that oaf Dr'ivn. He had been hired for his fighting prowess, and the fighting was over. Now was the time to balance the scales.

Lunging swiftly, Sopos shoved Dr'ivn hard in the back. Dr'ivn plunged over the side too quickly to yell. He cracked his head on the spider god's back, then slid bonelessly to the floor. Sopos stepped back in satisfaction.

Renner, seeing the flurry of motion and hearing the warrior hit the floor far below, looked down – then back at Sopos in horror.

"Sopos, what did you just do?"

183

"Killed a pig. We don't need him any more."

Renner's face paled. "You fool – he was wearing the protection amulet!"

Sopos stared at his leader, then at the westerner sprawled out on the temple floor far below. He swallowed. "We'll be safe. How dangerous can those spiders be?"

As if in answer, the nearest arachnids lurched towards them. Renner stood up, yelled a warning to the twins, and was knocked down by a man-sized spider. They rolled over the edge together; the splat that followed offered no difficulty of interpretation. Dassad swept out his sword and chopped two legs off a spider that had grown too curious for his liking.

"Sopos!" he yelled. "Back to back. We may be able to take them!"

Down below, one of the twins called out. "What's going on?"

"Spider attack," barked Dassad.

"We need the rope!"

Sopos knew then it was hopeless. His hatred had doomed them all. Well – maybe not all. The rope up the skylight was free of spiders. He abandoned Dassad and all thought of riches and dashed for the rope.

"Sopos! Come back. So – " The sound was cut off.

Sopos scuttled up the rope without looking back. It was a shame about the twins, he thought, but they knew the risks. He reached the top in safety and exited the skylight through the hole they had cut. Only ten paces across to the ropes.

He stood, only to be knocked sprawling by a mastiff-sized jumper. He felt the beast's weight on his back and desperately reached for his sword, but could not draw it before the spider's fangs sunk into his neck. He did not even have time for a final thought.

Dr'ivn smelled incense. He heard a quiet rustling and then heavy, deliberate footsteps. He opened his eyes to see his companion in roguery Jakar come into view, dressed in a black robe and bearing a jeweled scepter. Behind him stood two mailed temple guards, swords girt to their waists, torches in their hands. Dr'ivn tried to sit up and failed. He could not move his extremities. He settled for gazing impassively back at the priest.

"Well, my friend," said Jakar. "Thanks to your help, I am now master of this temple. Do not try to get up. You have been injected with a paralytic venom extract I feared it was necessary – I did not think you would be amenable to conversation otherwise."

Dr'ivn grunted. "Don't play with me, priest. Have done and kill me."

Jakar raised his eyebrows. "You recover much faster than I expected. But do not worry – I would not kill such a useful partner."

"What have you done with the others?"

Jakar was dismissive. "They received the reward that thieves deserve. But I feel a special kinship with you, and so I will give you the chance to serve me eternally and faithfully."

Dr'ivn gritted his teeth. He had been fond of the sisters. "Eternally is too long, priest. As long as I have two arms to wield a sword and shield, I would remain a threat to you."

"As long as you have two arms. Indeed. But what if you had eight arms instead?" He raised the ornate club. "The High Priest has the ability to destroy spiders – and create them. May Azoth bless you." Gently he lowered the scepter to touch Dr'ivn's forehead, invoking the name of the Spider God. As the scepter descended, for the first time in his life, Dr'ivn felt fear.

The fear lasted but a moment, replaced by a searing assault on his brain. His mouth froze in a rictus; he screamed, wondering how much he could endure.

Finally the pain stopped. Then came clarity, and horror.

His head swelled, as did his body, and his limbs bifurcated. Thick brown hair sprouted from every pore. His hands and feet dissolved and reformed into three-clawed toes with padded feet. He struggled to move, and lurched to his feet – all eight of them. He was turning into a spider, brown and gigantic.

His blurry vision disoriented him. He tried to make sense of it all. He had eight eyes! His brain could not yet process the information they sent. Movement blurred at the edges of his sight and he swiveled his head to the left to follow it. Now his centre eyes took over, and with larger-than-life clarity he saw one of Jakar's guards step backwards. More signals intruded, coming from a third set of eyes, telling him the correct distance to jump. Without a thought, he pounced.

Jakar gestured and an invisible force pushed him aside. He hit the wall five paces away and slid down gracelessly. Painfully he struggled to his feet. What was he doing? He was a man, not a spider. Yet arachnid sensations were assaulting his brain, overloading it with never-before-felt experiences. Vibration thrummed through the ground from a panoply of sources. He could sense the adrenalin of the temple guards. Outside of a limited circle he could only see in black and white. His fangs and incisors felt awkward in his mouth. Fangs? He felt sick. He was a man.

He scuttled up the wall, away from the priest. He was a man. His pads clung to the uneven surface effortlessly. Another spider came too close, and he struck with greater speed than he had ever known, bashing the monster off balance with his forelegs and jabbing him in the exposed throat with his fangs. His foe plummeted to the ground as Dr'ivn tasted spider-fluid in his belly.

He was a man! A man!

He climbed to the walkway circling the nave. Below, Jakar had turned away to inspect the statue. He was giving orders to three priests in green robes. Two sapphires were missing from the statue, and Dr'ivn wondered if the twins had escaped. He started to stalk the priest, his adjusted eyes providing the exact information his brain needed to strike.

But he was not a spider – this could not be happening! He edged away from a guard who was circling the balcony – the force emanating from the guard's amulet repulsed him. He remembered this magic. But it should not affect him. He was a man, not a spider – a man!

Dr'ivn had never been beaten. Every battle, every struggle in life, he had overcome. He had been raised among warriors, who gave nor took no quarter. This was just another struggle. The village crone of his youth had said that the power of magic was in the end simply belief. The truly strong could overcome it. Her words had meant nothing to him then, but now he understood what she had meant.

He was a man. He was a man a man a man a man a man... Unbearable nausea struck him, but he bore it, just as he bore down on the magic holding his brain. Sharp knives of light struck his eyes, stabbing and stabbing – but they were only stabbing two eyes now, and with a wrench of supreme will his spider form fell from him and he slid down the wall to the ledge – naked, sore, and unarmed, but human.

The guard who had just passed turned at the sound. From all fours Dr'ivn launched himself, wrapping his arms around the guard and taking them both over the same edge that Dr'ivn had fallen from before. They landed on the Spider God's statue, the guard breaking his back but cushioning Dr'ivn's fall. Dr'ivn clawed the guard's sword from its sheath, and holding it two-handed over his head jumped into the press of green-robed priests and red-clad guards, screaming the war cry of Kthath.

His sword reaped death. Adrenalin boosted his speed and strength, and his skill outmatched every opponent he faced. In seconds he reached Jakar. The other guards were too far away to help. He could see the fear and disbelief in Jakar's eyes.

"Impossible! How did you – "

The priest's words were choked off as Dr'ivn drove his sword through Jakar's breastbone and out his back. He withdrew it, showering the floor with blood. The great bejeweled scepter slipped from his nerveless fingers; Dr'ivn reached down and snatched it up. Still in a fury, he whirled and smashed the scepter against one of the statue's stone legs.

It snapped and the statue began to topple. The approaching guards stopped, startled. Dr'ivn crushed the scepter into another leg. It too crumbled, and the statue listed to one side. A moan came from the surviving faithful.

Driv'n shattered the scepter against yet a third leg and the statue crashed to the temple floor. The magic of its construction was released. The spiders in the temple, freed from sorcerous coercion, went berserk, swarming over the guards. Elephant-sized arachnids, larger than any seen heretofore, boiled up from hidden cellars.

Time to leave. But how?

Dr'ivn searched for an exit and a strategy. It was pointless to grab one of the amulets – their magic had been dispelled. The balcony overhead was out of reach. The windows were all high, barred, and spider-infested. He would have to escape from the ground floor.

If Jakar had spoken the truth, the only way out was through double doors and down a long hallway before reaching the temple gates. He grabbed a shield from a fallen guard, ducking a flying spider. From the corner of his eye he saw movement, spun, and punched a spider with his shield. The crippled beast reared back. Dr'ivn had his bearings now, and began to pick his way through the sprawling melee towards the exit.

"Dr'ivn!"

Fighting her way from a corner was one of the twins. She must have been hiding from the guards, but the failing magic had rendered her vulnerable. He wasn't sure which it was, but he took a guess.

"Nestra," he cried. "To me! We'll go together."

A few slashes of his blade brought him to her side.

"Jump on my back. Kill any spiders that attack from behind. Where's Jendra?"

"Spiders got between us. She made the corridor while I was bagging the sapphires. One for each of us once we escape."

"Agreed."

Dr'ivn wasted no more breath. He sprang forward. Nestra's body was but a small weight on his massive frame.

But spiders of all sizes were still emerging. Escape seemed impossible.

Dr'ivn had been tempered by battle, hardship, and privation since boyhood. Fifteen years in the Nibian wars and the killing grounds of Kyldar Peaks had refined his skills with the blade. But all his training, even combined with his size and quickness and the ferocious adrenal rush of fighting for his very life, would not have saved him that day.

But Dr'ivn had been a spider. He had felt what they felt, seen what they saw. He used that experience to cut his way through the arachnid maelstrom. Anticipating their reactions, he exploited their vulnerabilities and countered their attacks with a brilliance woven from human and spider intelligence. The pathway behind him was soon strewn with crippled and dying monsters, fodder which distracted the larger arachnids following.

Nestra screamed without ceasing, whether in terror or defiance he could not tell. It did not matter: if she could not protect his back, they would both die, and that would be that. But her guard did not fail, and Dr'ivn kept driving forward, always forward, clearing their way to safety through all the hell and horror of the Spider God's minions.

At last they burst free of the temple. The gilded gates beyond stood open. Priests and guards alike lay dead in heaps, gigantic spiders feasting on their corpses. Manitor had set, but light from Gainar and Kish showed that they could not possibly reach the exit without being attacked from all sides.

He could not fail now. He grabbed a hanging lantern and dashed it to the ground. The oil ignited, setting alight the nearby spiders to dance and thrash in maddened agony as they burned. Dr'ivn grabbed the only other lantern he could see and with a heave added its fuel to the fire. As spiders fled, Dr'ivn seized his chance and sprinted to the base of the nearest wall.

"Nestra! Get ready." He plucked the girl off his back and tossed her to the top of the wall. She landed lightly, grabbed a decorative spike on the top, then turned to look down at him.

"Give me a hand," said Dr'ivn.

He discarded his sword and shield as useless encumbrance. Spider instincts flashed back unbidden to his mind and he jumped. Nestra almost lost her grip when she caught his arm, but then Dr'ivn's desperate effort allowed him to grip a neighboring spike. He pulled himself up beside her.

Behind and below them a river of spiders poured from the temple into the city. The progeny of millennia of profane breeding broke free from their bondage. Kheled was doomed. On the other side of the wall, the estuary meandered broad and sluggish to the open sea, not twenty feet below them. A spice galley lay moored a bowshot away.

"What now, Dr'ivn?"

"We jump." They crashed into the murky, warm water and surfaced spluttering. Dr'ivn stroked towards the galley; Nestra kept pace. It was bad manners to board a ship unasked, but three years of piracy had made it second nature to Dr'ivn. They climbed up quickly and startled the watch.

"Who goes there?" The fearful cry came out of the dark amidships.

"Paying passengers. Get your captain now."

Dr'ivn learned long ago that if you were forceful and fearless, you could bluff through orders nine times out of ten. That tenth time a good sword came in handy – too bad he had left his behind. He waited dripping in the dark, his left arm wrapped around Nestra. Although the top of her head did not even rise to his chin, she held herself just as proudly as he.

At last a bearded Kheledan approached. Behind him came a score of sailors armed with cutlasses.

"What in Zheleth is going on?" he said. "Who are you, and what are you doing on my boat?"

"We are paying passengers, Captain. Look out there." Dr'ivn swept his arm towards the city. Monstrous black shapes still scuttled through the darkness. In the distance torches flared. Screams drifted towards them over the water.

"The city falls. The spider hordes of Azoth have been unleashed on Kheled, and its people are consumed. If you do not want to be the next course, you will unmoor and escape to anywhere but here."

"It can't be true," said the captain. "The priests have ever protected the city."

"The priests are dead, and the spiders crazed with hunger," said Dr'ivn "We have seen it with our own eyes. We have gems. We can pay for passage. Just leave, before it's too late."

The captain paused, surveying the city, beginning to believe them. "Show me a token," he said to Dr'ivn.

"Nestra?" asked Dr'ivn.

Nestra reached inside her cloak and eased one sapphire partly from the bag until it caught the light, then quickly concealed it.

"Satisfied?" she asked.

The captain's eyes flashed. "I'm Hymid, captain of the *Seraphid*." His voice was much friendlier. "Welcome aboard. You can use my cabin. We'll talk price in the morning." He turned to talk to his men. "Rasufad, make ready to cast off. Jaslar, set a course seaward, then around the coast to Khifir. The weather is nice there this time of year." He strode to the bow.

191

Dr'ivn led Nestra to their cabin and surveyed his surroundings. The single bunk would not accommodate both of them, and the captain's clothes were unlikely to fit either of them. Should they get out of their wet clothes anyway? He turned to Nestra.

"Any suggestions? You could take the bed. I won't fit. And we need to talk about the…"

"Ssshh", said Nestra, leaning into him. "No more talk." She stepped backwards and dropped her robes, eyes full of promise.

Dr'ivn heard a hubbub and his skull ached. The cabin door crashed open. He heard Hymid yelling. He opened his eyes to find for the second time in this long night that he was lying on a floor. Still groggy, he pushed his way to a sitting position. Hymid was livid.

"That wench of yours has disappeared. She incapacitated two of my men during the night and stole our ship's boat."

"Nestra is gone?" Dr'ivn was finding it hard to think.

"Yes. We don't think she stole anything else, but I am holding you responsible. I want you to pay for your passage now, plus hers, and for our ship's boat, or we are tossing you overboard."

Dr'ivn cursed. "Nestra had all the gems." He staggered to his feet, looking about. There was no pouch, just his own scattered clothing from where he had let it fall last night. He sighed.

"I can't pay you, Captain, but I can pull an oar with the best of them. I'll work my passage."

Hymid appraised Dr'ivn's deeply muscled physique. He would be worth two rowers, easily.

"Fine. You work three months' service and we'll call it even."

Dr'ivn considered making a fuss, but he realized he had few choices. "Agreed, Captain."

Hymid nodded. "Breakfast is in ten minutes. Get dressed. Then get out of my cabin." He banged the door behind him.

Dr'ivn dressed slowly, going over the night in his mind. Nestra must have left with the gems after he had dozed off. That was the most expensive night he could remember with a woman, and he had paid for a few. He wanted to feel anger, but all he could muster was a grin. What a woman! He was definitely going to track her down after he finished his service with the merchant. He threw back his head and laughed, a loud, uncontrolled laugh of pure delight. He was still laughing as he strode up the companionway to meet his new comrades.

Rush Hour

Tracie McBride

irgil heard something tapping on top of his computer monitor. He looked up. His teenage daughter Ginny looked back at him. Virgil checked his watch.

"Shit! Is it that time already?" he said.

"Language, Dad," Ginny chided.

Virgil's workmate Roger peered over the cubicle wall like a bespectacled meerkat.

"What's up, Virgil?" He feigned surprise. "Oh, hello, Ginny. Didn't see you there. You look lovely in white, as always."

"C'mon, Dad," said Ginny. "You know how bad the drive home can get if we miss the window."

"You should take the bus," Roger said smugly.

They found Virgil's car in the parking garage in a row of anonymous Japanese imports, drove down to street level, and eased into traffic. They were moving at a steady pace when the swarm hit.

The air was thick with wasps the size of a man's thumb. They splattered against the windscreen. Virgil slowed to a crawl and turned on the wipers, smearing gore across the glass. They could just make out screaming from the driver of a convertible one lane over who hadn't been able to get the top up in time.

"Poor sod," muttered Virgil. Ginny tugged at the cross around her neck and said nothing.

Then, as suddenly as the swarm had appeared, it dispersed, blown away by a wind that came up out of nowhere.

"Look," said Ginny. She pointed. "A tornado!" Virgil squinted as he tried to make out where it was centred. The smoky cone spiraled into the air, sucking up debris.

"Oh, God," he said. "It looks like it's over the dump!"

Ginny frowned. "Dad!" she said. "Don't blaspheme!"

The twister passed metres away, pelting cars with jettisoned filth and flipping less fortunate vehicles in its wake. Virgil ducked reflexively as his car shuddered, airborne rubbish bags striking the roof and bonnet. Slow-flowing slime oozed down the windows. A used diaper entangled itself on the wipers. It split, and the wipers laboured across the windshield as they smeared its contents back and forth. Ginny retched.

"Wasps, tornadoes and shit, and we haven't even made it onto the motorway yet," Virgil muttered. Just as he spoke, the traffic ahead sped up. He loosened his grip a little on the steering wheel as he headed for the on-ramp.

"Watch out for the dog," Ginny said.

"Oh, no – not the dog!" Virgil groaned.

The size of a small horse, it stood in the middle of the on-ramp, barking and snapping at cars as they swerved to avoid it. It had an impressive strike rate, to judge by the number of cars with punctures lining the verges of either side of the road. *Not surprising*, thought Virgil, *considering the mongrel has three heads*. A motorcyclist tried to do a U-turn, and the hound snapped; Virgil sped past as all three heads began chewing off the rider's legs at the knees.

He looked ahead and swallowed a curse.

They were approaching the bridge, and things were heating up there – literally. Magma, dirty red, seethed sluggishly in the channel below. Virgil stopped the car.

They waited. Out of the molten river spewed a series of eruptions: geysers of fire leaped high above the roadway. Burning rock splashed down, engulfing cars within liquid rock.

"Tell me when. I can never figure out the pattern."

Ginny nodded. She counted down: "Three…two…one…Go!"

Virgil slammed the pedal; tires squealed; the car surged into a tunnel of fire, hot as a broiler oven. They cleared the bridge with inches to spare. A blast of fire towered behind, flickering in the rear view mirror.

The road ran ahead cut across a swathe of sandy desert. Ginny gave a low whistle. "They've taken out a bus!" A forty-seater lay on its side, its tires pierced with arrows. The centaurs celebrated their kill, prancing about, hooting joyously and waving their bows in the air. A naked, muscle-bound giant with horns growing from his temples flexed hairy biceps as he forced open the doors and hauled out passengers.

A man in a knitted vest flew across their field of vision. "Isn't that Roger?" Ginny asked.

Virgil nodded, too absorbed in the spectacle to comment. Howling wretchedly in the burning sand, Roger struggled to find his feet and climb free. But new assailants, vulture-winged, swept down from the sky. Their human faces twisted in fury as they pinned him under strong talons and ripped his flesh with jagged teeth.

One harpy glanced up from her meal, hissed at Virgil. Blood dribbled down her chin and splattered on her sagging blue-veined breasts.

"You should take the bus," Virgil mimicked savagely.

"Dad!" Ginny exclaimed, and slapped his arm in reproof.

Once past the fallen bus, the traffic flow improved and for a span they made good time. Dense black clouds gathered overhead.

"Looks like rain," Ginny said.

The air in the car grew oppressively hot. Sweat beaded on Virgil's forehead as he struggled for breath. "This can't be a good sign," he said.

Fire began to fall from the sky, daintily at first, like the harmless spluttering of a holiday sparkler. Quickly, though, it intensified, soon coming down in thick napalm-like globs. Ginny closed her eyes and gripped the armrest. Her lips moved in a silent prayer. Virgil pressed down on the gas till his foot touched the floor and watched the needle gauge on the meter crawl downward into the red.

Then they were out of the squall and hurtling down the highway, smoke trailing behind them. Virgil eased off the gas.

"How's the car look?" he asked Ginny.

She shrugged. "Nothing leaked in that I can see. Hey – you better slow down."

They rolled to a halt behind a long queue of cars. Traffic was stacked up all across the expressway.

"What's the hold-up this time?" Virgil asked. "Can you tell?"

Ginny wound down her window and leant out as far as she could. She gasped, pulled herself back into the car, and quickly wound it back up.

"Road work," she said grimly.

Virgil swallowed hard. His hands trembled. "God help us," he croaked.

"Amen," nodded Ginny.

They crept forward with agonizing slowness. Bored, Virgil flipped on the radio: it was playing "Sympathy for the Devil." Virgil hummed along, but with a scowl Ginny flipped it back off. They inched along for the next twenty minutes in silence.

At last Virgil spotted the telltale orange cones. Seconds later, they were in chaos. Their single lane had somehow split into three, none of which was clearly marked. There was a burst of action as panicked drivers swerved toward any gap they could find.

Virgil cut off a blue Ford sedan and gained the left hand lane. Hulking man-like creatures in fluorescent yellow vests stood at irregular intervals. Green drool dripped from their grinning maws as they capriciously spun Stop/Go signs, sending confused motorists into slow-motion chain-link collisions. Ahead, some drivers had exited their cars to swap insurance details. Virgil leaned on his horn.

"Move it, deadbeats!" he hollered, then noticed movement to the group's rear. A team of bony little purple-skinned men wheeled a steaming cauldron into place behind the unsuspecting drivers.

"Look out!" Virgil screamed, but by then it was too late. They were knee deep in hot tar. They screamed and frantically tried to extract themselves, but the purple mutants were ready for them. Pitchforks in hand, they drove the howling motorists back into the tar, falling face-first to a fiery end. The little purple men applauded, waving their pitchforks forked tails with glee.

"We'll never make it," Virgil said.

"Have a little faith," said Ginny. "They must be due for a smoke break any minute."

As if on cue, the road crew dropped their tools. Some crouched in the shoulder and poured each other steaming cups of excrement; others shared out cigarettes from scarlet packets, lighting them from gasoline fires or the smouldering corpses in the tar. Virgil and Ginny waited.

Finally a bulldozer rumbled forward to push the abandoned cars out of the way, collecting several occupied vehicles in the process. Studiously avoiding eye contact with anyone, Virgil followed in its wake through the site.

Daylight and the sweltering heat of the road works abruptly vanished; they emerged into night and eerie calm. The headlights struggled to penetrate the darkness. Ice coated the asphalt. Virgil shivered in the sudden cold, and only narrowly avoided skidding off the road altogether.

They didn't see the figure in the middle of the road until they were almost on top of him.

He stood perhaps nine feet tall. At first he seemed to be wearing a full-length black coat, but then he flexed his shoulders and opened magnificent ebony wings into the night air. All Virgil could see of his face were his glowing red eyes. Virgil stared, mesmerized. His hands slid nervelessly from the wheel.

Ginny sighed. She wiggled close to her father, sidled her nearer leg into the compartment, and used her own foot to depress the accelerator. They rolled slowly by the black angel, Ginny steering awkwardly with her off hand. With eye contact broken, Virgil soon regained consciousness and resumed driving. Ginny turned back and watch the dark figure recede. She gave him the finger.

They reached their exit and turned off into tranquil suburbia. Virgil turned onto their street, then into their driveway. The streetlights cast a benign yellow glow around Ginny's head as she got out of the car. Virgil's wife greeted them at the door. He kissed her cheek.

"Sorry we're late, love," he said. "The traffic was hell."

God's Love

Alicia Rieske

 o one talks much when we walk. The creak of the handcart wheels and the soft crunching of hundreds of feet is hypnotic. Some days when the call to make camp comes it seems like the hours of travel never happened at all. Other days, when the wind blows bitter, or if a blister makes every step painful, it feels like years before Jonathan finally shouts the call to halt.

My belly sways with each step. Some of the brothers have offered me a seat in their carts because of my condition, but I have always refused. The baby seems more at peace when I'm walking. With the innumerable steps taken during this pregnancy, I feel she'll always crave movement and travel when she's born. I pray that despite this she will be able to find peace.

More and more I find myself at the back of the line. I don't mind. Emma stays in the back also. Jonathan is our leader, but she is our shepherd: she watches to make sure none are left behind.

At midmorning I am awoken from my walking trance by a murmur moving down the line. Several people point west.

At first I see only the same horizon we have been walking toward for the entire journey. The jagged snowcap atop the tallest mountains shines almost painfully in the early light. But then below that I see something else gleaming, like jagged gray teeth poking up from gums made of the morning fog.

As the day goes on and the mist disperses it is clear. The murmur rises to chatter. *Towers*, I hear. *City*.

I look at Emma. She is serene as always, but I think I see a burning brightness in her eyes.

As usual, it is a child – Lily Thomas – who voices first what we all are wondering: "Is this our new home?"

Her mother opens her mouth but cannot answer.

"Stop!" comes the call from Jonathan. It is repeated down the line until we are all still. "Circle!" comes the next command. This only increases the murmuring: it is way too early to camp. We haven't even had our noonday meal. But the men comply, carefully rolling the carts down the incline of the elevated road and constructing the same circle they've made every day for months – though never in full sun.

We gather inside the ring. Adults giggle like nervous children. The change in routine is almost more exciting than the sighting. Emma still says nothing, though everyone keeps looking to her for answers. A small smile dances over her face, filling us all with hope.

Jonathan enters the circle, still astride his chestnut mare – our only horse.

"Quiet!" he shouts, though we are already silent. He seems to assess each of us before continuing. "We are God's Chosen." He is not shouting any more, but his deep voice still reaches all of us. "He brought each of us together to continue His sacred mission upon this Earth. He chose me as the bearer of His Word."

Jonathan always begins his sermons this way. Many move their lips in time with his, so familiar are the words.

His voice softens as he veers from the standard message. "This journey has been long. It has been hard. We are tired. We are hungry. Our feet and bellies ache." Some of the people nod their heads. I want to tell them to stop – they will regret it. "Some have even *died* along this trail. They are buried alone, far

204

from anything they ever knew or loved, along this road we have followed so long we can barely remember the time before we walked it."

There are audible responses to this – *yes*, and *amen*.

"Perhaps you think – surely it is time to stop. Surely we can rest our weary feet at last."

They know better than to respond to this. They know now that this is a trap.

"This land in which we stand in today was once vibrant with life. Green fields grew where now we see desert. Millions and millions of people lived here opulently. But a great wickedness existed here. A wickedness so great it could only be remedied by purging the lives of all who lived here.

"And so, as in the times of old, God set His hand upon this place and destroyed it – utterly. Plagues ravaged the land. Earthquake; flood; fire; drought; famine; pestilence. What you see is what remains – a burnt-out shell of silent ruin.

"But past this evil place, beyond the mountains, is another city – one that is still green and intact. God has protected that city all these years, awaiting our arrival.

"God has sent us on the holiest journey undertaken since times of old. We shall find great happiness at the end, when the lands we left are scourged as completely as already the west has been. But first we must suffer."

He stops. His eyes cut into us. We are silent.

"We camp for the night," he says at last. He now sounds as if it were any other day. He prompts his horse and leaves the circle.

No one speaks while the fire is lit. There is not even any wind to break the quiet, and it's too early for the crickets whose instruments would ordinarily fill the air as we prepare camp.

But then Emma begins to sing:

When our pilgrims' lot seems futile, beset by storm and strife
and evil stalks the faithful and days seem black as night
God's love still shines upon us, a ceaseless perfect light
to guide us down the narrow way that leads to deathless life.

Her sweet voice calms everyone. We join in for the next verse and circle around the fire with her. I move my lips but make no sound, watching Emma as she sings. Her eyes are closed and she is smiling. Her face is perfect; unmarked by crease or wrinkle. But a single drop of sweat rolls from her forehead to run down the side of her face and fall away. She is human, then. My heart tightens, watching her sweat.

The fire blooms before us. I resist looking at it as long as I can – I'd rather watch the drop of sweat fall down to Emma's neck – but finally the vision engulfs me.

The flames have weaved themselves together while growing very tall. What emerges is a great glowing tower, taller than anything we've ever seen. So tall it goes up forever.

The details sharpen. It's not only a tower, but a temple. The single column has divided into two great turrets. Flaming stairs ascend toward a sparkling entrance. On either side, splendid angels stand, and point the way inside. They look like Emma, only with giant wings of fire growing from their backs.

Home. Emma's voice. It comes not from her mouth but from inside of us. While our bodies sit around the fire, our souls follow Emma into the temple. Inside it's warm as a womb. Light is all around. God's love envelops each of us and we join him in the place he has prepared for us for eternity.

I was a different person before I found Emma and Jonathan and their church. I was hardly a person at all. I was a creature that had never known love and whose only goal was to live another day. I'd walked hundreds of miles after leaving the man in Atlanta who'd raised and kept me for profit.

I'd gone north because I heard it was better up there. I learned quickly it was not – there was only less to fight over in the cold places.

I was close to dead when I came to the village. A man had told me I could get a meal there. Then he wanted something from me, but I scratched his eyes and ran away. He was stupid. He should have gotten what he wanted before giving what he had.

Two large men with guns stood outside the entrance of the Church. But when I approached they greeted me warmly and let me inside without asking any questions.

Many things were strange in that place. It was clean, and warm, and no one was yelling or screaming. The women all wore long dresses. But what struck me most was that everyone was smiling.

One of the women led me to a table and a steaming bowl was set before me. Hot stew with real meat. It was the best thing I'd ever tasted. Both instinct and experience told me that they must expect something from me in return, but I didn't care.

A hand touched my back. I flinched away and turned to look up at its owner, a smiling woman dressed like the others. Her golden hair was pinned up in a perfect bun, but for one loose yellow strand that drifted over her cheek. Her hand found my back again as I looked at her, and I began to feel very warm.

"You are special," said a sweet voice – but the woman's mouth wasn't moving. It sounded like it was coming from every direction, though it was very soft. "You deserve to be loved."

"My name is Emma." Now her lips moved, and it was the same voice I had heard in my mind. "When you have finished eating – please, have as much as you like – I would like to wash your feet, if you will let me. It is a sacred practice we have here – an act of humility we learn from Christ."

I nodded, not knowing what else to do. I still felt the odd warmth and I couldn't explain the voice in my head, but I couldn't make myself care. I suppose I should have been suspicious, afraid that the stew had been drugged – but I somehow felt complete trust for this woman.

My feet tingled as she washed them. Her golden head bobbed before me; the touch of her fingers sent shivers all through my body.

"I want to tell you about my husband," she said. She was looking down, so I couldn't tell if her lips were moving or not. "His name is Jonathan, and he has been chosen by God to be His Prophet here on Earth. His task is to assemble a community of the holy – those whom God will grant salvation. This world is filled with sin and pain, but God has chosen Jonathan to rescue us from despair."

Each word was punctuated with a touch: the stroke of a heel, the squeeze of a toe, the caress of an arch. Each sent waves of warmth throughout my body, all the way to the top of my head. She looked up at me. Her eyes seemed to be asking me something.

"This is what God's love feels like," she said. Her lips did not move. "Will you join us and become His Disciple?"

I didn't know what the word meant, but I nodded without hesitation. She was asking if I wanted to stay, and I did, badly. Food, shelter, safety: I would be a fool to leave. But my true desire was to stay with this beautiful creature.

I wake at dusk. The fire is out, and it is cold. Emma is no longer with us.

Waking from visions is always difficult. The world is so dark and sharp compared with the places we visit. But today is even worse. We have missed the noonday meal, and so are even more hungry than usual. Our clothes and hair smell like smoke. There is some bickering as we brush ourselves off and re-orient to an existence outside Emma's mind.

Eventually the fire is rebuilt and preparations for dinner begun. I am one of the last to stand. My lower back has cramped, and I concentrate on kneading out the stiffness with my knuckles.

I look outside the circle through a gap between carts and see Emma. She is staring out at the mountains. Movement catches my eye, dark figures in the grass beyond her. But then they are gone, phantoms of the twilight.

It's better when the fire blazes and we are eating our baked yams and biscuits. But the hunger remains. We are accustomed to being hungry on this journey — I've been used to hunger my entire life. But it's sharper now. Something is missing from the starchy meal.

I remember the last time we had meat. It was the evening before we left. We slaughtered the last pig and roasted it over a huge fire. I can almost feel the juice of it dripping down my chin. I stop myself. I've never had a craving so strong , not through my entire pregnancy. I've never even taken extra rations when they were offered.

Emma is here, but she seems distant. She has done nothing to comfort us since our vision. We sing no songs. There is no storytelling, or even gossip. The last bite of biscuit tastes like dust in my mouth and I struggle to swallow.

Finally Jonathan enters the circle. He doesn't eat with us. He only joins us to lead the evening prayer. I know we all prefer it that way — his is an unnerving presence. It's hard for us to be ourselves when he's around.

Emma introduced me to Jonathan soon after she washed my feet that first time, while I was still in a daze of deep relief. Somehow Emma had broken through the armor that I had spent my life building. 'Broken' isn't the right word: she melted it away like butter. But when she brought me to Jonathan and he looked at me, what was left of my guard went up.

His appearance was not particularly striking. He was of average height and build, and his features were too sharp to be attractive. He did not smile like his followers. His dark eyes bored into me with a look that was greedy and not unfamiliar.

"God looks at you through his eyes," Emma's ethereal voice said. This shook me. It meant that my new God must be a man, for only a man would look at me that way.

"Jonathan, this is Evelyn. She wishes to join us," Emma said in her normal voice.

"Evelyn," he repeated. His voice was deep and rich, as if it were coming from a much larger man. "That is lovely – after our Mother Eve."

I was baptized that day. Emma dressed me in a white tunic and led me outside to a stone fountain. It was old, left over from a time when people built things for no discernable reason beyond boredom and wealth.

He was waiting there for us. He put his hands heavily on my head and said a few words. I tried to remember them, but they disappeared in the shock when without warning he dunked me into the cold water.

I must have been under for a mere few seconds; but it felt so much longer. My hand tingled from where it had been wrenched from Emma's. My ears rang and my bones ached with cold. I no longer felt God's presence, which had seemed so strong when Emma washed my feet. For the first time I asked myself what I was doing.

Jonathan never joins in the visions either. I've never wondered why: it just doesn't seem right that he would. He is the Prophet. He gets his visions directly from God. He doesn't need Emma the way we do.

"Dear Father," he begins the prayer. "Protect us from evil as we sleep this night. Let us wake strengthened to continue our sacred journey, as we strive to do Your work. Keep foremost in our minds always the certainty of our destiny and the rewards which await us. Please forgive any who dared hope that our long journey had reached its end, for they wished only to please You, and knew not that we still have far to go. Amen."

"Amen," we all repeat, feeling chastened once again.

The circle within the circle disperses, and we each find a place to lay our bedrolls. As I am pulling mine from the back of a cart, I feel a hand on my shoulder.

"Prophet," I say, without even looking.

"Sleep away from the others tonight," he whispers in my ear. I nod, still not turning.

Jonathan came to me for the first time the night I was baptized. He said nothing, only took my hand and led me to his room. I didn't resist. I knew from the moment I met him what he would ask of me. I accepted it as the price of staying here, but I worried about Emma. I could not survive her displeasure.

But she was there, standing by the bed. Smiling, as always.

Jonathan led me to the bed, then stepped away. Emma came forward, taking both of my hands, then kissed me.

Something happened at the touch of her lips. The room changed. Where before it had been lit dimly by only a lantern or two, now a white, heavenly light glowed from every direction. I could no longer see the room, or even the bed beneath me – I knew only the light, and Emma. Her hands moved down my body. Behind her was Jonathan, standing casually on nothing, floating in the white light. He was draped in a beautiful robe, woven in colors too vivid to be real. He grew taller, his hair longer, his face more tender.

"This is his true form." Emma's voice came from every direction. I looked down at her and saw that she had changed too, but not as much. She now wore a gauzy white robe. Her hair was loose but for a thin golden band around her brow. But she was Emma. She was so beautiful.

Abruptly, I noticed that I was naked. My legs were covered with bruises and scratches. I had a long thin scar along the inside of my thigh, from a man's knife long ago. Then came a wave of shame; I felt so ugly before this angel.

Emma ran her finger along the length of the scar. I shivered. Her touch was pure pleasure – I have no other way to describe it. I closed my eyes involuntarily. When I opened them the scar was gone. So were all of the other marks. She smiled at me.

"This is your true form, Evelyn," her voice said all around us. Jonathan was still behind her, benevolent and holy, his robes rustling in a breeze that wasn't there. I wished he would go away.

For an instant, concern flashed across Emma's face. "I want you to love him as I do," her voice said.

"I love you." My voice was quiet and tinny compared to hers. It sounded like it came from another room.

She smiled kindly, and then put her mouth between my legs.

The room changed again. All around colors roiled and pinwheeled, their movements synchronized to the unbelievable sensations whirring through my body.

I tried to ignore the colors, to concentrate on Emma. Her golden head bobbed before me again – the way it had when she washed my feet. Soon it was too hard to keep watching her, and I lay back and let the colors of joy wash over me.

"Heaven is like this," her voice said.

I felt cold hands on my breasts and the colors dimmed. Jonathan's face was above mine – his original face. Emma redoubled her efforts and the colors brightened, pleasure intensified. I opened my mouth: it wanted to be filled.

Jonathan kissed me then, rough and hard, just as Emma's touch pushed me over a steep cliff of pleasure and I fell. Jonathan's tongue invaded my mouth as I bucked and arched my back.

As the colors melted away I found that Emma was behind me now. She pulled me into her lap and enveloped me in her soft limbs. She stroked my breasts with one hand, and gave the fingers of the other hand to my mouth, to nurse on like a newborn. Tears were pouring down my face; she kissed them off my cheeks.

Jonathan stood tall before me now. He flickered between the man I'd met and the man Emma had shown me. I still didn't love him, but I would follow him if it meant I could stay with Emma.

He entered me. Like the fountain baptism, it was quick and slightly painful. But I barely noticed. Emma was breathing into my ear, and I felt safe and warm and loved.

That was the night that God made the baby that grows inside of me now. I think of it as Emma's child. More than mine, and more than Jonathan's. That was the day I found my family and my purpose. My new brother and sister; my new husband and wife.

I sleep little. When I do, my jumbled dreams are stark and cold. No action, only images: bird skeletons splayed on frozen earth; hollowed-out eyes filled with cold, desperate fire; black blood oozing from between pale thighs.

I wake with a start and find Jonathan above me, stroking my hair. I welcome his warm body under my blankets; for I am chilled to the bones. His rough hands travel the globe of my belly before venturing into the warm place below it.

I open up for him, and let him do as he wishes. It is not unpleasant. The warmth and rhythm chase away the ghosts of my dreams.

He moans softly in my ear as he finishes and falls beside me. His hand rests on my belly.

"When do you commune with God, Jonathan?" I ask. "You're the Prophet, but I never see you speak to Him."

"I just did," he whispers. I feel his smile against my neck.

"And what did He have to say?"

"He said that you will be our salvation."

I laugh a little, but he doesn't.

I gaze at the sky and consider this, not sure how serious he is. We lay like this until dawn erases the stars and he leaves me.

I don't realize I've fallen back asleep until I awaken to screams.

It's Sister Mary Price. "Where is he? Where is he?" she keeps screeching.

Soon there's a crowd around her. It takes me longer to get close to see what's going on. Her baby is nowhere to be seen. She's frantically questioning everyone: "Did you take him?" She's met only with confused stares.

"He couldn't even crawl yet!" she bawls. "It must have been one of you!"

Finally one of the men kneels down and lifts her bedroll. Underneath, the bedding drips with blood.

Mary's wails grow even louder and she falls, rocking, to the ground, clutching her knees to her breast. I reflexively grasp my belly.

Jonathan pushes into the crowd, stopping short. He grows pale when he sees the blood.

After a moment he says, "It must have been a coyote. From now on we'll post guards at night. I'll take the first shift myself."

It's not clear whether Mary has even heard him. Two women lift her from the ground. Her face looks broken. I haven't ever seen such pain.

Then Emma is with her. I didn't even see her approach – she's just there. She places her hands on Mary's face and the tears stop. A few moments beneath her hands, and Mary is restored. She smiles, blinks at us curiously.

We burn the bedroll in the campfire. We all watch it like a burial, all but Mary, who hurries to pack up the rest of her things, shaking her head, as if we're doing something foolish and unnecessary.

I have my arms around my belly as we line up to leave. I hold Mary's face – the broken one – in my mind. Someone should remember it.

It's a relief when Jonathan gives the call to set off. The familiar rhythm of walking lulls everyone into silence.

The city in front of us is still exciting, even though we know now we won't be stopping there. It's at least a change from the endless plains we've been crossing for weeks.

By afternoon, the landscape around us has changed from nothing to something. Here are buildings, and more roads intersecting the one we follow. Our road becomes wider, then rises, lifted from the ground by huge pillars of stone. The men who pull the carts huff and groan and bow their heads in exertion, unaccustomed to the incline. Circular ramps divide off from our path and curl down to earth, where larger, taller structures cluster, strewn with stone and metal.

The pass rises directly ahead – a single road that pushes into the mountains. We will be through the city within the hour. I'm slightly disappointed: I'd hoped we'd have more to see than this.

As if on cue the line stops, then turns back on itself. When my turn comes to reach the bend, I see why. The road ahead has collapsed. Massive, cracked slabs lay fifty feet down, a multitude of rusted metal bars snaking menacingly from either end.

And so we circle our way down the closest ramp and descend into the belly of the city. The men's feet grind on the stone as they to hold back the weight of their loads.

We find ourselves among the tallest towers, craning our necks to see their tops. The scale of it all seems too grand for human builders. It is more like a place where giants once lived, thousands of years ago.

We walk, still west, through long corridors of stone. We will somehow have to get back on the raised highway to get over the mountains.

Shattered glass crunches beneath our feet. It is everywhere, crushed into a coarse, glittering sand. Now I regret my wish to see more of the city. Jonathan was right: this is not our home.

A great gust of wind rushes between buildings, ripping bonnets from heads and tarpaulins from carts. Children scream and clutch their mothers. I know what they fear: God – or worse – is angry with us.

But Jonathan won't slow down. We hurriedly reclaim our hats and go on.

Then he stops.

I know I should stay back. I am pregnant, awkward, slow. But I don't. Instead I move toward the front of the line. Something in me has awakened – I can no longer trust my life to these folk. The men I push through are frightened. Hats are held. Sweat pours down brows despite the chill.

At first it seems like nothing, a shallow black hole. But when I get closer I see that it is filled with ash. The concrete around its edge has been warped by intense heat.

A fire pit.

My heart thuds in my chest as I sort out the significance of this. Without thinking, I move even closer, holding my palm out over the pit.

"Evelyn," Jonathan warns.

Ignoring him, I gaze into the ashes. They dance in unfelt movements of air, rising and falling silently. The heat is unmistakable.

Something else catches my eye, and I reach for it. The ash clouds around my hand, making it harder to see, but I feel something smooth and slightly wet.

"Evelyn, stop!" Jonathan shouts.

I lift it, and it is visible to all. I drop it, but not before people begin screaming.

A skull. A human baby's skull.

Its fall unsettles the ash, revealing more bones in the pit. I can't stop myself from looking. There are hundreds. Most look human. What I had thought to be burnt sticks poking out of the ash are now clearly femurs, some cracked open to reach the marrow. I count five more broken skulls, all larger than the one I dropped. They are darkened from the fire, but there are marks all over them, as if teeth had scraped them clean of every last morsel of flesh.

Jonathan is yelling for quiet, but no one listens. Even the ones too far back to see scream, just because the others are.

"Emma!" Jonathan sounds much like a man calling for his wife to quiet a fussy child.

As is often the case, she seems to come from nowhere. She is standing right beside me, gazing into the floating ash.

"Who are they, Emma?" I ask her. "Who did this?" She turns to me and touches my face. She doesn't erase my fear, but I can't help relishing the touch in itself. Her fingers are warm against my cheek.

"They are God's children, just like us," she says, and smiles.

And then at once everyone is silent.

I turn around. The others stare back at me, serene as cattle. When I turn back, Emma is gone. I search the faces for her, frantic. Tears begin to prick my eyes, and I can feel my heartbeat quicken even more. But I don't see her.

Finally I look at Jonathan, who is already gazing at me with a raised eyebrow. He can tell. It didn't work on me – *she* didn't work on me.

He says nothing, instead calling us all back to order, to move on. I stand still as they pass me, hunting for Emma in the crowd. I even call for her, but no one listens, and she doesn't appear.

Finally I'm at the end, and I have to follow. I am filled with a fear much greater than the fear of the bones. Emma is not with me. Something is very wrong.

After only a few blocks I can't stand it anymore. The movement has none of the hypnotic effect it usually does – perhaps that was Emma too, the whole time. I quicken my pace, practically running at times, trying to get to the front. No one reacts as I push past them. They stare straight ahead, glass-eyed, taking in none of our surroundings. A deep revulsion for them grips me, so strong I am nearly nauseous.

"Stop," I tell myself out loud. These are your brothers and sisters. The only family you have ever had. My face burns from shame as well as exertion.

Just as I see Jonathan's horse in front of me, a cramp seizes my loins. I stifle my cry, but I have to stop and lean over. Sweat pricks my brow as I fall behind again. No one helps me or even notices.

Instead of subsiding, a stronger wave of pain washes through me, making my knees buckle.

"Emma!" I call – then, "Jonathan!"

The line stops almost immediately. I didn't even hear the call. Then he is in front of me, looking into my eyes.

"Are you having the baby?"

I shake my head, then gasp, "I don't know."

"Breathe," he commands. "You can't have it here."

I nod and try to do as he says. I never imagined it would be him, with his sharp tone and knit brows, with me in this moment. I always thought it would be Emma, holding my hand and giving gentle direction.

"Where is she?" I ask.

"Quiet – keep breathing."

I do. Finally the muscles relax and the pain goes away. I sigh with relief.

"You shouldn't walk. Get in someone's cart."

"No, I'm fine now."

"Don't be an idiot. If you have the baby here, the delay could cost us our lives."

He doesn't give me the opportunity to argue further. "Jameson!" he calls. "Make room in your cart!"

Though Brother Jameson is only feet away, he doesn't seem to hear. He is still looking straight ahead. It's only then that I realize no one is looking at us.

"What the hell?" Jonathan asks. It's the least prophetlike thing I've ever heard him say. He strides to Brother Jameson and slaps him in the face. The man doesn't even turn his head in reaction.

"Emma!" Jonathan shouts.

Nothing.

"She's gone," I say. My voice cracks in fear.

"Emma!" he screams this time. His voice echoes from the stone walls all around us. Once the echoes fade, the city is utterly silent.

"Traitorous bitch!" he growls. I'm shocked to hear him – anyone – speak of her that way. I want to defend her, but I don't know what to say.

Jonathan paces in front of me. "I think they'll still follow me," he says finally. "You get on my horse."

I'm doubtful, but with his help I manage to get into the saddle. I've only ridden a little, back at the village, but the mare is very well trained and doesn't give me trouble.

Jonathan makes the call to move. Everyone steps forward simultaneously and maintains a synchronized rhythm as we walk. The effect is eerie. The glass underfoot sounds like a giant creature crunching on bones.

Jonathan walks beside me. I watch him just for the comfort of seeing someone move like a real person. Occasionally he shakes his head, having some internal argument – with Emma, I imagine.

I try to pray. Emma always says that God listens to everyone, even if he doesn't always answer. Jonathan never said such a thing.

Dear Father –

Please. Please. Protect her – bring her back to us, I think. *Please –*

I can't continue. I've always had trouble praying to myself. The right words never come, and I end up feeling foolish.

I imagine whoever took Mary's baby grabbing Emma from the shadows. But I know that isn't what's happened. Why would she put the others in this trance if she didn't leave intentionally?

"This way," Jonathan says, pointing left. "We need to get back on the highway, up there." He points to the hulking silhouette of the overpass. I

220

can't help noticing how low in the sky the sun has fallen. We can't have long before it drops below the mountains.

Then there is a scream behind us, followed by many others. The horse, startled, kicks and turns, but I manage to hang on. I imagine an attack – something horrible and violent – but when I look I see nothing but the others. They scream and cry. Their hands clutch and scratch their faces. Some seem catatonic, swaying back and forth on their knees. Devastated children reach out to their parents but are ignored.

"Jesus Christ!" Jonathan yells. "Quiet!" It is as ineffectual as it was before.

Emma has fooled us all into believing that Jonathan is our leader.

I slide ungracefully from the horse as soon as it stops moving and try my best to comfort whomever I can.

"Emma! Emma! Emma!" Sister Karen screams. I grab her shoulders to try and get her attention, but she pulls violently away.

Mary comes up to me. "Evelyn!" she shouts. I am relieved that she even recognizes me. "Where is my baby?" she yells over the din. "I can't find him. I really need to find him!"

"Mary," I say. I take her hand. "Don't you remember?"

Her face crumples, and I know that she does. She falls to the ground, sobbing. I wish I had said nothing.

Was Emma's influence really so great that chaos could come so quickly? Apparently so. A sobbing child comes up to me with arms outstretched. I can't pick her up but I squeeze her to my side and feel her tears soak my dress.

"SILENCE!" Jonathan yells in his deepest, loudest cry. He is standing on top of someone's cart and finally looks like the Prophet he is supposed to be.

They obey, briefly, staring at him with stunned, wet faces.

221

"To your carts!" Jonathan yells. "We must keep going!"

Brother Christopher, a very large man, steps toward him. Tears cover his face. He takes another step, blinking fiercely, his brow knitted in an expression of fervent concentration.

He says something to Jonathan I can't hear. Jonathan's eyes widen, and he shakes his head. Brother Christopher repeats it, screaming now: "You fucked my wife! And I watched you!" He lunges at Jonathan, who falls backwards off the cart. The noise rises again, angry this time.

"Stop it!" I scream as other men converge on him. But my voice is not as strong as Jonathan's, and I can barely hear it myself over the noise.

I push through the men with all my strength to get to him.

Please protect us – please fix this. Please come back! I am praying again, but this time to Emma, not God.

Finally I am beside him. He's dazed, but conscious.

Help me, Emma. Give me your strength. Please.

Perhaps my prayer is answered, or maybe the men just don't want to hurt a pregnant woman, but I manage to lead Jonathan away from them.

I help him sit up. He touches the back of his head, then looks at his blood-covered fingers. I am surprised to see a wry smile.

I stand up. The people have quieted a bit, distracted from their longing for Emma by their anger towards Jonathan. I take advantage of the lull.

"Listen to me – we have to get up there." I don't shout, but my voice is firm. I point to the overpass. "That is our only way out of the city. We'll be killed here if we don't leave."

"We can't leave Emma!" someone shouts. A chorus joins him.

"Emma is waiting for us there!"

I immediately regret the lie. It's so pathetic I'm sure I'm going to lose whatever small authority I've earned. But they are quiet as they consider. Without even asking how I know she is there, or why she would be there, they resume their places in line.

They're so used to following. That's the only explanation. They're sheep. Poor dumb sheep. But for their sake I will do what I can lead them out of this place.

We turn down the street Jonathan pointed out. At the end is the ramp to the overpass. But blocking that is a wall of metal junk, piled fifteen feet high.

Another cramp seizes my loins, but I grit my teeth and force it to subside through sheer will.

"Unpack everything from the carts!" I shout. "We'll have to climb over."

They continue to obey me. I've never led anyone before and I am sure that each command will be the one they decide to ignore. But they unload the carts and begin to pack up bundles of supplies to carry on our backs.

Jonathan knows better than to intrude, though he is clearly sullen about his sudden fall from power. Without meaning to, I turn to him after each command I give, but he gives no sign of encouragement or dispute.

I gather all our rope together, then look up at the tangled mess of steel. "Someone needs to go up first to tie it," I say. I am only thinking out loud, but Brother Henry takes the rope from my hands and begins to climb. There are plenty of grips, and he scales the pile quickly. Relieved, I start to consider how to get children and supplies over.

But as Henry gains the top, a filthy hand with blackened nails reaches up from near his feet.

We scream, and he looks down just as the hand grabs his ankle and yanks. He falls, then abruptly stops as something sharp and bloody juts through his back. He has been impaled on a twisted piece of metal, several inches in diameter. Blood bubbles out of his mouth. But the thing keeps pulling on him. Each tug makes more blood gush from the wound and causes his head to loll more extremely from his neck. The rope is gone, dropped to where they are trying to take him.

The metal beam stabbing through Henry's chest finally bends under the weight of the unseen pulling. His body slides away and disappears.

Then the drumming begins. It is a low thudding noise, like a heartbeat that reverberates off the building walls. With the echo neither the direction of the noise nor the distance can be determined. It could be a mile away or right above us.

Some of the flock begin whimpering and holding each other.

"It's just a noise!" I yell, though my heart is pounding in my chest to the rhythm of the hollow beats.

It's too much. They flee in panic – away from the only way out.

I try to follow, but I can't keep up. Finally Jonathan, back on his horse, comes up behind me and pulls me onto the saddle behind him.

Several blocks away, they have all stopped. They are staring at someone who stands on the steps of a building.

She is filthy. Long, matted hair of undistinguishable color hangs over a face blackened with dirt. The lips are split and bleeding. By the concavity of the face, I know her teeth must be all but gone. But the black, red-rimmed eyes that look out from behind the curtain of hair are bright and avid with hunger.

She is standing so still that I might not have even seen her if it weren't for the dress hanging from her bony frame. It is a bright cornflower blue. It is the exact color of Emma's eyes, which is why I chose that fabric. I made that dress for her, a thousand years ago, when she was teaching me to sew back in the village.

The others notice too, and cry out. At the noise, she bares her teeth and hisses like an animal. Then she turns and runs into the building.

Only then do I notice what the building is: a stone church. Twin turrets reach up on either side. Below, a high arched doorway hangs open where the girl entered. On each side of the steps are life-sized angels, pointing inside. They're made of stone, not fire, and aren't nearly as beautiful as Emma, but they point toward the doors just as in the vision.

The others are already running up the stairs. There is nothing I can do to stop them.

I turn and see Jonathan, who stares up at me with frightened eyes.

"Why are they going in there?" he asks.

"Emma showed us this place, yesterday," I reply. "This is our home."

"No, Evelyn – no it isn't. It's a trap."

"But she's in there. She might be hurt."

"Look at me, Evelyn. We can still find a way out. Leave her."

But I am impatient, and already sliding off the back of the saddle. Another jolt of pain shudders through my loins. *Quiet darling, quiet,* I say to the baby silently. *We may both be dead soon. You are better staying inside, where you are warm and clean and innocent.*

"Evelyn," Jonathan says – not loudly, but with all of the power of his preacher's voice. "Don't."

I can see more of him in this moment than he could ever tell me. I see a life in which we escape this madness and make it to the mountains. I see him lifting our daughter from between my legs and weeping. I see him introducing me to the God who has called us all this way and making me understand why all of this has happened. I see us finding peace, and a kind of love.

But this vision stands no chance against the love I already know.

Emma was wearing the cornflower blue dress that beautiful day in spring, just before we set off on the journey. We were all so excited to see in person the amazing places that Emma had shown us in the visions. We couldn't wait to leave, but Jonathan kept delaying the departure to finish making preparations.

Somehow, Emma and I were alone. She usually had a flock of people around her, basking in her love. We were in the garden, digging up some early onions to bring with us. We were kneeling across from each other over a row, and I kept sneaking looks at a long smudge of dirt that ran down her cheek. Somehow it made her even more beautiful.

"These are strong," I said, holding one of the little onions to my nose.

"Yes," she said. "We'll appreciate it on the journey, when we need a little zest."

"Why do we have to go?" I asked, almost offhandedly.

She stopped digging and looked at me. I blushed, regretting the question. It sounded like a lack of faith, but I really only wanted to keep hearing Emma's voice.

"We must go because God has commanded it," she said.

I nodded quickly, feeling chided. I already knew all the reasons Jonathan had given. It was stupid to ask.

But then she went on: "God loves us too much to strand us here among the unbelievers. He has prepared a paradise for us – so great and beautiful that we will weep when we behold it."

We worked in silence for a few moments. Then I said, "This feels like Paradise to me."

226

She smiled at me. Our faces were inches from each other. I felt such relief at the kindness in her eyes, such overpowering love, that I kissed her.

The contact of our lips didn't affect our surroundings as they had that first night, but the simple, human warmth of it was just as heavenly.

She pulled away. "You mustn't," she said.

"Why?" I asked. This time the question wasn't offhand.

"If the Prophet isn't here, it's not a sacred act."

"Everything you do is sacred."

She said nothing, only shook her head.

I sighed, and we went back to our work, but I saw that her hands were shaking. I took one of them in mine. I held it to my face and looked into her eyes. Her pupils darted back and forth, looking everywhere but into my eyes.

"My love for you isn't a spell."

She finally met my eyes. Her hands stopped trembling. I leaned over and kissed her again. This time she didn't pull away. I pulled off her bonnet and let her golden hair free to shimmer in the sun.

Voices from the church. She jerked away, putting the bonnet back on. Determined, I pulled her up and away from there, leaving our onions to dry in the sun. I led her to the nearby river, hidden from view of the church by a copse. We dunked our hands into the cold water to wash away the dirt. I saw her shiver.

"I want to see you," I whispered. "All of you."

"Truly?" she replied. "You want to see me naked, of everything?"

"Yes."

She walked to a patch of soft grass and sat down. She took off her bonnet again, and took a deep breath with her eyes closed. I felt a bit like I had when Jonathan dunked me into the freezing baptismal. It was an awakening, and not a pleasant one. The sun seemed less warm, the afternoon's colors less vibrant. But when I looked at Emma I felt the same, and smiled.

She smiled back. She had small bags under her eyes. I went to her, and kissed them.

"We must hurry," she said. "The others won't be doing so well."

"They're free of it too?" I asked.

"Yes." She sighed again as I kissed her neck and began to unbutton her dress. "Goodness it feels nice to take a little break."

Under the dress I found a deep jagged scar running across her abdomen. I looked up at her, and she smiled sadly. "I can never have children," was her only explanation.

I kissed and licked it, cherishing the imperfection. "You're wrong," I said between kisses. I touched my belly, which was only barely beginning to swell. "This is your child too. It wouldn't have been made without you."

I moved lower and drank from her. She made little whimpering noises, her bare feet hugging my back. She tasted so very human. When she came, starlight in green and rose blinded me, and I could feel her pleasure in my own body. I cried out, and fell into her. She pulled me up next to her, and I gained my vision again.

"I'm sorry, I couldn't help it," she said. I noticed that her face was wet. She stared up at the canopy of trees and wept freely for a while. I held her – it was all I could do. I wished I had her gift just so I could comfort her.

Then she closed her eyes and took a few deep breaths. Her tears dried. The sun brightened. The world seemed warmer and kinder. But I already missed what we had shared.

"This was a great sin," she whispered.

"No," I said.

"I've forsaken the Grace God gave to me. I've been vain and selfish."

"No," I repeated, then – "When did God give you your...Grace?"

"When I was a child. I abused it at first, and would have lost it. But He gave me another chance by bringing Jonathan into my life."

Suddenly she jumped up and began grabbing her clothes. "I must repent for this."

Before I knew it she was gone, and I was left staring at her abandoned bonnet and missing the touch of her skin.

After that, things were different between us. She rarely spoke to me directly. Now and then I caught her looking at me, but when I met her gaze she looked away. I did not look away. Ever.

Like everyone else, I still took part in the visions, but I started to resent them. I would have given them up to be with her alone again, just once, back on the river bank.

I run up the stairs as fast as I can as Jonathan yells at me.

Inside is an open space, dimly lit by the sun's waning light through a big hole in the center of the ceiling. The others converge underneath the light in a huge mass. I know she must be among them, but I can't see her.

"Emma!" I shout.

The people give way before me, though I know it is not at my command.

She is naked and bleeding. She kneels, her hands and feet bound, on the filthy floor.

I have her in my arms before I have any awareness of running to her.

She is barely conscious. She can't hold up her head, but when I look into her face, her eyes meet mine and I know she sees me. A single tear leaks from her left eye. The blood is coming from her mouth, and between her legs. I want to scream to release my rage.

Instead I concentrate on the dirty rope that binds her.

"Knife! Who has a knife?" I shout after struggling futilely with the knots. Emma's head rolls on her shoulders and she gazes up at Brother Mitchell, who then puts a small knife in my hands.

It's awkward, but I saw her hands free. I am working on her feet when a loud slam resounds from behind us. The doors shut. Then a rattle of chains from outside.

The light already seems to have paled. It will be full dark soon.

As a child I was sometimes chained in a room for days. Strange men would come and go to use or beat me as they liked.

I thought I'd escaped that time. But now I am that girl again: small and trapped and afraid. Emma saved me from that life. And I came here to save her.

I focus on the rope. At last her legs are free, but she doesn't move them.

"You're hurt," I say. I take her face in my hands. The blue of her eyes barely shows in the light.

"I'm…fine," she rasps, then coughs. The bruises on her neck make a dark ring.

"I'll kill whoever hurt you," I say.

"You mustn't," she whispers. "They don't know what they do. I have to show them."

"That's crazy. They're animals – you can't save them."

"I can – I already have. See." She lifts her arm just enough to point to something behind me. I turn and see the girl in Emma's dress, staring at us solemnly. I had forgotten her.

"I have christened her…Naomi," Emma croaks. Despite how weak she is, excitement shines in her eyes.

"You've endangered all of us." My voice holds none of the anger I intended. "You've sabotaged our mission."

She shakes her head. "Jonathan is wrong. God's love is for everyone. God wants these people to know Him, too."

I look again at the filthy girl. She looks back with eyes filled with hate.

"I'll show you," Emma says. She grabs my arm with a surprisingly strong grip.

Uglyfatcunts, hisses in my head. *Fatnastyfuckerscocksuckingcunts.* I am looking at myself, in Emma's grip. But I am not myself, I am…Naomi. But Naomi is not my name. My only name is hunger, because that's all I have that is mine and no one else's, and it's been with me my entire life. I think about meat, because that's the best thing to think about. There is a lot of meat here, for me. I just have to take it. I…

Then I am back. Emma has released her grip on my arm.

"She's a monster," I gasp.

"No," Emma says. Her brow is wrinkled in the way I always loved, when she was trying to teach me something I just couldn't quite grasp. "You have to go deeper."

Before I can pull away — because the last thing I want is to enter that mind again — she has my arm once more.

I hear the horrible words and thoughts again, but they are softer this time. Over them is a thudding heartbeat, pounding as loudly as the drums we heard outside. Then it grows louder, until I can hear nothing else, and it explodes into a horrendous pain deep inside my chest, burning and yawning and terrible. The pain screams for something, but for what I don't know. It reaches a point that I can't take anymore. I want to tear at my breast to release it — and then it vanishes.

I fall on my knees, panting and pouring sweat. "What…what was that?"

"That is her need for love," Emma says. Her voice has recovered, or maybe she's speaking in my head. "Not so different from what I heard in you when we first met."

"It's too much. How do you stand it?"

"I can't stand it. That is why I have to fill it."

"But how? It's endless"

"I didn't think I could at first, but I've figured it out."

I turn to her. She is glowing, almost the way she did that night we were together. She looks so happy and righteous.

"What have you figured out?" I ask. An unease has risen in me, but I don't know why.

"The hunger is what is in the way — just like with your conversion. The first thing we did when you came to us is feed you. Feed the physical hunger first, then the spiritual hunger."

"I don't know what you mean, Emma," I say.

"Yes you do." She looks into my eyes. "I tried to save you, Evelyn. I didn't want to…bring you here. But you came anyway." Her eyes fill with tears, but she blinks them away.

"You can't do this, Emma. Please don't do this."

"I have to."

They stand around us, entranced. I've almost forgotten them. But Sister June now steps from the crowd and walks towards Naomi.

"No!" I scream. "How can you do this to her?"

"She is saved. She will receive the paradise she was promised."

I run to June and try to hold her back. She struggles with me violently, and finally elbows me in the chest, knocking the breath out of me. I let go.

Naomi actually looks a bit confused when June reaches her. Finally, Naomi lunges, as if June will try to get away. She doesn't. She falls to the ground, her eyes already closed. Naomi nuzzles into her neck. She could be kissing her, but then she pulls her head up sharply, tearing delicate flesh in her black teeth.

My stomach heaves and I bend over to vomit. Blood is already rushing along the floor towards my feet.

"Yes darling, that's it," Emma says, as if cooing to a child.

As I retch, the horrible sounds of Naomi's eating are drowned out by banging and scraping. The rest of our people are dismantling the church's pews and dragging them to the center of the room. They're doing what we've done every night for months: building a fire.

I try to calm myself and think. It's obvious, really, but I don't want to consider it. I accidentally look in Naomi's direction. June is in her lap, her head dangling at a grotesque angle. The blue dress is mostly red now.

Instead of letting myself vomit again, I pick up the closest thing at hand. Some sort of brass stand – it will do.

Emma watches Naomi eagerly. Her brow is still creased, and she is sweating. I don't love her one bit less.

The fire is lit. Everyone sits around it, as if it is any other night and the yams are about to be passed around.

The flames grow in the large pile of wood, lighting every corner of the room.

Then I see them and almost drop the brass stand.

There are dozens, at least, huddled around every edge of the room. I can see how I didn't notice them before: without a blue dress, they are nearly invisible in the shadows, all gray and filthy. But their eyes reflect the firelight, and their hunger is unmistakable.

The room seems to shrink as they all move forward, one step closer to the meal that awaits them around the fire.

"Emma!" I shriek. "Stop this now!"

"Yes, come out," she calls to the creatures. Their eyes dart from her to the others. She approaches one, a gaunt, naked man, and takes his hand. I can already see love growing in his eyes.

I want to say a prayer, but I don't know whom to pray to anymore. *Forgive me* is all I think as I bring the brass stand down upon Emma's golden head.

Chaos is immediate. My people are screaming and crying. Some are hyperventilating, others are running. Some have passed out.

The monsters wait no longer. They descend upon us with bared teeth, emitting a horrible screeching noise.

I swing wildly with the stand and manage to keep them off me. The others are not as successful. Already many are down. The feast has begun.

I finally am able to reach down and feel for Emma's pulse. It's weak, but there. I pull her to me, holding my weapon before me.

Brother Jameson jumps backwards away from a female and into the fire. Flames engulf him as he leaps back out of it and into his attacker's arms. They burn together, embracing. Then they fall upon another creature who is feasting upon Sister Anne.

I drag Emma towards the door. I swing at any creature that approaches, and they soon give me up for easier prey. There's plenty for everyone.

We reach the door. I kick at it, getting nothing but pain for my trouble.

It's beginning to get very hot. The fire has risen even higher, and more bodies are in flames. It smells like meat. One burning body I can't identify has landed against the wall, and a trail of fire moves from it steadily towards the ceiling.

I try pushing all my weight against the door. The chains allow a few inches of air.

"Jonathan!" I scream through the slot. I wedge my brass weapon through, trying to break the door with leverage, but then I feel a hand grasp at my neck. I yank the stand back out and it spears the midsection of the creature behind me.

I turn and shove the body from my weapon. My eyes dart around for another possible exit.

But then I hear a man's voice behind me, commanding: "Evelyn, get away from the door." Tears of relief fill my eyes. I fall to the side, pulling Emma with me, seconds before an axe blade bursts through the door where my head just was.

As he chops I gaze at the gruesome mess before me. The far side of the church is fully engulfed. Most of the noise now is either the roars of flames or wet chewing. I am crying but the heat dries my eyes before tears can fall.

Finally a chunk of the door flies into the room after a kick from Jonathan. There's just enough room for me to slide through and pull Emma after.

For over a minute I can only cough on the stairs in the night air.

"What happened in there?" Jonathan asks, but I can only shake my head and keep hacking. I don't think I'll ever be able to answer that question.

Emma wakes up screaming. "Why? Why?" she moans horribly. She writhes as if on fire.

Again, I cannot answer.

"We have to get away from here," Jonathan says. He throws Emma over his shoulder. She keeps screaming and wailing but doesn't struggle. "Can you walk?" he asks me.

I nod and let him take my hand. We return to where the carts were abandoned at the foot of the wall.

Jonathan lifts the tarp from an empty cart and hands us two bedrolls that surely belonged to people who are now being cremated in the church.

"Get in," he says. "We'll leave here in the morning. I'll keep watch."

We obey. I'm far from sleep, but I lie there next to Emma and gaze through the darkness, trying to make out her face. The smell of meat won't go away. It's in the air; on our clothes; in my nose. Emma won't stop weeping. Her shudders shake the entire cart, but I can't bring myself to comfort her.

Impossibly, I fall into a dreamless stupor. It is deep and perfect in its emptiness.

When I awake, light shines in pinpricks through the tarp above me, and Emma is gone.

Outside, Jonathan is loading his horse's saddle with supplies.

"You let her go," I say. He nods, and that is the last we ever speak of her.

It takes us most of the day to clear a narrow passage along the side of the rusted wall big enough for the horse. Jonathan chops at the rusted with his axe like he is hacking through briars.

Meanwhile I search for Brother Henry's body – I think I might find some peace if I can give at least one of them a proper burial. But he's either too deep inside the mangled wreck to be found, or he's been taken away.

Nothing disturbs our work. Just before the sun sets, we are finally able to coax the horse through the narrow pass and onto the ramp.

From the raised highway, in the red evening light, most of the city is visible. The church is an empty stone shell, but smoke still rises from it in an evil cloud. Beyond it, farther north, there is another fire glowing in the distance. A campfire – around which the newly faithful marvel at visions of God's majestic reward.

Sight for Sore Eyes

Aaron Kesher

hick mist made a dreamscape of the Obsidian City: slick half-formed trees thrusting upwards into a vague yellow sky. The temple flame was burning; the clouds flickered, heavy with sullen secrets. Out past the ancient break-wall, the black ocean rolled slowly, hugely, dissolving into a curved horizon.

Braesa stumbled and swore frantically, careening through the narrow, nighted streets. His mind was burning. "Too much," he thought. "Too much."

He paid no attention to where he was going. He saw the book in his mind, its hammered brass pages turning, turning, shining and seductive in the wash of candlelight. He grinned. He giggled. Urine ran down his leg, warm and wet, to soil his cotton hose. His shoes slapped and scraped on the cobblestones. "Braesa – you idiot!" he railed. "You shouldn't have read it!" But what other choice had there been? "Fool!" he yelled, but it didn't do any good.

He'd been lost before he even knew it.

The book had tormented him. He'd been on a special errand for one of the temple priests, in a section of the library where he wasn't usually allowed. He was only a clerk, a runner of errands, a transcriber of lesser scriptures. The book was almost buried in a niche. It caught his eye with a sudden metallic gleam. He stopped: reluctant, uncertain. He licked his lips and looked around. There was no one in sight. The silence was thick. Again he saw the gleam. Just five steps and he laid a hand on its cold cover.

He lifted it up. If he was caught here, he could be censured, even stripped of his clerkship. His wife would weep; his children look at him accusingly. He stroked the cover, tracing patterns on the blank metal plate. He wondered what was inside, why it was lying here covered by dusty, forgotten tomes.

Suddenly he heard footsteps, the jangle of keys. A priest was coming. Hastily he shoved the book back beneath the stack and wiped his hands on his tunic. As he stepped away, the priest turned the corner and saw him. Braesa noticed a white skullcap and the keys of a librarian.

The man called out in a stern voice, "Who are you? What is your business here?"

He stammered out his errand and presented the written order. The priest frowned, looked at him suspiciously. Braesa was sweating; his tunic was marked with dust. "This is not a good place to linger. Those with purpose had best move swiftly. Do you understand me?"

Braesa nodded, smoothed his thinning hair. The priest watched him as he left, but he felt as if it were the book that watched, peering from beneath its shining pages.

The book hadn't cared who he was or wasn't. It…called him, all night long, denying him rest. All day, ruining his work. He'd seen it once more, this time with no official sanction, but he was discovered before he could even touch it. He covered his face and ran, ignoring the commands to stop. His wife began to look at him strangely, but would only say that he'd been talking in his sleep. His children no longer wanted to sit on his lap and sometimes cried when he kissed them goodnight. 'Your lips are cold' was their excuse.

So he'd given in. Tonight after the last bells he had crept back inside. Softly gliding down little-known hallways, he'd crossed paths with a guard, battering the surprised man in the face with a club. Dragging the body into a side corridor, he forgot him and moved on.

The book was insistent. Its ancient whispering voice drifted down the cool stone corridors. Caressing its cold contours, he lifted it out into the flickering candlelight. With a sigh he pressed his lips to the cover. He opened it and began to read.

He read it all. It didn't take long. It was a slim volume, its message clear. But it had set his mind aflame, sent him running, clutching his head, a scream building all the way from the thick void behind his heart. He didn't dare release it until he was in the warren of backstreets behind the temple, where few would heed him.

Now his throat was raw. His whole body ached, and everything looked different. He knew so much more. The air smelled strange. His insides gurgled. He spat. It felt as if his ears were bleeding. Tears made cool tracks on his hot skin.

Ahead a light glowed, softening the fog. He limped towards it.

Lurching out of the alley Braesa found himself on a main street. There were people here, but they looked odd somehow. He stopped and stared. They were just normal people, albeit of the sort questing for coin or dubious pleasure at a late hour: prostitutes, drunks, city guardsmen. They looked like they always did, except…there was something else…

He stepped forward.

"Out of my way!" A black bulk reared above him, snorting, striking bright sparks from the stone. It was a man on horseback – an aristocrat by the cut of his cloak and the glitter of his mount's trappings.

Braesa fell flat against a wall.

"Do you make a practice of leaping out of alleys? I should have you whipped!" The man cantered around, shifting in the saddle to look closer. The dim light of the street splashed over him, and Braesa saw a neatly trimmed beard and dark eyes flashing, smelled the scents of horse and lingering jasmine, and something else…

"Answer me, fool!" said the man, sharp in his anger.

Something else…

Something fluttered. Something oozed, clicked into place. Unsheathed claws. Bone…

The man was different beneath his skin.

Braesa hissed, every muscle pulling tight. He leapt forward, thumping off the horse's chest, stumbling, regaining balance and running, running. "Wait!" the man commanded, wheeling his horse around. "Come back here!"

Crossing the street, Braesa ducked down another alley. He could hear the man thundering behind him, cursing furiously. "NoNoNo," he chanted, sucking in his breath, blasting it out through clenched teeth. "NoNoNo." He flew down the twisted byways, terror-quick. The sounds of pursuit grew faint, ghostly echoes ringing through the misted night.

Coming to a dead end he jumped and caught the top edge, sobbing and swearing at the splinters in his fingers as he scrambled over and fell heavily on the other side. Wiping the sweat from his face, unknowingly smearing blood, he listened, crouched against the wall, trembling. Nothing. No more pounding horse, no more screaming Thing atop it.

He released a long, stuttering breath and ran a hand through his plastered hair. Wincing absently, he pulled out some of the larger splinters with unsteady teeth. What had been wrong with the man? Why had he looked that way? Was it because of the book? The book had said…well, he couldn't really remember the words. There had been something inside the man, something that moved. It had leered at Braesa with hungry eyes from a bone-hard face. And claws, and something else, something…unstable. He fell to his knees and vomited in great wrenching heaves.

Leaning back, panting, he wiped his mouth. Unclear sounds wandered through the fog. He felt very alone, huddled in this dark corner. He was damp and sore, and had lost a shoe. "I don't understand," he muttered, licking his dry lips. He thought of his wife, his family. If he could only make it back home, he'd be safe. They could pack up and leave, maybe. He remembered his children crying as he kissed them. What if, the next time, something moved, something deep inside them, swimming towards the surface? What if he turned to his wife in the night and saw strangeness, hooked teeth, hot eyes, a dripping tongue? He almost laughed – he wasn't going to go back home, not at least until daylight, until he'd had time to think, to try and make some sense out of what the book had said.

Pushing painfully to his feet his joints cracked, his muscles protested. He wasn't used to this much running. Resting for a second, he listened again. Nothing. He glanced furtively around. No one. Satisfied, he moved, limping ahead between tall, black buildings.

He had gone only a few steps down the alleyway when a door opened in the wall on his left. Warm light spilled out into the night, washing over him, making him blink and jump back with a startled sound. A woman filled the glow, taking a step forward. "Oh!" she exclaimed, laughing. "I'm sorry if I startled you!"

By her dress she was an artisan's wife or daughter. But – there was something more… "Are you all right?" she asked, concern in her voice. "My goodness! You're bleeding! Can I help?"

Braesa could only stare. Beneath the woman's flesh something shifted. A gaunt dog-head, the wet shadow of scales, the rasp and scrape of lizard's legs. The forms swam and merged, tidal waters struggling against a single shore. A high keening ululated from his suddenly spastic mouth.

"What's wrong?"

She took another step. Braesa's emptied stomach lurched. He began to inch away, pressed up against the far wall in the dim end of the light. "Don't go," she said, a hand outstretched in concern.

Then something in his face gave him away. The woman tensed; her eyes narrowed, hand curled. The dog-head snarled. "What do you see?" she asked in a dangerous voice.

Braesa managed a sickly smile. "Too much," he said. He turned and ran.

"Wait!" she cried. Soon Braesa heard footsteps beating the cobblestones in pursuit. He heard doors pounded, voices raised in excitement. Torches flared in the gloom behind him. He had no idea where he was. All he knew was running, stumbling into walls, slipping and falling on the damp stones, scrambling back up and running again. The sounds of pursuit grew louder, disembodied voices floating through the fog, the drumming of footsteps, the weird flickering of muted light through the coiling mist.

This was the back of a building, however, and he couldn't climb. He tried, leaping frantically, but all he did was break fingernails. Nowhere to run. He turned, whining, and saw torches at the alley's entrance.

A wordless wail once again clawed its way out of his chest. Vague forms moved closer. He even heard the clatter of horseshoes, saw the light slide on a golden harness. His original pursuer had joined with the rest.

Closer they came, an unimaginable menagerie. Wings snapped the air, black tongues licked jagged teeth. Horns and claws gleamed, fluids dripped and circulated. Hooves tapped and scales scraped, tails thumped and writhed. They surged forward and surrounded him.

He screamed one last time, expecting death, but they only held him tight. He kept his eyelids clamped.

"Look," the woman said. "Look at me." He shook his head, snapping it from side to side.

"Open his eyes," said the horseman's deep voice. Fingers pried up his lids. His eyes rolled wildly, expectantly, glossy in the light.

"Why?" Braesa gasped. "Wha – what are you?"

"Legion," the woman calmly replied. Her scales rippled slowly as she pulled something from under her shawl. "I take it you read the book?"

Braesa nodded. The aristocrat spat an oath. The woman smiled grimly; the dog-head bared its teeth.

"Only a few copies are still extant. We didn't know there was one here. It is a troublesome thing." She shook her head; dog ears twitched. She moved forward.

Braesa struggled. Hysterical, he almost broke free, but was cuffed by a meaty fist (pincer). Dazed and defeated, he hung in his captors' grasp. "It will be all right," the woman said soothingly while the dog-head grinned. "Hold up his head."

Braesa was once again forced to look at her, much more closely this time. She held a simple mirror in her hands (paws). "Your new sight extends elsewhere. To truly understand, you must look more deeply." She raised the mirror. He saw only his own face, pale with fear, stained with blood.

Something else…

Scaling the Tower

Kristen Lee Knapp

wo hands throbbed against the tight skin of a drum, a slow beat pulsing through the den. Blue plumes of sweet smoke laughed from gaping mouths. Lights blinked from jostled brass lanterns hung on the cracked stone walls. A myriad of voices merged into an incessant oscillating tide of gibberish. The purple snake hung overhead, magenta-painted body writhing across the ceiling and walls, tail and jaw meeting over the arched stone doorway. Two red eye slits watched and its pink tongue lolled between bone white fangs.

Rykweh lay across piles of tasseled pillows, fingering the slim curved blade of a bone-handled knife. A sheen of cool sweat glowed over his earthen skin. His free fingers rubbed the coarse growth across his jaw and lip.

Cigleka's ringed fingers traced crisscrossing patterns of pale scar against the ridges of his back. "So many," she murmured. She brought the shisha's long nose to her lips and took a breath. A thousand bubbles thrashed in the water jar and she exhaled slowly, washing his shoulders with tendrils of smoke. She giggled, nuzzling closer, slipping her olive-skinned arm over his side.

He sliced her hand as it reached for the pouch at his waist. Cigleka cried out and recoiled, clutching it as a thin red line appeared across her knuckles. She whimpered coquettishly.

"He's late," said Rykweh, cleaning the knife against the cushion and leaving a jagged brown smear. He searched the crowd. A few Northerners, with long faces and skins pale as winter's first powder. Sailors baked brown from long toil on sun-drenched decks. Dark-skinned locals with hard eyes and faces like chiseled coal. Prostitutes, slim boys and buxom women, swimming the crowds like sharks.

"Are you waiting for your lover?" Cigleka's husky voice whispered in his ear. "Who is he?"

Rykweh heard the bitterness there and ignored it. He opened the leather throng around his neck, removed a few smoky leaves and chewed them.

"Tell me," she whined, dragging her vowels and pouting.

The clamor of the den faded as a bannerman walked in. Light glittered across his shirt of steel rings and a white silk frock painted with a red beetle was draped over his shoulders. A silver-buckled belt girded a longsword to his left hip. Blue eyes scanned the den under the lip of his imperious helmet. All eyes turned to him.

"Nice belt," said Rykweh, spitting.

"Who is that?" Cigleka's voice was incredulous.

"Excuse me," the bannerman said, raising a gauntleted hand. "Excuse me. I'm looking for Yazek. Has anyone seen Yazek?"

Rykweh grinned, grinding the sour leaves between his teeth.

The bannerman's eyes widened and he turned, abruptly leaving. Scattered laughs, taunts, and curses filled the absence. Conversations resumed slowly; the drum's pulse quickened.

"That's who you were waiting for, wasn't it?" she said, jewelry clinking as she stood. "But he knew you by a fake name."

"I don't give my real name to just anyone," he said.

Three raggedly dressed men slipped out, following the bannerman.

"Where are they going?" she said, large eyes following them.

"It was a nice belt." Rykweh spat the mangled blob of leaves from his mouth. "Kind of him to do my work for me."

"What *are* you talking about?" Cigleka shook her head and stood, reaching for her gauzy white shift. Rykweh hurled his dagger and the blade pinned the garment to the wooden post. Cigleka's face contorted into a scowl. "My pimp…"

Rykweh emptied a handful of copper, silver and gold bits from his purse: "…will be so proud of you."

Cigleka's eyes moistened. Her tongue flicked, tasting her lips. "You know I love you," she said, stretching like a cat down beside him.

He took his time with her, dragging his tongue across the faded bruises on her neck, down the smooth curve of her shoulders and the lengths of her arms. He stopped at the tiny scratch on her knuckles and pinched the skin until it bled again. He wrapped his lips around it and sucked it clean.

When he slid his index finger into the valley of her thighs he found her wet as a marsh. Her clawing, straining moans were genuine: she really did love him. The ludicrous fantasy of the idea made him feel momentarily guilty. He paused, taking the shisha in hand and sucking a deep breath.

"Oh," she moaned, impatient. "Oh, Fazeek."

Smoke and fumes from two million families conjured a green miasma above the city, hiding the moon and stars. Salt winds carried the putrid smell of low tide over the aged adobe huts and scrapwood shacks, enveloping the streets, ruffling dim flames burning in wrought iron braziers.

Rykweh followed the heavy, urgent imprint of the bannerman's boots in the sandy street. People passed him, families carting creaking wagons away from the market, cloaked travelers like himself. Someone was playing a qitara somewhere, dry fingers plucking an aimless, drifting melody.

He stopped, bending down. Scuffs in the sand: evidence of a struggle. He kicked around. A red slash of blood marred the dirt. Rykweh followed the trail, stepping briskly through shadowed pockets. He found two bodies in the street, each cloven by a heavy sword stroke. The trail of blood thickened. He followed it into a cramped alley between two taller adobe structures. Countless clotheslines were strung between them, hung with multitudes of sheets and garb.

A dismembered arm lay on the ground, fingers clasped tight around a silver-buckled belt. Rykweh stepped over it and knelt beside the bannerman.

"Hello Ngon," said Rykweh.

Ngon looked up. Sweat sluiced down his dark skin and his shoulders shook with short, sputtering breaths. A dagger stuck from his gut. "Yazek," he said, blood frothing from his lips.

Rykweh nodded. "I'm here to help."

"My…my master sent me," he said, moaning.

"I know," Rykweh said soothingly.

"I'm to say…*The scroll is within me,*" he said, moaning. "I don't know what it means. I…"

Ngon screamed.

Rykweh yanked the knife from his gut. He paused, looking at the blade. Iron, rusted, cord-wrapped hilt, notched edge. The weight was imbalanced, pommel a few grams too heavy, easily correctable. He glanced at the corpse which had once been attached to the dismembered arm, across the alley, and wondered where he'd come across it.

"I can't stand." Ngon reached up. "Please help."

Rykweh cut his throat with a single stroke. Ngon convulsed as blood pumped from his neck, oozing like a crushed tomato. He died quickly. Rykweh dragged off the bannerman's heavy hauberk and sawed his abdomen open. Blood flushed from the wound, soaking his hand as Rykweh reached through the gore, under the ribcage. His fingers clasped a strip of sealed parchment nestled in the heart cavity and he drew it out.

"Hey!" someone shouted. The dark shape of a watchman stood at the alley entry, sword in hand. "Don't move!"

Rykweh ran and leapt, planting the ball of his foot against one wall and springing to the other. His fingers caught the stone sill below a shuttered window and he pulled himself up, yanking his legs with him just as the watchmen's sword whisked by, sparking against the clay wall. Rykweh stood, jumped, caught a stone gutter and flipped over onto the roof. He took a quick breath and unrolled the scroll.

Rykweh,

Unfortunately this crude method is my only way of sending a letter in secret. I am forced to use my warriors as envelopes; I pray you were not harmed retrieving this. My power is failing. I do not know how long I can hold out. My enemy has become stronger. You have served me well, but should you accept this mission, I will not expect your success. Your target is the wizard Ciramus himself! Perhaps your steel will serve where my sorcery has failed.

Why should you risk yourself on such an errand when it is said Ciramus is as powerful as one thousand men? Because if you should meet success, the reward shall be your usual amount – one thousand times!

Ciramus resides in the White Tower. You must kill him tonight to save me, or it will be too late, and no one will remain to pay you your reward.

Yours in haste,

Ghaje, Wizard

P.S. If it is in my power to assist you in this endeavor, I shall.

Rykweh finished, sat and thought. Such an immense sum of money! Yet infiltrating the White Tower was said to be impossible. Northman warriors stalked the winged crenellations night and day like snow-tigers, and their claws were steel.

How many men are given such a chance?

The question appeared suddenly in his mind, washing in under a tide of doubt and terror. He folded the scroll and it ignited, disintegrating to a pile of ash. He sprang to his feet, running and leaping to the next roof, then the next, the next.

"Murderer!" a watchman shrieked somewhere, voice echoing against deaf walls.

Rykweh stalked through the nonsensical labyrinth of dilapidated slums, sickened by the smell of sour smoke and old feces. Dark shapes stood huddled around whimpering flames: cooking meat, dancing, singing ephemeral songs against the oppressive silence. Skinny boys wrestled and boxed in shadowed corridors. Older boys stood in semicircles in the street around sparring sessions, overseen by rigid-backed masters wearing circlets of gullfeathers. Naked teenagers wrangled, twisting wrists and elbows, kicking knees and ankles, learning to use the body's natural fulcrums and weak points in combat. Not so long ago, Rykweh was among them, learning his trade. The only trade.

He climbed up the rope ladder, quiet as a cat so as not to wake Azene in the shanty below his. He ducked under the doorway and into his room. A frayed wool rug blistered with dark stains covered the uneven floor. Flies senselessly orbited an overfull clay piss pot in the corner. A crude wooden idol stood atop a shelf, a dozen half-burnt candles arrayed around it. Three blades hung on the wall behind her. Pelzuk, a stabbing pugio he'd used to sever Chimek's spine. Gazija, a long-bladed stiletto that had pierced Rossert's heart. Piazz, an iron kukri which had severed Erk's hand. He took them all, lit the candles, bowed his head to the idol and left, leaping from his crude balcony and submerging into shadow.

Rykweh circled the pleasure district twice to think. He twice passed the arched entry of the Purple Snake, twice thinking of Cigleka, twice ignoring the thought. How could he infiltrate the Tower? He couldn't scale the outer wall. Even at early hours, guards would have to be both deaf and blind not to hear a grapple tossed onto the wall or to see him scaling it. And where would he find a rope long enough to reach over the moat?

He stopped mid-stride. *The moat!* The Tower's moat was not fed from any river nor from the nearby sea, but from the bowels of the Tower itself. One could infiltrate its defenses by swimming its own foul moat to the source. Yet some grim instinct made it painfully obvious to Rykweh that Ciramus would not place his trust in an intruder's sensitivity to cleanliness. What other dangers lurked in the moat?

The Tower rose out of the murky darkness, its circular stone wall emanating a lightless glow. Its surface was impossibly smooth, undoubtedly crafted by some wizard's inhuman tools. Rigid metallic shapes with pale faces marched atop the insurmountable whitewashed walls.

Rykweh scanned the tepid fecal soup of the moat, observing a rusty iron grate enclosed in a small culvert in the wall's base. A dozen questions came to mind. Was the grate rusted enough for him to pry loose? Perhaps a submerged gap? Would the sound draw attention? Was it too far to swim in a single breath? But one question repeatedly came to mind. *What was in the moat?*

Already he was taking unaccustomed risks.

He slid into the moat. The water was warmer than he'd expected and much thicker. His feet paddled and he waved his arms, yet he continued to sink, as though swallowed by the unending effluence. He fell, deeper, deeper, to his neck, his chin, his mouth…

His flailing foot touched bottom with his nose just above the surface. Not bottom. Rykweh knew at once that he stood upon a grimy ribcage. He tentatively prodded with his other foot, discovering more skeletons, then still more. A submerged bridge of human remains!

Rykweh stepped slowly, holding his breath as each pace jostled the bones beneath the surface, cracking ribs and skulls and femurs. He pulled himself over to the iron grate and hooked his arm around the bars. Feeling through the water, he found a gap large enough to swim through. He took a deep breath and plunged down, squeezing through.

Something very large thrashed somewhere in the water, rocketing near. A slimy shape bulled into him and jaws clamped around his gut, wrenching him as though weightless. Up, down, forward and back all lost meaning as he spun with the creature in the muck. Putrid water seeped into his nose, choking him. Countless tiny teeth ground deeper into him and long tentacles lashed his body like whips.

Rykweh slashed wildly with his stiletto, mauling the creature's gelatinous body. Its grip held, sinking deeper into him. A scream shook from his chest and his mouth opened, foul fluids flooding in. Berserk energy flared within him, like spirits poured over an open flame. He rammed the creature ceaselessly with his dagger until it finally shuddered, jaw slackening with release.

Rykweh swam blindly, the seconds lengthening, the dull thud of his heartbeat booming in his ears like a funeral gong as his last strength failed.

"You're awake now, yes?" said a woman's voice.

Rykweh shook himself from his daze and sat up on a stone floor. "What happened?" he said, voice hoarse as his sight began to return.

A pale-faced woman stood over him, silky white gown clinging to her voluptuous figure. Silver bracelets hung loose against the translucent flesh of her wrists. Her pale gold hair was bound in a jeweled knot and her eyes were like two chunks of ice chiseled from the blue face of a glacier.

Rykweh ripped his kukri from its snakeskin sheath. "Who are you?"

She propped a hand on her bare hip. "It's a good thing I knew you would accept the job, or that mokbeh would be sucking your bones clean right now." She pointed.

A fish the size of a cow lay near the edge of a bubbling river of brown filth. Its scaly body had been hacked open in multiple places and a long knife jutted from its left gill. Its cavernous mouth gaped and black eyes stared sightlessly at the wall. The memory of their battle made Rykweh's stomach twist. He ripped the stiletto from the mokbeh and sheathed it.

"I healed you as best as I could," she said. "However there is a limit to what I can do with such extensive injuries. I can cure them completely, later."

Rykweh looked at the puffy white tissue across his gut, an imprint of the mokbeh's jawline. Its tentacles had etched sinuous new scars onto his arms and legs, still inflamed. He spat on the beast.

"Ghaje must have sent you," he said. "My thanks."

"Dolt! *I am Ghaje!*"

Rykweh coughed. "Impossible! He's dark like me, and a man!"

She laughed. "What use does a wizard have for the human taboos of sex and color? Do you think I've never been a woman before? Or an owl, or an ant?"

Rykweh frowned. "Then you conjured this body?"

"Hmm? No! This is my new shell." She touched her chest, giggling. "Ciramus struck not an hour ago. He broke through my last defenses and slew my previous body. Fortunately, I escaped. I fled to the one place I knew he would not search: his very tower, in one of his own servants."

Rykweh stared at her, unable to connect her primped, dainty features to the ancient prune-faced Ghaje. "Who is she? Or who *was* she?"

"Her name is Isella. I told her of my plight and of Ciramus' normal use of virgin girls, and she agreed to my offer. Rather quickly." Her eyes shifted over to the wall, where an immense bronze demon's head was mounted. Endless black effluence belched from its horribly large grin, filling the moat below. "This is old," she said, approaching it. "An extinct people crafted it eons ago to defend their castles. They're rather effective, as you know."

Rykweh grunted, spitting again on the mokbeh. "Now what? How many guards are above?"

"None!"

Rykweh laughed savagely, invigorated. "Then this will be easy!"

"Ciramus does not need them," Isella said gravely.

Their footsteps scratched along the crystal steps like fingernails against glass. Tapestries of embroidered human faces rippled along the walls, hovering over white stones. The stairwell abruptly ended before a massive chamber. A smooth, polished marble floor emanated white light, reflecting the many burning torches with a flawless mirrored sheen. Three onyx statues stood sentinel in the center of the room.

One was the huge likeness of a savage warrior, blade in hand. His musculature resembled that of an ox, as did his fur-lined horned helmet. Sullen stone eyes stared forward from the rigid shape of his brutish brow and sunken cheeks.

Beside it stood another statue, taller and thinner, missing one arm. The remaining appendage clasped the swept hilt of a thin, curving blade. A long cape coiled from his small shoulders, the crest of a roaring wyvern carved into the stone.

On the far right stood the tallest statue, its lengthy shadow looming over the others. It was the likeness of an old man, large hands clasping the handle of a ludicrously large, rune-inscribed sword. Even though hewn from stone, the bearded face betrayed an aged sadness.

"Do not step into the room," said Isella, pressing a small hand against Rykweh's black chest. "Another step, and those statues will come to life!"

"What?" Rykweh rolled his eyes. "Statues are made of stone."

"You are in a *wizard's* lair," she said, eyes rolling. "Those are copies of three legendary warriors. Did you think we wouldn't be challenged?"

"Is there a way around?"

She shook her head.

"Then what choice do we have?" Rykweh palmed his daggers and strode into the room. He preferred any sort of foe to the wrangling mokbeh in that foul pit, and there was nothing fearful about statues. But why had his bowels suddenly turned to liquid? He stopped.

The three statues trembled, stone muscles fracturing and slipping to the ground, shattering in glasslike shards. The three figures emerged, climbing from their casts like insects from cocoons, bared steel in hand.

The horned savage roared like a bear and charged, hammering wildly with his polished iron sword. Rykweh jerked aside, gripped the barbarian's wrist and elbow, used his own momentum to flip him to the ground in an ignoble pile.

The old man cried in an ancient tongue and slashed, but the long blade was ponderously slow. Rykweh ducked and slashed at his hamstring. The kukri's serrated edge crunched against mail and the old man sunk to one knee, his leg dribbling blood.

One-arm confronted him, sliding lithely on long legs. His thin blade whistled as it struck, slicing, stabbing, cutting, seemingly everywhere at once. Rykweh

retreated on sandaled feet, barely able to parry the blows. Steel met iron with an ugly, wrenching shriek.

The old man shouted from behind. Rykweh spared no thought – only reacted – heaving his legs into the air and spinning aside, just before the rune sword swept below. One-arm did not dodge in time and the blade split his legs below the knee. He fell with a scream and evaporated in a swirl of dust.

Without pause the old man leveled his sword and thrust. Rykweh knocked the blade aside, but the cross followed through, bashing him in the temple and sending him sprawling. He scrambled backwards on his hands and feet like a crab as the old man's grey shadow loomed closer. Seizing his kukri, he hurled the blade. The long curved knife spun awkwardly and pierced the old man's chest. He fell with a deflated sigh.

Rykweh took a breath, dragged himself up. Across the room the barbarian stood with a grunt, raised his sword, and charged. Rykweh sidestepped again, but this time the savage was ready, turning his sword, cutting with a horizontal backhand. Rykweh drew his short pugio and caught the sword only centimeters from his flesh. The tremor of the impact numbed his arm.

The barbarian spun lithely on bare feet, thrusting. Rykweh hopped aside and slammed the knife into his wrist. Blood gushed and the muscle-corded hand dropped the sword.

A massive fist hammered Rykweh's face and the world went black. The ground flew up to smash him in the jaw and he felt the audible crack of a tooth snapping in his mouth. Endless blows plummeted against his skull, slowly turning his face to unrecognizable pulp.

A sword flashed. The barbarian's head vanished in a red geyser. His corpse slumped to its knees and toppled over. Isella looked at the old man's rune sword momentarily and then tossed it to the ground. She grabbed Rykweh's arm and pulled him up. "How did you learn to fight like that?"

"Necessity," he said, dizzily scooping kukri and stiletto from the ground. "If only I knew their names," he added, staring at the piles of dust and their forgotten weapons.

They walked on, up another crystal stair adorned with human artifacts, coming to an immense stone gateway shaped in the likeness of a serpent's mouth. Jagged fangs hung from the ceiling, mirrored below. Stone eyes stared down from above. Inside, a twisting stairwell spiraled upward. Isella didn't stop, simply walked past the fangs and began up the staircase inside. Rykweh stopped and stared up at the serpent's eyes, his thumb tapping the hardwood handle of his kukri.

"What's wrong?" she said, stopping. "Are you afraid?"

"No," he said.

"You were brave enough in the last room," Isella said absently.

"What happens when we reach the top?" he demanded.

"I know for a certainty we must pass a Virgin Door." She shrugged. "Beyond that, I do not know. Perhaps we can kill him, perhaps not."

"Perhaps?" Rykweh choked on the word.

She shrugged her pale shoulders. "Something will come to me or not. I don't recall dragging you along."

His fingers tightened around the handle of his weapon. "If we do succeed, you *can* pay, right?"

She looked at him. "When one learns the all the secrets of this world, creating gold is scarcely a challenge. Regardless of how large the pile."

Rykweh frowned, relaxing. "So what now?"

"We go up!"

"Too simple."

"Of course. Obviously this stairwell is enchanted in some way. I doubt walking up the steps will accomplish anything."

"So how can…"

"Quiet," she snapped. "All enchanted stairwells have solutions. They're large puzzles. I only have to figure it out. Let's go."

They began their ascent. Rykweh felt oddly disconcerted by the lack of flayed human skin on the wall. The architecture, he noted, was strange: it was difficult to discern individual stones or mortar in the bizarre, circular walls. Suddenly the ground seemed to shift and everything contracted, tightening. Isella stumbled and caught herself against the wall. She cried out, withdrawing her hands and staring at them. "Acidic," she mumbled, looking around. Her blue eyes went white. *"It's a real snake! Run!"*

They ran, Isella followed closely by Rykweh as the walls tightened around them like a clenching fist. Their sandals began to smoke, the edges of their garments sizzling when they touched the ground. A closing stone sphincter waited at the top of staircase. They leapt through just as it sealed shut.

Rykweh caught his breath and stood, brushing himself off. Isella groaned, sounding more irritated than injured. He helped pull her to her feet.

Two gargantuan doors of etched stone soared above them, their faces carved with spiral runes and geometric glyphs. A white sandstone saucer lay before them, splotched with dark red stains.

"Ciramus waits behind that door," she said, pointing.

Rykweh paused. "He knows we're coming?"

She smirked. "Rather difficult to sneak up on a wizard. Any wizard, for that matter." She undid the clasp behind her neck and her heavy breasts spilled free.

Rykweh blinked, breath catching in his lungs. "What are you *doing?*"

Isella gingerly stepped out of her gown. Pale firelight shimmered across her milky skin. "Only the blood of a virgin can open the Virgin Door."

"Do I…cut you?" Rykweh shuffled in place, pensive.

"Normally, that would work," she said. "Unfortunately, *my* blood also runs in these veins now. A tiny dabble of blood of a normal virgin girl would be enough to open this door, but I doubt Ciramus cares. He has no regard for human life, which isn't an altogether uncommon thing in old wizards. And he is the oldest. Over time, wizards have differing opinions of humans. At times we love or hate you. Most dangerously, we view you as livestock."

"I still don't understand." Rykweh shifted pensively on his feet.

She rolled her eyes. "There exists one bastion of pure blood left in this girl's body. Her maidenhood. You must break it."

"I refuse," he said, simply. A rift of silence split between them.

"I had not expected your reluctance," she murmured. "Very foolish"

"You said yourself wizards view humans as livestock," Rykweh said, pointing at her. "You're using her just like you used Ngon to send a message. Just like you're using me."

"Ah," she said, realization blooming in her eyes. "So it's some twisted notion of nobility." She shrugged. "Very well. She can tell you herself."

"Save your tricks," he growled.

Her eyes changed, and the difference was plain as the sunrise. The sharpness in her eyes blunted, the tenor of her lilting voice softened. "I am not weak, Rykweh."

"Is it…you?"

Her lips twitched. "I may be a fool," she said, "but I am no one's puppet. I agreed to the wizard's request when he showed me what Ciramus would do to me." Her voice faltered. "Ghaje showed me how strong Ciramus is becoming. He's *keeping* the souls of his victims. He's found some way to harness them like farm animals."

"Is that how you…I mean, Ghaje, was killed?"

She nodded. "I can't let that happen. All my life, I was bred for one thing. To be denied. You may come from poverty and misery, Rykweh, but there's no cruelty in this world to match the injustices I was dealt."

Rykweh opened his mouth and closed it.

"Wizards may treat us like animals," she said, tears throbbing down her flushed cheeks. "But *men* have treated me worse. I know enough to understand we'll probably die the moment that door opens, but I refuse to leave this world with a compliant smile. *I want to fuck*, because that was the thing I was to be denied forever."

Despite himself, Rykweh felt his skin simmer, felt the cool lick of sweat down his abdomen, iron-hard erection undeniably surging, pulling him toward her. His hands drifted from his blades towards her as though drawn by invisible wires. When his hands slipped over her thighs and touched her back, the cold of her flesh made him gasp, like he'd suddenly been thrown into a frozen lake.

Hot breath steamed from her lips as her cold fingers trickled down his back, urging him down on top of her. He took the pink dimples of her breasts in his mouth one at a time, gently grinding them between his teeth until her cries became desperate.

She cried out as he pressed the throbbing length of his cock inside her. He pumped his hips three times and they both climaxed, melting into one another. Blood dripped from Isella's thighs and onto the saucer.

The Virgin Door opened to the grind of sawing stones.

263

Ripples of nameless hue undulated from within, illuminating the walls of the chamber in an unending kaleidoscopic explosion. Bone chandeliers and candelabras held dribbling wax candles, all burning in ghoulish contrast. Gutted books lay open across the floor, disemboweled of their pages. Glass tubes and bottles filled with bubbling fluids of all colors stood in creaking wooden cabinets and iron stands.

A blackened iron pedestal rested in the center of the room, a white ball propped atop it. The pearlescent sphere shone with a soft inner light. A bright humanoid shape hovered beside it, white robes flowing like a frozen waterfall from its rigid shoulders. A jagged white icicle of beard hung from a jutting chin and emerald eyes burned madly from an ashen pale face.

Rykweh dragged the kukri from its sheath and charged. Ciramus turned, the weight of his eyes falling on him like a landslide of immense rocks. The kukri exploded in his hand, showering Rykweh's face with iron shards. He collapsed to the ground, thunderstruck with searing pain. Blood swirled from his face into his eyes and mouth.

"I never considered self-debasement a viable method of survival." Ciramus's voice creaked like the stretch of ancient wood. "Clever choice of host."

"Your tower's tricks were clever as well," Isella said, striding forward. "You won't find me so easy this time." Isella's eyes turned from blue to furnace red; her body shimmered like the air above hot coals.

"Fool!" Ciramus' face curled into a furious grimace. "You have delivered yourself unto the very crux of my power. You cannot harm me, no more than a mewling fawn can slay a lion." He began to shine, glowing tendrils of white light writhing from his body.

Bolts of black lightning sparked between them, wrangling spears and whips of energy coiling like snakes. Rykweh tried to open his eyes, but saw only blinding light through a syrupy, bloody film.

The light dispersed and the chamber was dark once more. Ciramus trumpeted with laughter. Isella wilted to the ground.

"I have killed tens of thousands," Ciramus said, dragging snaillike nails through his beard and laughing. "Millions of slaves bow before me! Kings tremble at the rumor of my presence! I am Ciramus, first child of Yagath. My memories are older than the stones of this world. I have heard the Creator's scratching madness as he scrawled the story of human existence on the scroll of time. You will not defeat me!"

One step, two steps…Rykweh stood – drew the stiletto – hurled it –

The wizard sidestepped the thrown knife easily. "I once believed it was bravery that made men challenge me. But I long ago learned the foolishness of such an idea. *Greed* forges your steel swords and stupidity brings you to wield them."

A horrendous, ear-splitting crack quaked through the chamber. The stiletto had missed Ciramus but pierced the sphere behind him. Cracks appeared in its glossy surface and it shattered, blasting a wave of pink smoke through the chamber.

Points of white radiance coalesced in the mist, hovering around Ciramus.

"Slaves!" he shrieked. "Return to your prison."

A voice spoke, one comprised of thousands. "No more," it said, and the lights converged, devouring Ciramus in a holy swathe of incandescent white. The stones of the tower shook, crumbling.

Rykweh tried to rise, then blacked out.

"Wake up already," said a voice. Someone pushed him.

Rykweh groaned, writing across a pile of soft cushions, knocking something over. "Hey!" the voice said. Familiar, somehow.

"What…" Rykweh touched his head, his face. "What happened?" His vision slowly returned. Dim lanterns. Indistinct dark shapes mingling, laughing, drinking. Mushrooms of sinuous grey smoke foaming from open mouths. A purple serpent with two red eyes.

"You fell asleep," Cigleka said, her eyes glossy with anger. "I've been trying to wake you for an hour." She irritably combed her lustrous black hair with her fingers. "Inhuman, the way you sleep."

"Asleep…" Rykweh shook his head. "Impossible." He touched his face, felt the memory of the pain as the shards of his kukri had ripped it open. But there were no wounds, no scars, no marks. He pulled open his silk vest. No scars from the mokbeh's jaws. "Isella. Ghaje. Ciramus." He clutched his head, cursing.

"The Wizards?" she said, chuckling. "Were you dreaming about them, Fazeek?"

"It wasn't a dream," he said. "And that isn't my name. My name is Rykweh. Rykweh."

She looked at him, then grinned. "And I'm Ghaje," she said, leaning in against him, pressing her plump lips to his neck.

Rykweh ground his teeth. A dream. The Tower, Ghaje, Ciramus. *Isella*. A dream. He exhaled slowly, eyes widening as he saw the two massive sacks behind Cigleka, filled with thousands of twinkling gold pieces.

Leprosaria

Andrew Knighton

 *eaving behind the bloodied remains of the Yorkshire Hill Witches, Sir Richard led us down into the valleys to a convent where he could seek healing for poor Adam. This place was a leprosarium, but Sir Richard feared not the devil's rot, for God himself looked over him…*

As the weary travellers approached St. Engelwald's they were greeted by the sound of distant singing: half a dozen cracked and broken voices trying to follow the soaring notes of their chorister within the monastery's walled grounds. Tobias slid from his horse, blisters bursting as his feet hit the dirt track. Fragments of Yorkshire flesh still clung to his toes.

"Next time we find a fight, can I keep my shoes on?" he said.

"We were in a graveyard," Sir Richard reminded him. "Would you sully holy ground with your filthy boots?"

Tobias thought back to the previous night, ash and embers dappling headstones slick with blood. He looked up at the knight adventurer, sitting calmly atop his noble steed, still sticky with sweat and gore but staring down with stern sincerity. Squire Adam lay unconscious still, slung across the mule's back with his head wrapped in a crimson-stained vestment.

"Of course not," said Tobias.

He turned and approached the oak doors with tender footsteps. A grimy brass gargoyle with a pox-ridden visage had been added sometime in the past fifteen years. He swung its bloated tongue with a series of loud thuds.

Echoes were returning from the valley when a sharp click announced the opening of a viewing hole.

"Yes?" lisped a pair of runny grey eyes.

"My name is Tobias of York, scribe and chronicler of the adventures of Sir Richard de Motley. My lord begs shelter and aid for our injured companion."

There was a second click, and a small wooden box appeared lower down the door.

"God aids those who aid his servants," said the eyes.

Tobias sighed and deposited two fake pennies looted from a Welsh bandit.

"Now can we come in?"

The door swung grudgingly open, revealing a hunched elder in weathered robes who beckoned them inside. The sound of bare feet slapping flagstones echoed back from the high roof and sandstone walls. The corridors were dark, lit mostly by grey morning light shining down through small arched windows below the eaves. Tobias could feel dust and debris beneath his feet.

Beyond the gatehouse lay an open quadrangle of packed brown dirt, enclosed on all sides by high walls encrusted with withered ivy. A narrow doorway led from there to the infirmary, a long cold hall with a wooden partition running down its length. On this side were a dozen closely packed pallets heaped with straw, heavily patched blankets, and the occasional patient. Richard gently laid Adam upon the nearest bed, then turned to face the holy brother waddling quickly up to meet them. The fellow was short and spherical, trailing an ill-fitting brown habit through the dirt. His protruding arms and wide grin created an air of child-like enthusiasm.

"What have we here?" he asked in a high-pitched squeal, ignoring introductions as he examined Adam. "No obvious boils, slightly pale, some difficulty breathing…tell me, how long has he been exhibiting symptoms?"

"About twelve hours," Richard replied.

"And when did it become clear that the problem was leprosy?" the monk continued.

"I don't think it did," Sir Richard said, face scrunched up as he scoured his memory.

"Then how did you know?"

"Know what?"

"About the leprosy?"

"What leprosy?"

"His leprosy."

"He doesn't have leprosy," Sir Richard exclaimed. "He's been hit on the head by a club. With spikes." He pointed to the improvised bandages swathing Adam's skull, which had become dislodged on the way in. Now blood seeped into the heaped straw on which the patient lay.

"Well, then it was very brave of you to come here," the monk said, beaming. "I appreciate the variety. Our regular patients offer me little practice at the surgical arts. Some cranial work will be wonderful."

Tobias studied Sir Richard. It was painful to watch the knight think. His face went slack as he looked slowly from Adam to the monk and then on to the other patients lying on their pallets. Just as his jaw began to slump open, something caused his eyes to narrow – the sign of a conclusion. He pulled Tobias to one side.

"You've been here before," the knight said. "Do you sense something odd?"

"Well, they weren't so specialised then," Tobias said, "but I'm sure they can help Adam, even if they have become a leprosarium."

"A lazar house?" Sir Richard asked nervously. There was a faint chink as he backed into the wall. Tobias could see a familiar expression beginning its journey of determination up from his jawline. Richard had only one response to worrying situations, and it couldn't help here. Tobias wracked his brain for a lever with which to move his master. A muscled hand was reaching down towards his trusty sword Nobility, and Tobias felt his gut lurch.

"See the monk, my lord," the scribe said, placing a calming hand on Sir Richard's shoulder. "Look, this man of God is in fine health, untouched by the taint amidst which he works. The Lord has blessed and protected him. Has God not guided and defended you also, throughout your quests?"

"Well, yes," Richard said, turning to his servant.

"Then He will protect you now," Tobias said, "for you are righteous and serve Him well."

"I do," Richard said, nodding earnestly.

Tobias saw muscles unclenching, fingers falling away from the weapon. Richard's head lifted to its 'inspired' look.

"God favours me," Richard declared. "I shall ask Him to aid Adam."

As the knight strode off towards the chapel at the end of the ward a cry rose from behind Tobias.

"I knew it!" the fat monk exclaimed, pointing at a boil on Adam's arse. "He is a leper!"

...Yet Sir Richard, eagle eyed and keen as the hound at chase, sensed something amiss, even in this most holy place...

With Sir Richard gone to the chapel and the portly physician off fetching surgical tools, Tobias took the opportunity to discretely slip back into his boots. The time had come to re-discover St. Engelwald's.

The patient next to Adam was happy to explain how the hospital worked. "The monks follow the Augustinian rule, and we are meant to as well. But as long as you give the nod to obedience, patience, and charity, they leave you be."

"You don't seem terribly sick," Tobias commented, noting the man's rosey face and round figure. The patient shifted uncomfortably, staring hard at his gnarly fingers.

"I may be getting better again," he murmured.

"How can you get better?" said Tobias. "It's leprosy."

"I get better all the time," the man replied with a shrug. "Then I get out to my wife again, and after a few weeks with her I feel the sickness returning. Brother Francis says my continuing presence is a divine mystery."

"Does he really?"

"But I am a leper!" There was a pleading look in the man's eyes now.

"Of course you are," Tobias replied with a grin. "The very model."

"I'm not," said a patient two beds down. He was pale and emaciated, with folds of pocked skin hanging from prominently protruding bones. Frenzied blue eyes stared out of dark, sunken sockets. "Five years I've been here. Came in with measles and a septic pinky," he continued, pointing to the gap where his left little finger had been, "but that waddling toad of a physician declared it leprosy and wouldn't let me leave. I can't sleep for worry I might catch the real thing here. Five years!" He batted a fly away with his twitching hand and sank back into bed.

The rest of the leprosarium bore a striking resemblance to the infirmary. Dark, dirty corridors inhabited by monks, pigeons, and occasional wandering patients, all of them clearly benefiting from the good health brought by regular bleeding and communion with God. They obediently kept quiet and charitably got out of Tobias's way. There were a further two dormitories for the monks, a storeroom with the distinctive sound of rats, and a small room of scroll-filled shelves that smelt of dust and urine – the latter smell possibly coming from the elderly monk who sat at a small desk amidst the parchments, carefully illustrating a manuscript with delicate illuminated letters and borders full of obscure and perhaps mythic animals. The dining hall was a clean room, otherwise much like the dormitories, but with heavy oak tables lined up its centre, crowded round with worn wooden stools. Tobias was pleased to find the letters 'A' and 'T' still crudely carved into the underside of one table.

"So this is the famed chronicler?"

Tobias jumped at the voice, bashing his head against the underside of the table. He emerged to see a tall figure in long dark robes, head shaven to a tonsure, frowning with authority behind a hooked nose.

"Arnulf?" Tobias exclaimed in surprise.

"Abbot Arnulf," the monk said, breaking into a grin. He strode forward and grasped Tobias's hand, pumping it warmly up and down. "It has been far too long."

"Surely an abbot should be…" Tobias let the sentence tail off.

"Older?" Arnulf asked. "Wiser? Uglier?"

"Not a petty trickster selling cracked earthen-ware pots as relics?"

Arnulf burst out laughing.

"Ah, the folly of youth," he said. "I have done penance for those sins, and many others we shared. Time has made me more devout, though I see that even the great Minster at York could not do the same for you. Come break bread with me, and you can tell of your travels. I hear you scribed a while at royal court…"

They spent a happy hour recalling old times and recounting new ones before Arnulf's duties called him to prayer. Tobias, feeling less devout, went for a walk in the countryside. As a novice he had learnt his letters in the abbey's echoing stone halls, but he had learnt far more in the wooded hills. Gossip and stories of adventure from local boys, the soft secrets of their sisters, the feel of the lash when he and Arnulf were caught shirking their duties. Here he learnt to test his own limits and those of the world, climbing trees, chasing rabbits, rolling in the bracken. He also learnt to dream of something more, and to work towards it, he and Arnulf scheming their escape to distant lands and lives of wonder.

St. Engelwald's did not draw visitors and their bulging purses like neighbouring St. Esther's, with its spring of hot healing water. At lunch, Arnulf had laughed off talk of the old rivalry, but an edge in his voice told Tobias that all was still not well between the two houses of God.

Esther's had long found fame and wealth through the miracles occurring there, but Engelwald's had its own resources. It had a great endowment of land, having been established under the aegis of Archbishop Lanfranc not long after St. Gregory's itself. A young lad could become lost wandering those hills, and that was how Tobias had discovered the crystal cave. Returning with Arnulf a second night he had watched with glee as his friend stared slack-jawed at the gleaming points that shone back the light of his small candle, hundreds of bright crystals embedded in the smooth grey walls.

Twenty years had passed, but Tobias was pleased to find that he could still slip between the boulders hiding the cavern mouth. As he squeezed through the gap he heard a noise ahead and instinctively slowed to a creep, thoughts of lighting a candle abandoned. Peering round into the main cavern he saw those same shining points, bright and fierce on the cavern walls, reflecting the light of torches held up by a half-dozen monks. A star had been marked out in chalk on the floor. Five of the brothers stood at its points holding burning brands aloft and chanting in Latin. A sixth knelt at the centre.

As Tobias watched, the central monk ran a long knife down the centre of his hand and let his blood dribble into a large brass bowl. Its trickling echoed through the cave, somehow louder than the rhythmic murmur of the torch-bearers.

Tobias backed away, down the passage and out into the light of dusk. His gaze ranged uneasily over trees and fields as he headed back to the abbey in search of Sir Richard.

Abbot Arnulf sat at a sturdy oak desk. In front of him, a brightly illuminated scroll lay open, ends weighed down by a heavy iron candlestick and an earthenware jug. He smiled at his guests as they entered.

"Sir Richard, I trust you have been provided with suitable accommodation?'" As he spoke the abbot sat back, twisting the large rings that decorated his left hand.

"The cells are most satisfactory, for which I offer thanks to the Almighty," the knight said gravely. "But there is another matter about which we must speak."

"Really?" said the abbot, smiling and rising from his seat. "Well, I am sure a dry tongue cannot aid you." He picked up three cups from a shelf and began filling them from the jug on the table. In doing so he turned his back, blocking the cups from view as he filled them. Below the glug of pouring Tobias heard the faintest of hisses.

"Please, take a seat," Arnulf said, gesturing them to a pair of stools. Tobias sat down and took the proffered cup, sniffing the rich, honeyed scent of mead. Tiny bubbles fringed the liquid, clinging to the cup's side. He held it to his lips without drinking, watching out of the corner of his eye as Sir Richard took a deep swig and licked his lips with satisfaction. The abbot smiled.

"What troubles you?" the priest asked. For a moment his gaze flicked to Tobias, before settling firmly on Richard.

"I have uncovered disturbing circumstances upon these sacred grounds," the knight declared. "Each one of your lepers is a charlatan, a common fraud scoffing at your benevolence as he suckles at the teat of mother church. Worse, your own brethren have been infiltrated by diabolists who commit their satanic rites on the abbey's holy ground. There is a dark canker at the heart of this place, Father Abbot, and I shall help you to root it...to root it... tooo rrrrr....."

The knight's head slumped forward and he let out a sleepy gurgle before tumbling to the floor.

"Perhaps we can talk properly now?" Tobias said, carefully setting aside his cup. Arnulf glanced down at the untouched mead.

"Was I that obvious with the drug?" he asked. "Then I suppose I shall have to resort to explanations. Come look at this."

Tobias walked over to the desk and stared down at a picture of the abbey grounds. A sprawling network of lines crisscrossed the land, wiggling across fields and woods. They centred on a large circle in the hill behind the abbey. Tobias leant closer, peering at the letters next to it.

"Esther's Womb," he made out, just before something collided painfully with the back of his head and the world went black.

...hidden beneath the monastery he discovered a den of Assassins and Wizards most foul, servants of Satan in league with the treacherous French. Though mightily outnumbered, he set about them with his trusty blade Nobility...

Sir Richard dreamed.

He lay broken upon the field of battle, foes strewn around him. Women came, angelic in their sweetness, robed in long grey gowns so elegant that the Holy Mary might have stitched their seams. They lifted him on high so that all might see.

From the crowd, a whisper was heard, "...hell is Arnulf thinking, he weighs a ton."

They bore him tenderly forth between high cliffs, and he could see the vault of heaven as it spanned the sky above. Then that too passed away, and there was the darkness of the Lord's sorrow. Every creature in the sky wept, and their tears washed his body clean.

"...never mind the river, we could practically drown him in the rain..." muttered a voice at his shoulder.

He swayed with the rhythm of his bearers, his mind drifting into the welcome of God's embrace. At last, the maidens paused before St. Peter, that Richard's soul might be judged.

"I need a breather," one of them declared gruffly.

And suddenly Richard felt himself falling endlessly down into a freezing darkness broken by burning red brands that closed in around him, the flames of hell circling ever closer. He felt Satan's minions draw nigh, clawing at his arms and legs. In desperation he lashed out, striking blindly with armoured fist and bare foot. He grabbed Nobility in his hand, the sword screeching in rage as he lashed out to beat back the flames.

"Run!" cried one of the imps, as they scattered back towards the pit.

With one last, desperate lunge Richard flung Nobility after the apparitions and collapsed into the grey morass of limbo.

Consciousness returned slowly to Tobias, though only black met his eyes. Had the monks blinded him? Waves of pain racked his skull, a souvenir of the blow that had knocked him senseless. Only a distant drumming sound suggested a world beyond this lightless patch of floor.

He tried to feel about him, but found his hands bound at the wrist with thick scratchy cord. Fortunately, years of misadventure had prepared him for such eventualities. Tobias reached down into his boot and grasped the pommel of a short, slim knife he kept sharp for just such occasions.

Liberated, he crawled forward until he felt the ground beneath his hands rise up to the coarse wall of a cave. Perhaps his sight remained to him, then. Using this surface for support he slowly pulled himself upright and made his way around the cave's perimeter in small, shuffling steps, wary lest the floor disappear from beneath his feet.

Rounding a corner he breathed a sigh of relief. A small, distant light flickered brightly at the end of a low tunnel. He had to stoop, sometimes scraping his back against the ceiling as it tightened, and soaked his leggings in an icy rivulet criss-crossing the tunnel's path in several locations.

After he crossed it a third time Tobias at last peered out into a larger cavern. The light shining so brightly through the all-consuming darkness revealed itself to be a small cluster of candles atop a barrel. After the long dark he took a moment to relish the very fact of sight. The distant drumming faded, and with a start he at last recognised its source: the beating of his own heart.

Straining the weary muscles of his neck, Sir Richard lifted his face from the stinking animal mud and looked straight into the eyes of a sheep. The beast stood a dozen feet away, staring accusingly at the fallen knight. He turned his head to survey his surroundings and another sheep caught his gaze, then another, and many more, all staring silently in the stark moonlight. There was a low, menacing bleat which echoed like a threat through his befuddled brain: *get off our field, stranger.*

With a long, sucking squelch he hauled himself up from the mud and lurched towards them. What sort of warrior could not best a mass of damp wool?

The flock parted at his approach, backing away, all staying beyond arms' reach, yet still staring. Eyes surrounded him now, boring into him from every direction. He turned swiftly, head spinning, and dashed at the nearest animals, armour clanking. They scattered before him and he flung his head back in laughter. But when he looked again they were back, encircling him in an ever-shrinking patch of cold, bare mud. He scrambled about in the clinging ooze, never taking his eyes off the throng as they pressed in all about him: clouds of icy breath rising in hungry snorts, teeth drawn back, mouths open wide. His heart was pounding; cold sweat ran down his shanks into the mud. *Always face your enemy – never let him catch you off guard*, recited Sir Richard silently. But the enemy was everywhere, closing in, murmuring plans to each other in soft bleats, grinding their teeth. He heard them behind him and spun to face them. But now the others were at his back, and he twisted round again, so close that their reek made him gag. Something nibbled at his jerkin. His fingers, clutching desperately, finally found the hard steel they sought. Caught between triumph and desperation, he drew his sword with a cry.

"Back, foul creatures!" He turned to menace each woolly villain in turn. "Away, hell-spawn, or I shall stain your fleeces red with blood!"

There was a distant rumble and icy wind blasted his face. Thick clouds drew across the moon. The field and everything in it faded first to grey shadows, then to black as the distant stars were consumed by darkness. He swung Nobility, trying to fend off foes he could no longer see. Thunder rolled over the valley, drowning out the soft fall of cloven hooves. As he turned again his foot slipped in a puddle and he fell to one knee, dizzy now and sightless, head spinning, mind reeling. As the first fat drops of rain pattered against his brow he felt something soft scratch his neck.

The monks' activities increasingly seemed more appropriate to a coven of wizards than a band of holy men, but whatever they were up to they had found a spectacular site for it. The candle Tobias had taken from the last cavern cast a flickering, erratic light down long, winding tunnels, their walls strangely smooth, rock hanging in streaks and folds like the hot wax running down his fingers. In places white layers hung across the way like petrified sheets, gouged and broken by the monks to create a path deep into the hillside. Rounding one corner he was faced with a wall that bristled with whisker-thin hooks and barbs formed from solid stone. No craftsman could have formed such a delicate array – but a hand had done its work here, for a swathe of protrusions had been swept away, leaving a dark stain of dried blood across their stumps.

Awed as Tobias was by nature's spectacle, he was yet more dumbfounded by what man had achieved. One cavern was filled with a myriad of coloured crystals, bright points of light dancing off the walls in such precise order that they formed pictures as his candle passed, images of strange beasts and foreign lands. Another was lined from floor to ceiling with shelves, crammed full of books and scrolls. The tight tunnels between showed signs of man's passage – soot-stains, boot-prints, torch brackets hammered into the walls – but it was not until the final cave that he saw the most intricate of their creations. Waddling duck-like from a low tunnel, back hunched, legs bandied, he emerged into a wide cavern filled from floor to ceiling with a scaffolding of timber and rope. It resembled the intricate web of a monstrous spider, bedecked not with dangling husks of flies but with gears and wheels, spindles and pulleys, linked in an intricately haphazard array across the entire cavern. At one end a stream flowed from the wall, turning a waterwheel which bucked and spun, passing its power to a rope, thence to a gear-shaft, and on into the hidden depths of the web, until that drive emerged as a rough metal blade gouging against the packed boulders of the cavern's far wall, sending a cascade of rubble and sparks into its shadowy corner.

Half a dozen monks prowled the machinery, muttering incantations beneath their breath. Tobias caught snippets of Latin and fragments of a foreign tongue that rolled with an eerie flow. Some of them were inspecting the gears, while others waved incense and daubed the beams with red-brown runes. The iron scent of blood mingled with the smells of sawdust and burning spice.

None of the robed figures were looking his way. Tobias snuffed his candle and slipped into the darkness beneath the construct. Steeling himself against the icy cold, he slipped into the icy subterranean river and waded across.

Tobias waded ashore at the far side of the cavern, not far from another tunnel mouth. This one was even narrower than that through which he had arrived, but he could feel a faint draft blowing from the entrance and hear the sound of distant thunder. He gazed into the pitch-black face of freedom, then up at the arcane works above his head. Arnulf stood at the pinnacle of the machine, watching the other monks, pointing and shouting above the growing rattle of gears.

Tobias saw the intensity of his old friend's expression and curiosity took control. Leaving his candle perched by the escape-route, he scrambled up the wooden frame, swinging swiftly to the uppermost beams, where he stopped, knife clutched in his hand like a protective talisman.

"Arnulf!" he called out.

The abbot turned to face him, as did the others, pausing in their weird work.

"Tobias!" Arnulf exclaimed, expression shifting quickly from surprise to unconvincing camaraderie. "I was hoping we could talk later."

"Much later, judging from where you hid me," Tobias said. "How about that explanation you promised, old friend? What is all this?"

"Isn't it obvious?" Arnulf replied. "We are alchemists, delving the mysteries of God's creation, and this place provides us with the perfect workshop. A sturdy monastery full of books and parchment; underground caverns filled with beauty and rare minerals. A place of seclusion that few dare approach, leaving us at peace to study. We have worked hard to be rid of any who might interfere. You remember Adam of Brook? He was so keen to remain that we had to invent a mission to Rome to get the old fool out from beneath our feet. No outsiders can know of our work – they would only ask ignorant questions and fetch meddling prelates down upon our heads."

"So that's why you knocked us out, to avoid our 'ignorant questions'?"

Arnulf nodded. "We could have talked it through, but there was not time. Tonight is important to us, the culmination of many years' work. You remember the hot pools at St. Esther's?"

Now it was Tobias's turn to nod. "We used to poach there."

"Remember the nobles and merchants who would visit, sitting in the shallows in hope of healing while their wealth piled up with the priests on the bank?"

"Didn't you snatch Lord Kettering's purse?" Tobias said, eyes narrowing.

"No, that was you," Arnulf replied. "But your action had a point. Such potential, frittered away by a band of elderly bumblers, using God's gifts for nothing more than pleasing the local landlords and paying for new beehives. Such a waste." He turned to look at the metal spike pounding away at the wall below. "But soon all that will end, ushering in a new era of power and grandeur in this valley."

Tobias followed his gaze. Heaps of jagged rubble and loose grit were piling up around the machine as it dug through the rock face. Robed figures scurried around it, dragging the debris away in rickety handcarts. Near the ceiling a trickle of water emerged, a thin dark stain growing beneath it.

"You're tunnelling under Esther's, aren't you?" he asked. "You're going to steal their water."

Arnulf beamed with pride. "Ah, Tobias, yours always was a wise head. Through that wall lies the spring from which the healing waters emerge, as divined by our ancient arts. Our digging mill will shortly break through, spilling the mystic power into our own tunnels. We shall gain a potent tool of holy healing."

"But why? Nobody here is actually sick."

"A fact for which I consider us blessed. But the water can serve other uses. Imagine hundreds, thousands of bottles, each filled to overflowing with this miraculous liquid. Like Christ with the loaves and fishes, we shall take something small and feed a multitude, our brothers carrying this water to every town and city in the kingdom. The lame shall walk, the blind shall see, lepers shall be whole and walk free across the land. The masses will pay well for their wonders and fill the coven's coffers, ensuring that our works continue until the very day of judgement."

Tobias stared for a moment, blinking as the words sank in.

"All this," he said, "the stolen convent, the so-called lepers, the arcane machinery, secret meetings and hidden works, not to mention the large bleeding lump on the back of my head – all this is so that you can steal and bottle spring water? I don't know who should feel more embarrassed – you for leading such a pox-ridden donkey of a scheme, or me for getting beaten up over it."

Arnulf's lips drew tight. A muscle twitched erratically at the corner of his eye.

"Do not mock what you cannot understand, scribe," he said grimly. "We are undertaking great works here, and magic does not come cheaply – lenses, crystals, parchments – you think the pittance we get from nurturing those buffoons upstairs pays for these things? It barely even provides their garlic enemas!" The abbot was almost spitting with rage now. "Each one of those scrolls in the hidden library was scribed by monks of a heretical order, on pages of spotless virgin vellum, risking life and limb in the Vatican's forbidden archives and smuggled out beneath the nose of the Pope himself. You think that kind of service comes cheap? This is not some petty cracked earth-pot con, it is vital sustenance for works of potency and genius. We paddle in the mud of commerce that we might rise to the stars of grandeur."

"How noble," quipped Tobias. "My head feels better already."

"Not for long," Arnulf snapped. Tobias heard something creak behind him and ducked as a stout plank passed through the space where his head had been. He rolled backwards, hacking with his knife at the ankle of his robed attacker, who howled and tumbled with a splash into the fast-flowing current below. Not pausing to look for the other monks, Tobias grabbed one of the supporting struts, slashed through the rope holding it in place, and pushed out towards the far wall.

He hoped the beam's slow descent would land him close to the tunnel mouth, but instead the wood slipped from its base, pushing back against the gears below, and the whole edifice began to buckle. The drill rose from its moorings, punching erratically across the cavern wall which gave way with a crash like thunder, spewing jagged stones and steaming water across the cave. Monks ran for cover as timber and rocks plummeted onto their heads, and as he hit the ground Tobias saw Arnulf plunging headlong into the path of the suddenly liberated waterwheel, his screams echoing around the cavern. The scribe grabbed his candle and scrabbled into the narrow tunnel as hot healing waters rose around his cold, tired feet.

…left and right he cut a bloody swathe, never resting though his arms ached and his legs trembled beneath him, until every heathen fell before his blade…

With one last heave Tobias dragged himself out of the steaming crevice and collapsed on cool, soothing grass. Overhead, white fluffy clouds drifted through bright blue skies. His eyes stung, but he felt his heart lifting in the pure light. He breathed the deep, fresh country air and stretched out each limb in turn, rejoicing in space. Peeling the last remnant of candle from a blistered hand he flung it away, watching it arch out over a drystone wall.

Something was amiss. A sharp, salt smell rode the breeze.

Tobias willed his aching muscles into action and staggered to the wall.

Gazing over those rocks was like staring into Hell's own abattoir. The grass was red with blood and littered with glistening crimson lumps. A dappling of white told of gore-sodden wool mingled in the morass. In the middle of this butchery, a blood-stained figure lay curled up in a ball, sword clutched close like an infant cradled to his chest, half a ewe draped over him for warmth.

Tobias approached the sleeper and tapped him on the arm.

Sir Richard's eyes fluttered open.

"W'appened?" he mumbled, taking his fingers from his mouth.

"Well done, my lord!" Tobias effused. "You have defeated the foul wizards who were corrupting this house of God. Look at the slaughter you unleashed upon them! Truly this is a victory that shall live in story and song."

"Wizards, eh?" the knight said groggily as they set off across the field. "Didn't I tell you something was wrong?"

With his work done, Sir Richard retrieved the good squire Adam and set out for Rippon. Such was his holiness that, where his blood had spilt, a healing spring rose up in that valley, which was known thereafter as Knight's Brook.

The Heist

Duncan Sandiland

nce I dreamt of wealth as the key to freedom. Little did I realize that vast riches meant trading the bronze shackles of poverty for the velvet cuffs of administration! Just this week I have had to fend off an efficiency review for the Elixir Thaumafacturey, a Revenue Committee appointment to the Privy Council, a shipping dispute arbitration request from the Trade Association, a blustery demand from Primarch Rainsford to revise his illegible, gaffe-ridden, apprentice-incinerating Manual of Arcane Procedures and Protocols, three tax collectors from two different countries, and a proposal of marriage.

Thus when Veslabag's letter arrived I gleefully seized the opportunity to take a quiet dinner with an old friend at my country estate. I had dismissed the staff early and activated all my magical wards to ensure an uninterrupted evening. As always, fowl and mutton were the chief courses. Clerics in the service of The Great Fovdat! observe a rigorous scheme of dietary restrictions, and over the years Veslabag and I must have shared a hundred variations on this theme. Yet there was never cause to complain, for Vez is a ceaselessly inventive chef.

In due course we retired to the study for brandy and dessert. The sideboard fairly groaned under a well-curated assortment of nuts, cheeses, sweet creams, pomegranates, chewing spices, and cordials of every description. I snapped my fingers and, with a barely audible *poof*, a merry blaze crackled up in the fireplace.

Veslabag stood by, examining my curios. "Ho, ho!" he cried, reaching for a coronet on the topmost shelf. "Where did you acquire this little prize?"

I poured out two flutes of Dorwinian brandy with a smile playing over my lips. "That trifle? Merely a souvenir of a certain enterprise in the City long ago." I handed him a glass.

"A souvenir!" he snorted, examining the coronet avidly. "The Great Fovdat!'s brass nose! A *souvenir*, you say. That's *mithril* inlay, and the emerald's at least five carats! Come now, Zin. How did you manage to add such a masterpiece to your collection?"

I now commanded his full attention, as I had hoped. Enjoying the moment, I settled myself into my overstuffed chair before elaborating. "Well, Vez," I said at last, "you have deduced the obvious: the coronet was obtained by somewhat unconventional means. It is, you might say, 'an ill-gotten gain.'"

"I thought as much," he muttered. "But from where?"

"As I said, it is a memento of a particularly exhilarating night on the town. It was before I met you – long before I was Lord Zin Fan'delle, Duke of Spavine – back in Faolan's pre-bard days, when he was just another sword-slinger.

"It had come to the attention of the Guildmaster – not Odo, of course; Ildor the Shrewd was master in those days – that a certain periapt of arcane potency had been secreted in a bank vault in the Silver Quarter. This was of interest for two reasons. First, the periapt had, until very recently, occupied a place of honor in the Guild's own collection – it was a relic of Leighber, an ancient and sainted Master Thief."

Veslabag puffed his cheeks appreciatively.

"The theft had been hushed up, and Ildor was anxious to see the periapt quietly returned, thus avoiding any awkward questions concerning Guildhouse security. Second, the banker had rejected Guild protection on multiple occasions, and Ildor.hoped to publicly demonstrate the consequences of defying the Thieves' Guild.

288

"So much for the reasons. Yet it is in the details that the majesty of the operation shines through."

"How so?" Veslabag asked.

"The bank took extraordinary precautions in its defense, so extraordinary that the chief banker had judged the customary Guild tax superfluous."

"For example?"

"Well, the safe-house was confined to a single story and had granite walls some ten feet thick."

Veslabag's mouth crinkled into a wintry smile. "Such a design is standard, and does not warrant your braggadocio. Moreover…"

I raised my palm to cut short his objections. "There is more. Much more. Indeed, the bank was most formidable. But I am getting ahead of myself. The location itself must first be considered."

"You mentioned the Silver Quarter?"

"Yes, on Putnam Square. The bank occupied a triple lot with no other structures directly adjacent."

Veslabag whistled. "A tony address!"

I nodded. "Just so. The neighborhood houses only folk of wealth and unimpeachable character. To falsify one's application for residence is a capital crime. Hence the populace is essentially incorruptible. Also, the Royal Constabulary maintains a barracks nearby, at the juncture of Bates' Dogleg. In the event of any disturbance, they would arrive in a flash.

"Now – to particulars. The aforementioned exterior walls were covered in six inches of quickstone, to protect the mortar and make any breach readily apparent. The perimeter had been cleared of all obstruction to a distance of fifteen feet and paved with massive flagstones. The floor inside was double-layered granite, putting tunneling out of the question.

"The only entrance was through the front door, a stout oaken portal formidable in itself and augmented by three complex locks. Beyond that was shut a iron portcullis, and to complicate matters further a vault-door of tempered steel served as the final barrier to entry."

"That does sound formidable," Veslabag admitted.

"Indeed. To negotiate the entire course would occupy even a Master Thief for an hour. Meanwhile, the grounds are well-lit and patrolled every ten minutes by vigilant watchmen.

"And no, the banker didn't employ the usual Slayer's Brotherhood bruisers. His guards were veterans, hardened men with many years of campaigning behind them. He selected them carefully, choosing only those few whose finances were already secure and worked mainly for pride and honor."

"So force was out of the question?"

I nodded. "You would have to hit them at once with poison or drugs. But such men have fought for years in the field which – as you know – often toughens the constitution. Such an approach had a high risk of failure."

"What of the vault?" Veslabag asked.

"Ah! The safe proper. Now *that* was a masterpiece. Half the dwarves and gnomes on this planet must have spent a year working on it. It was three feet thick, yet it spun on its hinges like a pirouetting ballerina. It had an intricate gearing system linked to two precision sandglasses in what the banker proudly called a 'timelock', the premise being that once the door was closed it couldn't be opened until the next morning. Quite an ingenious contraption, eh? To this date I haven't conceived a means to crack it – any force that could blast it open would destroy the contents as well."

Veslabag was perplexed. "But if you couldn't open it, how did you get the coronet?"

"What!" I cried, in mock umbrage. "You think I would stoop to using the door? Is my imagination so slight? I am wounded, my dear Vez, cut to the quick. For penance you will refill my glass."

Veslabag grinned as he picked up his own empty flute and strode to the sideboard. I waved a poker over to stoke the fire and arranged some chestnuts in a roasting pan.

"Apology accepted, noble cleric," I said as he handed me a fresh glass.

"Just so." He performed a stately bow, then plopped unceremoniously back into his chair. "And now, to cases. Tell me, how did you learn so much about this bank? And – more to the point – how did you secure the coronet?"

"Most of the information I just gave you was simple to obtain. Indeed, much of it came from the Guild's own dossier. But to learn certain details, a direct inspection seemed best. So I opened an account."

I had timed that just right: Vez spat his brandy. "You opened an account at a bank you were about to rob?" he gasped. "By The Great Fovdat!'s holy chickens, why?"

"Why not? No one was suspicious. I was known to be a full Guild Mage by then, and we are not reckoned poor folk. In conjunction with my deposit – two thousand golden royals, incidentally – the bank's principal, one Goodman Brinx, provided an exhaustive tour of the facilities.

"'The place is well nigh impregnable,' he boasted. 'I myself store a lifetime's earnings in this very vault.'

"I nodded agreeably. 'Your security measures are indeed most impressive. Still, one can never divine fate's intentions in advance. I'd like to take advantage of your insurance program and purchase a policy all the same.'

"'As you wish,' Brinx replied stiffly."

Veslabag's fish-faced expression was a slur of confusion. "You – what…" he managed to stammer.

I resisted the temptation to chortle, though it was a near thing. "Yes, dear friend. I actually purchased an insurance policy on my own account. Brinx offered full indemnity against theft at 2% of appraised value per annum. Given that the place hadn't suffered a loss in twenty years, this was a nice racket. As for me, I couldn't resist the chance to make another 2,000 royals in an insurance scam."

"I should have known," muttered Vez. "Anything you touch turns to gold, at least once it's out of sight. But I still can't see how you managed to break in."

"Ah, yes," I replied, cracking open a freshly roasted chestnut. "Well, the walls were too thick, the doors were too stout, and the floor impenetrable. Which left..." I cracked another nut and passed it to him while he thought.

"The roof!" exclaimed Veslabag in triumph. "But it too must have been well-guarded."

"Certainly. It had steel-reinforced solid stone rafters canted upward at fifteen degrees. The roof proper was overlaid in quickstone set with shards of glass and sharpened steel. Several rows of wickedly barbed steel spikes lined the edges so that ladders would be useless."

Veslabag was dubious. "Not necessarily. One might still leap across from a high rung and thereby gain the roof."

I dismissed his hypothesis with a debonair gesture. "Not so! Should he somehow reach the roof's center intact, the intruder would be in plain view of the frequent watch patrols. The arrangement was quite sufficient to deter even a Master."

"Which you were certainly not."

"Of course not," I replied, slightly annoyed. "I was good, but not that good. Yet you forget my other talents." I snapped my fingers. Acrid orange and purple smoke popped noisily out of the chestnut Veslabag was raising to his face. His sudden acrobatic leap might have been graceful but for the settee, which impeded his progress painfully. As Vez staggered to his feet my homunculus brought him a towel and put the furniture to rights.

292

Veslabag seated himself once more, daubing his chin, and spoke in an irritable tone. "I seem to have slighted your magic, or such is your implication."

I smiled graciously. "It is a common error. The banker made it also. Oh, to be sure, he took certain precautions, which he made a point of boasting about during the tour: Alarms that pealed should the doors be opened by spell; walls proof against scrying. He even installed anti-magical booby traps. Yet from certain casual phrases in his discourse I deduced that these protections did not extend to the vault's interior, so as not to corrode mystic metals or interfere with the auras of enchanted goods sequestered therein.

"Armed with that knowledge, I went shopping. After much wrangling, I prevailed on Shadowwolf to sell me a scroll of wall-passing, though I had to pay triple the going rate. I also had to solemnly promise that the spell would be used only to expand my repertoire, or in any case for nothing that might be construed in any way as nefarious. He relented only after a full afternoon's argument that left me altogether exhausted. In all candor, haggling with the Wolf may have been the hardest part of this whole affair."

Veslabag snorted. "That I can well believe."

I smiled and sipped the brandy, savoring its silky fire. "Next I visited the tent of Ondorio, a dealer in curios and adjuncts. There I bought a wand of metal and mineral detection I had tested and found genuine. From another vendor I purchased a large sheet of first-class oliphaunt hide. I also fetched a potion I had put aside for just such an occasion. Then I sought out Faolan and explained my plan."

"What of the split?" Veslabag asked.

I made an easy gesture. "Negotiations were exacting, of course, but Faolan proved a worthy cohort. He had been my student, you may remember, and we remained on good terms. More important, I had no doubts with respect to his loyalty and competence; and he could be counted on to follow my plan to the letter.

"We undertook the operation the first night of the new moon: Rogues' Frolic, as they used to call it."

Veslabag nodded. "A good choice. The watch is always overburdened."

"That was our thinking also."

"Still – only the two of you? What if you were spotted?"

"Ah! But you are right, my friend. I have neglected a vital detail. We did post a lookout: Oswald."

Veslabag guffawed appreciatively. "How apropos – a weasel to aid two skunks!"

"Now see here…"

He cut off my protest. "No need for all that. I withdraw the remark – I meant no offense to good old Oswald." I pursed my lips. Somewhere in his phrasing lurked a discourtesy. But he went on, in a pedantic tone, before I could tease it out. "*After all, it is well-known that familiars make the best lookouts And no familiar surpasses the weasel – his sense of smell is invaluable in conditions of darkness.*"

I did my best not to grin – the imitation was spot-on. How many times had I repeated this very claim? Striving to look solemn, I fetched the decanter from the sideboard and refilled our glasses. "I seem to have lost the thread."

"The new moon…"

"Ah, yes. Well, as we had hoped, the night was very dark when we arrived on Putnam Square. But we took further precautions. Did I mention the potion?" Vez nodded.

"Here was the moment for its use. We each took a draught and at once vanished from ordinary sight. We were invisible. After the watch was past us, we approached the rear of the building adjacent to the vault. I climbed on to Faolan's shoulders, took the hide from my bag, unrolled it and doubled it over. I now had a quilt of thick impermeable material, suitable for use as a protective mat. I tossed it onto the roof where it hung draped atop the spikes. Cautiously I pulled myself up. Faolan joined me presently, and we were perched directly over the vault. It was time to use the spell. I reached into my pouch…"

"And you drop the scroll – it rolls down the roof and wedges in a gutter! And look: here comes the watch! You will have to fight it out!"

"Not so!" I growled. "Events went very differently. Also, you have interrupted me at a crucial juncture. Do you lack all feeling for drama?"

"By no means. I was simply overcome by a spasm of ambient pathos. Please continue."

I did my best to control my irritation. Veslabag's conduct was not, after all, atypical. Every cleric of The Great Fovdat! had a duty to be irksome, and Veslabag was reliably orthodox.

Thus, when I spoke once more, my tone was mild. "I will have you know that bypassing walls is not accomplished with a simple cantrip. The flux is tricksy and easily fuddled." Veslabag cocked an eyebrow. "But in this case it went off without a hitch. There, beyond the portal's dazzle, the vault lay exposed. We secured a rope and scrambled down. We were in!

"But we had to work quickly. The portal would last a short while only. Faolan began at once to ransack the premises, while I set about concealing the portal in a web of illusion, so that it should appear intact to anyone who happened by. Unfortunately, the illusion required my constant attention, and Faolan had to do his looting without my guidance.

"Which he managed quite well. With the help of the wand, anyway. It pointed out the choicest stuff straightaway: strongboxes full of gold and platinum coins; individual gemstones wrapped in cheesecloth; and a handful of valuable oddities, including that coronet which caught your fancy.

"By the way, where is the coronet at present?"

"Here," said Veslabag, placing it on the side table. "It seems to have become tangled in my sleeve."

I smiled magnanimously. "A small mishap. You must be more careful."

He nodded sagely. "Just as you say. But again we run off track. What else did you find? More gold? Miscellaneous magic?" He licked his lips and leaned forward in his chair, his expression disconcertingly avid.

I shook my head. "No such luck. Mostly, there were papers. Boxes of papers. Wooden crates by the dozens, documents stacked neatly within. Faolan examined some at random by lamplight, in order to sort the wheat from the chaff, but got nowhere. There were far too many. Presently, he took to dumping whatever came into his hands into our sacks. The boxes he piled in the center of the vault.

"We'd been there perhaps half an hour before Faolan noticed the sweat pouring down my face. I was nearly spent. He hadn't realized what effort it took to keep an intricate spell going longer than ten or fifteen minutes.

"Did you apprise him of that detail in advance?" Veslabag inquired.

"It may have slipped my mind," I admitted.

"Then you are lucky he noticed."

"That's true."

"So what happened next?"

"Once he realized my distress – I could not speak without breaking the spell, you understand – Faolan acted expeditiously. First, he soaked the boxes and whatever papers were handy in whale oil. Then he loaded his packs with coins, gems, and jewelry. One bulging sack of documents he looped across my torso. The balance – what he could carry at any rate – he gathered below the rope. He nodded at me.

"Here was the weakest link in my plan. After such sorcerous effort it would take me some time to gather my senses. Meanwhile, the illusion was gone. If someone looked up during the interval, they would surely notice the shimmering portal. I had to rely on Oswald; he was our final line of defense.

"A moment later a voice tickled in a corner of my mind: *Clear!* Oswald's signal! I broke the spell and collapsed to the ground, sucking air. There were only a few minutes before the watchmen came back around to a view of our side. I forced myself to start moving, laying out a slow fuse leading from the oil-soaked pile to the lamp Faolan had used. Meanwhile, Faolan ferried our loot onto the roof.

"I lit the fuse and clambered up into the night air. Faolan was perched close by on the mat. We watched the fuse race towards the pile, its flame reflecting weirdly along the shimmering flux of the portal. Then, with a roar and an orange flash, the fire ignited the pile. Its sudden flare would surely alert the watch…"

I paused. Veslabag was poised on the edge of his seat, staring at me, wonderstruck. "Yes?" he cried. "Yes?"

"Well, then it was all over. Or nearly so. To cancel such a spell takes less than an instant. With the portal closed, the fire was for the moment concealed. The air in the vault would fuel a merry blaze, the scorched walls providing an indelible reminder to all of the folly of crossing the Thieves' Guild. We shouldered our loot, jumped down, rolled up the hide, and took to our heels. No one saw us."

"And that is the whole story?"

"Save for an epilogue. Shortly thereafter, the Lord Mayor resigned without explanation. His successor was a sea prince with much closer ties to the Guild. Further scandal struck just a week later: the suicide of His Lord Justice the Count Taraskhan, Impaler of Thieves."

Veslabag nodded. "Why do I suspect there's a connection?"

"Because you know me too well," I replied. "It seems that our greatly esteemed former Lord Mayor, who was so unyielding in matters of tariff enforcement, had been engaged for some years in the, *ahem*, clandestine import business."

"You mean he was…"

"A smuggler, yes. Perhaps the most successful of the modern era. As for the good Count, he seems to have been dissatisfied with his domestic arrangements, since he maintained several exotic mistresses whose combined fees were truly astronomical. To keep them he borrowed recklessly and fell hopelessly in debt. Certain of these loans were tendered by – shall we say – the wrong sort of people. Had the matter gone public, the family name would have been badly soiled. Apparently, he valued his family's honor above his own life."

"As I recall," Veslabag mused, "that was about when the Thieves' Guild's fortunes began their remarkable turnabout. And after so many years of decline."

"Vez, you are indeed perspicacious. From the perspective of the Guild, the contents of Goodman Brinx's vault were of a value that exceeds easy calculation. At the risk of melodrama, one might even say it was the difference between flourishing and extinction."

"The Great Fovdat!'s creed does not admit the concept of extinction. The essence of all things is preserved perpetually in the moisture of His Liver."

I poured the last of the brandy. Through the window, I saw the first timid hints of sunlight brighten the darkness of the lake. It had been a long night. I picked up the coronet and examined it anew. It glittered in the sunshine.

I said: "I know better than to argue doctrine with you, my friend. But it is safe to say that the operation was greatly to my benefit. I recovered my insurance claim, along with my share of the loot, including this bauble. The guild was so grateful that they even waived their customary tax. That's where I got the capital to found the Thaumafacturey. Furthermore, Faolan was inducted into the Guild on the spot, without the customary tests – a rare event, I can assure you."

"They should have been even more generous in your case – it was your plan."

"As indeed they were! I was granted a most precious sinecure: the status of Independent Operator. Ever since, I have been my own man. I answer to the Guildmaster alone. In fact, Lord Ildor paid me the highest compliment possible. He personally inscribed an account of my adventure in the Book of Legends, the Guild's history of perfect operations. The full details can be found under the title..."

I paused, smiling broadly. Veslabag cringed. "You set me up for this."

"...the Brinx Job."

Owasa

A. H. Jennings

wo old Surinamese women walking hand in hand bumped my elbow as I stared across the tarmac at the airport terminal. Several more figures drifted past me toward the terminal's open doors, silhouettes surrounded by buttery light.

I had never considered this place home, but here it was, open-armed, and I felt strangely comfortable in the vast and teeming night.

Was this the dry season or the rainy season? There was little difference between them – well, I suppose it rained just a bit more during the wet season.

Inside, Dutch businessmen and tired, well-heeled Surinamese milled around the airport's single working baggage carousel. Large black beetles dotted the terminal's linoleum floor like buttons fallen from a leather couch. There was no air conditioning.

I stayed to the back of the crowd, watching the belt for my own luggage. I checked my watch. Grove and Joyce were late.

The conveyor belt ground to a halt and an airline rep explained to me in the lazy, smoothed-over rhythm of Surinamese Dutch that my bags had never made it onto the plane in Miami. I was too tired to care overmuch.

Grove Van Meer appeared at the far end of the terminal. He was not what I had expected. Joyce liked tall, bespectacled boys with long graceless limbs, but Grove was square-built, with thinning brown hair and skin the color of dirty soap.

He asked my name, then introduced himself, and neither of us said much as he led me outside to a chocolate brown Land Cruiser. I paused, surprised, when I saw Joyce sitting in the front passenger seat. She was a small but heavy-set woman, her honey-blond hair streaked with strands of gray. She looked as if she'd been ill for a long time.

"Hey, love," I said as she rolled the window down and leaned out for a chaste kiss. "What kept you?"

"It's my fault, really," Joyce said softly as I climbed into the backseat. "I just couldn't find – I couldn't – *ha!* Welcome home."

Grove pushed the truck past sixty on the road to town. Most of this stretch had been paved sometime during my absence. Grove stared straight ahead, hunched over the wheel, and his manner would have set me on edge if I hadn't recognized the reason for it.

Every so often, the splash of headlights would reveal dark-skinned women walking in twos and threes beside the road. I could almost smell them as they moved from party to party in the dilapidated houses that dotted the roadside – the dark sweat of their dancing, the cardamom and curry powder caked beneath their fingernails. They reminded me of my mother.

"How's – ?" Joyce croaked, then made a noise to clear her throat. "How's Christiaan, then?"

"Christiaan is our son's name," Grove said gently. "He's away at university."

Joyce twisted round to look at me over the back of her seat. "Right," she said. "Christiaan went to ACS, just like you. I didn't mean him, I meant your brother. What's his name?"

"Theo," I said. "I don't know how he is. That's why I've come back."

The Torarica sat near the center of Paramaribo, glowering across the Suriname River. Theo and I used to ride our bikes by it every day on our way to and from school. The hotel had always looked to me like a great squatting time machine sent forward from the seventies.

My fourth-floor suite offered a balcony view of the river, and after checking in I stood out there a long time, watching colored lights move between the trees that lined the river's far bank. I tried not to think about the Interior. I tried not to think about Theo.

Theo had loved ACS. The religious instruction gave him a sense of purpose, and he seemed comforted by the notion of an invisible Father watching over him, protecting him from the horrors of the fallen world.

Personally, I hated ACS. Religion had never meant much to me: If God was all-loving and all-good, why had He allowed our father to die and forced our mother to marry a man I hated?

Despite our differences, Theo and I were always close. I led him into trouble and he tried to save me. I remember the rhythmic motion of his skinny legs as he pumped the pedals of his bright orange ten-speed. I remember the sound of his voice strained over a piss-poor telephone connection the night he called to tell me he'd been hired to work at the Summer Institute.

His words tumbled fast over the line, sliced lengthwise by his breathing. His excitement sounded a little like panic.

I blinked and sat up, wincing at the pain in my back and shoulders. I'd fallen asleep on the long canvass chair out here on the balcony, and now the sun beat down on me. My clothes were soaked with sweat, and for a moment I thought I'd wet myself.

Another knock at the suite's front door. I scowled, and headed inside, moving like an old man.

The bellhop was a tubby Hindustani whose uniform looked at least one size too small. "What is it?" I said in English, rubbing the sleep from my eyes.

"Mr. Ghiazi?" he chirped.

I shook my head.

"This is 414?"

"Yeah. It's –"

"Your luggage, sir." He stepped gracefully aside to gesture at a set of brown leather traveling bags.

"Ghiazi's not my name," I said.

"The airline call this morning, sir," he said. "Say your luggage here for you." He paused, watching me expectantly.

They looked like my bags.

I shrugged and stepped aside as he carried them into my room. He set them at the foot of the unused bed and turned to stare at me like a clockwork bird.

I reached into my pocket and withdrew a roll of guilder bills. I peeled off a fifty and handed it to the bellhop, who dipped his head in mute thanks.

It was only after he had gone that I realized I could have conducted the entire exchange in Dutch or Taki Taki for a better idea of what was going on.

304

A short examination of the bags left me certain that they belonged to someone else. Opening the largest of them let a breath of stale flowers into the room. I gagged a little, scowling as I pulled out a black guayabera.

The shirt looked like it would fit me, but I'd never seen it before. Where were my photographs? My maps?

Angry, and not a little unsettled, I resolved to address this matter at the front desk, but I knew I'd need a shower first.

I ducked into the bathroom, choked back a scream, and came out again, walking backwards, to fall into an imposing leather chair.

I put my head between my knees and clenched my teeth until my jaw hurt to keep from throwing up.

After a moment, I sat up and ran a hand through my tightly curled hair as I stared at the blank television screen. I wondered absently whether they had more than two stations these days.

Moving deliberately, I stood and crossed to the bathroom for another look into the basin.

Someone had piled it full of hotel ice. Two eyes, an unidentifiable organ, and a Negroid left hand sat there, carefully arranged as if for sale at a butcher shop. A thin layer of blood sat at the bottom of the basin – about as much as you'd find opening a chicken from a supermarket back in the States.

The hand was large and well-formed, with long strong fingers. It was the hand of an artist or a musician.

Idly, I thought to pick it up and check the fingertips for calluses. A wave of revulsion stopped me, and I went back to staring at it all.

What was that thing? A liver? What does a liver look like uncooked? Both of the eyes were a clear and startling blue.

It was not an easy thing, but I pulled my gaze from the basin to the mirror. I didn't look as bad as I thought.

Without thinking, I turned on my heel, left the suite, and headed downstairs to call a taxi.

The taxi dropped me outside a Mediterranean-style villa surrounded by a walled-in yard. Honeysuckle and bougainvillea branches spilled over the wall to hang down as if reaching for something on the cracked sidewalk.

From here, I could see the American School about a hundred yards away — its too-small but expertly manicured soccer field.

As usual, the afternoon air was swollen with moisture. I felt as if I stood at the bottom of a steaming sea. The smells of tropical vegetation and tobacco smoke sent me hunting for my cigarettes. My hand dipped into the front pocket of my batik shirt before I realized I did not smoke. I never had.

I looked up at the sound of tires churning gravel.

A beat-up white Daewoo sedan shot from the school's unpaved parking lot and fishtailed on the street.

The car raced past me to stop at the corner with a squeal of rubber on pavement. From my vantage point, I could see the driver — a small but heavy-set woman with honey-blond hair — stab the air with her finger as she shouted at the empty passenger seat.

My stomach clenched. Joyce?

It could have been anyone. All I knew, watching her back, was that this was a very angry White woman who was probably arguing over a cell phone, using an earpiece I couldn't see from here.

The woman stopped yelling to lean forward in her seat, fighting for calm as the engine chugged away.

After a moment, she straightened up and drove calmly on. I wavered for a moment, then unlatched the gate to number 21 and stepped inside.

For as long as I could remember, this house had served as the Paramaribo Headquarters for the Summer Institute of Linguistics. Theo and I used to come here with our father on his rare trips out of the Interior. Here, missionaries worked to translate the Bible and sundry religious tracts into several Surinamese languages.

I stopped by the little guard house at the end of the brick driveway and craned my neck inside. All I saw was a half-rotten swivel chair lying on its side, and the waterlogged guest registry sitting closed on the counter. In this town, only the American Embassy had decent security – and they used the U.S. Marines.

SIL's back entrance was locked tight, so I skirted the house to find the front door standing open.

The air conditioners were all running at full blast, and the place was freezing. It smelled like a meat locker where someone had decided to store rotten food. The roar of machinery combined with a high-pitched mosquito whine, adding to the sense that the house itself was terrified and in pain.

The place looked as if it had been hit by a storm. Pools of water had collected on the carpet, and the walls were streaked with brown. Broken computer monitors sat on the puddled floor, surrounded by ruined books and heaps of paper disintegrating from the wet.

The basement was no different – littered with broken furniture and unidentifiable pieces of equipment. I crouched over the wet linoleum and picked through a half-melted sheaf of paper for something, anything – a clue? – and realized I was talking to myself.

Suddenly tired, I shut my eyes tight and massaged my face with my left hand. This place was a loss.

Standing up, I noticed that my skin felt tight. The air of the room seemed thick and liquid – suddenly very warm. I moved slowly through it.

I mounted the stairs and went past the ground floor up to the second. I stopped at the first room on my right and pushed its door open. This would have been Theo's office.

Childish glyphs stood out nearly black against the peeling paint, and what furniture had not been removed entirely was pushed against the walls. Books, photographs, and framed certificates sat heaped for burning in the center of the carpet. Someone had either doused the fire or let it go out before everything had been consumed.

Looking at this, that blasted numbness I'd felt downstairs stole over me again, and I began to shake.

I tried to get a hold of myself. I thought of the letter I'd received last week, written in Joyce's odd, swooping script: "Something terrible is happening. Theo's gone. Pls. come quick!"

Pls. come quick.

"What's happened?"

I didn't cry out, but every muscle in my body seemed to contract, and my vision went a little gray. Very slowly, I turned to see Joyce standing just outside the room, her hands clasped below her belly.

"I startled you," she said.

"No. Yeah. Have you seen this place? Have you – ?" My voice sounded thin and shrill in my own ears, so I bit it off.

Joyce shook her head.

"Well, what the fuck, Joyce? Where is everyone? Where's Theo?"

"I don't know."

"Your…your letter. It sounded like you knew something, like you –"

Joyce bowed her head. In this light, she looked like a little girl. The faith of a child.

A brief flash of memory seized me, and I saw Joyce, twenty years younger, her pupils dilated as she laughed uncontrollably, sitting on a swing in the park down the street from our apartment.

"I don't remember a letter," Joyce said quietly, and that memory of her dissolved. "Is that why you came? Did I ask for you?"

Now rage heated my face and made me shiver. These – what were they, mood swings? – were becoming too much for me. I stood very still because I had no way of knowing whether I'd just grab Joyce and shake her hard or commit some act of terrible violence. The rage lifted after a moment, leaving me tired and empty.

"What…? What happened to you?" I asked. "What's wrong with you?"

"I'm sick," she said simply.

"Sick how?"

"I can't…my memory is going."

"Well – " I began and stopped short. We both looked up at the sound of floorboards creaking in the hallway.

"We did a lot of acid, didn't we?" Joyce said with a slight smile. "Maybe that's what's wrong with me."

A dark figure appeared behind her. "Hello?"

The voice was smooth and familiar – male – it conveyed an impression of authority, but I heard panic beneath its surface, and, oddly enough, that panic calmed me.

"Who's there?" I asked, and Joyce stepped aside so I could look.

309

"Sham Donald," said the figure. "And you are...?"

He stepped past Joyce into the room. I still couldn't get a good look at his face. It was obscured by a shadow that seemed to act independently from the others in the room.

"Wow," he said, and cracked a movie-star smile. "Oh wow. It's you! I haven't seen you in – God, it must be twenty years."

"A little more, actually."

"Well, what happened here? What is all this mess?"

"I don't know," I said. "I'm here looki–"

Over his shoulder, I saw Joyce give one decisive shake of her head.

"I just – I just got here and found all this."

"It doesn't look good. Crime." He frowned, and for a moment, seemed lost in thought. "You know what? The three of us should go somewhere and talk about what to do."

I didn't know what to say. Joyce shook her head again, but I felt Sham's eyes on me, and was afraid.

"Sure, we should – that sounds good, I guess."

I first met Sham when Theo and I started at ACS. He was an amazing liar. He lied not so much to obscure the truth, but because he was a natural storyteller, and that was how he entertained himself.

On our second day at school, he explained to us that he was secretly a prince in exile. His father was a movie producer who'd once refereed a bare-knuckle boxing match between Bruce Lee and John Lennon.

310

My clearest memory of Sham is from my fourteenth birthday party. My stepfather had hired two DJs and an army of caterers, and had our large yard decorated with crepe streamers and colored lights. Our real father could never have afforded such a bash.

That year I'd conceived a debilitating crush on Gladys Moessring, one of the girls from CLA, a rival Christian school attended mostly by Surinamese kids whose parents wanted them to learn English. Around nine or so, I left the outdoor dance floor and headed to the basement sitting room where a group of the CLA kids had gathered. I'd spent the night screwing up my courage, and now I intended to ask Gladys to dance.

The sitting room was mostly empty when I got there, but Sham and Gladys sat kissing on the overstuffed sofa.

I don't remember how it happened, but I ended up chasing Sham around the house. He was lighter than I was, quicker, and he didn't have to run full-tilt to stay beyond my reach – or he did, and I let him think that.

Up the stairs and through the foyer to the living room full of African masks and Surinamese statuary. Around through the kitchen where the remnants of my birthday cake sat in a stiff white box. Through the dining room and onto the patio where the DJs stood behind their turntables.

But the patio doors were closed.

I startled Sham with a burst of speed, and he glanced at me over his shoulder. I saw the doors in front of him – I must have – but too late. He ran through them with a clash.

Sham skidded to a halt on the dance floor, checking himself for wounds as everyone turned to look. He cut a stage bow and straightened again, immediately taking control of his audience.

"I'm all right, ladies and gentlemen," he announced. "Everything's fine!"

He stepped back inside, careful to avoid the glass.

"Your mother's going to kill us," he said with a shake of his head, and took a seat on our best sofa. "She's going to – She'll be *so pissed.*"

Both of us laughed at that, but I stopped when blood flowers bloomed through his shirt and khakis. Blood ran down his limbs to pool on the sofa beneath him. It looked almost as if he was wearing a diaphanous red skirt.

Sham looked down at himself and laughed even harder. Then the tremors set in.

Before long, anyone we knew who hadn't been there could tell the story word for word as if he had.

Funny thing, though: as it was told and retold, my role in the drama changed. I faded from the story until I found myself telling it not from the perspective of the one chasing, but from that of an eye witness. By the time we graduated, not even Sham, who told the revised version in his valedictorian address, remembered that I was directly involved.

But that's another thing; I never blamed myself for what happened. Surely I should have felt at least the barest pang of guilt – but I guess that's typical of me.

Joyce used to call me her Spaceman. When I came home to our apartment after our first and final argument, I stood in our bedroom doorway and watched her shove clothes into her largest suitcase.

She sensed me standing there, and said without looking round, "Hey, Spaceman: Why don't you just go home to Mars?"

Sham led us outside where we found his driver waiting beside a peach-toned Bentley. I was more than a little surprised when Sham told the man to head for Owasa. In my childhood, Paramaribo's premier country club adhered to a strict expatriates only policy. Even wealthy Surinamese like the Donalds found it impossible to buy membership.

"Will they let us in?" I asked as I slid into the plush leather backseat.

"I should hope so," Sham said with another cinematic grin. "I own the place, after all."

Owasa was a patch of jungle brought to heel by the old Dutch colonists and maintained through constant struggle. It was a riot of banana trees, tropical flowers, and swooping golf courses. These days, Dutchmen with tropical tans shared their garden with brown and beige Surinamese who sat sipping stroop beneath wicker bungalows. The smartly dressed staff treated us like royalty as Sham smiled gracefully and gave orders in rapid-fire Dutch.

After dismissing the club director, Sham led us through a garden full of aloe plants and faja lobis and up a set of marble stairs to a comfortable bungalow.

It was not long before a waitress, a short, fine-boned woman with olive skin, dark curly hair, and large arresting eyes, came to take our order. She listened carefully as she stood with her unusually large hands laced over her belly, and then bent to whisper something in Sham's ear. I found it difficult to guess her age, but the lines at the corners of her mouth told me she was likely much older than she looked. I could have sworn I recognized her from somewhere.

"Of course," Sham answered absently, and the woman withdrew.

Joyce shifted uncomfortably in her seat, wringing her hands as if she expected something terrible to happen. I wondered now whether what I'd taken for fear of Sham was not something else entirely. She aligned her body with his, watching him closely as he slid a brass case from his pocket and offered me a flavored cigarillo.

"No thanks," I said. "I don't smoke."

He made a "suit yourself" gesture with his neck and shoulders, then lit up, savoring the fumes.

Sham looked barely thirty years old, with nut-brown skin and delicately masculine features. There was a certain detachment to his gaze, as if his attention was continually focused on minute details that would have been invisible to anyone else. The one wrinkle between his brows gradually melted away as he stared across the lawn in the direction of the swimming pool.

"Did you know I went missing for six years?" he said.

"I heard something like that, yes."

"I'd like to tell you both what happened to me."

"Oh?" I said. "Well, first, do you think we might – ?"

"No," Sham said without inflection. "Listen."

It was not a request.

"I drifted through university without learning much of anything. I'd always been a gifted mimic as well as a natural liar, so it wasn't hard to tell my instructors what they wanted to hear. When I graduated at the top of my class all I knew was that I'd sooner slit my wrists than continue on to graduate school. Then, in the summer after graduation, my father died, and I suddenly found myself a very wealthy man.

"I'd always had a taste for narcotics – nothing habit-forming, but I could more than appreciate a mellow high. After my father's funeral, I bought myself a condo in Miami and spent as much time as I could under the influence.

"During that time, I read as much as possible – religious criticism, occult theory, anthropology – and it was through that reading that I learned of a rare psychoactive fungus rumored to grow in the Atlas Mountains. Rumor had it that if one were to ingest this mushroom, called by the locals 'the Word of God,' one could communicate directly with the Creator.

"Having nothing better to do, I sold everything I owned and set out.

"I headed first to England, and moved on only when I grew bored. I spent the better part of a year in France – I think I taught myself to produce records. By the time I reached Spain, I realized I was serious about my quest, and I left for Morocco after barely a week.

"At first, I found nothing at all there, but once I'd learned the language well enough to make sense of the differing dialects, my worst fears were confirmed. The Word of God was a fiction. It – "

"Wait," I said, leaning forward in my chair.

The waitress had set our drinks before us and I caught her scent as she stood over me – jasmine and something darker.

When she left again, I squinted and shook my head to clear it. "So – So what you're saying is that the Word of God didn't exist?"

Joyce opened her mouth to speak, but Sham silenced her with a look. "That's not what I said. I said I found that it was a fiction. Time is a fiction, you know, but time exists: it's just after two o'clock."

"Then you found it?" I asked, and as I crossed my legs, I noticed that the peculiar tightness I'd experienced earlier had returned.

"Sure," Sham said lightly.

"Well, did you take it? What happened?"

Sham made a pained face. "Absolutely nothing," he said with a shrug.

I worked hard to control my expression. "That's too bad," I said.

"Isn't it?" Sham said with a grin.

"But about the Institute…" I said tonelessly.

I looked up, startled, as the waitress took a seat across from me. She sat back from the table, and when she crossed her legs, I saw the dark thatch of pubic hair between her bare thighs.

"You remember Gladys, I'm sure," Sham said smoothly.

"Gladys – " I began. Of course. Of course I remembered her. Her jasmine perfume and the almost metallic aroma of her sweat made my heart beat faster. I had to bite my tongue to remind myself who I was.

"You look great for a man your age," Gladys said without a trace of humor.

Sham started speaking again, but I couldn't keep track of his words. Every so often, he aimed a comment in Joyce's direction, and Joyce reddened. I didn't care.

Very deliberately, Gladys uncrossed her legs and let them drift apart. My mouth felt stuffed full of cotton, and sipping my drink didn't help. I met her eyes and nodded slightly.

Before long, I made my excuses and left.

This is the sort of man I am: I knew as I left the three of them sitting there that Gladys would follow me to the Torarica where, if she let me, I would fuck her in the ass.

I couldn't remember my wife's name, or whether we'd had any children together.

Was she waiting for me to call home? How could I if I couldn't remember the number?

After our third round, I rolled onto my belly and felt on the end table for my cigarettes.

"You don't smoke," Gladys said gently, and I heard the snick of her lighter and the hitch of her breath as she drew in a lungful of dirty blue smoke.

I rolled onto my back and Gladys handed me a cigarette. I puffed placidly on it as I watched the wheeling blades of the ceiling fan.

"Did I hurt you?"

"Oh, no, I'm fine," I said lightly. I felt as if I'd just survived a beating.

"Don't lie," she said. "I wanted to hurt you, just a little."

"To tell the truth, I'm pretty sore," I said. "I need water. I need – "

"Get me some, too."

It was cold in here. Terribly cold.

"I need some – what are we speaking?"

"Mmm?"

"Are we? – Is this Dutch we're speaking?"

"Your Dutch is no good anymore," Gladys said. "You hardly remember it."

"I – yeah. Water."

It wasn't easy, but I climbed out of bed and padded across the room. I wavered outside the bathroom for a moment, my skin crawling as I remembered what I'd seen in there. Finally, I opened the door and looked into the basin.

Nothing. No ice, no hand, no organs. Someone could have come in and cleaned it. Someone...

Get a hold of yourself.

"What?"

"I didn't say anything," Gladys called.

I drank several handfuls of water directly from the faucet, careful not to look at myself in the mirror, then took a cup back to Gladys.

She sat against the headboard, her fine dark hair swept wetly away from her face. Her breasts were small, but perfectly formed, and a dusting of freckles or light brown moles stood out against her olive skin.

She took the cup from me and drained it almost at once. "Sham told you about the Word of God," she said.

"Yeah," I said. "He always did like to tell crazy stories. He's better at it than he used to be."

"It's a crazy story, yes," Gladys said, "but it's true. He brought the Word when he returned to Suriname. I've held it in my mouth, and it is sweet."

She set her cup on the night stand and watched me for a long time. She looked intently into my eyes as she took me in her hand and stroked me. "Are you ready?" she said.

"You want to go again?"

She shook her head. "It's my turn now. Come up here and kneel for me."

'Kneel'…? But it wasn't worth trying to make sense of her words. Better just to do as I was told.

"Relax," Gladys said as she positioned herself behind me. Her voice was lower now, and slow with authority. "Breathe, darling. Relax."

I realized when the pain began that the cold in the room was not in the room. It was inside me.

I swung my legs over the side of the bed and took a moment to gaze around the room. Shelves full of model cars and planes lined the sky blue wall above a smallish drafting table, and the wall directly to my right was a mural in which a smiling pilot guided an old-fashioned biplane through a bank of clouds.

I hunched over, elbows to knees, and pressed the heels of my hands against my eyes. Before long, I looked down at myself and saw that someone had dressed me for bed in a pair of briefs and a faded green teeshirt. The briefs were a little snug, and I usually wore boxers, but I was thankful for them.

I noticed the smell of cooking food and left the bedroom in search of the kitchen, concentrating on the sensation of the hardwood floor against the soles of my feet.

Joyce stood before the stove, and I considered the outline of her back beneath her white and yellow sundress. She turned with her skillet and saw me watching. She paused for a moment, looking as if she might say something, then slid the omelet onto an earthenware plate.

"That's yours," she said and turned away again to pour another helping of beaten eggs into the skillet.

I took my plate into the dining room and waited for her.

"You're feeling better?" I said as Joyce took a seat across from me.

"I have good days," she said.

I dug into my omelet. Caviar and cream cheese.

"How did I get here?"

"The police caught you at Zorg en Hoop. You were naked and out of your head, trying to steal a plane."

"Raving?"

"Oh yeah. 'Gladys is a man. She's a man and something worse.'"

319

"Ah."

"You were lucid enough to have the police call us, and when we explained to them that you were an American citizen, they took you over to the Embassy and had you examined by the nurse. She diagnosed your behavior as the result of a malarial fugue."

"Ah."

"How long have you had it?"

"Contracted it when I was nine, I think."

"And you never bothered to tell me."

"It's kind of – it's not something I think about," I said. "I've learned to live with it, and so…"

"I see."

"Don't do that," I said. "Don't."

Joyce watched me closely. "It's just that sometimes I can't tell whether it's that you're so full of shit that you believe yourself or that you think you're just that much smarter than everyone around you."

"Yeah," I said thoughtfully, and pushed my plate away. "Guess I'll be heading out, then."

"Samia called this morning. She says she's sorry she kicked you out. She didn't think you'd pick up and leave the country."

"Is that what this is?" I almost laughed. "Well, here is my official apology: I am heartily sorry for cheating on you when we were kids. I'm sorry you felt you had to leave and that we both married other people and that now you're sick."

Joyce smiled, and in her expression was all the charm and intelligence I thought her illness had stolen from her. "Don't kid yourself, Spaceman," she said. "Do you actually think I'd be better off with you?"

I couldn't help but smile back as I shook my head. "No," I said. "No, I don't. Good omelet, by the way."

It became clear to me as I sat cross-legged before my suitcase, packing the few clothes I'd used during my stay, that I didn't need any of these things. After all, I wasn't even sure they belonged to me.

I felt like myself now, but I knew that sense of wellbeing was only an illusion. I still wasn't sure who I was.

Joyce had mentioned my wife's name and the incident that had sent me running back here from the States, but I wasn't sure I remembered either of those things.

It was – You have to understand. I am only a man. Yes, I lie from time to time. Yes, I have been known to sleep with my students. And yes, I was with one of those students, a long, lean, androgynous girl from Colorado Springs, when my wife – Samia? – walked in on us.

But no one looks at himself in the mirror and says, *I am a bad man.* It's just a feeling one gets after a while, a suspicion that forms on the edge of one's mind. I'm sure good people have the same sense about themselves from time to time, and that their fears are largely unfounded.

Even the worst of men are able to convince themselves that on the whole, they act justly, adhering to some obscure moral code. Lately, though, I find it hard to deny that I have exerted a destructive influence on the life of every person with whom I've had more than casual contact.

And what is my excuse? That my father ruined my life? My father never ruined my life. I felt nothing at all when I opened the bathroom door to find him slumped over off the bowl, a bottle of lye fallen from his hand, the stink of shit and chemical death still thick in the air of the room.

I looked at him lying there until I was sure I wouldn't forget, and then I closed the door and went outside to chase cats with Theo.

Here is a picture of us together: I am twelve years old and oddly muscular, with dirty yellow-brown hair and a washed-out yellow complexion, sitting on Theo's chest as my fists strike him over and over with metronomic regularity.

His nose would run as he cried, and that made me angrier than I could explain.

I suppose now that he's gone I realize how I've hurt him.

Do I win? Is there a prize?

Suriname is two countries. There are the two major cities, and then there is the wild and seething mass of forest to the south, dotted with little villages.

The Brownsberg resort sits atop a mountain dominated by jungle waterfalls and a tangle of greenery. The year Theo entered the high school at ACS, our entire class spent a week there, learning to trust one another and work as a team.

My investigation had hit a wall, so it seemed logical – or not logical, but *appropriate* – to revisit a place Theo and I had known together.

I arrived at Brownsberg just as the rain began. It was about four in the afternoon. The sky, dark and swollen, would clear up once the clouds unburdened themselves and boiled away, giving me another hour or two of daylight.

I paid the driver and sent him back to Paramaribo knowing he'd never make it. He'd drive halfway there on red, rutted roads and find a place to stay till morning. I just wanted him away from me.

The resort was deserted, fallen to ruin. The lawn between the warped and hunkered cabins was overgrown and full of weeds. Soon, the forest would reach out to reclaim this place and no one would remember that it had ever been otherwise.

The main cabin was more or less intact. The subtropical climate had long since peeled the paint from it, and patches of gray-black mold clung to the bare wood. Another year or two and the building would lose its structural integrity, but it looked safe to enter for the time being.

The place was as badly wrecked as the SIL house had been. Pots, pans, broken furniture sat heaped against the walls, and a childish design about eight feet across stood out against the common room floor. I started laughing when I saw it.

Sham, I thought as my laughter turned to sobbing. *Sham did this.*

Thunder played ninepins in the sky as rivulets of dirty water ran through holes in the ceiling. The rain itself sounded like an army on the march. It can get like that here.

I remember riding home from school with Theo one day and turning the corner onto Indirastraat to find a column of heavy rain marching up the street to meet us. In the end, we were both drenched, but I didn't mind: I'd seen something secret.

The other cabins were empty. All clear of furniture, nothing on the walls…I made my way through all but one before I realized that Theo was lost for good.

I was no detective. I was a writer, an academic, and not such a sterling example of either species. The mystery of Theo's disappearance had taught me something important: sometimes the earth opens up and swallows people whole. Given enough time, it will swallow cities, nations.

323

Even the gods descend into the darkness of regret, and what then?

We used to play soccer in rain like this.

I stopped at the edge of the falls path and looked over my shoulder at the resort buildings humped sadly in the downpour. The rain we played in was never quite so intense, nor did it last nearly as long as this storm had.

For hours I'd sat by myself on the floor of the main cabin, trying to decide what to do next. Finally, I rose and searched through the place again, finding only a rumpled pack of cigarettes and a mercifully dry book of matches. I lit up, let the smoke fill my lungs, and as I did, my course revealed itself.

The rainforest trees swayed like backup singers for a blues band. If it weren't for the roar of the weather, I'm sure I could have heard them creaking. They waved their leaves, trying to shake them dry, and I wished I could speak their language.

I shrugged and lit another cigarette before starting down the trail.

The path was a mess of flowing red mud that ruined my shoes. I hesitated for a moment, then stooped to untie them and kick them off. I used my muddy toes to peel of my socks and kicked them into the underbrush before resuming my descent.

Farther down, I peeled off my shirt and tossed it aside as well. I looked back up the trail and watched the trees on either side lean over to share their secrets.

By the time I reached the falls, I was completely naked. I didn't even have my cigarettes anymore.

I waded into the pool and watched the cascade of dirty water. The lightning had ceased playing overhead and now colored flashes lit the iron gray sky. I shook my head, wondering.

When I looked around me again, I realized that the rain had *paused*. The falls themselves stood stiff as meringue, and fat tropical raindrops hung like marbles in the air. I reached out to grab a handful of them and took a sharp shocked breath as I rolled them across my palm and onto the backs of my hands.

Here you are.

Sham stood at the top of the falls – but this was not the Sham with whom I'd shared drinks at Owasa.

He was female now. I could clearly see the outline of breasts beneath his red striped polo shirt.

Sham became male again, and younger, as he descended the suspended spray. By the time he reached me, he was the boy he'd been at fourteen. His limbs were thin and knobby. His knees and elbows seemed to belong to someone else.

His presence seemed to disturb the water as he stood in the air above the pool. It trembled beneath him as if afraid. He smelled of that cloying incense the Anglicans use for mass.

My mouth opened, then closed with a snap as I realized I had nothing to say.

Sham bent and took my elbow, lifting me to stand before him. I couldn't look directly at him for long. Instead, I looked down at myself to see whether I had changed as he had. My slick yellow nakedness was entirely familiar to me.

I looked up again, on the verge of tears. "What happened to Theo?"

A sad smile raised Sham's lips and made him look older even than I was. "Sacrifices must be made if the spirits of progress are to turn the world. We are hungry when our eyes open for the first time. Ravenous."

"You devoured him?"

"Not I," Sham said with a shake of his head.

"Gladys."

Sham made a gesture somewhere between a nod and a shrug. "In her other life, she worked alongside Theo at the Institute," Sham said. "They were working a late night together when…when she made the final step. She might have consumed you as well if she hadn't recognized you for one of us."

"I'm not one of you."

"Of course you are," Sham said gently. "I told you before that time is a fiction. I've already given you the Word, and you have taken it a few minutes from now."

"I don't want it."

"Are you happy with the life you've led?"

"No, but – "

"This is your chance to be more than you are. How often do the old gods step aside for a new pantheon to take their place? But it is as I've said: I don't have to convince you. You've already decided."

He looked away for a moment, his smile serene. "Get a hold of yourself," he said, and then his eyes snapped back to meet mine.

"What will you do, then, if not this? Go home to your wife and beg for forgiveness you know full well you don't deserve? How has your trip been so far? Seen anything strange? Have you felt a different vibration in the air?"

Of course I had. Of course.

"You've come unstuck from time," he said. "You're being unmade."

"You're just trying to take advantage of the fact that I'm walking around in a malarial – you – none of this is happening! None of this…"

Sham crossed his arms over his breasts and just watched me.

"Fine," I snapped. "Fine. You want me to – ? Give it to me, then. Give me the Word."

"Fucking *finally*," Sham sighed, and rocked back on his heels.

He reached into his pocket, and I saw that he was grown again. His white linen summer suit gleamed in the twilight.

He withdrew a bundled handkerchief and handed it to me.

"Pronouncing it is the hard part," he said as I weighed the bundle in my hand. "For a while there, I was certain I'd never manage it."

"Is that what's wrong with Joyce?"

Sham shrugged. "Could be," he said. "You know her better than I do."

With that, he turned and stepped away into nothing.

I looked around at the frozen rain, the colored flashes in the sky, the waterfall waiting for time to pass again. So this was it. This was insanity.

I unwrapped the Word and examined it closely. It was hardly more than a thin fungal sheet, like something you'd find clinging to the wall of a darkened cave.

What if he was wrong? What if we weren't gods, but monsters? Was there a difference? What a horror a god must be in its infancy: male, female, abstract, and lacking all consideration for beings lesser than itself.

With a shaking hand, I tore a strip from the Word and popped it into my mouth.

Gladys told the truth. It was very, very sweet.

The Battering Ram
at Doom's Gates

Robert E. Keller

he trees showed their hatred from the moment Abrantus stepped into Council Wood, trying to drive him insane with whispers of madness and doom. He wanted to swing at them with his axe in whiskey-induced fury, but that would have just gotten him killed. It was evening and the demons were active, alert to his every move.

Besides, Abrantus hadn't come to do battle with the trees – he'd come to reason with them.

Twisted faces glared at him from trunks beside the trail. Over the decades, the trees had taken on the features of the devils that inhabited them. He shone his lantern on one. "I've been wronged!" he cried. "A demon has left the woods and made a home in my chicken coop. My chickens now lay foul eggs. I demand justice!"

"Your eyeballs will be popped by a sharp stick," a tree hissed. "They'll find your corpse with two bloody holes in the skull."

With a shaking hand, Abrantus sat his lantern down and took a swallow of whiskey to gain some courage. "Threaten all you want," he growled. "But my eggs are no good and can't be sold or eaten. I won't tolerate it!"

329

"We never leave the forest," said the tree. "You're a lying drunk."

Abrantus finished off the whiskey and smashed the jug against the oak that had insulted him. "And you're lying hellspawn," he said. "I deserve to have my complaint heard."

"We'll silence your nasty mouth," another tree said. "Just you wait."

Abrantus glimpsed a shadowy figure crouched in the brush to his right, its yellow eyes watching him. A twisted root ran from its head to the tree. Abrantus raised his axe in warning. The whiskey had given him a bit more spunk than he usually had, but he was still fighting hard to hold himself together. He'd been plagued by troubles over the past year – his wife leaving him for another man, his barn catching fire and burning down, and chronic gout in his toes that probably stemmed from his love of red meat and beer. And now, with his chickens laying worthless eggs, he'd been pushed too far – and had done the unthinkable venturing into this cursed forest.

But he was liquored up and ready to go down swinging, terror or no. "Back off, demon," he snarled. "I'll chop down every damn tree in these woods until I get my way. I want my chickens returned to normal!"

A quiet laugh reached his ears. "And maybe I'll stick my claws in your fat belly, human – rip it open and see what's floating around in there." The demon raised a branch, revealing fingers that tapered into fine points.

Keeping his eye on the demon, Abrantus continued on until he was out of reach. He stumbled over a root, agony flaring up in his swollen toe. Something scuttled across the trail in front of him – a wood spider. Normally, a wood spider wasn't much of a threat, as they typically left humans alone. But he'd heard rumors that some had been molded by the demons into aggressive servants, and something had looked funny about the one he'd glimpsed.

Abrantus paused, goose bumps breaking out over all his flesh. He shone the lantern toward the spot where the spider had left the trail, but nothing emerged. He continued on for a bit and then wheeled about on a whim to see what was behind him.

A spider was crouched in the trail, frozen in the lantern light. This was no ordinary wood spider. Its legs were crooked and much longer than usual, its flesh was pale and hairless like dough and webbed with crimson veins, and its mouth had been widened out into an oversized gap, revealing black fangs.

As soon as Abrantus glimpsed it, it leapt for his face. He brought up his axe and smashed it out of the air, driving it into the dirt. It shuddered beneath the blade, leaking dark blood, and then tore loose and staggered toward him. He hacked it again – a solid blow that splattered it into pieces.

Abrantus shone the lantern about. He caught glimpses of pale bodies and bony legs as more spiders circled him. With a shaking hand, he sat the lantern at his feet. He was a chunky man with graying hair, gout, and a whole lot of piss-poor luck – but he was proud and ready to die fighting. If he were going to go, it would be with his chin up – a Falenswor never shirked.

He hacked the first spider to charge him into twitching ruin with one stout blow. Another jumped on his back, but he brushed it off before it could bite him. Abrantus kicked a third spider with his swollen toe and sent it tumbling into a tree, a howl of pain escaping his lips. One bit into his leg from behind – not an accurate bite, just a slight pierce of the skin as its fangs got tangled in Abrantus' trousers. He shook the creature off and clove it in two.

A fire smoldered in Abrantus' belly, a battle lust he'd never experienced before. The pain in his foot receded, and he struck blow after blow in a berserk rage. He smashed three more spiders and stomped a fourth beneath his boot. But they kept coming.

Then blue sparks erupted in front of Abrantus, and three advancing spiders exploded into smoking ash. Sorcery hung in the air like spicy incense. A cloaked, hooded figure stepped into the lantern light. The other spiders quickly scurried into the trees.

"Hello, Abrantus," a muffled female voice said. "I've come to guide you to safety."

The strange battle lust that had consumed him was already subsiding. He lifted his lantern and stepped closer to her, trying to peer at her face under the hood. All he could see was shadow. Her breath smelled rotten. "Who are you? And how do you know my name? And what did you do to those spiders?"

"I am Lanatha," she said. "I live in this forest."

"Then you must be demon kin," said Abrantus, "for no human could dwell here. And furthermore, no human I know of makes spiders explode with blue fire."

"I was born a human," she said. "And there are parts of this forest where the trees are not infested. Come, I will lead you to my cabin, my unlucky friend. I know why you're here, and I have a solution to your problem."

Abrantus hesitated. Her breath smelled like decayed meat, but her hands were smooth and young-looking. "How do I know this isn't a demon trick?"

"Look, you fool," Lanatha snarled. "I just saved you from poisonous spiders. Now I'm offering you refuge and answers – and maybe some food and drink for that fat gut if you're in need."

"Let me see your face," he said. "So I know you're human."

"You don't want to see it, Abrantus," she said. "Trust me on that." Lanatha turned and walked away.

Abrantus limped after her, the pain returning worse than ever. "Hold on now, miss. I didn't mean to offend."

Lanatha whirled around. "But you did offend!" She seized his face and a shock surged through him. Abrantus found himself frozen in place. "Perhaps I'll drag you to the gates of doom and prop you up for the worms to feed on. What do you think of that, you bloated pig?"

Darkness took his mind.

When Abrantus woke, he was lying on a wooden floor in a log cabin, with a crackling fire warming his cheek. Lanatha was seated at a table eating soup.

Groaning, he sat up. "Why did you attack me?"

"I didn't," she said calmly, dipping bread in her soup and shoving it into the shadows beneath her hood. "I just shut you up so I didn't have to listen to you. I'm used to living alone, and I like my silence."

"You carried me here by yourself?" he asked.

"You were carried here."

Abrantus stood up. "For what? If you know what my trouble is, then you know I need somehow to convince the demons to release my chickens."

Lanatha cackled mirthlessly. "Yes, we can't have your chickens running around possessed. In fact, I'm making that my highest priority."

"Why do you mock me?" Abrantus asked, still wondering if she was a demon. He looked around for his axe. It was nowhere in sight.

"Because you're a joke," Lanatha said. "You have the blood of the fiercest warriors who ever walked this land inside you, and yet you worry about chickens. It's pathetic."

"What do you mean?" he asked. "I'm a Falenswor. We're farmers, blacksmiths, and shopkeepers. We do honest work. I know nothing of war."

"Do you even know your own history? Falenswor is a knightly name, and the men who bore it once served the King of Elsenmoln – the ruler of the land beyond the mountains. I too once served him as a knight. But I suffered a great misfortune, and now I dwell in this little cabin – talking to a fool who thinks his reason for coming here is to save his chickens."

333

"You confuse me, woman," said Abrantus.

Lanatha shoved her bowl away. "Maybe this will lift the fog." She went to a large oaken chest and took out a rune-covered hammer.

She handed it to him; he held it up. It was a heavy war hammer, beautifully crafted. "Looks like a good tool," he said. "What do you use it for?"

She sneered. "That is a weapon, not a tool. And I don't use it for anything. It was a gift from the king. Your ancestors once wielded that hammer."

Abrantus couldn't deny how right it felt in his hands. "Are you giving me this?"

"Do you deserve it?" She lifted a horned helm and some chain mail from the trunk and tossed them near his feet.

He put the armor on. The helm fit perfectly, but the chain mail was a bit tight in the waist. "These should help with the spiders," he said. "And I thank you for returning these to my family, if what you say is true."

"I'm not done yet," Lanatha said. "Are you hungry? Because if you are, you had better eat before I show you this next sight."

"I'm fine," Abrantus said. "Show me what you will."

Lanatha threw back her hood, revealing a nightmare in the firelight. Her face was partially covered in a sort of slimy bark, and a root seemed to have sprung from her left eye, where it hung twitching. Infected sores covered the flesh that remained. Her tongue looked like a piece of driftwood poking from between gnarled lips.

"The demons did this to me," Lanatha said. "I was sent here with a large company of knights by the King of Elsenmoln to free Council Wood from its curse. We reached the dark gates at the forest's heart, but were unable to advance further. We were taken from the rear, and my knights were slain. The demon lord bit my face and infected it with his evil. It gave me the power of sorcery, a power that allows me to command lesser demons – like the ones I sent to take possession of your chickens."

Abrantus' eyes widened. "So you're the one who caused my eggs to foul!"

"I needed to persuade you to come to the forest," Lanatha said. "I've known of your presence for a long time. But my curse keeps me bound to these woods. I am half demon myself now, able to walk free through the forest yet unable to set foot beyond it."

"What do you want from me?" he asked.

"I want your help," Lanatha said. "I still intend to carry out the king's orders and break this curse. Council Wood was once a sacred place. But the demons invaded and entered the trees, driving out the good spirits. They built a gate to guard the source of their power at the center of the woods – a gate protected by sorcery. But I've carved a battering ram from the limb of a mighty tree that was free of infestation. It's a dreary weapon, ugly with decades of rage, but that anger is exactly what is needed to smash those gates. And it's heavy – it will take at least two people to carry."

Abrantus gazed at her in admiration, his anger over the chickens forgotten. "So you intend to storm the gates and cleanse the forest? Can it really be done?" For an instant he was swept up with feelings of glory, envisioning their triumph. Then he came to his senses. "But why should I care what happens here? I just want my chickens to lay good eggs again."

"It's not about the forest," Lanatha said. "The demons are plotting something vaster, and they need to be stopped."

Abrantus nodded. "Well, good luck. I'm going home, and I expect my chickens to be back to normal when I get there."

Lanatha's face burned red. "You would abandon me? You would leave me trapped here while the demons carry out their plan?" She shook with fury. "You slimy bastard! I should have killed you when you were unconscious."

"Calm down," Abrantus said, shifting to a defensive posture. "All I'm saying is that I have no stake in this struggle. It's meaningless to me."

She turned away, hands knotted into fists. Then she wheeled around, pointing at Abrantus' leg. "I sense dark sorcery at work in you!"

He glanced down. "What are you talking about?" He realized his leg felt numb, the back in particular – where the spider had bitten him.

"You're poisoned," Lanatha said, sneering. "That venom will spread through your body and eventually kill you. Your death will be excruciating."

"What must I do to save myself?" said Abrantus, though he already guessed the answer.

"Come with me and break the curse. Then I will give you a cure. Otherwise, go and rot."

Abrantus' eyes widened in fury, and he lunged toward her. But she raised her hand, blue fire shimmering on her fingertips. "Easy there, fat man," she hissed. "Another step closer and I'll burn your greasy heart right out of your chest."

He stopped, knowing she had him snared. "Show me the battering ram."

Abrantus and Lanatha walked down the forest trail. Between them was a pale log carved from oak to look like a scaly serpent, with pegs from which lanterns dangled. A handle was carved into either side for easier carrying, one near the front and one near the back, but the going was still slow and awkward.

Abrantus could hardly bring himself to hang onto the piece of timber. It felt alive and slimy beneath his touch, like an actual serpent. It was also extremely cold. Thoughts of rage and hated swelled in his mind, emanating from the wood and into his body.

Finally he could bear it no longer. At his prompting, they laid the log down. "Can't do it," he muttered, shaking his head. "It feels cursed."

"It is cursed," Lanatha said. "It was carved from one of the few trees that somehow resisted the demons. It has grown spiteful over the years."

Abrantus gazed down at the log, his only instinct to set it on fire. How could something that felt so vile help them in their cause? "This is a fool's quest, woman. What good are two people against an army of demons? And my leg is getting worse." He rubbed the spreading numb spot.

"You'll hold out," Lanatha said. "Now keep up your side of the – "

A fat, deformed wood spider landed on her head, sinking its fangs into her scalp. With a cry, Abrantus raised the hammer, but he dared not risk swinging it so close to her skull. Chills crept down his spine and he whirled around to see several more spiders running toward him.

Once again Abrantus was overcome by battle lust. He killed two of the spiders in a single blow, sweeping the hammer in an arc before him. One of the rabbit-sized creatures leapt onto his face, filling his nostrils with a musty stink. Fangs probed for his eyes. Using his free hand, Abrantus ripped the spider away and flung it to the ground – just in time to see another scuttling towards his leg. He kicked it away and smashed it.

He turned to see Lanatha clutching her scalp and staggering about. The spider that had been biting her head was gone, but another was now attached to her thigh. Abrantus kicked it off her and then crushed it.

But there were dozens more, closing deliberately around the pair from all sides. Lanatha let out a piercing whistle. Two horned and winged demons flew from the forest and attacked the spiders, ripping most of them to pieces. Abrantus crushed the last two spiders and then faced the demons with hammer raised. But they flew to Lanatha and alighted beside her.

Lanatha slumped to the ground, moaning. "My mind is foggy. I'm very weak."

337

"Then let those demons carry the battering ram," said Abrantus, gazing at the winged imps in disgust. "They seem willing enough to serve you."

She hesitated, as if thinking it over. "I don't know if that's a good idea. I'm afraid – "

"What do you mean?" Abrantus growled. "Why should we bear this burden if those devils can do it for us? It would be good to have our hands free for the next ambush."

Weakly, Lanatha nodded. She pointed at the battering ram, and the demons lifted it.

As she struggled to her feet the imps let out piercing screams. Black smoke curled up from beneath their hands and they exploded into flames. They quickly burned into piles of gray ash while Lanatha gazed on in horror. The battering ram lay atop the ashes, smoke rising from its serpent's nostrils. Its eyes burned like crimson coals.

"What have I created?" Lanatha whispered.

"We should abandon this quest," said Abrantus. "We're both poisoned."

"The poison cannot kill me," Lanatha said. "I just need some time to recover."

Abrantus scowled. "That's all well and good – you recover while I grow worse."

"You were bitten in the leg," she said. "And it must have been a tiny bite, or you'd be dead by now. Just be quiet and let me rest."

Abrantus fell into sullen silence. Some part of him wanted to charge the gates and somehow see an end to the demon reign, but the more practical part of him realized such a quest was madness and he should return to his farm. But how could he persuade Lanatha of this?

Nothing came to mind. Finally Lanatha rose. "Come, let us take up the ram."

Reluctantly Abrantus seized the log and lifted it. His toes flared up again and made the going slow, and the hefty log tired his arms. They were moving into thicker forest now, and the trees began to whisper threats. The battering ram trembled beneath Abrantus' grip, filling his mind with a yearning to lash out.

As they entered a swampy area, filled with muck and mossy oaks, a towering demon leapt into the trail. It was a mass of shadow, vines, and roots, with a blue flame in the middle of its forehead that might have been an eye. "No one passes this way," it hissed at them. "Your blood will feed the trees." Abrantus was overwhelmed by a feeling of weakness that made him want to fall to his knees and surrender, as if his will were being crushed by the creature's mere presence.

"A greater demon!" Lanatha cried. "Ram the bastard!"

The two of them charged the demon, driving the log into it. The demon stood calmly, as if such an attack were meaningless. But when the battering ram stuck it, green sparks erupted and the serpent's head drove deep into their foe's chest.

With a howl the demon clutched at the log and tried to yank it free – and then the entire mass of shadow, root, and vine turned into a blazing green fireball that whistled and threw out bouncing sparks. In seconds, the demon burned to ash, leaving the ram fully intact.

The trees burst into frantic and enraged muttering. Abrantus was overcome by battle lust, and he raised his hammer defiantly. "Shut your mouths or I'll smash them shut!"

"Calm down," Lanatha said. "You'll work the poison more quickly through your system. Save it for when we reach the gates."

Abrantus lowered his hammer. "You should have just given me that damn cure – if you really have one." Suddenly, he was overcome with disgust. He dropped his side of the log. "I've had enough of this. Give me the medicine or I'm finished here."

"If you quit on me," Lanatha snarled, "you're a dead man."

He thrust his chin out. "I'm a Falenswor, and I won't let myself be jerked around by anyone." He tried to appear unyielding, but inside he was growing increasingly desperate. He cursed himself for ever coming to this forest.

Lanatha folded her arms across her chest. "Go on, then. Crawl off and die. I'll continue on alone to the gates, without the battering ram, and face what I must face."

"You stubborn devil," Abrantus growled. He grabbed the battering ram. "I suppose I'm in this until the bitter end. But I'm telling you – "

"Silence!" Lanatha commanded. She sniffed the air. "I smell demons." She vanished into the forest and quickly returned, flanked by three more imps.

"Why don't you just raise an army?" said Abrantus.

"I can only command the weaker ones," Lanatha said, "like these. And there are only a small number of them scattered about the forest. Consider it good fortune I found these."

They started off again. The forest grew even more ancient, trunks twisted and limbs sagging into mushy soil. Abrantus stumbled and dropped his side of the log.

"Take it up!" Lanatha screamed at him, as she pulled from the other side.

"Kiss my arse," Abrantus shot back, his annoyance starting to boil over.

For an instant Lanatha seethed with rage, her lip quivering. She closed her good eye. "We are not finished," she said with obviously forced calm. "The gates lie farther ahead."

Abrantus sat down in the path and rubbed his toe. "Curse you, woman."

Lanatha seized his throat. "Too late, I'm already cursed. Now get off your fat arse before I choke you to death right here in the trail."

Abrantus knocked her arm away. "You say you were a knight? Then start acting like one, instead of some filthy she-monster."

340

Lanatha stood up straight, her face cold. "I was a knight. Now half of me is monstrous. I can find little pity for you in my heart."

"But you won't kill me," Abrantus said, though he wasn't so sure. "I can see that. There's still honor in you, Lanatha, and your threats ring hollow."

Lanatha nodded. "You're right – I won't kill you. But I will walk away and let the poison do the job for me. The demons must be defeated, and I won't let this chance slip away. Now get up and let's get moving. What say you?"

Reluctantly, Abrantus once again rose and lifted the hammer and the battering ram. He limped worse than ever as he walked, every step a burning agony. His age and gout were getting the best of him. Lanatha too seemed weaker: her steps were slower and her body shook beneath her cloak.

"My body is conflicted," said Lanatha. "The demon half of me is not fond of what we're doing. I find myself battling it constantly. If I lose control for even an instant, the battering ram could destroy me as it did the imps."

With a crash of branches, a massive form leapt out into the trail. It was by far the largest demon Abrantus had yet seen – a blackened tree-like figure with twisted roots for legs and three smoldering eyes that glowered down at them. In one gnarled hand it held a small boulder. Lanatha's imps screeched and took cover within the forest.

"The demon lord!" Lanatha cried. For an instant she seemed to falter.

"Charge him!" Abrantus roared, and he started forward, dragging Lanatha with him and breaking her trance. They drove the battering ram at the demon lord, but he swatted it aside as if it were a walking stick. Abrantus and Lanatha went tumbling into the dirt.

Abrantus leapt up. He smashed his hammer into the monstrous figure, but it was ineffective against the tough tangle of bark and root. The demon lord swung the boulder at his head, and Abrantus barely managed to duck a blow that would have pulverized his skull to fragments.

Lanatha attacked with her sorcery, but the flames were drawn into the demon lord and smothered. It raised the boulder and made for her.

Then the winged imps flew launched themselves from the trees and went for the demon's eyes with their claws. With a roar, the giant creature swung the boulder at them, but they were too small and quick for it to strike.

Abrantus and Lanatha seized the fallen battering ram and drove it into the demon lord's leg. Green fire erupted. The fiend thrashed; the boulder slipped from his grasp. The demon lord seized the log and tried to yank it free, but the fire soon became an inferno, igniting several nearby trees and burning the airborne imps above its head to ash.

Lanatha stood watching, her good eye bulging with intensity. Abrantus seized her and dragged her away just as the blazing demon lord collapsed. Moments later, nothing remained but a large pile of ash and the battering ram – which still bore not even a mark.

Lanatha spit on the ashes and kicked them. Then she reached up to her face. The root still protruded from her eye, and the sores still covered her flesh. She dug her nails into her skin, and let out a moan. "The curse remains!"

She turned and gazed back along the trail. Abrantus gently tugged her arm down, sensing that Lanatha might be considering giving up. Now it was his turn to drive forward: slaying the demon lord had awakened his confidence. "You're still a knight, Lanatha. And we've still got our duty to discharge."

She gazed at him appreciatively; nodded. They moved on, crossing a stone bridge over a dark river. The shadows were deep here, and trees lashed out at them whenever they got too close. Beyond the bridge was a barrier made of wooden planks overgrown with moss and vine. It stretched into the forest on either side, forming a circular wall. Scowling demonic faces set into the ringwork leered out everywhere, cursing them and warning them back.

Overwhelmed by the terrible power radiating from the wall, Abrantus hesitated. Lanatha fell to one knee. The root protruding from her eyesocket dripped dark blood.

"Those are the faces of elder demons," she said, groaning. "It is their power that holds the forest captive. They're speaking to my demon half, trying to weaken my resolve."

"Get up!" Abrantus shouted. "Don't quit on me now."

Slowly, Lanatha rose. "This may kill us, Abrantus. I'm sorry."

Abrantus nodded. "I suspected as much. But we've made it this far, and we're going to see it through. Let's take them!"

With the last of their strength, they charged the wall. But as they drew close, vines shot out and entangled them – winding them in a crushing grasp. One wrapped around Abrantus' throat and choked him furiously, causing his vision to darken. For an instant it seemed they were finished, and then Lanatha's magic sprang to life one last time and burned the vines away.

The two pushed on as the faces screamed at them in hatred. They drove the enraged battering ram into the barrier with everything they had. There was an explosion of sparks, sending the two tumbling backwards, and the green flames shot up the wall.

They rose, watching as the fire engulfed the barrier. The demonic faces contorted with agony before burning away. Fireballs hissed through the air all around them, and Lanatha screamed as one of them struck her in the chest. She collapsed to the ground, burning.

"Lanatha!" Abrantus cried. He beat out the flames, but the damage had been done. Her chest was a charred and smoking pit.

"Return my body to Elsenmoln," she whispered, her eyes glazing over. "You will be knighted for this. Accept it with pride and honor."

"I will," Abrantus promised, kneeling beside her. "But how? I too am poisoned. Where can I find the cure?"

She managed to smile. "It won't kill you, Abrantus. You were not bitten deeply enough, or you would already be…" The smile faded in death.

Abrantus rose and faced the flames, hammer in hand. Beyond the collapsing wall, a crimson-barked, massive tree was thrashing about as the green fire tried to consume it. One huge eye gazed from the trunk, quivering with rage, agony, and determination. It spotted Abrantus, and its gaze became a crushing force, pinning him to the earth.

Abrantus clenched his teeth, his whole being focused on resistance. Meanwhile the green fire rose up like a hand to seize the crimson tree.

The tree fought the fire, but white tendrils sprouted from the crackling green and coiled around it. A massive cracking sound flooded the clearing, and the tree went still. The great eye closed; Abrantus was freed of its grasp.

Then the crimson tree ignited. Soon all that remained was ash.

It was a cool, misty fall day, and Abrantus rode into Council Wood on a white horse. He still wore the armor Lanatha had given him and still carried the hammer. The forest was peaceful now, with the exception of a few wood spiders. Having been cut off from the power that sustained them, the demons had perished, though here and there dead faces peered out from the trees – lumpy growths which yet recalled the vanquished infestation.

Abrantus paused before the sprawling ash pit, from which wisps of black smoke still arose even months later. A fire still smoldered at its heart. But something now held the demons back. The battering ram was still there, grim and terrible. It had spread roots throughout the pit, forever binding and tormenting the demonic forces that had nearly destroyed the old forest.

Abrantus nodded in satisfaction. He would return again in due time to make sure all was well and that Lanatha had not died in vain. And if somehow a demon did manage to escape from the pit, he would hunt it down and give it a taste of his hammer.

Rain began to fall. Abrantus turned his horse about and headed for the mountains, for Elsenmoln. There were great deeds to be done, and a family name to be restored to its rightful prominence.

The Walking

James S. Dorr

One must not discount the power love takes to itself; even in daylight.

hey were the day-watchers, Sumtum and Vlair and Pyfe. And there was one other who saw it too, that first sun-scorched evening: the corpse-train master, who had been forced out early that twilight across the Main Causeway that led to the Tombs, to make way for the more wealthy trains that would follow. But it was Vlair who first traded words with it.

He, with his companions, had just completed their final tomb-tour, pacing the broad-topped walls protecting the vast necropolis from those outside that might despoil it. Squinting through day-masks, their chadors safe-guarding them from the ancient and swollen sun's poisons to the extent that such garments could, they scurried rat-like from awninged gate-tower to half-shaded corner. They sought the telltale flicker of ghoul-lights assembling in shadows, blue and fitful, within the Old City to west and south; sought the possible dark-burdened forms of poachers – those too poor to even afford the minimum train-gift, risking the actinic sear of broad daylight to carry their dead themselves, seeking at Tombs' gate such rest as charity might then provide them – to east from New City across the great river. And, too, they sought the first of the corpse-trains: they knew this train master well, he of that first train, they having finished their work of the day and passed their duties on to the stronger, more numerous night-guard; he waiting for the

347

larger and richer trains that came on his heels to finish haggling over their cargoes so he could return to New City himself, perhaps to bring a new load across before morning. They, while he was waiting, sometimes sharing drinks with him, fermented from berries that grew over grave-plots within the Tombs' more shaded sectors. Sometimes sharing gossip.

But it was the old and long-since disused North Bridge that caught Vlair's attention this still sun-soaked evening, its swollen redness just now giving way to the star-speckled sky of night. "Over here, Sumtum!" he called to his captain. "I see some *thing*, walking."

"Ghouls?" was Sumtum's reply. "Should we call warning?"

Vlair shook his head, broad-brimmed sunhat rustling. "No," he called back. "It is only one, and no death-eater. Rather, it seems woman-formed — willowy. Clad in white gossamer, picking its way over jumbled stone…"

"Surely it is not simply a tomb-wraith — a heat-vision caused by the shimmering moonlight? The moon is not up yet. Could it be boat-gypsies?"

Pyfe called then, having spotted the thing too. "It is alone. And it is on the bridge itself — not on the water. And it is *all* white, not just its clothing, but also the pale flesh peeping through its garments. Except the hair: a chestnut red, deep as the color of blood."

"And lips as red as well, Sumtum," Vlair added. Sumtum now turned to see it himself, small and lonely below them as it walked across the bridge's ruined surface, jagged and half-collapsed, as were the structures to the west in the Old City, across the Tombs from them all, even now beginning to show their first blue ghoul-flicker.

But here, on the river side, scarlets and purples and yellows had started their own nighttime play, the lights of the New City flashing and pulsing, reflecting its arabesque towers and spires on the still, black water. Diffusing in mist that rose up from the river, condensing with night's approach.

Beneath and around the *thing*.

"How can she breathe, Sumtum?" Pyfe suddenly asked. "She has no mask. No mouth-guard nor filter, nor chador nor shoes nor stormhat. The river's toxins…"

But she was gone then! As if, with the mist, she had dissipated!

And then the bell-pulls of the Bridge Gate sounded – the first train's arrival! – and Sumtum and Vlair and Pyfe scurried east and south to the Main Causeway's entrance, down the steep-cut granite steps of its arched stone tower, to take their turns unloading corpse-carts, high-wheeled and waiting.

And, after, to share a drink with their train master – *who had seen this vision too*!

"She," the train master said in his cups – he had no proper name himself, as those of his trade seldom did, it being deemed more polite by New Citizens to give donations for those bereaved, gifts to secure their dead's place on the carts, in as anonymous a manner as one could – "is what you called her at first, Vlair. She is neither ghoul nor heat-wraith nor illusion, nor even a flesh-and-blood woman, but something the Ancients called just that: a Walking. We train masters know these things. We, who hear gossip on both sides of the causeway, dealing with clients of all ranks and stations. Though what we saw this twilight is deemed a rarity."

"But why, Train-Master? Why see it now?" Vlair asked. "If, as you say, it is rare…?" But then the call came; the carts were all emptied, the other trains gone, freeing the way for the train master's own carts to leave as well, hurrying, jostling across the causeway to bid for new cargo.

And then, the next day – not even at day's end, but intermittently throughout the sunlit hours – the Walking appeared again, pacing the North Bridge. She seemed to beg to be let inside.

But why? Vlair still wondered. And so, at day's end, when the others went drinking again with the train master, he sought another out, one who was wise and a scholar of sorts, one of the Tombs' curators.

This was an old man, ministering to those buried by right within the Tombs, as well as to those who shared amongst themselves the protection of marbled slabs against the heat of day. Many were those that lived thus in the Tombs: corpse-carers, grave-diggers, embalmers, ratcatchers – these for the tables of the living as well as for the dead's sake – artisans, stone-cutters, artists, engravers. And those who kept the Tombs' lore, charts and plot-maps, grave-goods and offerings – which went with what marker or stone mausoleum – the memories and histories. The knowledge of the Ancients.

Vlair came to him begging. "Curator," he asked, "can you answer my question? What is a Walking – and why is one here now?"

"A Walking," the old man said. "In olden times some might also have called it a ghost, although both those terms are somewhat in disuse these days, there being enough fresh death all around us. But it is a thing real enough, Vlair – not just some heat-vision. Not a tomb-wraith that exists only in your mind, but a true walking soul. Do you know much of souls?"

Vlair shook his head. "No. My job is only to watch for ghouls. To call the guard when they approach our walls too closely."

The old man nodded. "Souls, you must realize, are not simple things. There is, for instance, that which is most intimate with the body, which animates it – this is the part that leaves first at death, and which Necromancers among the ghouls can sometimes call back, to cause corpses to rise up. To do simple tasks before they eat them. But deeper than that there are other components: the *psyche* which governs that within the soul which makes it an individual – and which in death, under certain conditions, can make itself visible as it had been in life. So those who knew it can still recognize it. Its *will*, or life-force, which still can give it voice. Its *z'etoile* – fate-star – which brings all together, so that which should, *shall* be. All these things in harmony, each part with the others – at least while one still lives."

"But when one dies." Vlair spoke thoughtfully. "You said it is a ghost?"

"A Soul-Still-Walking, yes. When one dies the harmony between the parts is broken – the body, at least, is itself separated. To be honored by us as is our

350

duty, we who still survive! But other parts, too, may lose their way, become separated – from the shock of an early death, perhaps, or the sundering from *z'etoile* some thing that is its, these happenstances can also cause such rifts. Can rend parts of the soul away from the whole. Such as the psyche, which you say you have seen…"

"You mean, then, it's looking?" interrupted Vlair, who with youth often spoke out on impulse. "That is, *she's* searching for that which she has lost?

The curator paused before he nodded. "That which her soul needs, the will and psyche most likely in concert. But you are the one who has seen this vision, you and your fellow watchers-by-day. What do *you* think, Vlair?"

"How do I find out? That is, what she's looking for?"

This time the curator smiled. "There is a danger," he finally said. "You must warn your companions as well, although, if they are like you, they may not listen. But if you would know this – what this soul is searching for – you must go down to it, down to where you have seen it before.

"And then you must ask it."

Vlair heard the warning, and thought he had listened. He passed it on to Pyfe and Sumtum the next day as, chadored and sun-shielded, they walked their lonely rounds. Two and three times they walked the walls over, searching for ghoul-sign outside in the shadows until the sun finally approached its zenith, causing even the deepest to melt away.

Then Vlair made ready, snaking his ropes out above the old North Bridge gate. He warned his fellow day-watchers again: "You must not speak to it. No matter what happens to me, speak not to it through your souls' own will – lest *hers* be the stronger." He mentally reviewed his question, carefully memorized the night before, so he could utter it by rote. Through his mouth alone.

Then, wrapping his skirts about him, pressing his sunhat more tightly to his head, squinting through his day-mask, he lowered himself hand by hand down the tomb-wall, stone by stone to the old bridge's surface.

He saw nothing – not at first. Turning, he waved up to the others, nearly staggering in the sun's heat as he stepped one pace backwards, out from the wall's base and away even from such meager shade as it still offered, so they could see he was safe. Then he turned once more to face out toward the river.

And – just that fast! – she was there. Standing before him, smiling through crimson lips. Gossamer silks rippling in river wind, baring her legs, pale white despite the sun's scorching. Hair disarrayed now, still red as blood, long and lustrous, white shoulders gleaming, dark eyes flashing. Soft breasts jutting toward him, a darkness there too in the deep cleft between them – so near he could touch them!

Vlair forgot all his preparations then, all questions prepared by rote. Instead he stammered out his most heartfelt thoughts, from deep within – from inside his soul's own will – that which he *had* to say.

"Quickly," he stammered. "Come with me! Through the gate – my friends can open it! You are not safe here – the sun – the ghouls – but inside there will be shade –"

And, just that fast, the Soul-Still-Walking's will had captured his own, giving it voice in return. "I beg your help, sir," were the words she spoke, just as the others above on the wall forgot their instructions and shouted, through their souls' own wills, down to them both:

"Are you all right there?"

"Yes, let's get her inside through the old gate before her skin is seared."

"How can it be so white?"

"Did you say *ghouls*, Vlair?"

"Is she not beautiful?"

And so she had them all. "I am called Glom," she said, once she had come inside, then climbed with them back up onto the tomb-walls to walk with them on their rounds. She still in no more than her gossamer grave-shift, her legs and the curve of her breasts still bare; she who desired no protection from the sun's poisoned blaze.

She who was, after all, deceased already.

And she who, when Vlair asked her what it was she *did* desire – what she searched for, plying the old North Bridge, picking over its ruined and tumbled stones under the abandoned gate at its end – answered: "My lover."

"What is this lover's name, Vlair?" the curator asked – he would not speak to the Walking directly – when, the night having finally arrived, the four sought him out, the three young day-watchers and their pale companion. All four of them were of the same will now, Vlair and Sumtum and Pyfe seeking whatever it was Glom wished.

"Rantar," the Walking said, and Vlair repeated it.

"And where has this Rantar gone?" the curator asked, once again speaking only to Vlair.

"We were to be married, Rantar and I," the Walking answered. "He the most handsome and strongest of men in all the New City – though his family, like mine, was not rich – but then illness took him. A plague had ravaged the city that spring – he died, I think, of it. They took him, I knew not where. They would not tell me, fearing for my own health if the shock were too great…"

Here the Walking stopped, tears welling from her eyes, staining her grave-clothes, while the curator frowned and nodded. The others, too, were weeping.

"Then it is simple," the curator finally said. "What she seeks may be found in the Tombs' records. No doubt she has already searched the New City, its hospitals, alms-houses. Finally she has come here…"

"Then you will help me, sir?" Glom interrupted.

The curator shook his head, speaking once more to Vlair and his fellow watchers-by-daylight, he taking no chances lest his will be bound to the Walking's as well. "Tell her I help *you*, Vlair. Yes, I will search the records for you, in hopes that when we have found what the Walking seeks, she will release you. You and your companions. But I may need help too – the search will be long – "

And so he dismissed them, Vlair and his companions to wend their way to their nighttime quarters, to get such sleep as they could. Glom to continue her search if she wished, flitting from tomb to tomb, parsing inscriptions on mausoleums, but under strict promise – through Vlair as well – that she would take no more souls. Bind no more wills to hers.

Yet she did, in a way.

In the night's last hours, Vlair dreamed a strange dream. He dreamed of a time when ghouls teemed in the Old City, back before sun-spawned storms reduced their numbers – they, living among the ruins, having always been the least protected from such solar eruptions. He dreamed of a ghoul attack over the Tombs' walls, not by stealth as was now their custom, but by force as great hordes of them swept over tombs and through alleys. Searching, it seemed, until at last they met him and his fellows.

Then: "Make way!" a ghoul shouted. "There is a death-stink here."

Vlair shook his head. "No! There have been no new burials. None this night, anyway. I have a friend – a corpse-train master – one who knows such things…"

But the ghouls swept past, whistling, pointing…

They pointed at Glom, who now stood just behind him.

354

And, helpless, he watched as they reached. As they grabbed at her. She screaming, beautiful in the moonlight, with her long chestnut hair tangled in the wind, her delicate features marred by fear: "Help me, Vlair! *Please!*"

And yet – as the ghouls had her even now in their taloned grasp, *their hands passed through her.*

And then it was morning and Vlair and Sumtum and Pyfe took their posts on the already sun-speckled tops of the tomb-wall, and one of the night-guard paused to speak to Sumtum. "Have your men watch especially hard," he said. "There were ghoul-lights last night, massing about the walls. As if the ghouls had some expectation – some premonition of success, perhaps, divined by their Necromancers – and yet they did not attack. Rather, it seemed almost as if they were waiting for something."

The day passed without any sign of ghouls. Sumtum and Vlair and Pyfe's anxiety grew as the hours crept by, hoping for some word that night of the Walking's quest. Hoping their lives might soon return to them.

To drink with the train master. Once more to carouse with their companions.

But it was more nights than one before the search ended, nights in which other Tomb-folk searched as well, not because Glom had broken her promise – such promises, after all, even if given through intermediaries, were sacred – but rather because her natural charm, her beauty and grace, her old-fashioned ways had captured people's *hearts*.

Even if she was dead.

And so they helped her too, voluntarily, as Vlair would have himself had she only asked him, with no will-soul's binding.

He saw her sometimes as he came off duty, flitting over tomb-tops, inspecting obelisks, stooping – the front of her dress open wide to the moon-borne wind – to decipher crypt doorways. He stooping himself at such times to assist her, his lips sometimes brushing hers – *yet passing through them.*

Until one evening the curator called them in. "We have found what the Walking searches for," he announced, avoiding as always her name. "It is a grave in the Paupers' Sector, as might be expected, but, Vlair, this grave is two-hundred years old! Its headstone is weathered, its inscription worn away. That is why it took so long…"

Laughing, shouting, Vlair and Glom and Sumtum and Pyfe all but ignored the curator's last words as they, and others too, skipped down the hill to the weed-choked plots where the poor were buried – the dead whose families could offer no grave-gifts to secure their upkeep. Vlair's hand within Glom's, yet passing through it.

When they had reached the grave, Glom recognized it. "It is he," she shouted. "Thank you all – thank you! It has Rantar's feel to it. But…"

Now she paused as the curator caught up with them and the others, shaking his head slowly. "Ask her, Vlair," he said, "if this finding means her quest is finished."

"But surely it must," Vlair said, glad that at last his will would be returned to his own soul, but somehow also sad. Somehow uneasy.

He turned to Glom, seeing that she shook her head as well. That she had begun to weep.

"No?" he asked her.

"No," she answered. "Now we must find *my* corpse. It was, after all, Rantar's and my *bodies* that loved each other too." Kneeling, she clasped her hands to her breasts as if to prove her words, pressing them upward – gently caressing them – then moving downward. The curve of her hips. The softness of her bare thighs.

All the while weeping.

"But where?" Vlair asked.

She shook her head. "I know not. Not here."

The curator nodded. "Perhaps where she left it," he said, "in New City. It is a common thing among the poor there, that burial costs are offered as bride price – but on the assumption the husband will earn them. But if he should die before…"

"But are there not poachers?" Vlair asked. "Are there not those who carry their own dead across the causeway, receiving our charity? Surely they loved her – both families loved her – just as we love her here!"

The curator shrugged. "It was a time of plague – remember that, Vlair. Both sets of parents, if even alive, would have been frail. Enfeebled and elderly. They would have done their best for her, of course, but having already borne the expense of Rantar's death-toll so soon before hers, and physically infirm – they could not have been asked to do the impossible…"

Vlair nodded. "No, of course. But then how do we find her? Is this too in your records, Curator?"

"No, Vlair. Deaths in the New City are no part of my lore. For this you will need someone who knows the city. Who knows its people, its gossip…"

Vlair's face brightened. "Of course. The corpse-train master!"

So it was done the very next evening. Plied with bribes that all had gathered – in the event that friendship alone prove insufficient – the train master told them: "It will not be easy. We Train-Masters know these things – we hear the gossip. Of some who, so poor they can afford no burial, actually carry their dead to the Old City, leaving them there for the ghouls to consume them. Yes, even that is done – some folk making of it almost a religion, as if to propitiate the death-eaters so that, when their time comes, their own corpses might be spared."

Vlair interrupted: "Surely, though, not in this case, Train-Master!"

"No," the train master said, stretching his hand out. "Not if they loved her. But there are other things that the New City's impoverished do as well – all of these things done to cheat *us*, you understand, we, the corpse-fetchers, of our just train-gifts. I can be honest here. Some, for instance, are buried in basements – in well-guarded cellars beneath poor homes. In unhallowed ground, you see. Some they make mummies of, setting them into chairs, placing them thus around their tables as if they were still living. Pretending, as it were, that when they *truly* die they will do better. While others will even rent rooms in their houses, as habitats for the dead, taking in corpses of friends and neighbors as if they were boarders. All of this illegal, you understand, but…"

The train master made a particular motion, of thumb against fingers, and Vlair responded. "But for a well-placed gift or two, eh?" he said.

"Yes," the train master said, moving his hand then from table to pocket. Then back to table, before he continued: "It will be hard, you see. So many corpses – especially in plague years. And then so *much* cheating. This one's name is Glom, you say?"

"It is," Vlair told him, signaling to the others that gifts were gifts. And more yet might be needed.

"A common enough name," the train master said, "among the New City poor. One that is often given to daughters, its meaning is 'burden'" – again the thumb motion, hand stretched on the table – "and two hundred years, you say, since this death happened?"

Again the gifting, the pocketing.

"Yet I *do* hear gossip. And I have friends as well." Now the train master stood up abruptly, the call having come that the causeway was clear, that his carts were ready for their returning. Shouting behind him: "I'll do what I can, Vlair. Perhaps by next evening…"

And once more the day showed no sign of ghoul-plot. Again the hours progressed too slowly toward sunset. Vlair on the walls with Sumtum and Pyfe, each seeing in turn as they made their circuit the form of Glom, kneeling, alone near the old North Gate where she had first entered – the Paupers' Sector where they had let her in. And she, too, waiting.

Still dressed in grave-gossamer, weeping as the shadows that dimmed the grave-ground lengthened…

Pyfe saw it first. "Corpse-train approaching! The first of the evening! See! Look! It is on the causeway!"

"*Our* corpse-train?" Sumtum asked, rushing to join him, Vlair just behind.

"Yes – I believe so. Yes!"

"And our relief, Pyfe?"

"The night-guards approach as well, there, on the tomb-side. They, too, come early!"

And scurrying down the stairs Vlair passed the others, greeting the train master just as the gate was raised, letting the filled carts in. "Here," the train master said, handing Vlair down a bag, bulging and clanking. "It was not easy, finding the family – a name like Glom, indeed! Then tracing forward to find the descendants. Then wheedling, begging, explaining my mission to those that would hear me. Do you know, Vlair, that I had to trade *passes*? Free for the others we found next to *these* bones? My carts are half stuffed with 'em…"

"I understand," Vlair said. "Forgive me if I hurry, but I will be back. The others as well, I'm sure."

And, still running, he and Sumtum and Pyfe circled north to the paupers' grave-ground where Glom rose to meet them. "Thank you again," she said.

A crowd gathered, the curator at their rear. "Yes, I can feel them! These *are* my bones," she said.

But just then another shout rose from the west wall. *"Ghouls! Ghouls attack!"*

"They come in force!"

"We are overrun!"

Vlair snatched up his watch-staff, passing the bag to Glom who, as if not seeing what was around her, let it fall to her feet. Glancing back once, Vlair thought he could see her reaching within it, but then the ghouls were too near. He with the others – even the curator, elderly as he was – took up such weapons as they were able, the tools of their trades: the gravediggers their shovels, ratcatchers their nets and picks, even the stone-engravers their chisels. Slashing. Cutting. Pushing the ghouls back, at least for the moment.

But, just as in Vlair's dream, the ghouls were too many.

A new voice shouted above them all. "Hold!" it said. "I am Glom, the *Walking*. Is it not *my* corpse the ghouls seek?"

And, just as in Vlair's dream, one ghoul answered: "There is a death-stink here. And, yes, it is hers. Just as the Necromancers told us, she *is* a Walking. A rarity. Magic. Our masters wish for her corpse."

"A moment," Glom said. "Curator, remember the promise I made you?"

"Eh, what?" the curator said.

"That which you had me make you through Vlair, because you did not wish to ask me yourself. Will you now release me?"

Vlair understood then. He repeated the question. "Through me, Curator. Will you release her?"

The curator nodded, and the ghoul who had spoken before shouted. Facing Glom now, speaking to her directly. The others echoing. Horned, taloned hands reaching out to seize her.

"You, woman. You – *Walking*. Yes, you we shall take to our masters!"

But now Glom smiled. "No, you shall *not* take me, ghoul," she answered, "because it is not my soul's will that you do so. It is not my *z'etoile*. Rather my will is this: that you shall leave us."

And the ghouls stepped back. Slowly, to be sure, as if they still doubted – as if they struggled. But they *did* step back. And after that first step, the next one was faster, and the third faster still. Until they practically streamed back across the walls that they had breached before, panicking. Running. Their souls' wills no longer theirs. Back to the Old City from whence they had come.

Then Glom turned again, this time to embrace Vlair. Kissing him on the lips – *solidly* this time!

And then she fell, lifeless.

Afterward, the Tombs' dwellers found a new site for Rantar's grave, donating it for love, overlooking the wall and the river. Higher up on the hill where it would be tended. After they had exhumed his bones they added Glom's to them. They mixed them together, placing a stone on top – others adding grave-goods to the new tomb, jewelry and clothing to enhance Glom's beauty, flowers and brass coins, because it was she they loved – and on the stone wrote that just in the death that had come too soon they would now be joined forever.

And so life went on. Glom's quest finally ended, the day-watchers' wills were their own once more, subject alone to the dictates of their *z'etoile*. The train master found wealth, his reputation enhanced by the story. The curator busied himself with new records.

The sun grew more swollen.

And only Vlair still dreamed. He dreamed that he, too, had become a Walking, that sought only this: A kiss from lips crimson as blood. The embrace of pale flesh. The tangled feel of soft hair in the moonlight.

He sought the curator and left reassured that his will was still his own. Not captured once again, but yet, perhaps, still joined to some other's, but voluntarily, both his and its *z'etoile*. This led to still more questions –

And so he left once more, reassured now that in the Ancients' times – not that Glom nor Rantar were *that* old, but that there was precedent – sometimes a woman might be sufficiently rich in her soul as to have room for *two* loves. Such was, to be sure, a rarity – or so the curator told him.

But then, so too were Walkings.

Odin's Last Boon

Donald Jacob Uitvlugt

olgeir Ulfson shivered in his furs. For nine days and nine nights the rune-reader had kept his vigil. If anything were to come of it, it would be soon – before the tenth day dawned.

Already the branches of the great withered ash grew visible by dawn's first twilight, like the gnarled arms of a hundred giants striving against the sky. The sight sickened him but Kolgeir could not look away. Under his breath he cursed the gods for what he had suffered and cursed himself for what he had done. He tried not to look at the man-shape suspended from the ash or the spear in its side.

Kolgeir was an old man of fifty summers, bound to the old ways, the old beliefs. Storr Bjarnarson, his grandfather, had raised him as a warrior but taught him also the songs of the skalds, the sagas and lays. From Vegeir Bjarnarson, his great-uncle, he had learned to read the runes and the entrails of the stag, and other darker means of divination. Young Kolgeir's clan had kept to the wisdom granted man by Odin and Thor and Frey, and it had prospered.

Then Storr Bjarnarson died, shivering in his bed in the depths of winter, and soon after Ulf Storrson died at the hands of the Dane. The brothers of

Kolgeir's father quarreled with the brothers of Kolgeir's mother. The wolves and ravens fed well on Kolgeir's kin.

Though scarcely twenty summers old, it was Kolgeir who seized power and in due course was crowned jarl. By his uncles' cairn, Kolgeir knit together the remnants of his clan by means of solemn oaths sworn to the old gods: to Odin and Thor and Frey. Soon thereafter Kolgeir led his people out of the blood-stained land of their forefathers and into the north.

This new life was also hard, the winters long, the growing season short. There were few settlements for the fighters to raid. But the very hardness of life there united the clan. If Kolgeir's people did not spread across this new land from horizon to horizon, they did not starve either. By the fifth spring the men were felling trees to fashion dragon-prowed ships of war. That autumn they returned prosperous from their raids and joyfully named the babes their wives presented to them. For a time, life in the north went well.

But in Kolgeir's fortieth summer the blight came. Crops withered in the field; the thin soil bore no grain at all. The clan survived solely on what their raiders could snatch. The next year's crop was also bad, and the one after that, too, but by then Kolgeir had learned to close his ears to the grumbling of hungry men and, in the winter, to the whimpers of starving children. The clan grew fewer and fewer.

Kolgeir prayed to the gods. When prayers brought no help he turned to curses. The runes told him nothing, or spoke in gibberish. He spilled the entrails of a twelve-point stag onto the ground. Its intestines writhed like serpents, and the liver and heart were black with disease.

The next year even spring was late in coming. Amid mutters of *fimbulvintr*, Kolgeir realized he must try something desperate.

When the brief summer finally arrived, Kolgeir waited for the time when the honeybees swarm. Just after midsummer he came upon a buzzing mass, sheltering in an old oak. With a torch of smoldering ash he smoked them out and captured them in a wicker basket.

He took the basket to a field where, that prior winter, he had killed a wolf. Wind and weather had shrunk its carcass until there was nothing but hair and skin and bones. Kolgeir split the wolf's breast with his axe. He placed the basket of bees in the chest cavity of the wolf; then he waited.

For two years running he returned at midsummer to ensure that the hive had indeed established itself in the wolf's flesh. Those years were hard ones: quarrels leading to bloodshed, warriors deserting the clan. No newborn lived past three months. Their crops failed yet again.

At the end of the third summer, Kolgeir smoked the bees out from the wolf's remains and hacked the comb from its ribs. The honey within was dark as congealed blood. To this honey Kolgeir added certain herbs in the manner his great-uncle had taught him and brewed a mead from the mixture in an iron kettle, all the while murmuring ancient songs. When it was ready, Kolgeir closed the mead in three jars and set it aside to age for the winter.

Then came spring. Kolgeir called the whole clan before him. "My people," he said, "we have faced hard times. Yet the sagas speak of times still harder, which our ancestors long endured, yet survived. You fear that the gods have deserted us. Your faith waivers. So it was with them, too.

"But I tell you that the gods have not deserted us! I go now to petition them, far into the north, to the place where spring does not come. There I will offer again the old sacrifices in the old way and so win us their favor once more. Who will go with me?"

Men shifted uncomfortably. Women looked at the ground, pulled their children closer to their skirts. At last a young warrior stepped forward.

Kolgeir's eyes blazed. "Only one? No more? A single boy to fight for his clan?" Silence. Kolgeir spat at their feet. "Very well. I shall return to you with a message from the gods to shame your cowardice – or not at all."

Having already prepared three years for the journey, it took Kolgeir only a short while to gather what was needful. They departed without further talk, the youth afoot while Kolgeir rode a gray mare that dragged behind her a pole sled bearing their provisions. Fear rose in Kolgeir's heart: that he would never again see his people. He pressed his fist against his breast to strangle the thought.

The pair traveled in silence, though there was much Kolgeir wanted to say to the young warrior. About the sagas and lays. About the old days and the old ways. About the old faith. But he found that he could not speak. Instead he scanned the northern horizon, looking for the landmarks that led to a place Kolgeir knew only from the tales of Vegeir Bjarnarson, his great-uncle.

Their provisions grew lighter and lighter, the grass underfoot shorter and coarser. In due course they reached lands untouched by spring. Snow drifted on the wind above lichen-covered rocks. They donned fur-lined jackets from the sled and marched on.

A hidden crevasse broke the mare's leg. That night they ate well. Thereafter, Kolgeir and the youth took turns dragging the sled.

They went on. After a time even the horseflesh was exhausted. Only the jars of black mead remained. Again the fear rose up in Kolgeir; again he stifled it.

On the third day without food he sighted their destination. They made camp nearby. Around a blazing bonfire made from the poles of their sled, Kolgeir and the young warrior celebrated the near-completion of their journey.

Kolgeir opened the jars of mead and poured the contents of the first out into two golden goblets. The youth did not notice that he alone drank.

The young warrior's cup was filled once more, and a third time, until he sank into a stupor. When he was sure the youth was thoroughly unconscious, Kolgeir stripped off his clothes. It took the remainder of the night to drag him up the high stony hill to the blasted ash with branches like the arms of a hundred giants who strove against the sky. There Kolgeir lashed him to the tree and, as a new day dawned, plunged the warrior's own spear into his side.

And so began Kolgeir's vigil. The fourth day had been the worst. The mead had worn off, and Kolgeir must sit silently and listen to that golden voice cry out for mercy. Intimate pleas, coarse invective, groans of despair: he ignored them all. By morning of the fifth day, the youth spoke no more.

Past midnight of the sixth night, Kolgeir was awoken by the young man's final rattling breaths. His chest convulsed, then rose no more. Kolgeir's fear returned, much stronger now that the deed was done. Was this unwisdom after all? Soon he would know. He prayed to the gods to hasten his vigil; yet again the gods did not answer his prayers.

Just before dawn on the tenth day, Kolgeir rose on legs weary with cold and his long vigil. He unsheathed his knife and carved a mystic sign into the youth's dead flesh: the twelfth rune. It gaped red and angry, but no blood spilled forth. Kolgeir murmured a final prayer to Odin Alfather and stood back.

Nothing happened. A growl started low in Kolgeir's stomach. He flexed his hands in impotent rage.

And then the first ray of the new sun lit upon the corpse.

Its head fell back and its eyes snapped open. One was clear and blue, staring down at Kolgeir with a cold intensity. The other was covered by a dark film. Its jaws opened and closed a few times, experimentally. And then the corpse spoke:

"Who seeks counsel with Ygg on his gallows-throne?" The voice was low and resonant, as if issuing from a deep pit.

Kolgeir willed his legs to stop trembling, and spoke. "I am Kolgeir, son of Ulf, son of Storr. My people wither and die. We still follow the old ways, we still hold fast to the old beliefs. For our many years of faithfulness I ask a boon, my lord."

The corpse regarded Kolgeir without expression. The rune-reader could read nothing there: he wondered what it saw from behind that clouded orb. Powdered snow dusted his shoulders but did not touch the ash. At last the voice spoke again.

"I have little to give, my son. Our time has passed, we Æsir and Vanir. The hanged God from the south drives us out, and the great twilight has fallen on us in ways unexpected."

"So my faith has been in vain? And so my people die?" growled Kolgeir in disbelief.

"I did not ask for your belief. Your plight – and your people's – belongs to you. But there is honor in your sacrifice; I will give you what I can."

Kolgeir nodded and stepped forward. "And what boon can Odin Alfather give me?"

"Come close. I will tell you what I whispered in the ear of Baldr my son as he lay upon his bier."

The voice spoke its great secret, then fell silent. The sun broke above the horizon. The spell was over.

With tears in his eyes, Kolgeir took the body down from the blasted ash. He sank to the cold earth, cradled the corpse in his arms, and rocked slowly back and forth. The final words of the god echoed in Kolgeir's head.

There is no rising. After twilight is only darkness.

A cry rent the cold dawn air. Kolgeir Ulfson wept over the body of Valdram Kolgeirson.